ROGUE

ROGUE

by Robert Cameron

FIRESTEP
Press

FireStep Publishing
Gemini House
136-140 Old Shoreham Road
Brighton
BN3 7BD

www.firesteppublishing.com

First published by FireStep Press, an imprint
of FireStep Publishing in 2015

ISBN 978-1-908487-49-0

Designed by FireStep Publishing
Cover by Ryan Gearing
Typeset by Graham Hales, Derby

Contents

Acknowledgements

Everybody who has helped me in getting the
Sterling trilogy published:

Ryan and the team at Firestep for believing
in the project

Christine Howe for her advice

My family for their support

And Aga, who reads my work and keeps me right

Thank you

www.rcameronbooks.com

This story is fictional

Persequor Persequi Persecutus

Rogue

The room came into focus. Static crackled as the camera switched on. Dirty white tiles gave it an air of emptiness. Whatever was lighting the room illuminated the bare walls efficiently; strands of light glinted back at the lens.

From behind the camera a figure emerged and went to a chair, placed in the centre of the room. The chair legs scraped the floor as the figure took a seat. He leaned forward, resting his elbows on his knees, fingers interlocked he looked at the ground. His frame grew a few inches as he inhaled and filled his lungs with air. Still staring at the floor he exhaled loudly, the warm breath formed a visible cloud in the cold room. He looked up directly at the camera, opened his mouth to speak but paused, unsure of how to start.

"Well," he said eventually. "By now you know what's been going on." He sighed again, his right leg twitched nervously. "I think you've had suspicions for a while now." He looked down again and tapped his fingertips together as he struggled to verbalise what he wanted to say.

"So, if you're watching this you've worked everything out and…" He returned his attention to the camera. "I'm probably already dead."

Chapter 1

Tuesday 19 March 2013
1400hrs GMT

Humidity hung in the darkness and drenched everyone in their own sweat. There was no wind, nothing to provide a break from the heat. The wood and mud brick buildings were like ovens to the troops stationed there.

The man in charge stood at the open window to his wooden hut, he looked out over the other structures in the village. He had chosen this hut as it was the highest point in the village and he had three hundred and sixty degree vision of the small town. He scanned the area in front of him and drummed his fingers on the wooden window-ledge.

Perfect circles of light randomly floated over the village, lighting up small adobe houses and tight alleyway entrances. Their source: powerful spotlights on the rooftops of the sturdier structures. The alleyway entrances led to what was no more than a rat warren, which zigzagged through the village like an un-mapable maze. He had his guards constantly patrolling, looking for this 'intruder' he had been tipped off about.

He stepped back from the window and stretched his back. His green, sweat-soaked shirt stuck to his body. He pulled it off his skin and attempted to allow some air to circulate, but there was no relief in the warm, sticky air. He pulled a battered packet of cigarettes from his breast pocket and flicked the bottom, producing one cigarette. The Zippo lighter sparked a flame, which illuminated him through the window. Only for a second, but long enough for attention to be drawn to his location. From then on, when he drew in a lung full of smoke, a small red dot glowed as he inhaled. He knew better than to make himself a target, but he was tired of this now, night after uncomfortable night had eroded his enthusiasm.

His second in command emerged in the doorway to the hut. The two men looked at each other. He gestured with his hand as if to ask the same question he had asked over and over. The second in command shook his head and he turned back to the window. Saying nothing, he slipped away, leaving his boss leaning on the window-sill, gazing aimlessly out over the village.

The cigarette smouldered between his fingers. He knew he would not be popular with his decision to break the rules and light up, but he didn't care anymore. He flicked the cigarette out of the window and watched as is tumbled down towards the street below. The cigarette end hit the ground out of sight of the window, but he could still see the feint orange glow as it burned down to the filter.

The discarded, half-smoked cigarette lay on the cobbled street at the entrance to one of the alleyways. In the shadows, just inside, but out of view, a pair of black boots was visible in the glow. One of the boots emerged from the shadows and stepped on the cigarette, extinguished it and returned to the pitch-blackness of the alley.

The owner of the boots, now back in the safety of the shadows, allowed himself a peek out of the alley. He had been dodging patrols all night but was slowly getting closer to his target. He was dressed in black and was practically invisible; he wore night vision goggles and a covert earpiece. A silenced pistol was strapped to his thigh, his hand never to far away from the grip.

"Is he smoking again, Al?" said the dark figure quietly.

"Yeah, that was his," said a voice directly in his ear.

"Someone should have a word with his supervisor."

"Huh yeah," laughed the invisible voice. "I'll make a phone call. You're close, he's directly above you."

"I figured as much, any movement?" said the shadowy figure looking up and down the street through the night vision goggles.

"No," said the voice. "There's one other person up there with him, but I think you can handle them both. Just stay out of the lights." The figure ducked back into the alley, avoiding one of the spotlights as it swept past.

"OK," he said quietly, exiting the alley and cautiously moving down the street. "Moving now." He silently walked along the street towards a set of wooden steps that led up to the hut. His target was located. He stopped short of the steps as another spotlight unexpectedly changed direction and beamed towards his position. He stepped smoothly into a doorway alcove and closed his eyes to avoid the light burning his retinas in the bright green glow of the goggles.

"I'm at the steps Al," he said after the light had passed. "Making my way up." He stepped onto the first wooden tread and shifted his weight forwards. It creaked under the weight of his equipment. The second step did the same, and the third.

"We need lighter kit, Al," he said, carefully taking each step one at a time. He tried to walk at the edge, near to the rail, but it didn't help. The higher he went, the more unstable the structure seemed. "Is there no other way up?" he asked, stopping on the platform where the steps turned one hundred and eighty degrees to continued up.

"Not without going all the way back," said the voice, dashing any hopes of an alternate route. He continued up.

The increasingly creaking steps began swaying side to side. He grabbed for the rail for support, but support did not come, instead the wooden steps buckled under his feet. The step he was on splintered and he began to fall. He turned and reached back for the platform where he had rested for a brief second. His gloved hands scrambled for a handhold.

Hanging high above the ground he gripped onto the platform, but the weight of his body armour, equipment and weapon proved too much and he slowly slipped to the edge, until only his fingertips were clinging on to the shaking platform.

"Oh shit!" he mouthed quietly as his grip gave way and he plummeted to the cobbled street. He slammed onto the ground, winding himself and knocking off his night vision goggles. The guard force was on him instantly, surrounding and covering him with automatic weapons. The spotlights all zoomed to where he was lying, gasping for breath.

"Al," was all he could get out through the short sharp intakes of air. The guard commander appeared at the top of the destroyed steps and looked down at the mess of troops and debris below him. The figure in black squirmed on the ground surrounded by troops. The enemy commander burst into laughter.

"Cam you dickhead," he roared. "What the fuck you doing?" The figure on the floor managed to raise his hands and make a time out signal. "Alright," he sniggered. "Endex everybody. Get him up." The troops lowered their weapons and helped him to his feet. The night turned to day as hundreds of lights were turned on.

The fake village was now illuminated under the roof of a huge hangar-like structure. The town had been constructed with every effort on detail; it was an exact replica of a small village in South America.

The troops dusted off the man who had fallen as the duty medic arrived to check him over. After a quick examination he was given the all clear. He looked up at a glassed balcony high in the rafters of the hangar to where the control room was situated. He made eye contact with a well-dressed man who was looking down on them all. He shrugged his shoulders as the man in the suit turned away.

"Well," said the man in the suit. "Not the best demonstration, but I think it goes to show the type of operations that we conduct and the problems that come with them." He looked at each of the visitors who were sat watching the exercise, in the control room high above the exercise arena. The room offered the controller and, on this occasion, the visitors, an unobstructed view of the action.

"Is he alright, Al?" asked one of the female visitors looking concerned. They had been watching the exercise unfold on the many monitor screens in the control room.

"That was Sterling," said Al, "or Cam to his friends. Don't worry about him he's quite resilient." Al looked down and saw one of the guards pat Cam on the shoulder and walk away laughing. "He's been with the Asset program for a while now," he continued, turning back to his audience. "He's got a good track record with completing near impossible tasks."

"What is your success rate on operations Al?" asked another visitor.

"Pretty good," he answered. "Considering we're normally sent in on ops where we are expected to fail."

"Expected to fail!"

"Yes. That's why none of our operators officially exist," Al said leaning back on a desk. "When the task is thought to be near impossible and there is no other way but to send in a human, we are the ones to come to."

"And who does come to you?" asked the woman.

"Any nation with an operative in the program," said Al shifting his gaze back to the women. "We have British, Americans, Australians, Canadians and most of the European nations represented in the program. The team playing the enemy down there right now have two Scottish operatives, a Greek and an Italian."

Al looked over his shoulder for the second time. The team playing the enemy were busy teasing Cam. " We have one of our operators in Poland right now helping out with one of their operations, in the hope of recruiting some Polish troops. In fact I'm heading over there myself once we're all done here."

"Why Polish?" asked the woman.

"They have a group called G.R.O.M, damn fine soldiers and would be a great addition. Also Polish nationals could pass as Russian if needed, not that most of them would want to, but it would be handy to have a team able to blend in that corner of the world."

"So no Russians in the program then?" she asked sarcastically.

"No," snorted Al. "Nor countries like North Korea, China and Belgium."

"Belgium?" said another member of the group.

"Oh yes," said Al enthusiastically. "Nothing against them, but Belgium is a hot bed of espionage. And I know we are supposed to be all friends at the moment," he continued making air quotes. "But we have more acts of hostile espionage from Russia and China now than we did during the cold war."

"Really?" said the visitor. They all looked surprised and started to mutter amongst themselves. Al let them for a moment then interrupted.

"So!" he said. Raising his voice a fraction. "We are handed a task, we select the team, normally one of the already assigned four-man teams. Set up a training environment in one of our training hangars like this one. And then when the approval is granted, we go in."

"How many of these do you have?" one of the visitors asked.

"Training environments or teams?" asked Al.

"Well, both."

"We have twelve teams of four. When not on operations they are training. They play enemy for each other, just like you witnessed downstairs there."

"And training environments?" persisted the visitor.

"We have two other training environments exactly like this one," Al gestured to the hangar space below him. "We set up replicas of the targets and we can control the environments, hence the heat in here, for which I apologise." The group of visitors shuffled in their seats, adjusted their clothing and fanned themselves. "We have one operational control room, with a similar set up to this one. From the control room we can get imagery from CCTV, satellites and unmanned drones for real time intelligence. We can keep track of our teams; we now have better communication equipment and are always in contact. We simply guide them in."

"So the guys on the ground will get up to the minute support whenever it's needed," said the woman.

"Yes," he said answering her question. "I have amazing tech support, intelligence and a full-time linguist. You might meet him later. His name's Donald he was one of my operators but got injured on an operation. He's an excellent linguist and we need him on most operations so he's available through our control room at any time."

"So Al," said one of the visitors cautiously. "What operations do you have on at the moment?"

"That I can't really talk too much about," he said. "We have two full teams out at the moment. And half of Sterling's team is out too." He turned, looking over his shoulder through the window, down to the exercise area.

"Half?" enquired a visitor.

"Yes," he said turning away after seeing Cam sitting on the smashed stairs stretching out his back. "It's rare but we sometimes split teams. One is trying to recruit the Polish guys and one is out in Afghanistan."

"Afghanistan!" he said. "What's he doing out there?"

"Now that's something I really can't go into."

Chapter 2

The 173rd Airborne Battalion Combat Team were nearly halfway through their fourth tour of Afghanistan. The 'Sky Soldiers' had a long history dating from the First World War. They had fought in most of America's wars since, earning many unit citations for combat in Vietnam, Iraq and Afghanistan. Most of the members had been to Afghanistan before and were veterans of the combat patrols similar to the one being detailed to them now. Nothing was out of the ordinary, except the extra man tagging along. He sat at the back of the briefing tent and said nothing as the officer delivered the orders.

The paratroopers turned in their seats every so often, checking out the man with the scruffy beard. He was dressed the same as them: desert combats, desert boots, body armour with various pouches attached and the standard issue US pistol strapped to his thigh. He did however, have a different unit patch to theirs. As opposed to their Airborne Brigade insignia, he wore a US Navy S.E.A.L trident over his left breast pocket. This was causing rumours to circulate amongst the seated paratroopers.

The rumours were fuelled even further when the officer referred to him as a member of the C.I.A, attached for a one time only purpose. This patrol was to locate a suspected Al-Qaeda bomb maker who had taken up residence nearby. They were to find the man and photograph him. The C.I.A man was there to identify the target. The briefing ended and the troops stood up still discussing the stranger, most were nearly kitted up. In an environment such as the Forward Operating Bases like Altimur, it made sense to be ready for anything. They shuffled out past him to prepare for the early morning departure.

Once the tent was empty, apart from the officer who had conducted the briefing, he himself rose to his feet. He acknowledged the officer who nodded back to him and he too exited the tent. His name was Bull, one of Al's Assets. He was a member of Cam's team back in the UK. However, this time he was on his own. He had been for three weeks now.

Bull entered the cold night air and his breath formed a mist. Stars littered the sky. Groups of paratroopers still hung around talking about the morning's patrol. When they noticed Bull they dispersed, returning to their tented accommodation.

F.O.B Altimur was a small outpost in central eastern Afghanistan. A rectangle shaped camp on the main route between Kabul in the north and Gardez in the south. The camp was mostly tents: accommodation, briefings, supplies and chow hall all under canvas.

The surrounding mountains, topped with snow at this time of year, created a wide valley. Altimur sat in this vast valley. The F.O.B was on a slope, giving the camp a three hundred and sixty degree view of the surrounding landscape, most of it desolate. Bull headed back to his tent; he had been given one of the officers' tents. The officer had moved reluctantly to shared tent alongside a colleague. Bull's purpose there demanded privacy and the officer didn't complain, especially when he saw the S.E.A.L emblem, which the C.I.A operative wore.

Bull had been a member of S.E.A.L Team Six, an elite group who referred to themselves simply as The Teams. S.E.A.L Team

Six had conducted the raid that killed Osama Bin Laden. Bull had been involved but had never talked about it. He had come into contact with the Assets by chance when he had been asked to assist with an operation. He had been impressed and, when he was asked, he jumped at the chance to join them at their new headquarters in Oxfordshire.

His wife, Dee, was over the moon at the move. Her dream of visiting Europe finally realised after years of marriage to a serving S.E.AL. They had met at school in Queens and married not long after leaving. Bull's job meant long periods of loneliness for his wife. He had missed all of his young daughter's birthdays but joining the Assets would give him more time with his family. Dee had always been supportive and they were as strong as they ever had been.

He would be home soon, back with his family and back with the team he enjoyed working with. But for now he had a patrol to go on. He walked past the vehicles being prepared, the M.R.A.Ps' diesel engines roared and kicked sand and smoke into the air.

These Mine Resistant Ambush Protected vehicles would keep them safe from the thousands of IEDs that littered the surrounding countryside, probably put there, the most part, by the patrol's target.

Pushing through the tent flap he took off his body armour and flung it onto the camp cot in the corner. He looked at his watch; he had six hours until he would have to report to the vehicles. He would be able to get a decent few hours of sleep if he could block out the engines being revved only a few metres from his tent.

0305hrs AFT

Bull pushed the tent flap to one side, slung his rucksack over his shoulder and took in the view of the busy compound. Wrapped up warm against the cold morning, he made his way into the havoc that was erupting around the vehicles. The M.R.A.Ps had been lined up ready to go, fumes filled the air adding some warmth to the area.

"Sir!" shouted one of the Paratrooper sergeants. "You're over here with us, Sir." He waved Bull over to the vehicle second from the lead. "In here, Sir." He pointed into the back of the vehicle.

"You don't have to call me Sir, Sarge. I'm no officer," said Bull in his New York drawl to the Sergeant stood to attention at the side of the vehicle. "Call me Bull." He patted the Sarge hard on the shoulder, knocking him out of his military stance.

"Hope you don't mind, but we got a couple of new guys in here with us today," said the Sergeant. "The driver crew are experienced though, just thought the new guys would benefit being with us on this one."

"Sure, no problem," said Bull gruffly. He placed his rucksack on the floor of the vehicle, in front of his seat.

"What you got in there?" asked the Sergeant pointing to the bag Bull had so gently put on the floor.

"Just camera equipment," said Bull. "For recording evidence." The interior of the armoured vehicle had soft lighting, allowing Bull to find his way around the inside of the metal beast. At the back of the vehicle the two new paratroopers arrived and were talking to the Sergeant. Bull couldn't hear what was being said over the noise of the engines. He knew it was about him and the new guys kept looking over.

The troops climbed aboard and slammed the rear doors shut, sealing them inside the belly of the armoured vehicle. At four in the morning the convoy started to leave the F.O.B, heading south along the main Kabul to Gardez highway.

The plan was to head south then double back on themselves, attempting to confuse the enemy spotters. As soon as they left Altimur the chatter started. The voices coming in over the radios were that of the enemy, watching troop movement and warning their people to hide or set up ambushes. Normally this information was passed through interpreters, but Bull understood what was going on. Afghanistan had been his war, and sometimes he thought he knew Afghan better than some States back home.

At just over half a mile the convoy broke track and doubled back on itself. Heading back towards Altimur, with the main road on their right and the river on their left, the vehicles kicked up dust into huge clouds. The chatter increased, the enemy passed information on the change of direction.

Bull listened to the enemy voices attempting to pass complicated information, the language of the spotters faltered and began to change, slipping into English. The more complex the commands the more the enemy showed who they were. Bull had now lived in the UK for two years and could recognise the accents. West Midlands and Yorkshire accents were obvious. More evidence of home-grown terror, Bull thought. There had been strong intelligence of UK nationals fighting for the enemy, but this was the first time he had witnessed the evidence first hand.

Veering west, the convoy crossed the river at a point that was fordable. The V-shaped hulls of the M.R.A.Ps cut through the desert landscape. These hulls would protect them from mines and other buried ordnance. The armour on the exterior of the vehicles could withstand Rocket Propelled Grenades and a hail of 7.62mm fire. The convoy snaked towards the road that ran west towards the town of Daber. They would be travelling over a mile on this road and it was the most dangerous part of the operation.

The crews did not like using obvious routes and this was one, a long straight road with hills to the south, a perfect ambush point. The call came over the radio for top cover and one of the young paratroopers stood up and opened the hatch in the roof. He pushed through and emerged into the open taking control of the .50 cal turret.

The convoy increased its speed along the road, hoping to get clear of it as soon as they could. The passengers felt every bump in the back of the vehicle as it bounced down the potholed surface.

The sun was rising and the terrain was more visible to the gun turrets of the vehicles.

"I got movement south," came a call over the net. "Anybody else see that?"

"Shit yeah," confirmed another of the vehicles' gunners. "Dust trails to the south, in the foot hills. Eight, can you see what it is?" The gunner was asking the eighth and last vehicle in the convoy if he had a better sight of what was causing the trail.

"Looks like some sort of pick up truck," came a reply to the request. "Possibly some sort of flatbed."

"Shit! Stop, stop, stop." The convoy slowed to a standstill. "We got disturbed ground on the road up ahead." The lead vehicle had noticed rubble on the road and didn't want to pass it. "Any enemy chatter?"

"No, nothing," said the Afghan interpreter. "Not about an IED strike anyway."

"Might be nothing," said one of the vehicle commanders.

"Yeah but we can't take the chance," said the convoy commander. "Get the Buffalo up there." The Buffalo broke ranks from the convoy and moved to the front position. The E.O.D variant of the M.R.A.P vehicles stopped, taking the lead position.

"All round cover?" asked one of the E.O.D operators. After confirmation that the gunners had eyes on, in every direction, he exited the vehicle. "I wanna know if that flatbed stops," said the operator, swinging shut the face visor of his helmet. He slowly made his way towards the rubble in the road waving the metal detector over the road surface.

Moving slower as he reached the rubble and, under the weight of the extra body armour, he studied the area of ground that had forced the convoy to stop. It did indeed look like it had been placed over the road. He methodically cleared the area, ever mindful of the danger he was in.

After what seemed like an age, he called back to the convoy giving the all clear. He had made safe the road that was strewn with rocks, also the edge of the road going out a few metres to the sides, protecting the convoy from possible secondary devices. The vehicle creating the dust trails had disappeared into the distance having never stopped.

The E.O.D operator de-kitted at the back of his vehicle, with the help of his number two.

"Nice work," said the convoy commander over the net. "Should we still go round it?"

"No," said the E.O.D operator looking in the direction of the commander's vehicle. "I've cleared through it. That's now the safe route we should use. I didn't clear round it."

"OK, straight through it is." With that, the convoy ploughed through the rock on the road, resuming the patrol. The turret gunners stayed vigilant, ever mindful that an ambush could happen at any moment, as it had in the past.

After a mile the road turned to the right taking a south westerly direction. The convoy broke track again and headed north west. The target was located in a compound that they would pass by on the north side, making it look like they were heading straight past into Daber. Then, at the last moment turn south and be on top of the compound giving the target no chance of escape.

The convoy commander took the place of his turret gunner and scanned the compounds in the immediate area, looking for movement and anything out of the ordinary. The mud walled compounds had a tendency of all looking alike, making it difficult to find the right one.

This time however, the compound was unmistakable. One of two separate enclosures, close together with a dust track running between them. Their target compound was the more northerly of the two.

Once they had made it appear that they were passing by they turned south and were on top of the compound within minutes. The first two vehicles went straight for the entrance and blocked it. The other vehicles took up strategic positions around the compound to stop anyone trying to wander off. Most importantly they were there to stop anyone from the other compounds, only a few hundred metres off to the west, from becoming too nosey and possibly causing trouble.

Only one side of the compound was built up with mud brick buildings and wooden structures; the other part was dusty fields where the occupants scratched out a living from the land. Bull and the passengers from his vehicle headed for the mud brick buildings. The other vehicle's passengers supported by providing a visible presence in the grounds.

"Bull hold up," shouted the Sergeant as Bull went to bang on the shabby wooden door into the building. "I'll call in the interpreter."

"No need," said Bull pounding on the door, knocking cladding off the brickwork. Bull shouted something in Afghan, then repeated it a second time. He pounded on the door again and was about to shout for a third time when the door opened. A filthy-looking local stared back at the American soldiers. Bull said something to the man and pushed past him into the building.

Amongst protests by the local man, the Paratroopers followed Bull into the building. Two other local men joined the grimy man, shouting and screaming at the American soldiers. Bull pushed all three into a room and yelled something at them, which shut them up immediately.

"Have a good look around," said Bull bluntly to the paratroopers. "Check every room but for God's sake don't move anything."

"You heard the man," ordered the Sergeant. "Get going. Be careful what you touch." The three Paratroopers started a search of the building. Bull moved in close to the three Afghan men who backed themselves against a wall. He eyed them up and down. One of them, Bull knew, was his man.

Bull said something to the one who looked the least confident. The man stood next to him tried to answer for him but was stopped by Bull. He asked again but the man stayed silent. He moved to the man who was yet to speak, keeping eye contact with the noisy one as he moved. He asked a question in a politer manner. He asked again when met with silence. As he asked the second time he pointed at the noisy man. All three remained silent.

Bull nodded and stepped away from the three men lined up against the wall, swung his rucksack off his shoulders and opened the top flap. From the rucksack he pulled out a digital camera and readied it for use. He pointed it at the noisy man in the middle who instinctively hid his face from the lens. Bull yelled at him in a threatening manner until he lowered his hands.

Bull took three individual face photos of the men; he then looked at the LCD screen of the camera. The faces of the men flicked up on the screen and the camera isolated the images of the men's eyes. Bull kept a wary eye on the men as the camera did its work. The camera indicated it was searching its internal database.

The first photo he took eventually reappeared on the screen along with the words 'known target, eliminate' in red. The others came back with the same message. Bull put the camera away in his rucksack and turned to face the men who were now shifting uneasily with this American's attitude towards them.

Bull unzipped his tactical vest's left-hand side zip and reached inside. He pulled out a silenced pistol and in one smooth motion silently shot each of the men in the head. They fell lifeless to the floor, their knees buckling underneath them. Bull looked at the crumpled pile of bodies for movement as he zipped away the pistol back in its hidden holster.

He turned and exited the room closing the door behind him and sealing in the evidence of his actions. He fished out a packet of cigarettes and lit one, taking in a long drag. The Sergeant approached Bull with a confused look on his face.

"What's going on, Bull?" he asked, getting within speaking distance. Bull stood leaning on the closed door, cigarette in the corner of his mouth.

"You find anything?" he said, answering the sergeant's question with one of his own.

"No, none of us did," he replied. "Place is clean."

"Not surprised," said Bull. "Wrong guy."

"What?"

"Wrong guy," he said again. "Get your two and lets get the hell out of here." The Sergeant shouted for the young paratroopers who came running back to their Sergeant. He told them about the mistake and the four of them went to leave the building. One of the young troopers made a move to open the door to check on the local men, but Bull slammed his arm across the doorway stopping him from opening it.

"I said let's go!" he said sternly at the trooper. The young paratrooper didn't want to upset whoever this man was and left the building without a look in at the locals. The crew of the two M.R.A.Ps loaded themselves into the vehicles and moved out of the compound. The young trooper looked at Bull as they pulled out, but Bull made no effort to acknowledge his inquisitive look.

The convoy linked up and began the journey back to Altimur. Bull knew that as soon as they were back in the F.O.B there would be a helicopter waiting to take him to the next location. Then, the whole process would start again. The hunt for the bomb makers had stepped up a notch and it was Bull's job to locate and terminate.

Chapter 3

The airport on the outskirts of the city of Szczecin looked more like a large bus station than an international airport. The flight from London had landed and the passengers were now lined up slowly going through passport control. Al handed over his passport to the man who scanned it, the computer bleeped and he handed it back without saying a word.

"Thank you," said Al taking his passport and slipping it into his suit's breast pocket. He stood for a second smiling at the man behind the bullet-proof glass who simply stared back. Realising he wasn't going to get a response he nodded slightly, muttered something under his breath and turned away towards the baggage carousel.

Al pulled his wheeled suitcase off the conveyor belt, set it on the floor and extended the telescopic pull handle. He looked around for the exit then followed the crowd through the corridors, a set of glass sliding doors opened and he stepped out into the foyer.

A number of people stood in the foyer waiting for friends and family members. Al looked for his driver amongst the crowd. Above the heads of the anxious people trying to spot their loved ones he saw a small flag rise into the air. Once in plain view it started to wave feebly from side to side. On the small white flag, in crudely written black marker, was Al's name.

He snaked his way towards the flag, weaving in and out of the crowd until he came face to face with the flag bearer.

"Hello Rory," said Al to his old friend. "How are you doing?"

"Good mate," he replied with his thick Dorset accent. Rory had known Al for many years, before the Asset program had started. They had met up again two years previously when he was tasked to help on one of Al's operations and since then had been part of the program. "Car's outside, we can talk on the way."

Rory was an outstanding soldier, started as a marine and progressed naturally into the S.B.S. He had taken part in so many classified operations that he struggled to remember most of them. He was tall, broad shouldered and had sun-bleached, messy curly hair from spending too much time in salt water. He always had a large smile on his face and had an ability to find humour in any situation.

Rory led Al out into the morning air and across the car park to his car. Al followed pulling his baggage across the bumpy ground. The case bounced from side to side on the small plastic wheels and Al struggled to keep it upright.

Rory opened the boot of the car and picked up Al's case, threw it in and slammed the boot shut. He walked round to the right side of the car only to stop himself short.

"Sorry, sorry. Still getting used to left hookers," he said, doubling back to the other side.

"Doesn't bode well," said Al, climbing into the passenger seat. Rory started the car and drove to the exit barrier.

"Wait here a min," said Rory climbing out of the car. "Gotta pay." Al sat in the car and watched as Rory inserted coins into the paying machine. Al had sent Rory to Poland two weeks previously to help out in one of their operations. He knew few details of the op, only that it was to do with the Polish intelligence base at Stare Kiejkuty. This old Nazi outpost had been turned into a Polish base after the war; from there the C.I.A had gained permission to use it as one of their subject detention, and probably interrogation sites. Since the Americans had started this, the Poles wanted them to finish it. Now the Assets were international they had been asked to help out and smooth it over.

For this reason he sent one of his best, his ulterior motive being he wanted to recruit the G.R.O.M team working on the task into the Asset program. Rory was the perfect choice. He was a professional warrior but also a likable guy with a sense of humour most people warmed to.

"So," said Al as Rory climbed back in. "How's it going then?"

"Good mate," he replied, his voice muffled by the parking ticket in his teeth. He pulled forward up to the barrier and slotted the ticket into it, causing it to lift. "We got a good team, I think they'll fit in well."

"Good," replied Al. "Have you told them much about us?"

"Some, not much," said Rory pulling out of the airport car park onto the main road.

"Rory! Right, right!"

"Sorry!" shouted Rory, swerving the car back onto the correct side of the road. "Like I said, still getting used to it."

"Right, now that we might make it to our destination. Tell me what all this is about."

"Simple," said Rory. "The C.I.A black site at Stare Kiejkuty has come to the attention of A.Q, or a Chechen Muslim cell anyway. We only assume they are A.Q," he said, looking over at Al. "They're in Szczecin waiting and planning something. What however, we don't know."

"How come?"

"It's difficult," Rory continued. "They're holed up in a block of flats. The flats are very small and there are about six of them crammed into it. We conducted a recce the other night but because it's so tight in there any noise is very noticeable. We've just secured the flat next door. We're going to work on it tonight."

"What's the G.R.O.M's theory as to why they're here?"

"The black site's been used rarely since it was exposed after Bin Laden was taken out, but we think these guys are waiting until a prisoner comes through."

"What for?"

"A break out, we think," answered Rory. "Prisoners are transported from the airport we just been at the three hour drive to Kiejkuty. Normally hog-tied in the back of a van. We think this cell are planning on breaking the next one free." Rory indicated and took the exit for Prawobrzeze/Szczecin, almost crossing the centre line onto the wrong side again. Realising his mistake he righted his course onto the right lane. "See, getting the hang of it." Al raised his eyebrow and slightly nodded his head in acknowledgment.

"Tell me about the team."

"Well, I'll start at the top," said Rory driving through the town towards Szczecin, where the G.R.O.M were watching the cell. "We got Jerzy, he's the team leader. They refer to him as 'Tatus' or 'the Daddy'. He's a typical Polish S.F, you know dark curly hair, moustache. Tough old guy but tends to stay in the background controlling things rather than getting in the mix. Not that he can't hack it, if he needs to he can still kick some ass."

Al nodded, listening to Rory, but taking in the surrounding scenery. The sun was now high in the sky lighting up the lake on the right. The car left the town of Prawobrzeze and headed for the old industrial city of Szczecin.

"We have a guy called Karol, good guy," said Rory looking over at Al. "Dependable and strong as an ox. He works mostly with the Daddy, who's not so hot with new technology. Karol keeps him right."

The car travelled along the road, the city looming in the distance. On the right the disused shipyards came into view, ghostly empty. They drove over bridges spanning large rivers, a network of waterways that, back in the eighties, would have been full of ships. The roads became increasingly bumpy as they entered the city suburbs.

"The two younger guys do most of the leg work," continued Rory. "We got Radoslaw and Mateusz."

"Christ," said Al finally turning his attention back to the conversation, "say them again."

"Don't worry we call them Radek and Mats. Radek's slightly older than Mats, he's the gobby one. If we need to talk someone round he's the one, especially the ladies." He paused to think. "Reminds me of a young me."

"Huh, yeah," laughed Al. "How are the ex-wives by the way?"

"Anyway," said Rory clearing his throat. "Mats is the youngest but still capable, he's a wiz kid, the techie. Anything with computers he can do it."

"So do you think they'll be open to joining us?" asked Al.

"Give them a good deal and I'm sure they'll be more than happy. Why are you after them anyway?"

"Well, we're still getting problems with the Russians, more than before in fact." Al looked at Rory who was concentrating on the drive through the crowded city streets. "We may need them in the near future, if we're to believe the latest threat assessments."

"Really?" asked Rory. " I know these guys speak better Russian than English, probably what you need eh?"

"Yeah, also China and North Korea, but that's another ball game. Not so easy to get our guys in there."

"World's going to shit."

"Mmm," said Al turning his attention to the outside again. "Not just A.Q anymore. It gets more complicated by the day." Now deep in the city centre Rory had to concentrate on the roads and the road users. Cars and other vehicles overtook and crossed lanes erratically. "People don't seem to drive by the rules do they?"

"Not here mate, no," answered Rory, fully focused on what was going on around him. "The cell are in a block of flats in the centre of the city, near a shopping mall called Galaxy Centrum." Rory applied the brakes suddenly to avoid a van that swerved in front of him. "You'll be pleased to know we'll be there soon."

1040hrs CET

Rory parked the car up outside the shopping mall and led Al to the front entrance. They stopped under the awning of the main way in, people walked round them as they stood in front of the sliding glass doors. Mingling with the pedestrians, Rory pointed towards a block of flats across the wide road.

"That's where the cell is," said Rory as a tram clattered past. "Busy isn't it?" Al looked around at the mass of activity: cars beeped their horns, people pushed by one another and street vendors shouted their wares.

"Yes it is," said Al thoughtfully. "Might make it easier for us though."

"Right," said Rory dragging Al out of his thought process. "Follow me, we've got an empty room in the radio station on one of the higher floors. It's our best view of the flat. Still it isn't great."

Al followed Rory into the shopping centre. Music played over the mall's speaker system and the smell of deep-fried, fast food filled the floor space between the glass-fronted shops. The main hall of the centre had long escalators on either side leading up to another two floors of shops. In the middle of the hall was a climbing wall, the shape of a tooth, with both children and adults climbing or dangling from it.

"Back here," said Rory, making his way behind two Mercedes cars, displayed in an arrow head formation for a competition. He opened a door in the wall and both he and Al slipped inside. Rory bounded up the staircase taking steps two or three at a time followed by Al who, by the time he got to the top, was visibly out of breath.

"You need to work on your cardio," said Rory, leading off down the corridor. He pushed his way through some double doors with the radio station's logo above them and waited for Al to catch up. "Do you need some time to compose yourself before we go in?" giggled Rory as Al passed through the doors being held open for him.

"I'm fine," huffed Al.

"Good, right. Got the Daddy and Karol in here. The young lads are down on the street parked up watching from a different angle."

"OK," said Al. "I'd like to have a chat with them, explain why I'm here and try to get them interested."

"No problem, Karol speaks the best English out of the two," said Rory opening the door to the makeshift observation post. "Hey guys," he said, approaching the two men sat by the room's window.

In front of the men was a vast array of surveillance equipment and a bank of inactive monitors.

"Hello Rory," said Karol, turning to face the two visitors. The Daddy grunted a greeting but didn't break sight of the flat.

"Guys, this is Al," said Rory introducing his boss. "Al, this is Karol, and Jerzy." The Daddy finally turned away from his binoculars held up close to the window on a tripod. The three men shook hands and exchanged pleasantries. "Al would like a word with you," interrupted Rory. "I'll keep an eye on the lads if you want."

"Yes, this is OK," said the Daddy. The three walked to the corner of the room and made themselves comfortable on some chairs that had been stacked against the wall. Rory sat in the seat in front of the window and took a look through one of the pairs of binoculars.

Rory squinted through the lens to see a view of the street on the other side of the flat. Radek and Mats were clearly visible sat in the front seats of a plain car parked up across from the block. They looked bored. Rory thought back to the days when he worked surveillance – long boring days where nothing would happen, followed sometimes by a short burst of excitement.

He shifted to the other set of binoculars, which had a view of the cell's flat. The view was terrible, only showing the front door that exited onto a long balcony that ran the full length of the block linking all the front doors. This was the best they could find. Either the members of the cell knew what they where doing and selected the flat well or were just plain lucky. All the G.R.O.M could do was watch the front door and the street from the car. However, that would change tonight as they had access to the flat next door.

Chapter 4

George was concerned, Al had never asked him to do this before. Al must have been worried about Cam to have him keep an eye on him. He drove the last few miles thinking, back to all the time he had worked alongside Cam. Had he been changing? Al seemed to have thought so.

George had been with the Asset program from the beginning, he had been one of the first that Al had recruited. He had run into trouble in his homeland, the Republic of Ireland, and Al had helped him get out of that trouble. He had lost his family, his wife and son; they left because their lives were in danger just because they were connected to him. George knew they had a safe existence now. He still missed them but finding them would only put them back into danger. They were best without him.

Since that point in his life he had worked with Cam many times, all over the world, sometimes barely getting out alive. Two years ago he had teamed up with Rory, Bull and Donald and gone to Iran, since then they had been working together. Donald had been badly injured on that mission and was no longer operational but was still a excellent linguist in the Asset program.

Rory too had been injured, shot in the back by a sniper. Rory bounced back as he always did, shrugging it off saying it was nothing more than another scratch. The four-man Asset team of George, Bull, Cam and Rory was one of the best in the program. George thought back through the two years since Iran and all the tasks they had been on. Perhaps Cam was having problems. Anything annoyed him these days. He had developed a bad temper and his views of the world were becoming more extreme day by day.

George spotted the red road sign up ahead. The sign said 'Works Access Only' and indicated a slip road off the motorway. This sign was the way into the Assets headquarters and training site. Although the site itself was huge it was hidden from the road by nothing more than a long track. If anyone took the turning they would soon turn and head back to the motorway thinking it led nowhere.

He drove up the single-track road between open fields until he came to a battered old looking metal fence. He climbed out of his car leaving the engine running and searched his pockets for the key to the lock. It opened easily, the lock being used daily by people coming and going. He drove through and repeated the process in reverse, locking the gate.

He continued on along the track and slowly the large hangars came into view, six in all, huge in size. They contained the training facilities where they could practise for their assignments, the headquarters and control rooms, a state-of-the-art range and skills house and accommodation areas for when they had to stay over.

George knew Cam was on the range today so he headed straight for the building containing the range and armoury. He pulled up at the anonymous, old shabby building and stepped out of the car.

"Hey George!" came a shout from behind him. George looked over his shoulder to see Speedy and his team walking towards him. George knew what this was about and sighed as he locked his car door.

"Hello speedy," said George waiting for the jokes to start flowing. Speedy and his team had been playing the enemy in demonstration the previous day. Al had told George all about it over the phone when he expressed his concerns for Cam's state of mind.

Speedy and Lugsy, made up half the team. Both from Scotland, Speedy was a funny guy from the highlands. He looked and acted accident-prone but was a great operator with varied experience. Lugsy was from Glasgow, a decent guy, but found fault with everything.

The other two were from the continent, Kostas was from Greece, he was ex-Greek special forces and Luca was from Rome. Both fine operators. There was a healthy rivalry between the two teams, George's and Speedy's. Both thought they were the best and competed with everything they did.

"Did you hear?" said Speedy getting close to George's car with a large grin across his face. "Did you hear what happened yesterday?"

"Yeah, I heard."

"You should have seen it, it was bloody brilliant." The other members of Speedy's team sniggered . George looked at the four men in front of him, they were fully kitted out ready to enter the skills house.

"Cam in there?" asked George knowing the answer, trying to cut short the volley of insults that were bound to follow.

"Aye, what you doing here?" said Speedy.

"Need to speak to Cam, can you give me some time in there?"

"Why? What's going on?" enquired Speedy.

"Yeah, if something's happening and they need the top team in the program, here we are," said Lugsy jokingly whilst motioning to his team.

"Nothing's going on Lugsy, I just need to speak to Cam."

"Well, whatever it is, I'm sure Al will see sense and send his 'A' team," said Kostas. "Your guys are split all over the place."

"I'm sure you'll be first choice if anything kicks off," said George. "But for now I need a few minutes."

"Fine," said Speedy. "Let's get a brew on guys." Speedy and his team spun round and made their way back towards the accommodation block. George watched them until they were out of sight. He didn't want them to double back and come up with any practical jokes, for which they were known.

George could hear shooting from in the range. He entered the building and made his way through the corridors to the viewing platform, which was above and behind the firing point. George stood leaning on the handrail and looked through the bullet-proof glass that protected onlookers from wild shots and ricochets.

Cam was in the middle of a practice shoot with a HK53 sub-machine gun. George had a good view down on Cam as he fired round after round at the targets at the other end of the twenty-five metre range. He had the stock folded in and was pushing the weapon out against the strap.

He was firing short, three-round bursts into the wooden figure-eleven size targets. When the twenty-five round magazine was empty he performed a well-drilled magazine change. He continued firing and started moving in on the targets. Walking front on, he fired more bursts into the target, which splintered as the rounds cut through, entering the sand behind.

The next magazine was slid out of his tactical vest and inserted into the weapon. Automatically Cam slammed the cocking handle forward from its locked back position, loading the first round in place. This magazine was emptied in two or three longer bursts as he closed in on the targets. When that magazine ran dry he slung the weapon and pulled his Glock17 pistol from his leg holster and emptied the seventeen-round magazine into the target followed by another.

When the shooting was over he stood only a few metres away from what was left of the target. He holstered his pistol and pulled off the high impact, noise-cancelling ear defenders. Still staring at the smashed target George could see him take a deep breath. He turned and Cam immediately saw George up on the viewing platform.

The two locked eyes and George nodded to him, Cam nodded back, his face still expressionless.

George left the viewing platform, placed his hands in his jacket pockets, and walked down the metal staircase to the ground floor of the range. He opened the door to the firing point to meet Cam who had come back from the far end of the range. Cam stared blankly at George. George, with his hands still in his pockets, beckoned with his head. He and Cam left the range.

1525hrs GMT

"So," said George placing the cups of coffee on the table. "How's things, mate?" He sat by the wooden table where Cam was already seated. Cam looked at the mugs and then at George.

"Since when do I drink brews?" said Cam.

"Yeah," George snorted. "You're probably the only man in the mob who doesn't." Cam didn't reply, he just shifted uncomfortably in his chair. They had retired to the back office of the range, an old dusty room, used more as a target storeroom than an office. Still it was a place they could sit and talk in private. "Look mate," sighed George. "What happened yesterday was just one of those things."

"I don't give a shit about that," said Cam. "Putting on a show for some bullshit V.I.Ps isn't what we're all about." He slumped down in his chair and rested his forearm on the table. "So what's Al saying?"

"He was fine about it, showed them the difficulties we face." He looked at Cam and studied his demeanour. "So what's up?"

"What do you mean?" Cam shrugged.

"Come on," said George sipping his hot coffee. "You're not yourself mate, something's bothering you."

"I'm fine!" said Cam abruptly.

"I know you Cam," said George warming his hands with the hot mug. "I think you forget that. And so does Al." Cam shook his head and slid his mug of coffee around on the table by its handle. "Four years mate, four years we've been working together."

"I know, I was there," he said sarcastically.

"Do you know what?" said George with a slightly raised voice. "We're only sitting here today because at some time or another we've saved each others lives." He stared at Cam who stared back. "I would have thought you would be able to talk to me if something was bothering you."

"You want to know what's bothering me?" Cam matched George's volume. "God damn everything! That's what!" George inhaled and held it, then leaning on the backrest of his chair he breathed out. "This isn't the same organisation we started with George!" shouted Cam. "Even you should see that!"

"It's improved if anything," said George at a more conversational level. "Look at what we've got around us." Cam scanned around the cluttered, cobwebbed full storeroom.

"OK, bad example. But we have everything we need here."

"I liked it how it was," said Cam crossing his arms. "When the teams didn't come into contact with each other and there wasn't all the crap that comes with this place."

"There's no crap here Cam," George said in disbelief.

"What!" he exclaimed. "Are you blind, George?" Cam sat forward. "Do you know what I was doing before the range today?"

"What?" George sighed.

"A lesson!" Cam looked at George across the table. "A lesson on the national decision-making model."

"The what?"

"Exactly!" he answered. "The process of how to make a decision. Some bloody police lecturer Al's brought in to teach us how to make decisions. How to gather information, what to consider, what to do if things go wrong." George sat opposite, listening to Cam who was now ranting, making air quotes with his fingers. "If I think about all that shit I'd be shot dead."

"Look I…"

"But do you know what the most ridiculous thing was?" Cam interrupted.

"No, what?"

"He said that we do it automatically!" He raised his arms in the air to show his contempt at the lecturer's statement. "So why teach us it? I breathe automatically, nobody teaches me to breathe!"

"OK, I understand but…"

"And equality and diversity!" he added. "The Human Rights Act! Us! The Human Rights Act," he repeated. George stayed quiet. He knew he would be interrupted again if he didn't. "Do they even know what we do? Does Al?"

"Of course he does," said George.

"Yeah," he snorted. "Sometimes I think he forgets. Come on George, some of the shit we've done and they are harping on about human rights!"

"Everyone has rights, Cam."

"Fuck off, George! You hanged someone and made it look like they killed themselves." George looked uncomfortable at the statement that had just been made. Cam paused to compose himself. "I'm not sure I want this anymore," he said eventually. "We kill the enemy abroad no problem, no questions asked. But here at home, no. Here we can't do shit all. Human rights! Christ the home-grown enemy have us by the balls, nobody's willing to risk offending them."

"Yeah," agreed George quietly. "We all think the same mate."

"Do we?" said Cam. The room fell silent for a short time. "Remember that Mosque in Birmingham?" he said, breaking the silence. "It's always Birmingham, right?" he asked. "Just before we met in fact." George looked back at Cam who fidgeted in his chair. "Bomb factory, brainwashing facility. It all went on there. I'd like to burn that place to the ground!" Cam's voice sounded grave.

"Cam, mate, Al's concerned about you," George said in a way to hint that a problem might be on the horizon, and to give him the chance to stop before he said something he might regret.

"Is that what this is about? Al's asked you to check up on me. See if I'm mentally stable." Cam made another set of air quotes.

"Are you?"

"Tell him anything you want." Cam stood up, pushing the chair across the floor. "I couldn't care less." He walked off leaving his full coffee cup on the table. George remained, staring at the cold drink. After a few minutes thinking, he too got up and left the range.

Once outside he walked over to his car. He opened the boot and then his kit bag that he had packed with a view to staying on site for a few days. From the bag he pulled a bottle of Jameson whiskey. Bottle in hand he made his way to the accommodation block.

The block was ghostly quiet. All the teams were out on tasks, they could be anywhere in the world. The block had a simple layout: two floors, a long corridor with rooms off each side, a communal kitchen on one end and a sitting room on the other. The individual rooms were of a good standard for a military type accommodation. They had a bedroom, bathroom and a small study with a desk and chairs. Each man had their own room, which they could use when needed.

They all had their own homes outside the site and some of the team members had families but not Cam, neither did George. Those who had families did their best not to let their home lives and work lives come into contact. It was the individual's choice how much they told their relatives about what they did for a living.

George arrived at Cam's room. He knocked, but there was no answer. He tried the handle and the door opened. Inside, Cam was standing by the window, staring at his reflection. He turned to face George who lifted the bottle of whiskey. Cam snorted a laugh, opened one of the cupboards and reached inside. He slammed two glasses on the table and sat down.

George opened the bottle and poured a large glass each. He replaced the cork and sat down opposite.

"When's he back then?" asked Cam.

"Al?"

"Yeah."

"Tomorrow morning." George lifted his glass copying Cam. "Cheers."

Chapter 5

Mats turned the key in the lock and the bolt clanked open. He pushed the heavy door into the cold, bare corridor. They were in. They let the door close itself on the slow return spring. Quickly they climbed the stairs to the top floor, striding two or three stairs at a time.

They reached the top landing breathing heavily from carrying the cases full of surveillance equipment. Rory led the way along the landing to the third apartment from the end. He moved past the door and stopped to listen. The lights of the Galaxy Centrum shone in the background. He heard Mats inserting the key in the lock of the door and turning the mechanism. He looked up at the coloured lights to where the other G.R.O.M and Al were.

The door opened and Mats slipped inside, Rory followed carrying the cases. Mats closed the door carefully, pushing the door fully into the frame. He let the door handle return to its natural position and it seated without a click.

"OK," whispered Mats feeling for the light switch on the wall. On came the lights causing them both to blink after being in darkness for the last few hours. "Put the cases on the desk."

48

Mats pointed to a table in the middle of the small apartment. Rory gently laid the cases on the table and opened the clasps one at a time using both hands, avoiding the click. Inside the first case were a number of drills, other equipment and a laptop. The second had a recording device in it.

Mats stepped up onto the old sofa that was against the wall adjoining the flat next door. He put his ear to the wall and listened, and after hearing nothing through the thick wall, he slid his open hand over the surface. He gently tapped the wall in a few locations near the corner of the ceiling.

"Here I think," he whispered whilst still assessing the wall. "The detector." He looked over at Rory who picked out the pipe detector. Rory handed it to Mats who returned his attention to the wall. He swiped the detector over the wall surface, checking for pipes and electrical wires. He watched the small LED light that would alert him to any metal objects hidden within the wall cavity.

"Looks good," whispered Rory.

"Yes, drill," said Mats quietly, marking a small cross on the wall with a felt pen he pulled from his back pocket. Rory picked the small, hand-operated drill from the case and moved to where Mats was perched precariously on the arm of the sofa. Rory handed him the drill and he placed, gently, the tip of the drill bit in the centre of the cross.

Mats turned the handle of the mechanical drill slowly and plaster, ground to dust, began to fall to the floor. Rory squatted down and leant on the wall, pressing his shoulder hard against it. He wanted to absorb as much of the small vibrations into his body as he could whilst facing the door to the apartment, their only route out.

He pulled his pistol from his shoulder holster hidden by his jacket and felt the row of spare magazines lined up in the belt rig. In this squatting position they dug into his torso but he wanted to keep eyes on the only way into the flat. Mats continued grinding into the wall, every few centimetres he retracted the drill and blew into the hole.

"It can not be far now," he said. "I have no idea what will be on the other side."

"Do you want sound?" asked Rory in a hushed voice.

"I think so, I would like to avoid a surprise." Rory moved from his crouched position and picked up the other open case. He placed it on the floor near the wall and picked up some pads that were attached to the device by coiled wires. He peeled off the sticky back of one of the pads and stuck it to the wall. He repeated the process until all the pads were on the wall, spread as far as they could, stretching the wires as much as possible.

"OK, we're about to have sound." Rory's hand hovered over the switch on the recording device. Mats nodded giving approval for the sound to come on line. Rory flicked the switch and turned the volume up from its pre-set position at zero. They heard nothing.

Mats continued with the drill, cutting further into the wall. At every half turn of the mechanism he checked the hole, mindful he was nearly through. Rory listened, hoping not to hear a clatter of a picture falling to the floor or an ornament being knocked over. Mats' choice of the corner of the room would hopefully negate that possibility.

"I think I'm through," said Mats peering through the hole. "Lights are off so it is hard to say." He didn't blow into the hole in case he blew some dust into the apartment. He inserted a special brush that has bristles that are retracted until it's pushed through the hole. With the brush, he cleaned the hole of dust. "OK," he sighed. "Let us put through the camera."

Rory took the tiny camera from the case and gave it to Mats. He then returned to the case and opened the laptop, connected the camera cable to the back and switched it on. The laptop booted up quickly and a view of the apartment they were in appeared on the screen. The view jerked as Mats moved it into position, and then the screen went dark as he inserted it into the hole in the wall.

"Switching to night vision," said Rory, selecting the NVG option via the mouse pad on the laptop. The screen lit up a dull green colour showing what looked like a tunnel with a circular opening at the end. Mats pushed the camera centimetre by centimetre through until a picture of the next-door apartment came into view. "OK, that's enough." The fisheye lens was only as far as it needed to be for its purpose.

Both men stood looking at the screen of the laptop. The view was as good as it could be. The living room was fully displayed; two people were asleep on the room's sofas. The rest of the room was unremarkable, old and tatty. A door in one corner seemed to lead to the bedroom, the other corner had an area that was the kitchen and next to that was the front door. An exact, albeit opposite, copy of the apartment they were in now.

Rory reached into his pocket and pulled out a mobile phone. He swiped it into action and tapped in a number.

"Who are you calling?"

"Someone who can help," he replied. "Donald, Rory." In the silence of the room Donald's voice could be heard coughing through the phone's speaker.

"What the hell. Do you know what time it is?" said Donald between coughs.

"I need a favour, mate."

"Couldn't it wait? And why are you whispering?" Donald finally cleared his throat. "I can barely hear you."

"It's a long story, mate," answered Rory. Donald sighed.

"Do you know what? I don't care and don't want to know. What do you need?"

"I might be sending you some audio, could you translate for me?"

"Sure, when?"

"Don't know, as and when, mate."

"No problem, I'll be waiting."

"Sweet, check your email." Rory hung up, letting the tired Donald get back to sleep. Mats looked at his watch.

"I do not know what Tatus will think of that," said Mats.

"It's just a bit of help with translation mate, that's all." Mats flicked open the edge of the closed curtains; it was nearly five in the morning and the sun would be up soon. For now, they could only wait to see what the day would bring.

1145hrs CET

"Wake up!" shouted Mats. "For Gods sake you are snoring!"

"What?" said Rory, waking up with a start and looking around frantically. The street outside the block of flats was crowded with pedestrians going about their daily business. The day was passing with still nothing happening. Karol and Radek were inside the flat and the Daddy was still in the shopping centre's radio station.

"Can not stand it anymore." Rory had taken Al back to the airport and now they were taking their turn watching from the car, ready to follow anyone who might leave the flat. As Rory needed sleep Mats had taken first watch, but the snoring had been too much to take.

"What? I'm just making sure you're staying awake," said Rory, snuggling into the corner of his car seat. Mats huffed and picked up the radio that was sat on the dashboard.

"Tatus, czy cos sie tam dzieje?" he said into the radio mic.

"Nie, nic. Przygotowuja obiad."

"Zrozumiane." Mats threw the radio back to its original position on the dash.

"What was that?" asked Rory with his eyes shut.

"Still nothing." Rory could tell his colleague was getting impatient. The pair sat in silence and Rory began to drift off again. Mats stretched in his seat straightening his legs under the steering column and arching his back. "I'm hungry." He looked over at Rory but he was fast asleep.

Mats grabbed the radio after a message in Polish was sent across the air. Rory was instantly awake. From the tone of the voice, something was wrong. Mats listened, his eyes darted around the interior of the car.

"Problem?" asked Rory. Mats didn't respond right away, he was still listening, gathering information from the short hurried messages.

"I think they have found the camera," said Mats turning his attention to the flats. More frantic messages came over the radio. Rory waited for an update, leaning forward so he could look out of the windscreen, up at the flats. "Cholera!" Two members of the cell exited their flat and began kicking in the door to the hide next door.

The pair in the car could do nothing but watch as the door was kicked in. A volley of shots echoed across the street. People on the streets stopped and all turned in the direction of the gunshots. More shots followed as the two terrorists fired into the flat where Karol and Radek were. Then the screams from the civilians drowned out the shooting as they scattered for cover.

"No!" Rory grabbed Mats' arm when he went for the door handle of the car. "We have to wait!" Mats turned to Rory, panic etched across his face. "They can look after themselves." Now the streets were virtually deserted and the gunfire could be heard again. To Rory this sounded like return fire, Glock17s. The two terrorists fell out of sight from the view of the car. "See," said Rory. "Told you."

More cell members ran from the flat, firing indiscriminate shots into the flat as they jumped over their fallen colleagues, and raced for the stairwell. Rory patted Mats on the shoulder and the two climbed out of the car keeping low. Mats joined Rory on his side of the vehicle. They watched the main entrance to the block.

In their peripheral vision the two on the ground saw Karol step out of the flat, smoothly and with his pistol up on aim. Radek followed him and the two moved cautiously to the stairwell on the southern end of the block. Karol made eye contact with Rory and Mats, and he paused hoping for some instructions. Rory held up his hand indicating for them to stop.

Karol and Radek held their position at the top of the stairwell. Rory and Mats took aim in the direction of the entrance. The heavy entrance door swung open and two cell members flew out onto the street. Rory waited until the others were out before opening fire. When he did, the two on the top floor heard the shots and they entered the stairwell, bounding down the stairs.

The four cell members panicked and ran north up the street towards the Galaxy Centrum. The range that Rory and Mats were from the cell members sent their shots wide, ineffective. Karol and Radek reached the ground level and opened fire on the fleeing cell. On seeing this Rory and Mats pursued on the opposite side of the street, under cover provided from the others.

Taking cover behind a parked car, Rory and Mats took over the fire from the others, who ran forward changing magazines. The four cell members ran flat out for the shopping mall, they had no choice but to keep going. One of the cell grabbed an old lady who was hiding in a doorway and held his gun to her head.

Karol slowed to a walk steadying his aim. He yelled something at the hostage taker but it was inaudible to Rory and Mats. He closed in on the terrified cell member who was pushing his pistol into the old lady's temple. Radek moved off to one side, creating an L shape on the enemy, he too was up on aim. The hostage taker switched gaze from Radek to Karol and back again. The old lady's face was contorted with fear. Karol edged closer.

The hostage taker, in sheer panic, extended his pistol in Karol's direction. One shot rang out hitting Karol in the left shoulder; he returned fire hitting the enemy in the head. The cell member fell to the floor and the lady collapsed to the ground covering her face with her hands. Radek rushed in and pushed her back into the doorway. Karol approached the dead terrorist and put one more round in his head, his left arm hanging limp by his side. From up ahead, the three surviving cell members had re-grouped using the time provided by their, now dead, colleague. They began to fire on Karol and Radek.

Radek held the old lady in the doorway, keeping her safe and out of harm's way. Karol advanced on the enemy, defiantly down the middle of the street. He held his pistol up with one arm and fired repeatedly on the terrorists, who hid from the onslaught laid down by the visibly pissed-off Polish soldier.

Empty cases, ejected from Karol's Glock17, bounced off the walls and windows of the shops that lined the street. When the pistol ran dry, its top slide was held open by the empty magazine, signifying a mag change was needed. With a well-rehearsed drill Karol pressed the magazine-release button with his thumb, ejecting the empty magazine from the bottom of the pistol grip. With one arm out of action, he knelt down placing the pistol in the crook of his leg, trapping it between his thigh and calf muscle. Now, with a hand free, he pulled a fresh magazine from his belt rig and slid it in place.

Raising the pistol back up into the aim he released the top slide, loading the first round into the chamber. Karol was back up and firing, moving within seconds. The terrorists had no time to get back into the fire fight, still cowering behind the cars near the entrance to the shopping centre. Rory and Mats now joined the shoot out and all four of the team moved in on the terrorists. Rounds punched into the metal work of the cars and some began to penetrate. Shocked, the terrorists ran into the centre.

The team rushed to the sliding door entrance, the two fire teams either side. Karol holstered his pistol under his jacket and gripped his shoulder feeling for the wound. His hand came away covered in blood; he winced in pain as he felt the injury. Rory looked at Karol, he appeared pale and in a bad way, but he would never leave the team.

Screams emanated from within the shopping centre. The team had to move. Rory knew Karol should fall back, but they needed everyone if they were to re-take the centre. They could be anywhere, hiding, waiting for them to make an entrance, ready to take them out.

"We should go!" shouted the ever impetuous Mats. "Szybko, ruszajcie sie!" he shouted to the other G.R.O.M motioning them forwards.

"OK, fuck it. Lets go!" said Rory, doing his best to keep calm. Rory went for the sliding doors and moved inside the centre. "Radek, Karol, push right!" Rory and Mats jinked, zigzagging to cover.

People ran all over the centre, terrified, not knowing what to do or where to go. The team found their cover and, when safe, peered over it hopeful of locating the enemy. Above the screams Rory heard a car engine revving.

"What the hell's that?" said Rory, scanning the shopping centre for movement that wasn't civilians running for cover. "Can you hear that?" he said to Mats who looked blankly back at him, eyebrows furrowed. Rory straightened up to gain a better view of the centre floor. "Oh shit!" He grabbed Mats and pulled him away from their cover as two silver Mercedes cars smashed through the shopping centre's booths and kiosks.

The vehicles knocked everything out of their way smashing debris all over the centre's floor. The glass doors shattered as the terrorist cell burst out onto the street. Rory and Mats looked at each other then back at the destroyed doors.

"Ruszaj sie!" shouted Mats, sprinting for the entrance. Moments later Rory ran after him.

"Where the hell did they get the keys?" he shouted, running after him. After a few paces he stopped and looked back at the others. Karol was struggling to get to his feet even with the help of Radek.

"Radek!" Rory shouted back. "Take care of Karol. We got this." Radek gave him the thumbs up sign and Rory continued after Mats who was now half way down the street. Rory stopped at the entrance and saw the two Mercs disappearing into the distance, driving the wrong way against the flow of traffic.

Moments later Mats skidded to a stop outside the centre, having reached their parked car and racing it back to Rory's position.

"Do samochodu, szybo, ruszaj tylek!" Mats called out, running round to the passenger side of the vehicle. "You will be driving. I speak on radio." Rory ran from the foyer and climbed in the driver's side of the car entering via the door that Mats had left open. Slamming it shut he stamped on the accelerator causing the wheels to spin before they took and the car sped off after the two silver cars.

"We'll never catch them in this piece of shit." said Rory, dodging in and out of the vehicles scattered in disarray after the Mercs had come through. Mats gripped the radio pressing the pressel and spoke to the Daddy.

"Tatus," he said. "Ktoredy Oni sie przemieszczaja?" The Daddy could be heard replying.

"Lewo! Na lewo, mijaja Radisson." Rory knew he would be watching from satellite view. It had been available but they'd had no reason to use it as yet.

"Which way, mate?"

"Left, past the Radisson." Mats indicated down the street signed Pilsudskiego. Rory slid the car left, tyres screeching. Still headed against the traffic, which was already at a standstill caused by the cell. Mats continued with the comms from the Daddy, getting more directions.

"Right!" shouted Mats. Instantly he was forced to grab at the roof handle to steady himself as Rory skidded round the corner back onto the correct side of the road.

"There they are!" screamed Rory. "I see them." The two Mercs were having trouble pushing through the traffic. Rory caught up as they struggled to weave in and out of the cars waiting at the lights. Mats leaned out of the car and fired on the Mercs.

The Mercs started to bash their way past in response to the incoming fire, causing unwanted attention from the police station on the intersection. The police joined the fight, firing on Rory and Mats, who ducked back into the vehicle. Rory slid down in his seat and turned the wheel to the right mounting the pavement. People jumped to safety, bins and other street furniture bounced off the bonnet smashing the windscreen.

"Stop, stop, stop." shouted Mats. "We have gone past. Go left, they gone left." Rory performed a series of manoeuvres still under fire from the police near the station.

"Fucking hell!" shouted Rory. "Do all your police have guns?" He sped away from the police station down the cobbled street. The cell were still heading east towards the river. "Christ!" he said as they escaped the reach of the police's guns. "Hope you took the full cover out on this thing." Mats grabbed the radio that had fallen into the foot well of the car during the fire fight. He frantically asked for information through the radio. He held it up to his ear staining to hear the instructions.

"Which way, mate?" asked Rory. "T-junction! Which way?" The junction loomed, Rory didn't want to slow down and lose momentum. He needed to keep up with the Merc's powerful engines. "Which Way!" he demanded.

"Lewo! W lewo skrec."

"What?" shouted Rory as he swung left, heading north up Jarowita.

"How did you know to go left?"

"What you said started with an L," he said, concentrating on the pursuit. Up ahead Rory could see one of the Mercs going with the flow of traffic. "Where's the other one?" Mats spoke fast and loudly into the radio. Again he held it up to his ear.

"Kurwa! On our right!" he shouted. Out of the side street on the right came one of the Mercs. It clipped the back of their car slewing it towards the museum building. Rory spun the wheel left correcting the course of the vehicle as the rear window shattered.

Mats turned in his seat to see the enemy passenger firing on their vehicle. Mats slumped down and returned fire from between the front seats. Rory scanned the street ahead for the front vehicle, it had disappeared right after the museum. Also upfront, a tram headed towards them down the tramline in the middle of the street. Rory saw his chance.

He slammed the brakes on for a second, only to flash the brake lights. The Merc braked hard and Rory saw it wiggle in the rear view mirror. Rory slowed his car, under control, and moved right. The Merc came up on their left and Mats fired shots into the vehicle's wheels and tyres. Rory slammed the car left into the side of the Merc pushing it onto the tramlines. Once on the tracks, the Merc struggled to escape the tramlines and the tram hit them head on. The Merc was destroyed, it's bonnet pushed into the driving compartment inflicting fatal injuries on the occupants.

Rory accelerated at the next junction; he had seen the vehicle go right, east towards the river.

"One more, there's only one more." said Rory. "We can finish this right here." The river came into view.

"Right, go right," Mats said, relaying instructions from the Daddy. Rory took the corner and saw the Merc. His driving skills were better than the terrorist and he gained ground fast. The Merc's brake lights came on and the vehicle skidded side on to their vehicle. Rory saw the driver raise his pistol and take aim on their car. He was going too fast to stop and with the new threat of incoming fire he swung left.

A small restaurant on the other side of the pavement loomed into view, crowded with people hiding around their tables where, only a moment ago were enjoying their teas and coffees. Rory swung further left onto the concrete steps that led down to the river. The underside of their car raked down each step destroying the exhaust and suspension of the vehicle.

The momentum of the fall down the steps kept the vehicle moving as it smashed onto the flat ground by the riverside. Mats flew forward as the car hit the ground slamming his head off the smashed windscreen. The force of the hit deployed the driver's airbag pushing Rory back into his seat. Mats slumped back in his seat whilst Rory fought to keep the car out of the river.

"Ahhhh shit!" Rory shouted against the deflating airbag as the car's right wheels went over the embankment and entered the cold waters of the Odra river. The car had gone too far and toppled over into the dark river. Up-turned, the car began to sink beneath the surface. Both without seatbelts, they were now lying on the roof of the vehicle. Rory grabbed at and pulled the door handles but they wouldn't open. Water poured into the vehicle, fast through the open rear window.

Rory held his breath, coughing from the powder from the airbag, as the car sank fully under the water. Only then did the doors open as the pressure inside the vehicle equalised with the outside. Rory grabbed Mats' shirt collar and pulled with all the strength he could muster. The water was dark and Rory couldn't tell which way was up. He blew a few bubbles for reference and followed them to the surface, pulling an unconscious Mats behind him.

When he broke the surface, he tried to lift Mats' head into the air. Watered-down blood leaked from his head wound as Rory gasped for breath, treading towards the shore. He threw Mats' arms onto the concrete shore and lifted him onto the land causing himself to go under the water. Rory spluttered after taking in the foul-tasting salty water of the Odra.

He climbed out and collapsed next to Mats who was still not moving. Breathing hard he wiped the gluey powder from his eyes to see a man approach from the side. Rory thought this person had come to help but instead pointed a gun at his face. It was the last member of the cell. Rory felt for his pistol but he had lost it in the crash. The Arab-looking man said something and straightened his arm ready to fire.

Rory, unable to defend himself, spat at the man, drawing from the back of his throat. "Fuck you, asshole!"

Chapter 6

The skills house in the HQ was a collection of corridors set over three floors with doors leading off into rooms at random intervals. Some rooms had doors leading off into other rooms, giving the assault teams something to think about. Furniture was scattered about the building and could be moved from one room to another. Every so often they would re-arrange the layout, providing a new building for the teams to practise in.

Cam and George sat in one of the rooms on the middle floor, nursing sore heads. Speedy's team were practising building clearances and they were playing the enemy. They had been sat waiting for over two hours now and boredom was beginning to set in. Their weapons, loaded with training simunition, lay on the rickety table. Cam and George lounged on sofas that they had pulled from other rooms to create some kind of sitting room.

"I feel like shit," said George.

"Yeah," grunted Cam. "Me too." He stretched out his legs and rested his heels on the table near to their pistols. "Where the hell are they? I can't be bothered with this."

"Two hours," George sighed. "They should be in by now."

"I haven't heard anything, have you?"

"Not over the bells ringing in my head I haven't." Cam shakily got to his feet. He rubbed his eyes and ran his fingers through his hair.

"I'll have a look," he said, moving over to the window. He peered out of the glassless window-frame; the skills house was a building within a building. This huge hangar, similar to the other training hangars, contained the skills house and the range. He saw nothing except the mock-up of a street on the exterior of the skills house.

"Anything?" asked George.

"No," he said looking around. "Nothing." Cam stumbled back over to the sofa and collapsed down into the old, flat cushions. "Christ, I'm getting old." George laughed under his breath. "Did you hear my knees crack there?"

"Happens to us all I'm afraid," said George. "This is a young man's game, only exceptional people can keep it going."

"Like Bull, the man's a machine."

"Yeah. But it'll catch up to him too, eventually," said George.

"Is he still out in Afghan?"

"Yeah," George replied. "Hunting the Taliban." He stood up and arched his back, reaching up towards the ceiling. "Do you think I can sneak out and get us some scran?"

"You can try," said Cam. "I think they've forgotten about us." George walked to the doorway. He stopped and held on to the frame.

"Do you want a coffee?" He looked back at Cam slouched on the other sofa. "Oh, oh yeah. Course you don't." He turned to exit the room but stopped again. "Wait…" He turned his head listening intently to the corridor outside the room that contained the staircase down to the ground floor. "I think I hear something."

"What?" said Cam once again rising to his feet. "Are they coming?"

"Yep, yeah. I hear them," he said, ducking back into the room.

"They're in, they're downstairs."

"How the hell did they get in so quietly," said Cam. "We barricaded the doors." Cam picked up both pistols and handed one to George who was still listening.

"I can hear them moving," whispered George. "They're about to come up the stairs." George spun round to the other side of the door, Cam took his place. Cam peeked round the doorframe and looked into the corridor, he could see the stairs, not the full flight, but halfway down to the lower floor.

"There," whispered Cam. "Movement." George nodded in acknowledgment. He slowly pulled back the top slide on his pistol, loading the top, 9mm training round from the magazine. Cam did the same, silently making ready his pistol. He sneaked another look, ducking back inside the room when he'd gathered enough information. "They're on the stairs."

Cam could see the helmets of the team members on the stairs. Brackets fitted to the front to hold night vision goggles and cut out ear cavities where the noise-cancelling ear defenders fit. They were also wearing respirators with blacked out eyepieces, a tactic used to completely remove any humanity from the assaulters.

"Now!" said Cam who immediately swung round the doorframe and opened fire, George joined him. The firing from the two pistols didn't last long; the seventeen rounds from each pistol were empty in seconds. George threw his pistol down at the advancing troops on the stairs.

"Un-armed! I'm un-armed!" he screamed. Cam followed suit. Now they knew the team should arrest them as opposed to kill the un-armed enemy. "Un-armed!" He screamed again as he ran to the sofa he had been sitting on. He began sliding it to the doorway as the team outside stacked up on the door, preparing to make a room entry.

Cam joined him, lifting the end of the sofa up and flipping it out the doorway, leaving it half in and out of the room. The lead man clambered over the sofa followed awkwardly by the second man. Cam could tell the lead man was Speedy, he stepped over the sofa his feet ripping through the innards. His leg disappeared into the sofa slowing the assault.

The other team members tried to clamber over their colleague in an attempt to get into the room, the second man fell to the floor landing on his back, the back plate of his body armour banging loudly on the floor. Cam and George stood with their hands raised in surrender, giggling at the team's trouble.

"Fuck this!" came a muffled shout from one of the last two members of the team. The respirator-wearing assaulter aimed his MP5 and fired. The automatic fire spread simunition across the room hitting Cam and George in the thighs.

"Awww! Christ!" shouted Cam falling to the floor. George too was now on the floor holding his leg where the crayon-type bullets had hit. "For God's sake. Didn't you go to the human rights lesson?"

"Naaa. Fuck that," said the assaulter, firing further shots – one each into the enemy on the floor.

"Alright! Alright!" shouted George. "Enough!" The assault team finally climbed over one another into the room and, whilst gasping for breath through their respirators, began to zip-tie the offenders. The assault was cut short by the site's tannoy system barking into life. The Assault team stopped, as the message was transmitted across the entire HQ.

"Message for George and Cam," came the echoed voice with a hint of static. "Please report to my office. It's Al." Cam and George looked at each other from their position laid flat on the dusty floor. The assaulters released the pressure off their backs and allowed them to get to their feet.

"Ahh, I knew something was going on," said Speedy, ripping off his respirator.

"Yeah, what is it?" asked Lugsy. "We want in."

"Al didn't ask for you did he? He's the boss, he knows what's best," said George sarcastically. "Tell you what, you guys tidy up round here a bit." George motioned at the floor. "Maybe sweep up, it's a bit dusty in here." George was exiting the room as he spoke, trying to time it right so to make a retort difficult.

"If you think it's too much for you to handle," shouted Speedy after George and Cam. "Just give us a shout, we don't mind babysitting you guys." They were out and away and pretended not to hear Speedy's remark.

"What the hell do you think he wants?" asked Cam.

"Don't know," said George. "Could be anything, mate."

1105hrs GMT

Al was sat on the edge of his desk. His office was a large room with a huge wooden desk in the middle. The blinds were closed in the windows for privacy as they normally were, only opened when he had no visitors. He beckoned the two guys in and motioned to a couple of comfortable looking chairs nearby.

Al forwent the usual pleasantries and avoided eye contact and looked at the floor. Cam and George sat down apprehensively. A silence filled the room and Al took in a breath through clenched teeth. He clicked his front teeth together as if looking for a way to start the conversation.

"I've uh," he said eventually. "I've been sat here thinking of a way of saying this." He looked up and made eye contact with both of the men. "And there is no easy way of saying this, so I'm just going to come out with it." George and Cam nodded, hardly breathing. "Rory's dead."

He left that information with them for a few seconds. The nodding stopped.

"What?" gasped Cam.

"He um," Al sighed. "He was shot by the suspects in Poland." George sat forward in his seat and mouthed a silent 'what?'

"The observation point was compromised and the suspects made a break for it."

Al stood up and started to pace back and forth across the carpet. "After a short contact where a G.R.O.M operative was shot, Rory and another G.R.O.M put up a chase by car. They killed all but one, then it all went to shit and they ended up in the river."

"So how the fuck was he shot?" asked George angrily.

"Rory dragged the G.R.O.M out of the sinking car, and by all accounts the suspect approached them on the shore and shot him there and then."

"Him!" said Cam. "Only him, what about the other one?" Al stopped pacing and shrugged his shoulders.

"He survived." He looked over at the two shocked men. Cam stood up.

"He survived? Why didn't he get slotted?"

"Don't know," answered Al. "Maybe he thought he was already dead? I don't know I'm only guessing. But maybe we can get some answers out of him when he gets here."

"Here?" said George standing alongside the others.

"Yes, I've got him sent over to us so we can get some answers first hand," said Al.

"Good, I wanna speak to him!" said Cam.

"No, you'll have nothing to do with him."

"OK," nodded Cam. "So I'm going to Poland to finish the job. Get that bastard who killed Rory."

"No," said Al. "Nobody's going out to Poland, another G.R.O.M team have been assigned to it, they can handle it."

"So what the hell do you want me to do?" said Cam, getting annoyed. "Just sit around doing nothing?"

"Cam," said Al in an attempt to bring him back down. "I want you to take some time off, get away from here. Go back up north and do whatever it is you do up there."

"What!" shouted Cam. "Someone just killed Rory! You want me to just leave it?" Cam paused and looked in turn between Al and George. "Oh right, I see. I get it. You two having little talks about me behind my back are you? After everything we've been through!"

"Cam," interrupted Al. "You're getting this all wrong." Al looked over at George for a split second. George tried to avoid direct eye contact.

"I saw that," said Cam. "Now it makes sense, you turning up at the range yesterday. Asking me what's wrong and how I'm doing."

"Cam, you're in no state of mind to be getting involved with this task. Not after what's just happened."

"Oh right! And he his?" Cam pointed at George. "We're in the same situation. Except I'm being told to get lost."

"Cam…"

"No. That's it. I've had enough. I'm out of here." Cam opened the office door. "But that's what you want isn't it?"

"Cam," said George. "Don't do this."

"Do what?" Cam paused in the doorframe, "you just told me to go." He looked at them both. "I'm just doing as I'm told. Just like I've always done!" He stepped through the doorway. The door slammed behind him, making the closed blinds rattled on the frame.

"Should I go after him?" asked George. Al rubbed his face then pressed his closed eyes with his fingers and thumb.

"No," he sighed. "Just let him go, I can't trust him around this G.R.O.M guy when he gets here."

"Well it's a bit suspect isn't it?" said George, opening the closed blinds and looking out of the office. "Rory getting shot and him being left alive."

"He was unconscious when Rory dragged him out of the car."

"Still, you would have thought he would have made sure they were both dead."

"Look George," said Al in a serious manner. "Cam has been acting strange for a while now, you must have noticed."

George let the blinds snap back into place and turned to face Al, who nodded after considering his statement. "Also, there are a couple of extra things I can't go into right now."

He fixed a stare at George, a stare that George knew all to well.

"So," said George, realising he didn't need to be party to this extra information. "What's the official story?"

"Same as ever," said Al sitting down on the edge of his desk as he had been when they entered his office. "Training accident."

"And Cam?"

"Let him calm down whilst we get some information from the G.R.O.M. Decide what to do from there." Al was back in deep thought, staring at the floor again.

"What if he doesn't come back?" Al looked back up from the floor.

"I don't know mate, I don't know," he said, shaking his head. "I've got Bull on his way back from Afghan." George silently acknowledged. Words seemed to be failing him. "I'm sending Speedy and his team to replace him."

"Huh," laughed George. "He'll love that."

Chapter 7

Thursday 21st March 2013
1900hrs GMT
Keswick, Cumbria, Northwest England

The sun had set. Keswick was as beautiful and fresh as always. Cam stopped on the way into town to pick up a few supplies at the BP petrol station. He paid the attendant and loaded his shopping into the plastic carrier bag. The doors to the station slid open and he stepped out into the cool damp air. He paused to take in the scene; across the road the windows of the timeshare apartments glowed through the waving trees. The river Greta babbled over the rocks as it passed under the bridge behind Toll Bar Cottage.

Instead of driving through town he doubled back the way he had entered, back to the bypass. He followed the A66 to the north of the town and passed the small hospital on the way to Derwent Water. Following the shoreline he looked over towards Lord's Island and the other islands that towered out of the lake.

After a few minutes drive he took a left and began the ascent up towards Ashness Bridge. The narrow winding road led to the place Cam had called home for five or six years, or at least the closest thing he could call home. He had once lodged here. His landlady had left it to him when she died and he had been coming and going for the past two years.

The place looked old and tired, it had been slowly slipping into disrepair, as Cam couldn't find the time to up-keep the property. He parked up in the driveway and stepped out of the car. The main building sat to the right. The kitchen window, where his landlady had always stood, was dusted over and covered with cobwebs. His old cottage lay to the left of the driveway, this too looked old and dilapidated.

The front door to the small cottage creaked open, the key sticking in the lock. The interior was shrouded in darkness, Cam knew the layout like the back of his hand and strode across the living space and felt for the mantelpiece. The matchbox, he had left last time he was there, was still lying on the shelf above the fire next to two large candlesticks. He shook the box and slid it open.

The front room of the cottage flickered in the light created by the candles. Cam knelt down in front of the fireplace. He had left the hearth ready to be used, packed with logs he had splintered outside in the yard. Kindling was stacked in the centre ready to be lit. The first match broke but the second caught and the kindling and old newspaper blackened and twisted into flames.

Cam pulled the oblong table across the stone tiled floor and sat himself down in front of the flames. Mesmerised by the dancing flames Cam felt himself slightly relax, he hadn't experienced that for a long time. He ran his hand over his unshaved face and rubbed his closed eyes with his index finger and thumb.

The bag of shopping lay on the floor, inside the front door. Cam left his seat on the coffee table and lifted the carrier bag onto the counter in the kitchen area of the living space. Some tins of food that he could heat up on the hob clanked against the bottles of whisky as he set it down.

He placed one of the bottles on the counter and hunted for a glass, he found one in the sink and wiped it clean. He snapped open the screw top and poured a healthy double. After taking a swig direct from the bottle he replaced the cap and took a sip from the glass.

The glass of whisky was placed on the table in front of the fire and Cam walked over to the old sofa at the far end of the room. From underneath the sofa he slid out an old wooden footlocker. From it he retrieved a box file and carried it over to the table. The area in front of the fire started to warm up and radiated throughout the room. Cam opened the file and flicked through the documents.

Before pulling one from the box file he finished his glass and slammed it down on the table exhaling the burning whisky fumes. He re-filled the glass and opened the folder. Details of a person of interest in the form of random notes filled the file. Cam thumbed through them one at a time. Printed details, photos and Cam's own handwritten notes made up all the information he needed.

If Al knew he was up to his old tricks he would face serious consequences. He had lost faith in the Asset program since it had become more mainstream. Since it had come to the attention of the US and the wider world they had been under the microscope. It had become harder to complete their tasks whilst conforming to health and safety and human rights. Long gone were the covert assassinations and the underhandedness of the old days.

Before Al had recruited him he had been hunting terrorists alone. He had kept notes from his days in the army and used them to kill the enemy on his own terms. Now the process had started again. He had been executing terrorists his way for over a year now. This time he would see it through to the bitter end, however it may turn out.

He downed another full glass and replenished it from the bottle. He studied the photo of the man; he hated this man. He was, to Cam, the epitome of evil. He was what was wrong with the country. A radicalised Muslim preacher – one that gave sermons in the streets. He would stand on British soil and preach hatred of the western way of life.

Cam swallowed another shot. Instead of re-filling the glass he picked up the bottle and drank from the neck. Freedom of speech, he thought. It seemed OK to spread hate and incite violence for him and his weak-minded followers, but God forbid anything is said about them. That would be racist! Attempts to deport the man had been tried and failed. Some bullshit stories about being afraid to return home or sent to America for fears of torture.

Cam stood up, throwing the photo onto the table; it slid across the surface and fell to the floor. Cam picked up the bottle and took a dram. He paced around the living area, attempting to calm down. A series of deep breaths didn't help, he rubbed his forehead and forced his eyes tightly shut. He gulped more whisky and flung himself down on the sofa kicking the footlocker out of the way.

Cam had another target! He would enjoy this one. Birmingham again! He thought. Why always Birmingham? Home grown terrorists, is there anything worse? Born here, live here, happy to drain the country dry but still hate us! Jealousy, that's what it is with these bastards. Forbidden to live our way when that's all they want, so they hate us for it. Freedom, that's what they want but they're denied it.

"Fucking animals!" he slurred, hauling himself to his feet and cutting the rhetoric in his head short. He took another swig. He wandered over to the table with the file strewn over it. He bent down to pick up the photo that lay staring up at him from the floor. "You're dead, asshole!" He let go of the photo allowing it to flutter to the table-top.

He rooted around in the box file; something else was in the back of his mind. Searching for the next file he found his spare phone and picked it up. This smartphone was the one he would use when on his own tasks. It was untraceable to him, bought and registered under a false name. He had a backup of all these paper files stored in the phone's memory, for use whilst away. His Asset phone had a tracker in it; this would be left here in Keswick when he went on tasks. He slid his own phone into his pocket and put the Asset phone into the box file.

He found the file; it read 'Szczcien, Poland.' He took two gulps from the bottle, whisky dribbled onto the floor. He staggered backwards to the sofa and fell onto the cushions. He opened the file and the contents fell, spilling and sliding across the floor to the left and right.

"Which one of you bastards did it?" he said under his whisky breath. He gathered the photos of the six men. He lined them up on the sofa next to him. The men had been secretly photographed, some in the street, one getting out of a car and two talking to each other sat at a restaurant table. One of them was still alive; one of them had killed Rory.

Cam shakily got to his feet, one hand on the arm of the sofa for support, one hand grasping the nearly empty bottle. He took one more gulp, brought the bottle up to his eye and rotated its body, sloshing the remaining liquid around the base. He necked the remaining whisky and walked over to the kitchen counter.

He dropped the empty bottle into the sink where it rolled around the square basin. He reached for the full bottle, and in his state, misjudged the distance. His fingertips pushed the bottle an inch along the counter. He unscrewed the cap and tossed it into the sink alongside the empty bottle.

He turned and leaned on the counter. He took the first sip and the moon caught his eye shining through the dusty window. He put down the whisky bottle. Taking a rag from the draining board he wiped the window, breaking a few spiders' webs in the process. A spider scuttled away into the corner of the frame.

The clouds outside the window were dark blue and moving fast. The moon shone through, creating a tunnel, breaking up the clouds and lighting a circle around the moon. Reminded him of being out at sea, chasing ships on ridged raiders. He and Rory had conducted many operations out on the waves. He couldn't tell if the swaying motion was the effect of the whisky or was he back out at sea, chasing oil tankers and cargo ships. He shook the thought from his head and turned back to the bottle. The room, shrouded in darkness, was lit only by the flickering flames, which evoked further memories. That cave had been lit by a low fire. He had found himself alone. Where was his team? Cam ducked down behind his kitchen counter.

"Swanny," he whispered. "Swanny." He looked quickly over both shoulders along the length of the counter, his back pressed firmly against the drawers. "Swanny," he said again. "What's going on? Where are you?" He shuffled along the counter's drawers to the corner.

He peeked around into the living space. Shadows danced on the walls and across the sofa. "Boss. Glenn." He listened for a response that would never come. His heart rate rose, he could feel it beating in his chest. He needed to find his team. He stayed crouched and spun round the corner into the living room. He darted across the living room floor, keeping low. He almost ran into the footlocker, which sat in the middle of the floor space.

"Fuck!" he said, the word catching the back of his throat. He took a short sharp intake of breath. The raised lid of the footlocker took the form of a gravestone. The name read Neil Swann. He wanted to retreat, back away from the hallucination but two bar stools under the counter held the names of Glenn and the boss.

He scampered backwards away from the three gravestones to the corner of the room. He curled up into a ball and held his face in his hands. He rocked back and forwards.

"No, no, no, no, no!" he mumbled. "Not real, it's not real," he told himself. He slowly slid his hand from his face and looked through splayed fingers out across the room. The graves had gone, replaced by the locker and two bar stools. He stayed curled up in the corner of the room, too terrified by what his brain had tricked him into seeing.

Most of his friends from before the Asset program were dead. Now so was Rory. He had been through so much with all these people. He had trusted his life with them and they too trusted him. He had let them down and now they were dead. But he wasn't. He had to avenge them; he had to kill the enemy. He stood guiding himself to his feet with the palms of his hands against the wall. The room spun and he shook his head and brought it back to normal although still blurred from the alcohol. He stumbled to the counter and the open bottle of whisky.

He leant his forearms on the counter and took control of the bottle. He threw more whisky down his neck; he needed to dull the memories. Behind him, he could feel someone. Someone looking at him. He turned his head and peered over his shoulder. The photo of the preacher stared back at him.

"Fucker," he said, taking more whisky. He took the bottle to the photo and knelt down by the table. He could hardly see the man's features, so blurred was his vision. He was barely holding on to consciousness. All he knew was this man's time of spreading hate was nearly over.

He blacked out, still knelt by the table, his eyes rolled in his head. The night passed in a blur of headlights, dotted white lines flashing past, orange streetlights streaking above him. Was he moving? He couldn't tell but motion filled the night.

Friday 22nd March
0900hrs GMT
Birmingham, England

Light exploded into his painful head. First the light glowed red through his closed eyelids then, once he opened them, the light burned to the back of his skull. He screwed his face trying to open his eyes fully but he couldn't. His head pounded, his mouth was dry, he tried to swallow but his throat felt like sandpaper.

He could feel that he was sat up, but where, he couldn't tell yet. Very slowly his eyes adjusted and his head accepted the pain the light was causing, he gradually started to see the world around him. He was sat in his car, the sun was up, and he was in a place he had never been before. He looked around the inside of the car, hoping for some answers. All he saw was a bottle of Lucozade in the foot well of the passenger seat.

His head felt like it was going to burst as he leaned over to pick up the bottle. The thirst he had was overbearing, he needed the drink. At first the bubbly drink stabbed at his dry, closed throat but seconds later it provided relief. It was gone in no time. He threw the empty plastic bottle back into the foot well and searched, praying for another.

An old, already open can of Coke, flat but still drinkable provided extra necessary fluid. With one need fulfilled, he started to try to piece together the chain of events that led to him being here.

He remembered being in his cottage, he remembered the hallucinations and he remembered planning his next hit. Could he remember the journey here? Yes, it all came back as if it was rewinding in his head. He had driven here. He remembered the lights of the motorway. He remembered the photo on the table and he remembered the drink. He was surprised he had made it here, considering the state he had been in.

Could it be? He thought to himself through his misty head. Could it? He reached into his inside jacket pocket and pulled out the phone he had taken from the box file. The maps application showed his location. Birmingham. He exited the app and opened the PDF document with the preacher's information. He was! He was on his street. It was however, a long street and he was nowhere near to the house he used as his makeshift Mosque. But he was there.

Cam felt there was more in that pocket than just a phone. A second search of the inside of his jacket revealed a hip flask. He opened it, had a sniff then a swig. Whisky! He almost balked.

"Ughhh, Christ!" he said loudly, but it didn't stop him having another nip. "Hair of the dog." He took another and remembered packing the boot of the car. He was ready for the kill. He was aware that he was still massively drunk but he didn't care. The preacher's days were numbered. Today was his day, it wouldn't bring back Rory but it would make him feel better. He fumbled for the keys that were still in the ignition and turned the engine over. It started and the aircon automatically kicked in. Normally he would turn it off straight away but it felt good on his face. He left it flowing the cool air around the car.

He released the handbrake and pulled out of the space in which he was parked, parallel between two cars. He cautiously, like a learner driver, drove down the road towards the preacher's house, being careful not to sideswipe the parked cars that lined the street. He had to concentrate, and fight to keep control over his still intoxicated head. Up ahead, there was movement, mostly centred round one house. That was his; it had to be.

Still a distance from the preacher's house, he stopped. In his state he didn't feel confident he could parallel park again. He wondered how he had done it after his drink-fuelled drive from Cumbria. He would wait here in the road. It was quiet and with little traffic. He could sit and watch.

He was in an area of the city populated predominantly by Muslims. And locals were hanging around the house that was now less than a hundred metres in front of his vehicle. At least two of the people loitering around were, what Cam assumed, some kind of doormen. They were watching the others and not paying any attention to the house.

The doormen allowed only a couple of the slowly growing crowd to enter the house. After a few minutes, and more people arriving, some passing Cam's car on foot, the doormen started to control the crowd. They started barking commands and waving their arms, shooing the crowd out of the house's front garden and out onto the street.

The doormen took up a position either side of the metal gate that blocked the path to the house. The crowd jostled, each person wanting the best position for whatever was about to happen. Cam watched through his pain-filled eyes. Clouds provided some temporary relief from the early morning sun.

The door to the property opened, and the crowd settled. Out of the house stepped two Asian men, followed closely by a man in a long black overcoat over white robes. This man had a long, wiry, scraggy beard and a pair of glasses balanced on a large hooked nose. Cam recognised this overfed man with dirty-looking skin immediately. His target had presented himself.

Cam remained in his car – this man would routinely preach for over an hour. His hate-filled messages would fire up the crowd and incite their hatred of the western way of life. How evil the infidels were, how they persecuted the Islamic world and they were the punch bag of the British government.

Cam was too far away to hear the words of this creature but knew the probable content of his sermon. He re-opened the hip flask to calm his rising hatred for this man and his followers. His mind was full of how they lived off the country like parasites. How they were known members of terrorist organisations with proven criminal pasts and still left to incite violence against their adopted country. How they sent their sons to Pakistan to training camps to return home to plot acts of terror.

Cam drank from the hip flask remembering how the Asset program would have put a stop to things like this. Not now, not anymore, since they had become known to the powers that be. Now they were forced to conform to the rules of engagement that continued to make the country weak and targets for these animals.

Cam could take it no longer. He finished the flask and flung it onto the passenger seat. He swung open the door and climbed out of the car, nearly falling onto the road. He walked to the back of the car using the roof to steady himself. He opened the boot and grabbed at the felt flooring that covered the spare wheel compartment. Under the false flooring and in place of the wheel, Cam saw a range of weapons that he must have placed there that night before leaving his cottage. Not only weapons, but also a bag lay in the boot. He unzipped it and inspected the contents. It was then that he remembered what he had planned.

Chapter 8

The Ridgeway was a track that extended across the southern part of England, an ancient road that has been used for thousands of years. This raised portion in the chalk ridge of the Berkshire Downs was close to the Asset HQ and was often used by the operators as a running route.

Bull had been welcomed back to the UK by George the previous evening at R.A.F Brize Norton. He had spent the night at home with his family in Oxford. If it had been under any other circumstances it would have been nice to get home early from a deployment. Still, his wife and young daughter had been pleased to have him home.

Bull had woken early and had driven to the HQ to find Al. However, he was nowhere to be found. He met up with George who explained he had seemed to be avoiding everyone the past few days. With little to do, and with the events that had passed recently, prominent in their minds, Bull suggested a run. George agreed and they went out on a quick nine miler that was a favourite of theirs.

"So how was it out there?" asked George as they ran along the Ridgeway.

"Same as ever," replied Bull. "We're really starting to clean up out there though."

"Yeah," panted George. "Shame we can't do the same back here." Bull ran ahead of George. Bull might have been stocky, but he could move fast when he needed to, a typical S.E.A.L. George was older than Bull, but would keep up through sheer stamina.

"It's easier out there, bud," said Bull in between breaths. "Rules don't matter, especially if we want to win."

"We're never going to win out there," puffed George.

"Nah, not with our ways." said Bull, controlling his breathing. "If the Russians couldn't do it with their huge numbers and hard-line methods, then what chance do we have?"

"Yeah," gasped George, keeping on the heels of the American.

"They only understand violence, that's how they've lived for so long, it's how we need to treat them." Bull jumped a large puddle and changed direction down a gradual decline, much to George's relief. "The simple answer is, we need to kill as many as it takes to stop them; it's the only way." Bull stopped running and put his hands behind his head to suck in the air. "Then maybe they'll stop coming."

Bull turned to face George who was a few metres behind him. George breathed deeply trying to get his breath back while he could. He was pleased to see sweat running down Bull's face. He was just as tired as he was, but George had a few years on him.

"So, where the hell's Al?" asked Bull.

"Don't know mate," answered George. "He's been around but not getting involved with anything since Rory died." Bull nodded.

"That's not like him," said Bull. "How did Cam take the news?"

"Not well," said George. "He and Rory went back quite a few years, before the program." George paused for a second. "Al asked me to keep an eye on him."

"How do you mean?" asked Bull.

"Not really sure, he was very vague about the whole thing." George sighed. "I just don't think he's handling everything so well anymore."

"It'll get to us all eventually." George agreed with a silent nod. He went to add to the conversation but was cut short by the buzzing of his phone. He had it strapped to his arm like an Ipod. He read the message and looked confused. "What is it?"

"It's Al," he replied with a quizzical look on his face. "He wants us back now." The two men started back the way they had come. The return journey was done in silence, each man thinking about what it was Al could want. What couldn't wait so much they had to come back now?

They got back in no time at all and made their way straight to Al's office. Al was waiting and he looked stressed, similar to when he had to deliver the news of Rory's death. Bull and George stepped into his office and shut the door behind them.

"Blinds," said Al curtly. They span round and twisted the blinds control rod, shutting themselves in to the office. "Sit down." The unusual tone in Al's voice put the two men on edge.

"What's going on?" Bull asked in his thick New York accent.

"There is about to be some breaking news," began Al, who was nervous and choosing his words carefully. "I've tried to hold it off for as long as I could for damage control reasons but I can't stop it for much longer." Al paused as if he didn't want to voice it, like if he was never to say it, it hadn't actually happened.

"What is it, Al?" prompted George. Al looked surprised to hear the question and stared at the two men sat in front of him.

"Do you remember when we first met Cam?" asked Al talking directly to George.

"Yes, yes I do."

"So you remember what he was up to?" George replied with a raise of his eyebrow.

"He's at it again," blurted Al. He waited to allow the information to sink in.

"What!" George sat forward in his chair. Bull remained at ease but watched the reactions of his two colleagues. "He's what?"

"And he's been at it for a while," added Al.

"What!" repeated George.

"Is someone gonna fill me in?" asked Bull, reclining in his chair.

"Umm, yeah," said Al clearing his throat. "We umm, we found Cam about four years ago. At that time he was in a mess, out on his own hunting down and killing known terrorists. I recruited him into the Asset program because of his military past. And everything's been hunky dory since then."

"So you allowed a murderer into your program?" said Bull calmly.

"He was doing the same work we were," protested Al. "We may as well have been using his talents."

"And he turned out to be one of our best," said George in Al's defence.

"Right," said Al thanking George for the support. "But after Yemen, he seems to be struggling with everything."

"We all know that he drinks heavily," said George. "He does it to block memories of what happened to him and his troop in the Waziristan caves."

"The caves?" asked Bull. "He was in the caves?"

"Yeah," replied Al.

"Shit! You guys had a rough time out there. I know some guys who assaulted the other caves."

"Well, he never really got over it," said Al. "But alcohol seemed to work so we left him alone with it."

"Still, Al," said Bull. "It ain't a great combination is it?"

"No, no it isn't."

"What about Yemen?" George asked.

"That's when he started again."

"Two years!" said George surprised at the length of time. "And you knew and have been letting it slide?"

"I know it looks bad," said Al. His open hands appealed for their understanding. "But he was doing it so well. He would never have been caught and we needed rid of these targets, so I let it go."

"Does Cam know you were on to him?" asked Bull.

"No, I don't think so, at least he never let on."

"How many?" enquired George.

"A fair few," said Al. "Started with the Saudi diplomat in Malta who kicked off the whole Yemen situation.

"Christ! I had no idea."

"No, nobody did," said Al. "Well, except me." Al sighed and looked at his two operators who themselves sat stunned at this information. "Now," he continued. "There's this." Al picked up a remote control and flicked on a monitor on his desk. The screen fizzed into life showing nothing but static. "This will be aired within the hour." A further press of the button and a news report burst into life. George and Bull leaned in, closer to the screen. Al began to pace the room; he had seen enough of the report.

The breaking news music filled the room and Al quickly turned the volume down and resumed his pacing. The female reporter introduced herself and announced some news just in.

"Friday morning at nine am," she began in her newscaster voice. "An ordinary street in Birmingham has been turned into a scene reminiscent of the St Valentine's Day massacre." The screen changed to some grainy CCTV footage showing a man walking down a street carrying a submachine gun and a bag slung over his shoulder. The man appeared to be stumbling slightly as he walked. George and Bull recognised the man as their friend Cam.

"The man you are seeing, calmly walked down the street and opened fire into a crowd outside the home of a radical preacher, well-known in the area." The man walked out of the view of the CCTV camera. The picture remained until people ran past in panic away from the direction Cam had walked.

"The sound you are hearing," said the reporter, "has been taken from footage recorded on a mobile phone. It has been deemed too graphic to be shown on TV." Gunshots could clearly be heard as the picture stayed on the empty street.

"Fifteen people were killed in the attack including the preacher who has yet to be officially named." The picture changed to a zoomed-in, pixelated, but still recognisable face of the gunman. "If anyone recognises this man, they are urged to contact police immediately." Al stopped the report where it was, Cam's face still on the screen.

"I have the mobile phone footage here." Al pressed more buttons on the remote and the footage started. Al turned away as if he didn't want to see it again. The footage had been taken from a house across the street from where the sermon was taking place. It clearly showed Cam walking up to the crowd and opening fire indiscriminately into the bystanders. The person holding the phone, purely in an act of natural self-preservation, ducked down behind their window for protection and the view was lost. Then the camera phone operator raised the phone up above the level of the widow-sill and the street was yet again in view.

People ran screaming in all directions. The doormen pushed the preacher back towards his front door and bundled him inside. They pulled weapons and tried to fire on Cam but he was too fast and shot them down with three-round bursts of his rifle.

Before opening the gate to the front garden he shot lengthways down the street at the people who had formed the crowd. Once they were out of range he swung open the gate and stumbled down the garden path to the front door, which he started to kick open.

After a few badly aimed kicks the door was smashed in and he again raised his weapon and fired into the house. Cam, in view of the CCTV camera, changed magazines in the threshold of the door throwing the empty one into the garden. Then he entered the house and disappeared from view.

"That's all we got for now," said Al pausing the video, "except for some scene-of-crime photos from inside the house, which I'll show you in a minute."

"Christ Al," said George. "How the hell we gonna get out of this one?" Al looked directly at George and sighed.

"I'm not sure we can, George," he said sullenly. "This is about to go national, I'm afraid Cam is on his own now."

"You've been shielding him up until now," said Bull accusingly.

"He's on CCTV, killing on national TV," said Al, defending himself. "I'm out of options." George went to say something but Al raised his hand to stop him. "Look! I haven't showed you what he did inside the house yet." George cut short by Al sat back in his chair. "This is what the scenes-of-crime officers found inside." Al reached into his jacket's inside pocket and handed a collection of photos to George.

George leaned over, taking the photos, all the time focusing on Al, trying not to see the images until he was ready. George sat back in his chair, deciding if he wanted to see the photos. He lifted them into his field of vision, under the watchful gaze of Bull. George stared at the first photo, for what seemed an eternity. He then flicked to the second then the third.

"Jesus Christ!" exclaimed George. Bull sat forward and took the photos from George's hand. He hardly reacted to having the photos taken from him.

"Well you're right about that!" said Bull, viewing the scene-of-crime photos. Bull saw the preacher slumped on the floor, his back braced against the wall where he fell, killed by a hail of bullets from Cam's automatic fire. The preacher had been hit by more shots than was necessary, as if shot over and over again. His features were almost unrecognisable, but that wasn't the worst image on the photo. He had been crucified.

Sat up against the wall, his arms outstretched and hands nailed. His head flopped forward, his palms taking the full weight of his fat body. The metal spikes were close to ripping through his hands under the dead weight.

Bull flicked to the next photo and rubbed his forehead with his free hand.

The second photo was of the living room wall above where the preacher sat slumped on the floor. Cam had painted a message on the wall with what looked like a spray can. The message read, 'You pollute the minds of the world.' And on a second line the message continued. 'You will not take this country.' The messy message, crudely written over the wall, was in red spray and drips slid down towards the dead preacher.

"Crucified," said George swiping back the first photo from Bull's hand. "Why crucified?"

"Best guess is he wanted to insult the religion," said Al. "Dying in that way sends quite a message in itself."

"Islamic State have been known to use crucifixion as a method of executing people," Bull lowered the photos out of his view. "Maybe that's his message?"

"Could be," Al agreed. "Those are the next lot we'll have to be dealing with."

"World's gone to shit." Both Al and Bull looked at George, neither said anything. They all knew what he had said was the truth.

"I've done all I can," said Al breaking the silence. "He's on his own now."

"Do you know where he is?" asked George, waking out of his trance. Bull flicked through the photos again.

"No," answered Al. "He's disappeared off the grid."

"Yeah, he's good at that," said George.

"He's clearly intoxicated on the footage," said Al, George looked at him. "You saw it!" said Al, abruptly. "Look," he sighed. "We've been tasked with finding him. And when we do, we have to stop him by any means."

"Shit," said George. "You want me and Bull, don't you?"

"You guys know him best," he replied. "Apart from me that is."

"If you don't know where he is how the hell do you want us to find him?" said Bull. Al took a seat on the edge of his desk and stared hard at the two operators.

"We wait," he said eventually. "He'll show himself when he wants to."

"Any trace at all?" asked George. "I mean where do we start?"

"Do you remember when we first found him?" said Al looking at George. He nodded in a positive response. "The house he was living in is his now. The old lady died and left it to him."

"That's where he goes to isn't it?"

"Yeah, we've traced him on most of his little outings. Anyway, I want you to head up there and check it out. Take Donald with you. He needs a break from here too."

"What about me?" said Bull in his gruff voice.

"I got a replacement for you to take a look at." Al picked up a folder from his desk and handed it to Bull. "Everything's in there. You'll meet him on Monday night in Oxford. In the meantime have a few days at home with the family but keep your phone close by. OK?" Al gave Bull a slight smile, acknowledging his efforts in Afghanistan, also knowing he deserved some time at home. "Right, I've got to go. Still working on this mess." Al stood and straightened his suit jacket.

He walked over to the door of his office and stopped. He placed his hand on the door handle and before pressing it down he turned back to his operators.

"George, be careful when you're up there. We don't know what state of mind he's in. OK?"

"Yeah, sure," agreed George. "Just see if you can sort this out before it's too late." Al turned the handle and pulled open the door.

"I'll do my best." With another forced smile he left the office, leaving George and Bull sat in silence. George took in a deep breath and let it out in an audible sigh.

"Can't believe this," said George staring into space. "First Rory, now Cam. Feels like our team is falling apart."

"Mmm," replied Bull. "And now looks like we're getting a replacement from outside." Bull opened the folder and read the front page of the document. George got up from his chair and went over to Al's mini bar. He poured two whiskies from the crystal decanter and swiped two Cuban cigars from an open wooden box. He handed one of each to Bull and re-took his seat.

"Who we getting then?" he asked cutting the end of his cigar.

"Guy called Rigg," said Bull speed-reading the profile. "Looks like ex-Navy, got some pirate hunting experience. Then went off to S.R.R, one tour in Northern Ireland and two in Iraq and one in Afghanistan. Now he's back in the UK and seems to want to leave the military rather than go back to the Navy."

"Fair enough," said George, listening and lighting his cigar at the same time. Bull put the folder down and cut his own cigar. "You can't replace someone like Rory," he continued between puffs.

"No," said Bull taking a drag and a sip from his whisky glass. "Big shoes to fill." He sat back in his chair, allowing the springs to take his weight, glass in one hand cigar in the other. George took a long drag from his cigar and some ash fell from the tip into his lap. He wiped it off with the palm of his hand, let out a snort through his nose and shook his head.

"What's so funny?" asked Bull.

"Do you remember last year?" George snorted. "When we were called in here and Al told us we were going to the Antarctic." George let out a throaty chuckle. "The look on your face was priceless."

"Christ, don't remind me." Bull squirmed in his chair at the thought. "I've said it many times; I don't do cold weather."

"Do you remember how Rory got us out of there?" George struggled to control his laughter, fully aware it could be seen as inappropriate.

"Are you kidding? He nearly killed us." Bull started to snigger. George tried to control himself and held it in. Bull snorted a laugh and set George off. They sipped Al's whisky and smoked his expensive Cubans, both men reminiscing back to the previous summer.

Chapter 9

"I don't do cold!" said Bull loudly. "I've lived in Virginia for most of my career. I've been operational mostly in the Middle East. He flicked his view between the members of his team. "I don't do cold!"

"You're the only team available," said Al in a compromising tone. "I'm sorry Bull. Take a seat." Al motioned for Bull to sit next to his team mates. George, Cam and Rory grinned at Bull's misfortune. Rory, next to the empty seat, patted the chair and smiled one of his huge smiles.

"Have a seat," he said. "Take the weight off your feet." The others giggled like children.

"What the hell do you mean by that?" said Bull abruptly.

"Nothing mate," said Rory. He had been slowly working on Bull, trying to give him a complex. Bull was a stocky guy, but certainly didn't need to lose any weight. Rory needed a long-term project and he decided to mess with Bull. "Sit down. Christ, I thought your type was supposed to be jolly."

"Enough!" interrupted Al. "Bull, sit!" He took his seat next to Rory.

"Did you just say enough bullshit?" asked Rory.

"No! Bull, sit." Al said emphasising the individual words.

"Oh, right." He turned to Bull. "Good boy, Bull," he said as if talking to a puppy. He went to pat Bull on the head, but he swiped his hand away before he managed to get to him.

"Rory!" shouted Al. "Just shut up. For five minutes, please, just shut up." Rory sat up straight in his chair like a naughty schoolboy in front of the school head teacher. "Right," exhaled Al. "As you know Speedy's team has been in the Antarctic for the past few weeks now."

"Yeah," said George. "What the hell they doing down there?"

"They're watching the Argentineans," said Al. "As you might know, most countries have their own bases down there. But what you might not know is that the 1961 Antarctic Treaty, signed by fifty countries now including Argentina, forbids military activity. Apart from peaceful purposes that is."

"Let me guess," said Cam. "Those Argies have broken that treaty." Cam sat, arms folded, listening to the brief.

"Yes," stated Al. "Well, sort of."

"Hmm, figures," said Cam arrogantly.

"They are the only country whose Antarctic research centres are predominantly operated by their military. And, their activity has been steadily growing over the years."

"Why?" asked Bull.

"They have a claim to the Antarctic. You know what they're like," said Al.

"Yeah, they have a history of trying to take stuff that don't belong to them," said Cam.

"Their claim is based on many reasons: they have the oldest permanent base, conduct more rescue missions and the Antarctic peninsula is geographically part of the Andes."

"So it's not about their claim to the Falklands," said Cam.

"Maybe, they are quite persistent with that," continued Al. "The area with the most military build up is also claimed by the

UK. Coincidence?" Al looked at the team before him as if to ask a rhetorical question. "The San Martin Base is the westernmost base on the Antarctic."

"Western?" enquired Cam. "So the nearest one to the Falklands?"

"Yeah," said Al raising an eyebrow. "It's gotten out of hand, been going on for years and has come to the attention of the international community. They've enough evidence to be suspicious of them and approved a pre-emptive strike. You know, to serve as a warning."

"Sweet," said Cam. "Might actually enjoy this one."

"We've had Speedy watching the base. They've done a few close target recces and have asked for assistance with the assault. They will provide intelligence and sniper assistance. You will conduct the actual assault."

"What are we looking at down there?" asked Bull.

"A population of between eighteen and twenty, civilians. Possibly up to one hundred military, a mixture of Army, Navy and Air Force. Two buildings, one large hangar and another complex of buildings. This is a soft target, that's why it's been chosen."

"How free are we with this?" asked Rory.

"Take out the military, try not to kill the civvies," said Al. "Now, no identifying markers. We don't want anyone to know who conducted the strike. That's why they have come to us. We've considered putting you in Argentinean uniforms and using their weapons."

"Yeah, whatever's easier. What are they using?" asked Bull.

"M16 and M4," confirmed Al.

"Fine," said Cam. "We'll use the same; we can carry less ammo then. We'll use theirs as we take them out."

"What's our way in and way out?" asked George.

"Ahh," said Al taking his usual sitting position on the corner of his desk. "As we need to keep this under wraps we are going to drop you in from low level." He looked at each member of the team in turn. "From under their radar."

"What?" exclaimed Rory. "That's like, less than two hundred feet."

"Yeah." Al nodded.

"That's too low for chutes," said Bull. "You gonna chopper us in?"

"No, it's too far for a chopper. It'll be a Hercules drop." The team looked at each other, for answers.

"We can't use chutes, it's too low," said George matter-of-factly.

"You wont be using parachutes," smiled Al. "It's been trialled," he continued. "During the war they dropped special forces directly into thick snow drifts at low speeds." The team members sat back in their chairs not convinced by Al's story. "MI6 have had some agents zipping about the tundra finding an appropriate drop point. The best they've found is an easy two-day trek from the base."

"Simple as that," said Rory, smiling and looking at the two either side of him, grinning.

"Yeah," agreed Al enthusiastically. "Easy. Won't be picked up on radar. The assaulting troops dressed in Argentinean uniforms using the same weapons. In and out. Warning given with no trace of who did it."

"This is crazy," said George, a hint of amusement in his voice.

"So crazy it'll work." Rory laughed. "Let's go." He stood up with a clap of his hands. "When are we leaving?"

"Now. Get yourselves to Brize. Your flights leave in…" Al checked his watch. "Just over an hour."

"How long is the flight?" asked Bull.

"Nine hours. After a short stop over on Ascension you'll fly to the drop zone and 'fall' in." Al made air quotes as he spoke. "Get going, time is short."

2100hrs GMT
Royal Air Force Base, Ascension Island

"I am sweating my arse off!" said Rory. The team of four operators stood under the fake lights of the airfield. Each man was fully kitted out in arctic clothing, their Argentinean uniforms temporarily covered by white, silk over trousers and coats.

"I'm not sure I like this," said Cam, looking at a reflection of himself in a land rover window. He didn't like wearing the enemy's uniform. The sun was setting but the temperature had remained high. The small volcanic island held the heat of the day in its rocks.

"Well, that's the last we'll see of the sun," said George, watching it set over the tail of the waiting Hercules aircraft. The Antarctic, in the southern hemisphere, was starting its winter and was in perpetual darkness. The sun wouldn't rise again on the southernmost continent for months. Temperatures of between minus twenty and eighty were the norm, and Bull wasn't happy with the thought of it.

"It's gonna be God damn freezing!" he said, shaking his head.

"Just think how Speedy and his team feel," said George. "They've been out in it for weeks now."

The engines of the Hercules transport aircraft kicked into life with a whine and the propellers started to spin. The team looked over at the aircraft on hearing the four huge prop engines start up.

"Guess that's us," said Cam. One of the aircraft's crew walked down the open tail ramp and looked in the direction of the team. He held up his thumb as if to ask a question. Cam replied with the same gesture and he and his group of operators made their way over to the open back of the transporter.

They climbed up the ramp, following the crew member and entered the belly of the aircraft. The crewman indicated an area of canvas netted seats that lined the fuselage. They took a seat each and buckled themselves in, ready for take-off. The crew rushed around preparing the aircraft for the flight as the wheel brakes were released and the plane jerked forward.

The engines revved up and down as the pilots taxied the aircraft to the edge of the runway. The ramp was still down and the team could see the sun setting on the horizon; the colours changed as it shone through the thin wisps of cloud. Amazing red, orange and purple colours filled the skyline where the sun was disappearing. The operators watched, knowing there was no sun where they were going. They didn't notice the ramp closing until it shut out the fading light with a clunk, which knocked them out of their dream-like state.

With the aircraft prepped, the engines roared and the transporter was pulled forward along the tarmac. The plane accelerated towards the southeast end of the runway, the nose lifted and the aircraft left the ground. The undercarriage was retracted with a buzz of motors and the pilot initiated a sweeping right hand turn, giving his passengers a good view of the small rocky, equator island. Once on the right course the plane levelled its wings and climbed higher into the darkening sky.

After a few minutes of climbing the crewman, who had seated himself near the front of the aircraft for take-off, re-started his checks. As he passed the team of operators he shouted something to Bull. The others couldn't hear the message above the noise of the engines and vibrations of metal on metal. Bull leaned forward so everybody could see him; he gave another thumbs up indicating they were free to roam around the aircraft.

They unbuckled themselves and each man began their own personal checks. In the middle of the aircraft, ready to be pushed out the back, were the supplies they would need to complete their mission. Weapons, food, water and arctic survival equipment all packaged up in a pair of pulks – toboggan-like devices designed to be towed behind them as they skied to their destination.

Once the checks were complete, the men had many hours of flight ahead of them so they set about finding comfortable places to bed down for some shut-eye. Rory had brought along his Hercules survival kit, a small net hammock, an Ipod and a set of ear defenders. He strung his hammock up and climbed in, put in his earphones and placcd the ear defenders over the top. Like a professional soldier, he was asleep in no time.

Rory only woke when then crewman shook him by the shoulder. He looked at the crewman who shouted something to him. He didn't hear through his ear defenders and music. The crewman made a gesture with his hands to indicate they were coming in to land.

They had started the plan of deceiving the Argentineans into believing the Hercules was landing in the Falklands. The idea was to fake a landing and to carry on to the Antarctic under the height of Argentinean radar. There they would be dropped and the Herc would return, still under the radar, to the Falklands.

Once the attack had gone in, they would secure some Argentinean transport and evacuate, along with Speedy, to the nearest British Antarctic Research Base and simply fly out posing as some researchers. It seemed an easy operation, with only one difficulty: the actual drop.

The Herc flew low over the frozen sea, north of the Antarctic continent, skimming the mix of waves and ice flows. When they made landfall the Antarctic desert came fully into view. The snowdrifts were clearly visible, lit up under the moon. The vast, frozen desert was blanketed under a smooth-looking layer of soft snow. MI6 had been out finding a suitable drop zone for this experimental drop. Every one of the team hoped they had done a good job.

The crewman waved to get their attention then beckoned them forward, towards the rear of the aircraft. He raised his hand and extended his fingers and mouthed the words 'five minutes.' The team prepared themselves mentally for the drop. Each one lost in their own thoughts; none of them had done this before.

'Two minutes,' mouthed the crewman. Rory being either brave, or simply interested in how this drop would turn out, volunteered to go first by taking up the position directly behind the pulks. 'One minute.' The rear ramp opened and the cold Antarctic air blasted in through the narrow crack between the ramp and the aircraft's hull. The crewman, attached to the aircraft via a long reinforced canvas strap, braced himself ready to push the pulks out the back.

The crewman signalled thirty seconds as the ramp stopped moving. The ground looked far too close for comfort, Rory involuntarily began to breathe faster. His hands shook out the tension in his arms and he shifted his weight onto each foot in turn. He watched the red light and waited for the green. The crewman moved in his peripheral vision and the pulks shot out the back of the aircraft and disappeared into the darkness.

Rory followed a split second later; he wanted it over with. He leaped off the ramp holding his breath as he went. He fell into the buffeting trail created by the Hercules and tried to stay in a seated position as he fell, but his arms and legs flailed as he dropped to the desert.

Rory waited for the impact; falling backwards towards the snow he closed his eyes tight. The buffeting stopped as the aircraft continued on its flight path, leaving Rory and the others hurtling to the snowdrifts below. The intense ride, now smooth, lasted seconds only. Rory plunged into the snow, disappearing below the surface.

Chapter 10

Mist clung to the trees and a light drizzle hung in the air. Soon spring would come to this area of the Lakes and the trees would turn a lush green, right now they were still bare. Donald and George could keep a good distance from the cottage and still see through the sparsely leafed branches.

"Well," said George in a hushed voice. "Doesn't look like anybody's home." Both George and Donald crouched in the bushes that were abundant in the surrounding forest.

"Are we sure he's not in the area?" asked Donald.

"Nope," he replied without taking his eyes off the cottage. "That's the thing, nobody knows where he is. When he left the scene he left his car, phone, pretty much everything."

"How the hell do you just disappear?" asked Donald. "You know, without anything at all. How do you do that?"

"That's what he's good at," replied George shrugging. "But that's what we're here to find out. Maybe we can find some answers in there."

"Yeah," agreed Donald. "Well then, shall we take a look?" George nodded and got to his feet. He beckoned with his head and Donald followed as George slowly crept towards the cottage.

All the way, they watched for any movement and tried to keep obstacles between them and the windows.

They paused at the edge of the forest for one last assessment from the tree line. George looked over the entire property. The driveway was nothing more than a dirt track. It looked like nobody had driven up the track for a couple of days. Both the cottage and main house looked abandoned; the owner who had rented the cottage to Cam had been dead for two years.

"So this is where he's been working from then," said Donald.

"I'm not sure work is the right word Don," said George. "More like…" George paused trying to put his thoughts into words. "I…" He sighed. "I don't know what it was. It's fucked up whatever it was."

"Yeah, a hell of a mess."

"Come on," said George. "Lets get this done." They made a beeline for the front door, George knelt down at the door handle and Donald faced out keeping watch. George reached into his jacket pocket and pulled out his lock pick gun. He inserted the picks and pulled the trigger, the picks vibrated and raked at the pins inside the lock. The barrel turned and George un-locked the door.

He re-placed the snap gun into his pocket and rose to his feet. He took out some latex gloves and put them on and gripped the door handle but didn't turn it.

"What?" asked Donald, looking over his shoulder. "What's wrong?" George placed his other gloved hand on the middle of the wooden door then moved his ear close to the panel. Donald watched, a confused and anxious look on his face. "What is it?" he whispered.

"Not sure," he whispered back. "Got a bad feeling." Donald's eyes flicked from the door to the exterior of the house. George pulled his pistol from his shoulder holster. Donald, with his lack of field experience did the same. "OK, stay alert."

George turned the handle, millimetre by millimetre. The dead bolt clunked as the old, warped wooden door slipped and the hinges took the weight. George cracked the door open, it creaked. He stopped and examined the tiny gap that he had created. Starting at the top and working all the way round the door, he looked for anything that might be some kind of trap or anti-intruder device.

"What you looking for?" asked Donald in a hushed voice.

"Absence of the normal, presence of the abnormal," said George solidly. He worked his way down and around the door. "OK, clear," he whispered. He swung the door open, pointed his pistol into the cottage and followed the arc of the door as it opened. With the curtains drawn the interior of the house was dark, George couldn't see much, but what he could see was clear.

"Put these on," he said, handing a pair of plastic overshoes to Donald. Once Donald had stretched the elasticised overshoes in place he put a set over his own shoes. "Come on." George entered the cottage and Donald followed. Behind them George closed the door. "Stay put."

George left Donald by the door and proceeded to clear the rest of the cottage. He left Donald's view for less than a minute as he checked the building. Donald waited, his pistol pointed at the floor.

"OK," said George re-appearing. "Clear. Lets have a look around." Some sunlight sneaked in through the small gaps in the curtains creating thin shafts of light. Dust sparkled in the bright columns, thrown into the air by the front door being opened. The living space was untidy, in disarray with furniture all over the place. Empty whisky bottles lay on most of the surfaces, some stood upright, some on their sides. George moved past the counter that separated the kitchen from the living area, his eyes scanning the bottles as he went.

"I knew he liked a drink," said Donald finding another empty in the sink and one on a window-sill. "But this is ridiculous." Donald picked up the bottle, disturbing the curtains. The light that flashed into the room caught George's attention.

"Try not to touch anything mate." He said. "I want to leave it as we find it."

Donald replaced the bottle carefully. George approached a computer desk in the far corner of the living space, which had a laptop open on its surface.

"Who's this?" said Donald, looking at a photo in a wall-mounted frame. "Mum and Dad?" George turned his head to see what Donald was looking at.

"No," he said returning his attention to the laptop. "That's the old lady who used to own this cottage and the larger house."

"That's odd," Donald added spotting something small in the corner of the frame. "There's a small mirror in the corner of the frame." Donald leaned in, placing his face close to the small make up mirror.

"I got the same over here," said George examining another small, round make up bag mirror stuck on some Blu Tack. The Blu Tack putty had some twist and turn marks in it as if the mirror was moved to allow a view of the room behind the computer.

"They're everywhere," said Donald, finding another one attached to a frame of a second window.

"I think Cam was suffering with a bit of paranoia," said George, noticing that the web camera on the top of the laptop was covered over with a small square of black tape. Next to the computer, a cardboard document file lay on the desk. "Here we go," said George.

"What?" asked Donald walking over, joining him at the desk.

"Got the documents," he said. "At least one of them anyway." George wanted to open the file and see what it contained but resisted the urge.

"Why did he leave it lying around?" asked Donald.

"He was drunk on the footage, you saw him staggering around," George said. "I'm not sure he knew what he was doing when he left here."

"You mean he did it all on impulse?"

"Possibly," he said. "Might explain why this place is in the state it is. And why he seemed to leave everything behind. It's like he was completely unprepared. And we both know that's not like him."

"Mmm," agreed Donald. "What do we do with it? We can't leave sensitive stuff like that lying around."

"We'll let Al decide. Give him a call, mate." Donald took out his phone and swiped at the screen. George scanned the room looking for anything out of the ordinary. He walked to the doorway that led to the corridor connecting the kitchen/living room to the rest of the cottage.

As he passed the doorframe he noticed another mirror tacked to the wooden frame. He could see Donald in the reflective surface with his phone up to his ear. He left him pacing back and forth in the living room waiting for Al to answer.

George didn't know what he was looking for; it was clear to him that Cam had lost control.

All he wanted to know was if they should take the file when they left. Anything else he found now might help to reinforce his suspicions. He stopped next to a cupboard door that was slightly ajar. He peered in, it was dark and he couldn't make out what it contained.

With the sound of a conversation coming from the living room, he took out his own phone. He un-locked it and turned on the torch function. The LED camera flash lit up bright and illuminated the contents of the cupboard. In it, he discovered a second cabinet. This one was metal and was secured to the ground, George recognised it as a gun cabinet.

This too was open and some of the weapon slots were empty. George nodded to himself and shut off the torch light. Donald rounded the corner into the corridor, his hand inside his jacket pocket, returning his phone after the call.

"These mirrors are freaking me out," he said noticing the others that were dotted around the cottage.

"What did he say?" asked George with a sad tone to his voice.

"We take them with us."

"Thought so," he said. "There's no way material like this can fall into the wrong hands."

"It already has," sighed Donald. "How do you want to do this?"

"However we want," George said. "It doesn't matter now. Come on we're gonna have to trash the place." George and Donald proceeded to search the entire cottage. Every piece of furniture was turned over; everything was opened or cut open.

During the search Donald entered a room attached to the rear of the building. The room was different from the rest of the cottage, completely tiled with white porcelain tiles. In the middle of the room was a video recorder on a tripod set just below head height.

Donald looked through the lens viewer; he stooped and closed one eye. White tiles filled the screen. The only other object in the field of view was an old chair, positioned in the centre of the room. Donald straightened up and looked around the room, empty apart from the camera and chair.

"George!" he shouted. "I think you're gonna want to see this."

"What?" The sound of George's voice echoed through the empty cottage. A second later he appeared in the doorway to the tiled room. "Whoa," he said taking it in.

"Digital camera," said Donald. George approached the camera feeling inside his pocket. He pulled out a specially designed flash drive, located the USB port and inserted it.

"This'll take everything on it," he said, watching the device working. "Oh," he said when the small green light stopped flashing. "That was fast, can't have been much on it."

"Might be useful," said Donald with hope in his voice. "Anything else?"

"Nah, I think we must have everything by now," said George, pulling the flash drive from the camera.

"Yeah, I'm done," said Donald. "How many do we have?"

"Bloody loads mate," said George, counting the files he had collected from around the cottage. "Come on, back to the car."

Both men left the cottage closing the door behind them. They quickly crossed the muddy driveway and entered the forest. After a few hundred metres their car came into view through the trees. George bleeped the doors and entered the vehicle.

As soon as he sat down he took out his mobile and dialled a number.

"Hi Al," he said into his phone. "Just a minute I'll put you on loudspeaker."

"Am I on?"

"Yeah," said George hearing Al's voice through the loudspeaker. "Al, what do you want us to do?"

"You got the files?"

"Yes, there's loads of them. Don's going through them now." Donald flicked through the files whilst listening to the conversation.

"Get them back here, we need to analyse them to try and figure out where he's going."

"You think he's still going through with these?" asked Donald.

"No idea, Donald," replied Al. "All we do know is he doesn't give up easily. And he's done this type of thing before."

"Don't you want us to keep watch on the cottage? I mean what if he comes back," said George.

"I doubt he's going back there but I'm going to get Cumbria Constabulary to watch it."

"He'll take them apart if he does come back Al," said a concerned George. "Sure you don't want us to stay?"

"No, get yourselves back here. If we get a lead on where he is I'm going to need you guys to get after him. I'll tell the Bobbies not to get involved with him just to report back to us."

"Check this," said Donald holding up one of the files. "This is the one he just did."

"Get them back here," said Al. "The answer might be in those files."

"We're on our way," said George. "See you tonight." He started the engine and released the handbrake. "This is messed up," he said.

"There's so much stuff here," said Donald still going through the files. "I haven't heard of half of these."

"Yeah, and he's still got hold of them," said George with a hint of sarcasm.

"You don't think Al was allowing him access to these do you?" asked Donald after a short pause.

"Don't know mate," said George. "It does seem that Al was letting him away with it. Maybe it was a way of disposing of problems we couldn't deal with."

"Christ, I hope not," Donald said, staring out of the window and taking in the Lake District countryside.

"Like I said, this is really messed up," said George navigating the twists and turns of the narrow B5389. "This can only end up badly."

"You got that feeling as well have you?" said Donald. "Do you have any feelings about where he is?"

"No mate, he could be anywhere."

Chapter 11

Since the European Union had opened the borders it had become increasingly easy for people wanting to stay off the radar to travel un-noticed. All Cam had to do was get out of the UK, made easy by the many identities and passports that he had acquired over the years.

Cam stood in his south-facing hotel room on the top floor of the Radisson Blu. He tried to picture the chase Rory had been involved in, difficult from this height. He needed to get higher. He turned from the window and walked over to the bed, his bag perched on the bottom corner.

The only possessions he could bring were ones that couldn't be traced to him. His car was left behind in the UK, his phone still in the glove box. He had managed to visit a camera shop and print off the documents he had backed up and stored in the memory card that he had taken from it. He would need these documents to track down the targets he had marked.

He scanned the room – there would be things he could use. On the table, he found a welcome folder, inside were some brochures and a map of the city. Under a desk he found the mini bar. He sighed when all he saw were miniature bottles of vodka.

He pulled one from the door rack. It clicked as he pulled it free, a small button released as it registered the sale to the room's bill. He sighed again.

As he'd now paid for the drink he took it back over to the window with the map. He slid the bottle into his pocket and unfolded the map. He knew where the chase had started and where it had ended. He folded the map so that only the area in question was showing.

Still facing the wrong direction he found no further info from the view, he would have to go out. He decided to walk the route and get higher – he knew the perfect place. The map was placed in his back pocket and the bottle snapped open. He pulled a face and looked at the bottle, he never could take vodka but finished it anyway.

The front of the hotel, curved in a half moon shape, almost hid the Galaxy Centre where the chase had started. Only the top portion was showing, the round tower and radio mast loomed over the hotel. He studied the map and set off for the steps by the riverside, the other miniature bottles lifted from the bar clinked in his jacket pocket.

With the aid of the folded map it only took ten or fifteen minutes to find the spot where Rory died. Behind him stood two large buildings that looked like museums or some sort of government buildings.

In front was the river Odra, some vessels of various sizes were moored up against the shore. The road he was standing on was lined with leafy trees and had some pleasant cafes, busy with people sitting outside in the sunshine.

Four days ago this place was the scene of a horrendous crime. A man had been gunned down in the middle of the day, the surrounding streets smashed by a car chase and a gunfight in the street near the Galaxy Centre. From where he was stood he could see floral tributes to the victim, lined up against a metal railing erected to protect the crime scene.

Cam walked past the café where people sat with cups of black tea, enjoying what was probably the first warm day of the year and down the steps to the waterfront. He couldn't understand what they were talking about but he knew from their gaze and hand movements that it was about the car chase.

He didn't want to get too close, as it was obviously still an area of importance to the local police. From where he was he could see some broken concrete steps and an area of floor stonework that had been scrubbed clean.

Cam twisted the metal top off the next bottle of vodka. He took another nauseating gulp of the liquid and the rest he poured on the ground. One last dram for his lost friend. He tossed the empty into a nearby bin, shook his head and left, ascending the stone stairs back to the road.

He followed the route of the chase. The damage was easy to follow. Smashed shop fronts, out of action tram lines and damaged signs and lampposts lined the streets. He walked over the cobblestones and took a right and headed towards the police station. He didn't know if what he saw was the norm but there were police everywhere.

Armed coppers swarmed the station on the corner of the street. They watched everyone as they passed. Cam saw the bullet holes in the walls of the buildings, they were scattered as if the firing had been indiscriminate. He passed the station, staying as nondescript as he could. The signs of the chase led round to the right, he followed the road taking him past his hotel.

Trying to blend into the crowd as he slipped past the police station had made him aware that his walking trousers and walking boots made him stand out like a sore thumb. The locals all had a certain look and he never felt so English. He needed to do some shopping. He found himself at the block of flats in which it had all started. The Galaxy Centre was only a few hundred metres away.

He entered the centre through the smashed glass doors, which were under repair. Music played over the centre's sound system and it was business as usual for the kiosks and fast food sellers. Cam stopped at one of the food kiosks and ordered, through broken Polish, two Paszteciki, a deep-fried mixture of meat and vegetables. He'd been to this part of Poland a couple of times and each time he made a point of getting a couple of Paszteciki .

The centre buzzed with shoppers going about their business. Most of the clothes shops were on the upper floor so he stepped onto the escalator. As the centre's floor sprawled out underneath him he could see the hustle and bustle as the shoppers rushed from shop to shop. People of all ages dangled off the climbing wall and representatives tried to entice customers to their stalls.

Cam spent some time buying clothes to allow him to go about his business un-noticed. He studied the local guys and bought clothing that would make him look similar. Walking trousers turned to jeans and boots to trainers, a bland looking jacket completed his outfit. Time to get to height.

He slipped back into the crowd feeling a little more incognito, he made his way back outside and walked back towards the block of flats Rory and the G.R.O.M were staking out. Police and men in suits were still in and around the two flats on the top floor. The investigation was obviously still going on. His investigation would focus on a different part of the city. The last surviving member of the Chechen cell could be holed up in another flat southwest of the Galaxy Centre.

Café 22 was on the twenty second floor of a tower near to the shopping centre. This would allow him a three-hundred-and-sixty degree view of the city. He would be able to orientate the map to the ground and get a better idea of what he would be facing. He waited for the elevator in the foyer, hands in pockets. The door opened with a ping and he stepped inside the mirrored lift.

He was alone in the elevator except for the reflections of himself. A handrail ran the length of three mirrors. A hatch in the roof of the lift would give access to the cables in the lift's shaft.

He could use the handrail to climb up into the void if needed. He couldn't see a reason why he'd need to but old habits died hard, an impulse to note features such as these were part of his make up.

A second ping signalled the lift had arrived on the twenty-second floor. The mirrored doors slid open and he stepped out. A central bar surrounded by tables, almost all full with customers, seemed quiet. He did a lap of the café. Waitresses ferried food and drink form the bar to the customers. He felt at ease, nobody was paying him any attention and the place had a relaxed atmosphere about it. He ordered a pint of Lech and sat at one of the tables that lined the windows, facing south he looked out over the city.

He spread the map over the table, spun it around to orientate it to the panoramic view before him. To the southwest the buildings disappeared over the horizon, one of them was the hideout of the last surviving terrorist. Cam had information that he took from Al. He also knew that they hadn't shared all information with the Polish security services. This meant that they may or may not have someone watching the place.

Cam took out a luminous highlighter from his jacket pocket and began marking streets with possible routes in and out. The city was huge. The roads ran away from a central point like spokes on a bike wheel. He tried to commit as much to memory as he could. His elevated position allowed him to visualise the streets in his head.

He finished his beer and left the restaurant, taking the lift back down to the ground floor. It was now afternoon and the streets were still busy – this was the type of city that would never sleep. He joined the crowds and walked the selected route to the target.

2130hrs CET

Cam looked at his watch then at the skyline of the high soviet-looking block of flats. The light was fading fast and the streetlights had been lit. Cam was sat on a low wall within sight of the flat's entranceway. Trams thundered down the centre of the street between the two roads, periodically blocking his view.

He had been watching for hours now, moving position every so often so not to attract attention. Everything looked as normal as it should, except for a black transit van parked a few doors down the street. The van hadn't moved since he had been in the area. Advertising marked it as belonging to some kind of skilled worker, a plumber or electrician, but there was no sight of any work going on anywhere on the street.

The block of flats itself looked formidable, only five storeys, the windows were tall indicating high ceilings. This gave the building extra height. The entranceway to the grey building was more like a tunnel, big enough to drive a car through, leading to a courtyard where, presumably smaller doors would take you up to the individual flats.

As the light faded further, a group of youths began to gather at the entrance tunnel that was lit up by bare light bulbs. This, coupled with the dubious transit van, ruled the traditional entrance out of play. A quick check of his map showed the blocks were the same all down the street and the one behind on the adjacent street was a mirror image. Cam decided it was worth a look.

He skirted around to the other side of the target block to find the same layout, but this entrance tunnel clear. He decided to go for it. Head down and hands in pockets, he went for the entrance. As he entered he realised the only difference was that this tunnel was in darkness; someone had smashed the light bulbs. With a hint of apprehension he walked through the darkness.

He could see a slither of light ahead, the wooden doors that led to the courtyard didn't quite connect. A corridor came into view on the left of the tunnel. In it a door sat elevated slightly by three steps. Cam ducked into the door's recess, to stop for a second and listen for any other movement.

He stood still, taking in every sound and trying to block out the ambient sound of the street. He left the recess and moved on to the wooden double doors, pushing one open with the palm of his hand. He entered the courtyard, where he found two cars parked. Two doors, one either side of the courtyard, were the entranceways to the flats and a garage-type structure at the far end of the yard seemed to be for the residents' bins.

This courtyard was separated from the one he was interested in by a wall about twelve feet tall, the building containing the bins being part of this wall. He covered the courtyard at a quick pace and, using the corner where the wall met the main building, bounced off the brickwork and vaulted to the top of the wall.

After speedy assessment of the new courtyard, taking in as much detail as he could, he dropped down into the shadows cast by the light from people's windows. This new yard was an exact copy of the last. He remained stood in the darkness waiting to see if his climb had attracted any attention.

After a short time listening Cam moved along the wall, keeping to the shadows, towards one of the entrances to the flats. He ducked into the doorway. The buzzers on the wall showed numbers 9 to 16. This was the block he wanted, from his intel the target should be hiding out in number 16. Top floor.

To enter, he either needed to buzz a door or enter a code into a keypad. He studied the keypad for signs of wear and tear that might indicate which keys were pressed more often, but the metal keys provided no clues. He could wait to be allowed to enter by the next local, but he wouldn't be able to converse with them. He would be questioned and couldn't answer back. Too dangerous.

He had to do something. He could not remain in the doorway. He had to go. Then the wooden doors to the tunnel entrance swung open and in stumbled an obviously intoxicated man. He walked shakily to the middle of the courtyard mumbling to himself and, just as Cam was getting concerned he would be found, he veered off to the other side slamming into the opposite door.

The drunk poked at the keypad, which beeped as he entered the wrong code a number of times, until he got it right and the latch clunked open. He pushed the door with his shoulder and nearly fell into the stairwell. The lights went on behind the closing door. Cam seized what could be the only opportunity he would get that night and crossed the courtyard. He stopped the door from closing with his foot and waited to give the man time to climb the stairs to his flat. Cam slipped inside and quietly clicked the door closed.

He found himself in a stairwell. Brownish yellow painted walls either side of a wooden railed staircase led up to the landings, with numbered doors on either side. The first door, numbered 17, he climbed past and headed to the highest landing. The door on the second landing, number 20, was slightly open. Cam assumed this was where the drunken man had gone. He continued past to the landing of 25 and 26.

Each landing had a small window facing the way of the courtyard, some with old stained net curtains. This top floor had a net curtain that Cam could use as cover from view. Suddenly the lights went out. Cam hadn't noticed any switches as he'd entered the stairwell. He looked around for light controls. He found them, plunger controls designed to give only a certain period before turning the lights off automatically. Probably best to stay in the dark, Cam thought.

Cam watched the building on the other side of the courtyard through the dusty, old net curtain. It had to be the place. Al had information that each of the terrorists had their own individual hideout.

This was the last surviving one's place, the one who had shot and killed his friend. Cam didn't have many people he considered friends, but he had known Rory for a long time. He wanted revenge.

Someone was home, he could see flickering light through the window as if a television was on. He had worked out from the block he was in, the probable layout of the one across the yard. The target's flat should be the one on the left of the stairwell.

An hour passed. Cam kept watch, drinking the last two miniatures to pass the time. Waiting for some proof his target was in there. Cam's eyes widened when a figure approached one of the windows of the flat. He locked on to the man's face as he opened the window. He saw him only for a brief second before he slid the curtains closed. The man he saw could have been a Chechen.

That was all the proof he needed. In a city like this, people of ethnic backgrounds were few and far between. In fact, Cam thought, he hadn't seen anyone who looked foreign since arriving in Szczcein.

Satisfied, Cam left his observation position and descended the stairs, exited the building and hopped back over the wall to the neighbouring courtyard. He was tired from the day's activities and the long journey that had brought him there. It wouldn't make sense to run in unprepared. It could wait till the next day. All he wanted to do was return to his comfortable hotel, and although sleep usually eluded him, he had to at least try.

He walked back onto the street and took out his map. Looking at the street signs he found himself on 'Ul Getta Warszawskiego.' It was one of his highlighted streets, so he knew it would take him home. He walked along the street to the next crossroads and looked again at his map.

"Hej ty!" Cam heard a voice from a concealed area behind him. He didn't move, with a bad feeling he continued to study the map for the way home. "Hej ty, mowie do ciebie!" Cam didn't understand but gathered it was directed at him. He lowered the map and slowly turned round.

Out of the dark doorways of the shops that lined the street stepped three lads who looked like thugs. Shaved heads and low browed. "Nie lubimy byc ignorowani," said one of the lads. Cam looked at them, knowing what was about to happen.

Cam said in broken Polish that he didn't speak the language, which the three of them found overly funny. Their over-exaggerated laughter made Cam raise an eyebrow in their direction, which they didn't like. The laughter stopped abruptly and their demeanour changed to a very threatening one. They threw back their shoulders and swung their arms out to the side, attempting to make themselves look bigger. They made angry looking faces trying to intimidate their intended victim.

"What do you want?" said Cam, refusing to take a step back as they encroached on his personal space.

"English boy! What you doing here?" said the largest of the Neanderthal looking thugs. He moved in on Cam, chest to chest. Taller than Cam he looked down, curling the corners of his mouth down into an exaggerated leer. Cam tried not to react. The thug pushed hard on Cam's shoulders shoving him back. Cam shook his head and looked at the floor, waiting for the inevitable strike. "Money!" said the thug making a cash sign with his fingers.

"No," said Cam, making eye contact again with the thug whose expression changed slightly as he cocked his arm back. Cam saw this coming a mile away. The arm went back, the shoulder twisted and the fist came forward as the haymaker flew at Cam's head.

Cam waited, although only a millisecond. He anticipated it and had time to calculate his response. As the punch came round in an arc Cam raised both arms to protect himself then, both arms were forced forward at the thug. His right forearm slammed into the thug's clavicle bone, snapping it. His left forearm blocked the punch and the force of Cam's well-rehearsed defence threw the thug backwards off his feet.

With one thug on the floor, incapacitated and writhing in pain, he turned on the others. He stayed low in a combat stance: arms outstretched, elbows bent ready to strike.

The attack came. The thug went for Cam. He tried the same thing as his punk friend. Cam wondered if this was the only way they knew how to fight. Cam simply retaliated in the same manner, only this time he caught the thug's punching arm under his armpit, trapping it. With the second thug trapped, he hit him with the underside of his fist just below his jaw on the carotid artery. The thug blacked out instantly and collapsed to the floor.

Cam turned to the last thug, remaining in the stance in which he'd taken out the others. The thug turned on his heels and ran, leaving his friends. Cam straightened up and turned his attention to the casualties he had created – one moaning in pain, the other out, unconscious.

Cam went through the conscious thug's pockets. He protested as his intended victim stole his possessions.

"Shut the fuck up!" said Cam, slapping him with the back of his hand. Everything he found he stuffed into his own pockets, he would rake through it all later. Cam moved to the next thug and checked his pulse as a good blow to the carotid artery could have killed him.

He was fine. Cam took everything he had before heading in the other direction from the fleeing thug. He may be going for backup Cam thought. He melted into the shadows of the tall buildings that ran the length of the street. Soon he would be back at the Radisson for a well-earned rest.

Chapter 12

Monday night was still busy. Although the weekend was over, students were out. Oxford University had the wealthiest students. Rich kids away from home for the first time ran wild through the streets. Togas, superheroes, vicars and nuns wandered from pub to pub.

Bull sat against the wall facing the main entrance in the Irish pub. The streetlights had been on for a while and the fake orange light spilled into the bar. Rain had forced more people inside than usual and the tables were all full. Behind Bull, the walls were lined with pictures of Irish bands playing their instruments, and other random paraphernalia.

Bull took a sip of his pint of Guinness as the song playing changed to Spandau Ballet's Gold. He was putting his pint down on the scratched, beer-soaked table when the door opened. The newcomer closed the door and looked around the pub, shook the rainwater from his coat and approached the bar.

He ordered a drink as he had been instructed in the mysterious message he had received. Holding his drink in his right hand he spun around to face the revellers sat at their tables. The only other instruction he had been given was to find the contact in the bar, he rested his elbows on the bar behind him and scanned the faces of the drinkers. Bull paid him no attention. He simply sipped his drink.

The latest visitor to the pub picked up his drink, took a gulp, and walked straight at Bull. He arrived at the table, pulled the wooden chair from under it and sat down. Bull sat still, his hand on his glass, watching the man that wasn't a stranger to him.

After an awkward silence that lasted less time than it seemed, the stranger shrugged and shifted his facial expression into a question. Bull took another sip from his Guinness, leaving froth on his moustache, which he removed with his bottom lip.

"Why'd you come to me?" asked Bull gruffly in his New York accent.

"You're an American?" he said, surprised.

"Well done!" said Bull sarcastically. "Maybe you are the guy for the job." Bull raised his hand to attract the attention of the barmaid. In some pre-arranged plan set in place earlier by Bull, she delivered two shot glasses and poured a measure of bourbon. Bull sank his and his new companion did the same. The barmaid poured another and the process repeated itself.

"So! Colin," said Bull after the barmaid left. "Tell me about yourself." Bull turned the full shot glass with his fingertips.

"I'm not telling you anything," he replied.

"Well, should I tell you what I know about you?" said Bull. He waited for a response but none came. "OK," he continued. "Colin Rigg, Navy, S.R.R, tours of Afghan and Iraq." Again silence. "Sent home and now you are thinking of leaving the Mob." Bull picked up his shot glass and clinked it on Colin's, which was still sat on the table. The bourbon in Colin's glass jumped and splashed onto the table. "And we can't let that happen."

"Why not?" Colin downed the remainder of his shot.

"Because you're too good at what you do," he said answering his question. "I mean it, I've read your confidential reports." Bull paused his explanation as the barmaid returned to re-fill the shot glasses. "Plain and simple, we need you." He continued when she was out of earshot.

"Me!" he said surprised. "Why me?"

"Like I said, your confidential reports are exemplary. You're one hell of a covert operator and that's what we do."

"And who are you?"

"We're the Asset program." Bull waited to gauge his reaction. He hid it well but Bull noticed the slight change in expression. Any member of their community would have heard of the Asset program, whether they believed it was real or not was up to them. "So, you know who we are then."

"Yeah, I know. Nobody's sure if you guys exist or not."

"Well, here we are," said Bull, taking another shot. "Look, you can go back to Abingdon and sit around in the Intelligence section there. Or, you can join us and give someone else that position. I know there are plenty of people who want that posting."

"Look," said Colin. "I'm only wanting out because they've pulled me from ops and given me a desk job. I want back in the field, if you can give me that then I'm in."

"Well, I can get you back on operations. Drink up." Colin had his shot that had been left behind after Bull took his. Bull signalled the barmaid for a re-fill. "Tell me about what happened in Afghan," he said after the barmaid replenished their drinks.

"If you're trying to get me to gob off and tell war stories, that's not going to happen," he said in response to Bull's inquiry. "No matter how much of this stuff you give me." Colin picked up the shot glass and downed it in one. Bull gave a slight smile barely visible under his beard, picked up his own and followed suit.

The barmaid passed by and went to re-fill the shot glasses, but Bull waved her off. He cleared his throat and sat back in his seat, stared at Colin deep in thought.

"How many bar staff are there?" he asked in a quick question. "Without looking!" He added as Colin went to turn.

"Four, including the one filling me with whiskey."

"What's her name?" he followed up with.

"Anne."

"Sure that's her real name?"

"That's what's on her name tag anyway," he said. "However!" he said, stopping Bull before he could ask the next question. "When I ordered my drink the guy's nametag said Tom. But when I was stood there I heard him being called Dave. So, can't be sure."

"Exits?" Bull said, impressed.

"Front door, trade exit over the bar, fire escape round the back."

"What about the toilets?"

"No," he said confidently. "They're below ground level. Even though I haven't been down there yet, it'd be my last option."

"Who are the most dangerous people in here?" Bull said. He leaned in, placed his left elbow on the table and picked up the remainder of his Guinness. Colin leaned forward, his hands stayed under the table.

"We are," he said.

"I think you'll fit in," Bull said snorting through his nose. He finished his drink removing the froth with the back of his hand. "Col, welcome on board," Bull said, sliding sideways along the bench and getting out from behind the table. "Tomorrow, nine o'clock." He threw a scrap of paper onto the table in front of him.

Colin picked up the scrap of paper, gave it a cursory glance and stuffed it in his pocket. Bull left the table and walked past Colin. He sat still but watched him leave the pub, out into the rain.

Colin sat back in his chair and pondered what had just happened. He knew his life and career had just taken a strange new twist. As he sat thinking the barmaid who he thought was called Anne approached the table.

"Hi," she said enthusiastically. "That'll be £34.50 please." She smiled, clutching the silver metal tray to her waist. Colin relaxed further into his chair and smiled a thin wry smile.

"Son of a bitch!" he said under his breath.

Chapter 13

Cam had done this so many times, it felt familiar to him. He felt he was back on track. He was finally back finishing his plan from all those years ago. The tasks with the Assets had not been him. He had wanted to break free long ago and complete his mission, although the moment never presented itself. The death of his long time friend had been the last straw. Now was the time, he would finish this.

This man he was after tonight was responsible for the death of his friend, he would take great pleasure in tonight's activities. He had packed in his rucksack everything he would need to get into the man's apartment. He shifted it on his shoulders displacing the weight.

He looked up at the top of the block. He had to crank his neck right back as he was at the foot of the building, his hair brushed the top of his bag. This was the building that was adjacent to the one the target was in. Soon he would be on the roof, the best and safest way to get to his target.

It was time. He was excited about killing this man. He had a real hatred for him. He walked through the tunnel entrance to the centre courtyard, swapping the orange streetlights for the natural light of the moon. The courtyard was empty, as expected this time of night. He crossed the yard to the small outbuilding that housed the bins and skips.

He jumped up onto the roof of the outbuilding using some discarded street furniture. Crawling across the corrugated tile roofing he looked up at the flat that was his destination. It was in darkness, it wouldn't matter if the target was up or not, he was going to die tonight. If he wasn't in, he would wait. If he had anything, he had time.

The separating wall that cut the two courtyards in half was a narrow brick wall that extended either side of the outbuilding. He stepped along the wall, heel to toe until he was against the wall of the block. Out to the left, about half a metre away was a metal drainpipe. It was of strong construction and fitted solidly to the wall. This he had noted the previous night.

He reached out to the pipe and fumbled for a good handhold. He felt out with his foot and it found a bracket bolting the pipe to the bricks. In a fast movement he shifted his weight and brought both his feet and hands onto the pipe.

He bounced slightly on the brackets of the piping. Checking the security of the pipe work, it seemed strong enough. Standing upright, the pipe close in at his chest and looking up, he followed it towards the roof. Leaning back, his feet placed firmly against the wall, he began the climb.

The rough wall helped the climb. The pipe held firm and he was at the top before he knew it. The top of the building was flat and the guttering ran along just below the level of the roof. Cam had strained to reach up and get a good hold of the roof-top. His fingertips were all that held him from the fall to the courtyard below. He scrambled his feet against the rough brickwork until he could throw one arm over the top, giving himself the first safe hold of the climb.

With relief he pulled himself over the top of the raised brick edge. Once over, he rested, breathing deep to get his breath back.

He dusted the fine layer of dust from his hands by rubbing them together. The dust had dried his hands, giving his skin a rough, dry feeling. He turned and looked down into the courtyard, still empty. The lights from the drunk's flat were still on from last night. For a moment he wondered if he was OK but the moment passed.

He stayed low and moved along the rooftop until he was above the flat he wanted to be in. He looked over, leaning right out to see the windows below. He shuffled to his right, still looking over the edge, stopping when he was directly above one.

He turned and sat, taking in the layout of the roof. It was flat with some raised built up areas that could have been old skylights or ventilation chutes. He opened his bag after slinging it off his shoulders and un-doing the drawstring. He pulled out the ascending and descending kit he bought earlier in a climbing shop and slipped into his climbing harness.

He looped the climbing rope and tied it off so the end wrapped around one of the vents in line with the selected window. He slowly lowered the other end over the side of the building, he watched it creep down past the window and stop half way to the ground. He clipped the descender onto the rope but kept the second part, the ascender, in his bag. He might not need it but it was with him in case he did.

Climbing onto the low wall that ringed the roof he turned his back to the courtyard below. With the descending equipment attached to the front of his harness, by a karabiner, he gingerly leaned backwards. He turned the control on the descender and, with his feet planted, he started to assume a horizontal position on the wall.

When he was happy with his position he began to walk backwards down the wall, the climbing equipment controlled his speed. He tightened the screw control and stopped his descent when he was just below the height of the window. Studying the window, he realised it wouldn't cause much of a problem to open.

It was an old-fashioned window with two handles clipping it shut. With a bit of force, his knife moved the latches out of the locked position and the window swung outwards.

He opened the window as far as it would go and he slipped into the apartment. Once in, he closed the window over. He didn't want to change the air pressure within the flat and cause any other doors or windows to slam shut. He waited there, beneath the closed window, listening for any movement. His natural night vision adjusted to the darkness of the flat after the light from the streetlights outside.

Inside the flat he was met with silence, only the ambient street noise could be heard through the single paned window. He stayed crouched beside the window, hidden in the shadows of the room he found himself in, until he felt secure he hadn't been noticed.

Confident he was either alone in the apartment, or the target was asleep, he stood. It was time to have a good look around. Carefully he moved through the apartment, checking the rooms methodically for the target. Cam knew he had to take great care; the target was a dangerous man. He had read the file he had taken before he had absconded.

Cam turned the door handle to the last room in the flat. As he twisted the handle down he pulled it towards him, pulling it into the door fame. Once the handle was fully turned he pushed the door open from the middle of the panel. These techniques stopped the mechanisms from snapping and the hinges from creaking.

He stopped the opening when the room came into view through the crack. There he was, tucked up in bed. He was unaware of what was going on, that he was being hunted. Cam wanted to kill this man. Revenge was going to be sweet. He was going to enjoy this hit.

Cam opened the door enough to slip into the room and shut it silently behind him. The room was as bare as the rest of the flat. It was nothing more than an emergency rendezvous for the cell if things went wrong. It was leased under a false name and should have remained empty, but things had gone wrong, and he was now hiding out until he could figure a way to escape the country.

Luckily Al had access to all intel from each country that had a member in the program. Al knew everything about the cell, and if Al knew, Cam knew. Many documents he had secretly copied and taken. He may have left the physical documents behind in his cottage but he had them backed up digitally, and these documents had led him to this bedroom.

He stood inside the door and stared at the Chechen, still deep in slumber. He pulled his pistol from the shoulder holster hidden beneath his jacket and approached the bed. He kept a constant eye on the target, watching for any sign of movement, no matter how slight. Even though he was deep asleep, he was still a dangerous man.

He took in a deep breath and leaned in close to the target's ear. He readied himself for the coming reaction. He double-checked the extractor claw on the side of his Glock. It protruded, proving there was a round in the chamber.

"WAKE UP!" he screamed into the Chechen's ear. The Chechen jumped, his muscles contracting at the sudden noise. His face contorted as he spun trying to find the source of the noise. Although still close to his target, Cam was ready, his pistol covered the man's movements.

The Chechen was quick. Years of fighting the Russians, then the infidels, had made him battle hardened. He swung the pistol that he had been sleeping with towards Cam. Cam acted on instinct. He blocked the Chechen's arm with his forearm and trapped the pistol under his arm and torso. He thrust his pistol's muzzle into the target's face splitting his cheek wide open. Blood gushed from the Chechen's face as Cam slammed his Glock17 down onto his opponent's bicep. The Chechen dropped his weapon, his arm numb.

Cam sideswiped the now un-armed Chechen again with his pistol, knocking him onto his back. Cam kicked the dropped pistol to the skirting board and turned to the Chechen who was holding his face with both hands. Blood seeped between his fingers.

Cam spotted a towel draped over the bottom headboard; he picked it up and threw it at the Chechen. He blindly grabbed the towel and mopped at his wounds. He cleaned the blood from his eyes and stemmed the flow from his cheek.

Cam turned and strolled over to a wicker chair in the corner of the room. He tipped the discarded clothing off the chair and took a seat crossing his legs and resting his ankle on his knee. He gripped the pistol, shifting its weight on his thigh and stared at the bleeding Chechen.

The Chechen swung his legs over the side of the bed, sitting up. He blinked, his eyes only just cleared of blood. He held the soaked towel to his cheek and stared back at the man now sat in the corner of the room.

"Do you know why I'm here?" said Cam quietly after a long silence. The silence continued. Neither man wanted to be the next to speak, the psychological games had begun. Cam held his silence. He had time and wanted to control the conversation.

"Who are you?" grunted the Chechen with hatred in his voice.

"I'm asking the questions here," Cam retorted. "Why do you think I'm here?" He said empathising each word.

"Fuck you," said the Chechen defiantly, his accent strong.

"OK," said Cam calmly. "Let me tell you what I know." Cam cleared his throat. "You were planning some kind of attack," he continued. "I don't give a shit what you were planning, only that it didn't go as you wanted. Right?" The Chechen said nothing, he only returned the stare. "You killed someone, by the riverside." Cam paused to gauge the reaction.

"I defended myself," said the Chechen.

"Defended," laughed Cam. "You're a terrorist."

"You people are the terrorists!" shouted the Chechen. "Your leaders, every single soldier in Afghanistan." The Chechen paused. "You!" he continued, accusingly.

"One man's terrorist is another man's hero," quipped Cam. The Chechen snorted in derision. "Well the man you killed was one of mine."

"And you're here to kill me, is that it?"

"Yeah," smiled Cam getting to his feet with a sigh.

"And how many people have you killed?" said the Chechen, anticipating what was about to happen. "How many faces are stuck in your mind? You're no different to me."

"I am nothing like you," said Cam, keeping calm. "Me and you," he said, pointing between himself and the Chechen with the barrel of his pistol, "are natural enemies. We don't get on, we never will. Our people are too different."

"Our differences are what will allow us to triumph over you sinners. You can't win."

"One question," said Cam as if he were having a conversation with a friend. "Why didn't you kill the other guy dragged out of the car?" The Chechen searched for the answer, his eyes flicked from side to side.

"He was already dead." He shrugged.

"Mmmm," said Cam. He raised his pistol and fired, hitting the Chechen between the eyes. He slumped back on the bed, lifeless. Cam walked over to the body. He looked down on the dead Chechen. The small entry wound dribbled blood that slid down the side of his face into the gash on his cheek.

Cam snarled as he thought about this creature killing his friend. He forced the barrel of his pistol into the mouth of the Chechen, smashing his front teeth. He angled the barrel of the pistol upwards breaking more teeth, he then pulled the trigger blowing the top of the dead Chechen's head clean off. His brains splattered onto the wall on the far side of the room and slid to the floor.

Cam, satisfied with the degradation of the body, breathed in the revenge. He turned and picked up the Chechen's pistol. He examined it, an MP-443 Grach, standard Russian issue, probably taken from a Russian soldier. A fine trophy, he slipped it down the back of his belt.

Cam walked to the front door. When he reached it he paused and felt in his trouser pocket, pulling out one of the wallets he took from the thugs who had tried to mug him. In the wallet was a till receipt, he dropped it, allowing it to flutter to the floor.

Next, he un-bolted the front door and left the flat. He climbed the staircase to the attic floor that was being used as a drying room for the residents. At the far end of the drying room was a ladder that took him back up to the roof. He removed the rope he had used to descend to the window, shoved it all back into his rucksack, and made his way back down to the street.

Chapter 14

Thursday 28th March 2013
1320hrs GMT
Asset HQ, South Oxfordshire, England

Al sat behind his desk, blinds closed sheltering him from prying eyes. He didn't want to be seen deep in thought. He had failed to keep the story from breaking, now the whole country was aware of what had happened in Birmingham. Cam was a wanted murderer and being hunted by the authorities. Al hoped he and his Assets could find him first.

If that wasn't enough, there had been more developments that he wasn't sure how to handle as yet. Perhaps when his team arrived they would have some suggestions. He expected them any moment now. Still, he wasn't sure how to begin talking about it.

The knock on the door rattled the closed blinds against the doorframe. Al shouted for them to come in and close the door behind them. Bull, George and Colin settled down in the chairs that surrounded the low, oval glass coffee table.

"So. We've seen the news," said George when Al failed to speak. "I guess Cam's deep in the shit now." Al sat and only managed a nod.

"What's next Al?" asked Bull.

"We have to find him," Al said finally. "And soon, before anyone else does." Al tapped a pen on the desk as he spoke.

"How we gonna find him?" said Bull, narrowly beating George to the question.

"There's been a development," said Al tentatively. Bull and George waited patiently for what was coming. "The survivor from the car chase in Poland has been killed – murdered, apparently."

"The guy who killed Rory?" asked George. Colin looked around not knowing the full story.

"Yes, killed by a known local criminal." Al sifted through the paperwork on his desk. He found a mug shot of the thug and passed it to George who reached forward out of his chair to take the photo.

"And they've got him in custody?" asked George, scanning the photo and handing it to Bull, who only gave it a cursory glance before dropping it on the coffee table in front of Colin. "I don't see what this has to do with us. Except that we don't have to do it now."

"Well, there might be more to it," continued Al. "That guy," Al motioned to the discarded photo, "was arrested because they found a receipt for some goods bought using his credit card at the scene. CCTV footage checked by the Polish police, shows him at the shop in question paying and placing the card and receipt back into his wallet."

"So they have him banged to rights," concluded George.

"Maybe not." Al sifted through the paperwork again. "What do you make of this?" Out of the mess of documents Al handed George another photo.

"Shit!" George exclaimed, passing the photo fit drawing to Bull. "You're not serious?"

"God damn it," said Bull, staring at the face photo fit. "Where did this come from?" Colin leaned over so he could see the photo.

"That was taken during interrogation, from the man they have in custody." Al motioned for the photo back. Bull handed it over. "I think we all know that it bears a passing resemblance to Cam," said Al, flipping the police drawing around so they could all see it.

"That's one hell of an understatement Al," said George. "It's a bloody dead ringer. How did he? I mean, how?" George struggled.

"He claims the person in the drawing stole his wallet and phone," explained Al. "His friend's too."

"Guy's I'm lost here," said Colin finally getting a word in.

"We'll have to fill you in later," said George. "This is complicated and has a history to it." Colin nodded accepting that he would spend the rest of the conversation in the dark.

"OK, OK," added Bull, getting back to the point. "So, we're saying Cam killed the Chechen cell member and planted evidence that would frame this guy?" Bull pointed to the photo of the thug on the table.

"Yes, also," Al put the photo fit down and leaned on his desk interlocking his fingers, "I've been monitoring passport control at every possible way out of the UK. And narrowing the search within certain parameters, I found this man." Al passed yet another document to George. "Do you recognise him?"

George studied the photo that had been handed to him, he didn't recognise the face but the details of the man rang a bell. He squinted his eyes and searched his memory.

"Caleb Goodman," he said quietly. "Why have I heard that name before?" Al waited to see if George could remember.

"You heard it in Yemen," said Al when it appeared George was at a loss. "Caleb Goodman was the C.I.A agent you tried to rescue from the Al Shabaab pirates."

"Yemen," repeated George. "Christ yes! I remember. But I didn't have anything to do with him. I was providing cover for Cam and Rory."

"Mmmmm," said Al thoughtfully. "So you didn't see the body?" George shook his head. "So only Cam and possibly Rory, who's now dead, had any contact with the C.I.A agent."

"Yeah," confirmed George. "Shit, you don't think we found him alive and Cam just saw an opportunity to take an identity do you?"

"That doesn't matter," Al waved his hands in the air as if washing them of the possibility of another murder. "What matters is, Cam is travelling under the identity of a dead C.I.A agent. He's in Poland now, and he's killed the guy who killed Rory." Al looked at his colleagues. "We need to get to him, and fast. I've sent the G.R.O.M team to the police station and they are going to keep the photo fit out of the investigation. They're also at the closest airports watching for him."

"I thought they were on their way here?" said George.

"Yeah, well I had to put a hold on that for now," said Al. "They are the only ones in the know and I want to keep this as small as possible."

"Al," interrupted Bull. "You said he took that guy's phone. Have we looked at tracking it?"

"Yeah, all done and nothing," answered Al. "GPS has been disabled, we tried to take a snapshot of the user remotely via the provider. But looks like the camera lens has been covered over or disabled."

"He'd done the same on his laptop in his cottage up north," interjected George.

"What's next then?" asked Bull.

"There's not much we can do," said Al. "We wait, hope that he tries to travel on the passport again. The G.R.O.M are watching for him."

1445hrs CET
Goleniow airport, near Szczecin, Poland

Cam stood outside the glass windows of the airport terminal. Through his tinted sunglasses, protecting his hung-over eyes, he peered through the reflection of himself into the airport departures lounge.

Cam had spent the remainder of the previous night pillaging the mini bar and hallucinating about his old friends. Now he was trying to leave the country but what he was seeing in the vestibule area had stopped him in his tracks. The lounge was under surveillance, he saw all the signs and his spider senses were tingling. It didn't feel right.

Stood, unassumingly in one of the corners of the arrivals lounge, was a covert operator. At least he seemed to be, it took one to know one. He was stocky. He looked handy and had one arm in a sling. With his free hand he held a mobile phone, Cam had watched him make at least three very short phone calls. Cam backed off into the car park. He needed time for his throbbing head to think.

He pulled out the passport he would be travelling on, flicked it open to the ID page at the back. He was using the same name but a different nationality, would it be enough? Was he busted? So soon, was that possible?

Sceptical he had been located that quickly, he looked around for a way through the departures lounge. He scanned the car park for what he needed. There she was, a lone female getting out of her car and struggling to lift her cases out of the car boot. She fitted the bill perfectly – she wasn't so good looking that nobody would believe they were a pair. They could plausibly be a couple. A stunner would always draw attention. He approached the sliding glass doors, timing it right so they walked through at the same time.

He walked closely beside her as she pulled her wheeled bag to the ceiling-mounted televisions displaying flight times. While she located her flight number Cam removed his sunglasses, confident they would be concentrating on lone males. He confirmed that he had gone un-noticed. The covert operator was still scanning the lounge. He had dismissed the couple on entry.

Cam rubbed the stubble on his face and cracked his neck, stiff from sleeping rough, where he passed out intoxicated on the floor of his hotel room. He replaced the sunglasses and sighed an alcohol fumed sigh at the possibility of skipping the country. He followed the lady to the baggage check-in and joined her in the queue.

He waited patiently, the line was for all destinations, which helped him with his illusion. When the lady came to place her wheeled case onto the carousel, she struggled to lift it. Cam saw his chance to complete his deception. He smiled and assisted her with her case, lifting it onto the conveyor belt. She said thank you in Polish, Cam hardly responded, continuing the bluff they were a couple.

The crowds moved as a group but Cam stayed with the lady, not too close as to freak her out but close enough to carry on the rouse. The next hurdle would be the security team and the metal detectors. He had placed the Russian pistol inside an X-ray-proof bag in his hold luggage, his Glock17 was in another X-ray bag in his hand luggage.

As he approached the X-ray machines he assessed the operators. He chose his preferred operator, a girl who looked inexperienced and was surrounded by male security employees. She was obviously distracted as each of the young security guards was attempting to hit on her. He joined her queue and prepared himself by removing all metal objects from his person.

He placed his hand luggage on the conveyor belt and watched it travel through the X-ray machine. She hardly paid it any attention as one of the guards made a flirtatious comment. He smiled to himself and passed through the metal detector, picked his bag up on the other side and retrieved his metal items from the plastic tray that had followed his bag through the X-ray. He was home and dry. After a short wait in the lounge, he walked along with the other passengers, across the pan to the waiting aircraft. He left the pack and speed walked past everyone to the rear of the plane.

He climbed the ladder and entered the aircraft saying hello to the flight attendant at the top of the staircase. Directed to his seat by the attendant he moved back towards the front of the aircraft and sat down. He opted to place the bag at his feet, due to its content. From the amount of people in the throng he knew the flight was probably full. He waited to have someone sit next to him, knowing his luck with air travel it would probably be the most annoying person on the manifest.

The aircraft took off. The lady coincidently sat only two rows in front of him. He took a few miniatures of whisky from the duty-free trolley and snapped the first one open. He downed it and cracked the second. Immediately he knew he would need to order more. The person sat next to him shifted uncomfortably in his seat at being sat next to the drunk on board. This time Cam realised he was the undesirable person on this particular flight.

He caught the attention of the trolley attendant on her way back and took six more miniature whiskies. The attendant begrudgingly served her customer under the concerned gaze of the person sat next to him. Cam continued his drinking under the blast of cold air from the aircon system above him.

He reached up and attempted to turn it off by twisting the control, but the cool airflow failed to turn off. He sat back in his seat and downed the miniature bottle of scotch. He shook his head as the memories of his former colleagues returned. He sat in silence, under the cold aircon. The cold air flashed him back to a flight he had been on last summer, although that flight had been a one-way journey. Could it have been that long ago?

Chapter 15

Thursday 12th July 2012
0200hrs ART
East of Barry Island, Antarctic

Cam blinked, twice. His eyes darted around the snowy hole. He was down, safe and unhurt. He breathed out the tension in a cloud of frozen air. The mist rose towards the crisp night sky and out into the open air.

He was comfortable in the cushion of snow that had enveloped him when he plunged into the Antarctic desert. But he had to move, even though the adrenalin leaving his body wanted him to rest. Impacted snow, stuck to his clothing, began to melt as his body heat warmed it.

He kept low in the crater and was surprised to learn he had sunk five feet into the snow. He poked his head up into the air and scanned the surrounding area. The surrounding desert was as flat as it possibly could be, smooth and with no disturbances. Where were the others? He had seen them, and the pulks leave the aircraft, he had been last out. The sky was littered with stars, millions of them, lit like diamonds. There was no moon and no wind. It was still, and cold, so very cold. He spun three sixty looking for any trails left by the aircraft. He had become disorientated in the vastness of the Antarctic landscape.

In the clear night sky he could see the Hercules in the distance, only a spec now, making a left turn and heading back to the Falklands. He put his back to the departing plane, his team must be somewhere in that direction. One by one, three heads poked up from the ground at equal distances leading away from his position.

Looking like meerkats, the heads of his team mates swivelled, also checking out the landscape. Rory was the furthest from his position. Being the first out of the aircraft he would be closest to the pulks. They held all their equipment and needed to be found. Rory stood in his impact crater and waved, his standard wide smile barely visible due to the distance.

Cam climbed out of his hole. Sinking into the snow on the surface, he crawled out. He stood and looked towards his team, they too were scrambling out of their holes. He could see, now that he was stood on ground level, that there were small disturbances on the surface of the snow where the others had landed. They hadn't been visible from ground level. Relieved to see the others Cam started towards George's position, he struggled to take steps as he sunk up to his knees in the soft snowdrifts.

"That was intense!" said George when Cam was in earshot.

"Certainly was," replied Cam still approaching him, lifting his feet high to take steps through the snowdrifts. George stood, up to his knees next to his snow hole. "You sank in pretty far too then?"

"Yeah," he laughed. "Thank God it was deep enough." Cam snorted a laugh in response and beckoned his head towards where Bull was standing. One by one they converged on each other's position until they all stood together, near to where Rory had landed.

"Well," laughed Rory. "How deep did you guys go?"

"Deep. Too deep," said Cam, scanning the horizon.

"I bet you went deeper than the rest of us," said Rory pointing at Bull and smiling. "Didn't you." He looked at Bull hoping for a response. "Did he?" he said to the other two when no reaction came.

"Come on," said George changing the subject. "We need to find the pulks." He led the way they assumed they must have been. The four team members trudged across the deep snow looking for ripples on the smooth landscape. Then, they saw them. Two craters close to one another, the pulks had landed within fifty metres of Rory.

They dragged them from their pits and began the process of turning them into sledge-like devices. George and Cam released some straps that attached two sets of skis to the top of each pulk. Each man took a set of skis and poles and attached them to his ski boots.

"OK," said Cam. "I'll take a pulk and Rory, if you have the other." Rory nodded. "George you take point, then me, Rory and Bull. OK?" Cam looked for some agreement. It came by the men moving to their positions. Cam and Rory attached the pulks to their belt kits and looped the ski pole straps around their wrists. "Right," he continued. "We'll do twenty-five minutes march and five rest."

"Yeah," said Rory. "The last thing you want to do is start sweating. It'll freeze and you'll start to suffer."

"Yeah, so we'll take it easy for that exact reason," continued Cam. "We have plenty of time. We'll stop in about five hours so we're only travelling at night."

"Night?" said Bull.

"Figuratively speaking," said Cam. "We'll bed down during what would be working hours and get to the base for silent hours, for a dawn attack."

"Cool," said George. "Lets get going."

"Yeah man," said Bull. "I'm God damn freezing! Wanna get moving." The moisture in his breath had already started to freeze, forming ice particles on his beard.

"Right," said George. "Follow me."

After five hours skiing, the team had stopped for some rest. They needed sleep. They hadn't had much time for it since leaving the UK, only a few hours on the crossing from Ascension. The tent had been put up and snow packed around the base to keep it secure. Shelter would be important if the weather came down on them.

They had taken it in turn to stay up and keep watch. The one awake was also boiling snow, so they would have enough water to drink before setting off again in the evening. Rory was taking the last shift and was still boiling water.

"Hey," said Cam with a croaky voice. He slowly sat up still wrapped in his sleeping bag.

"Hey," said Rory. "How are you this fine Arctic evening?"

"Antarctic, Rory," said Cam yawning. "We're in the Antarctic."

"What's a difference? It's still cold as shit!" he said, shrugging the remark off. "Do you want a brew?" he asked motioning towards a small, burning gas stove. They had decided to keep it going throughout the day, to keep the temperature up in the tent, since they shouldn't need any more gas after the attack.

"I don't drink brews," he said, unzipping his sleeping bag.

"Yeah I know mate," said Rory lifting a small plastic pot. "I brought some concentrated juice. I know you, remember."

"Cheers mate," said Cam as Rory put a metal mug full of recently melted snow water on the burner.

"I'll have one too," came a voice from deep within a sleeping bag.

"Make that three." Instinctively everyone's natural body clock was waking them up. Soon all four were sat up in their sleeping bags sipping hot blackcurrant juice from hot metal mugs with only a small strip of black tape on the rim to stop them burning their lips.

Condensation, from their breathing, had settled on the inside of the tent and frozen in a thin layer dripping icy water from the canvas. The wind had picked up during the night and was rocking the tent back and forth, the whipping sound making it seem worse than it actually was.

"Did we all get enough shut-eye?" asked Cam with both hands gripping his mug, his fingers uncomfortably hot but not really caring.

"Mmmm," grunted George, with Bull nodding silently next to him, his eyes transfixed on the steam rising from his drink. Cam had never seen Bull out of his comfort zone before. Arctic warfare was obviously not his speciality.

"I've been thinking," said Rory cheerfully.

"Christ, here we go," moaned Bull, his gaze never leaving the steam twisting up to the top of the tent.

"It's about how we describe periods of time on the radio," continued Rory undeterred by Bull's comment. "As we all know, no comms system is completely secure."

"Yes," said Cam unsure of where Rory was going with this, if he was sure of anything he knew it was probably going to be a joke of some sort, but with its basis making at least a little sense.

"Well," he said. "When we say how long we'll be or when something is going to happen, we give away intel to a potential enemy listening in." Everyone sat in their sleeping bag, lethargic from the cold, too tired too participate in Rory's conversation. "So, I've come up with a system to confuse the enemy," Rory said, looking particularly happy with himself.

"Of course you have," said George, playing along.

"I propose that we describe units of time as movies and episodes." Rory paused as if to let his genius idea sink in. Instead he was met by a series of blank-looking faces, cheeks drooping from fatigue.

"What?" asked Bull finally.

"Well, a standard movie is about an hour and a half and an episode usually lasts half an hour. So if you're going to be an hour you say, I'll be two episodes. If your going to be two hours you'd say I'll be a movie and an episode." More blank faces stared back at him. "What do you think?"

"Is he being serious?" asked Bull, turning to the others.

"Like I've said before mate," said George. "It's hard to tell." He finished his drink with one last gulp burning his throat. "What about small measures of time like five minutes? How would you say that?"

"Got that covered mate," he said holding up his finger as if to indicate a good idea had come to mind. "We'd say I'd be a porno."

"Eh?" said Cam.

"Well, you only watch porn for about five minutes anyway." He looked around the group for approval. "Don't you?"

"So you'd say for thirty five minutes, I'll be an episode and a porno," Cam said.

"Yes."

"And for two hours five minutes you'd say I'll be a movie, episode and a porno?"

"Yes," smiled Rory.

"You're insane!" said Cam without a hint of emotion in his voice.

"I think it'll work," said Rory, clearly hoping the group might adopt his idea.

"Anyway," said Cam, steering away from one of Rory's inner madness. "We should get packed up and on our way. We have about a five or six hour march ahead of us."

"That's about four movies," Rory said.

"So lets get going," said Cam, ignoring him. The team began to unzip their sleeping bags and sort themselves out. "Rory, stick on some boil-in-the bags."

Rory placed a metal mug with some water on the burner and plopped in two silver foil meal bags into the mug. The water poured over the side of the mug and fizzed as it hit the blue gas flame, almost extinguishing it.

One at a time, Rory fed his team as they prepared themselves to move off. Before exiting the tent they opened the lukewarm, boiled meals and dug at them with their spoons.

The meals, high in calories, would help see them through the march ahead.

Cam unzipped the tent and let in a blast of freezing Antarctic air. Bull swore and pulled his clothing up around his neck. Without another word said, they crawled out into the darkness. The weather had turned. The stars were hidden behind a blanket of clouds that dropped large snowflakes on them. The wind, which was bitterly cold, seemed to rub at their skin giving a sensation of burning.

The edge of the tent had been buried by the snowdrift during the time they had been inside. The team set about pulling down the tent.

"What the fuck!" said Bull. "How God damn cold can it get?"

"We're well under minus ten," shouted George over the wind. "Breath in hard through your nose. You'll feel your nose hairs freezing and feeling sharp." Bull tried it. "That's how you can tell we're under minus ten. But I think we've busted that by at least another minus twenty or so."

"This is why I never volunteered for Arctic training!" shouted Bull. The tent was packed away and stored in the pulks. Bull held up his hands and looked at them. "They're bloody numb! They feel twice as big as they should be!"

"Don't worry mate!" shouted Cam, his face feeling the same as Bull's hands. "We'll get going soon and you'll warm up." Bull didn't look impressed by Cam's optimism. "Come on, lets get moving. We'll stop for five minutes after every hour."

"That's a porno after every couple of episodes," said Rory, still hoping it might catch on. Making no reaction they clicked their ski boots into their skis and were off, hoping to warm up as they moved.

2350hrs ART

Snow fell from the clouds creating a pinkish/blue haze around the four men stood by the frozen ice. They had been marching for hours now and were not far from their target. It lay across the water, frozen from the Antarctic winter. Snow began to pile up on their shoulders and backpacks, cooling the backs of their necks. They shook it off and gingerly skied onto the ice.

They had their backpacks slung over one shoulder only, in case the ice should break and they be forced to ditch them. The ice should be metres thick at that time of year but it was standard practice when crossing over ice. They kept a greater distance from one another. Should one go through the rest should be safe.

This was the last part of their journey. The crossing to Barry Island from the main Antarctic continent would only take them half an hour to an hour. Rory had already converted it into his new time format for them. They only felt safe when they finally crossed onto the powdered snow of Barry Island. Bull breathed a silent sigh of relief.

"OK," said Cam. "We are literally only a few hundred metres from the site. Up there, " he pointed to a slope ahead, "is a summit that will give us a good view of the San Martin base."

"Where's Speedy?" asked Bull, shivering.

"On another part of the hill, they'll provide us cover. We'll contact them once we have eyes on the site."

"Right," said George. "Break out the guns, we can leave all this crap here. MI6 will gather it up once this is over." The pulks were opened up and weaponry was handed out, M4s and Browning pistols to match the enemy's weapons. "Ditch the whites," he said. The silk coveralls were taken off to reveal Argentinean Army uniforms.

"Doesn't feel right, wearing this shit!" said Cam, clearly unhappy displaying the Argentinean flag on his shoulder.

"At least we'll blend in, make it confusing for them," said Bull, looking down at himself. "How do I look?" he said, turning to the team.

"Um, well fed," quipped Rory. Bull looked like he wished he'd never asked.

"Are we ready?" asked Cam. A round of nods signalled they were.

"Earpieces guys," said George, placing the standard Asset communication device into his ear. The rest copied him. With their skis back in place they slowly herring boned their way up the slope to the ridge. As they approached the top they lowered their profile so as not to skyline themselves against the light coloured clouds. Now crawling through the snow they saw their target: two main buildings set in the snow, one a large barn type structure the other, some sort of living and working building, both of a red coloured wooden construction.

"What's that doing there?" said Cam, on spotting the Argentinean military Bell 205 helicopter sat on a landing pad to the south of the buildings.

"No idea," said George. "Al said nothing about that."

"No," said Cam pressing his earpiece and activating the push to talk function. "Speedy, Cam. Can you here me?" Cam spoke clearly, looking into the distance and wondering where Speedy had dug himself and his team in.

"Where the hell have you lot been?" Speedy's voice joked through their earpieces. "We've been freezing our asses off out here."

"You're from Scotland, you should be used to it!" replied Cam.

"Not even Shetland gets this bad."

"Speedy, when did that chopper turn up?" asked Cam.

"Yesterday, a high ranker must be visiting." Cam listened to Speedy and contemplated their next move.

"What's the plan mate?" he asked, knowing Speedy had been on the ground for a couple of weeks now and would have a better understanding of what was happening and what should be done.

"I'm estimating about eighty to one hundred military personnel and fifteen to twenty civvies. I'll stay here and guide you in and keep you up to date with what's happening in real time. Lugsy will be sniper support and Luca and Kosta will put in place a cordon and stop anyone escaping."

"No civvie casualties, Speedy," said Cam

"Sure, we just needed you guys to help out. A hundred of em is a bit too much to handle."

"Yeah, we're getting a little sick of bailing you guys out of trouble."

"Nice one. One thing – if two of you take the office type structure and two take the barn. In the barn are some snowmobiles. They are our ticket out of here. Don't shoot em up. OK?"

"No problem. When do you want to go?"

"Give it a few hours, let em get sleepy."

Chapter 16

Thursday 28th March 2013
2230hrs GMT
Woodstock, Oxfordshire, England

The village of Woodstock sat a few miles north of the city of Oxford. Seventeenth century buildings made of old bricks and timber beams were laid out in a scattered fashion around the narrow village streets. Steeped in history from royals to poets and politicians, this was the place Bull had chosen to live with his family.

His wife Tracy had found it amusing to be living in a place called Woodstock. They had been there for two years and had been enjoying the slow pace of life and the safety of the village. His daughter Molly had been enrolled in the local school and was flourishing.

Bull had tried hard to keep his family life away from his work with the Assets. Tracy had never met any of his colleagues. She had made friends around the village and had given Bull a social life completely separate from his work. With the exception of what was happening with Cam, life was near perfect for the ex-Navy S.E.A.L.

Bull sat in his favourite chair angled slightly towards the low, flickering embers in the fireplace. He sipped on the cold beer. The condensation dripped off the bottom of the bottle as he raised it to take a sip. Tracy was upstairs, putting Molly back to bed after another of her trips downstairs. She was always making excuses trying to stay up late.

The staircase creaked. The old wooden planks ground against each other as Tracy came back down to her husband. She stopped in the door to the living room when she caught a glimpse of Bull sat wide-eyed, staring into the fire. Normally aware of everything going on around him, he daydreamed, un-characteristically.

"You don't seem yourself these days Dwayne," she said dragging him away from his thoughts. "Do you want to talk about it?" Tracy took a seat next to his comfortable armchair. Bull placed the beer on a wooden table. Tracy picked it up and put it back down on a coaster.

"Can't really talk about it, Trace," he said. "Anyway, it's not that interesting. What you been up to? We haven't had much of a chance to catch up."

"I went into town today," she said. "I love it there, now the weather's improving that is."

"Yeah, you go a lot I've noticed."

"I love wandering round the old universities," she continued. "I was thinking, now Molly is settled in school and taking part in afterschool activities, that maybe I could get a job." Bull looked surprised.

"You want to go to work?"

"Well, yeah. There's a job going at the library at Balliol College," Tracy explained.

"Balliol College?" Bull asked. "Is that one of the big ones?"

"Yeah," she replied. "It's one of the main universities. The library is open twenty-four hours a day. But I'll only be mornings and afternoons."

"That'll be great, you'd enjoy that," Bull said. "When's the interview?"

"I've already had it," she said, smiling. "I got it, but I haven't accepted it yet. I wanted to ask you first."

"Take it, Trace!" he said, slightly confused at her asking his permission. "Well done, when do you start?"

"Not sure, I'll call them tomorrow," she said excitedly. "And you, what about you? Are you around for a while?"

"Well, I am for now," said Bull. "I am until we get some more info on something. I guess you could say I'm waiting for a call." The second he finished the statement his phone rang, buzzing on the table next to his beer. Bull shrugged and made a face hidden beneath his beard. "I'll uh, I'll be through there." He picked up the phone and hurried to the kitchen, pressing the accept call button as he moved.

"Hello," Bull said, closing the kitchen door behind him.

"Bull, it's Al. We have a development." Al sounded out of breath. "He's in Rome."

"Rome!" exclaimed Bull loudly. "Rome," he said at a quieter level, hoping Tracy hadn't heard him. "How did he get to Rome?"

"He flew, from Poland to Fiumicino. I need you and George there now. And take the new guy with you."

"I'm out the door as we speak," said Bull pacing the kitchen. "But Al, you had guys at the airports. And we were watching for his ID to pop up."

"Yeah, it took a little longer to come to the surface. He used another passport. Same name but a different nationality." Al sighed.

"It only came to us after he had landed in Rome. I tried to get the Carabinieri there in time to intercept him at baggage reclaim, but somehow he just slipped away."

"Do we know what he's wanting in Rome?"

"There's a few possibilities but we don't know for sure. That's what I need you guys to find out. I'll email you everything I have on possible targets in Rome but you're going to have to work it out on the ground."

"What are the arrangements?" Bull asked, going straight to the point.

"George is waiting for you at Benson," said Al. "Get yourself there as soon as you can. Keep me updated." Before Bull could say anything else the phone signalled the end of the call with a soft tone. He slid the phone into his pocket.

"Trace," he said going back into the living room before he saw his wife still sat by the fire.

"You off then?" Tracy said twisting herself round towards the kitchen door. She always put a brave face on when Bull left but it was growing harder to hide the emotions created by never knowing if she would ever see him again. Bull nodded looking down at the floor before meeting her gaze again. Tracy stood up and embraced her husband.

Bull closed his eyes and breathed in a long slow breath through his nose, knowing he may be gone for a long while he wanted to take in as much of his home as he could. The smell of the burning kindling, the old English house beams and the warm hold of his wife.

"You know I..."

"Shhh!" She whispered placing her hand gently in front of his lips. "I know, but never say that before you leave. It's just asking for trouble."

"Too many movies Trace, this one is nothing at all." He always said that before he left but Tracy had heard the stories from the other wives before leaving the States and knew exactly what type of jobs he was sent on. "I'm gonna give Molly a kiss before I go." He said moving towards the creaky wooden staircase.

"Quietly!" She said in a hushed voice. "Just got her off to sleep, try not to wake her up again."

"I'm as quiet as a mouse." Bull feigned shock at the comment then started up the stairs.

"Sure you are," she said after him unsure of whether or not he heard her. "That's why they call you Bull is it, Dwayne?"

The Internet café didn't blend into the buildings on the Roman street. Cam had asked the taxi driver to drop him off at the closest Internet facility to the accommodation he had booked before leaving Poland. He sat in front of the computer. He had chosen one that the other customers couldn't see. While he waited for the computer to log on, he decided to get hold of a small laptop for himself. There were plenty of Wi-Fi hotspots around he could jump on and use.

He inserted the memory stick into the USB port and connected the mobile he had stolen in Poland into the other port. After copying and pasting the documents from the stick to the phone's memory card, he sat back and waited for it to complete. After dumping his phones in the UK, so they couldn't be traced, he now had this one to view the stolen documents on the move.

The process finished, he removed the devices from the computer. He opened the computer's control panel and clicked on system restore. He chose to roll back the system to an earlier point, removing all trace he had used the computer to transfer the documents. He slid back on the wheeled chair and stood up. He grabbed his bag and left the café.

The owner of the apartment he had rented worked in his own leather shop beneath the apartments. He was still working late, probably waiting for his new tenant.

Cam disturbed him from his work when he entered the shop. He soon completed the paperwork, signing under a false name and followed him up the stairs into the flat. There was a small cage elevator in the stairwell but it seemed quicker to use the stairs. There was a shared kitchen but the room had its own bathroom. He dropped his bag on the floor and reached for his wallet. The leather craftsman waved his hand saying he could pay later, but Cam paid upfront. He didn't want any further contact with the owner of the apartments.

Once alone, Cam opened the sliding sash window. The light from the streetlights seeped through the wooden slats of the outer shutters. Sounds of a city that never slept joined the lines of light. Cam unhooked the latch and concertinaed the double folding shutters inwards.

He leaned out and looked down over the street. He closed his eyes and drew in the night air. One of the cleanest cities, he thought, even though the traffic never ceased. The night was cool – Rome was enjoying a mild spring. He left the window and sat on the bed, leaving the window open, allowing in the sounds of cars driving and horns beeping.

He pulled out the stolen phone and drew the pattern on the screen to un-lock the device. He smiled to himself remembering the ease of unlocking it after taking it from the thug. His dirty, sticky fingers had left a trail on the screen. Cam simply followed the trail to unlock it. After only a few attempts the stolen phone had become his. He had disabled the GPS and covered the camera lens and it was ready to go.

He swiped through the documents with his thumb until he found the notes for Rome. Scrolling down through the information, most of which he had committed to memory, he found the photo of the main player he had come to Italy's capital for.

The man in the photo looked back through Cam, his focus on a distant object. He had been unaware he had been under surveillance when the photo had been taken. Hakem Al Hammed, an Egyptian national, had spent most of his adult life travelling between Afghanistan, Jordan, Pakistan and of course, the UK.

He was one of A.Q's fund runners, moving funds between A.Q sources and the cells in the UK. He had come to the attention of the security services and was arrested. However, the judge threw out the jury's guilty verdict and he was set free. The story on the news had angered Cam so much he had taken it upon himself to collect information on this guy, one of Cam's assignments Al probably knew little about.

The US had been interested in extradition and was secretly looking into getting him to the States. His superiors had ordered him to disappear, as he knew too many details about key personnel. So, he had been in hiding in Rome but was still at work. Fund raising by exploitation.

He would bring in migrants and force them to work for their travel to wherever they were trying to get to – probably the UK. These migrants sold crap to tourists or dressed as Roman centurions for photo opportunities then fleeced the tourists for as much as they could. This money then went to fund terrorist activities. The migrants would never get to where they wanted as he took most of the money and only gave enough for them to survive on.

Cam closed the document and threw the phone onto the bed, sighed and stood up. He paced the room a few times. Thoughts of how to find him swirled round his mind. Tomorrow he would visit the main attraction. His migrants wouldn't be too hard to spot. Maybe one would lead him to his target.

Cam returned to the window, he was tired. He leaned on the window-sill and took in the scene below him. A scooter shot down the street and a group of pedestrians walked northwards. Cam leaned further out and watched them move past the front of the leather shop. With his head and shoulders out of the window he looked back south, he needed a shop that would still be open this time of the morning.

A light was still on a couple of buildings down, souvenirs were still outside hanging on revolving hangers and filling wire baskets. Cam reasoned there was a strong possibility of alcohol being sold from there. Grabbing the phone he bounded down the bare concrete stairs past the elevator, stationary on the second floor. He stepped out onto the street through the large double wooden door and stood underneath the streetlights.

A quick sweep of the shop and it became apparent that the supply of drink was limited. All he could find was a fridge with bottles of cold beer. He opened the glass door and picked out a bottle of Peroni. Not exactly what he had in mind but it would do for tonight, after all he needed to sleep.

Returning to his room, with a carrier bag full of bottles clinking together, he filled a sink with cold water to keep the bottles cool. Taking one, he opened the jagged cap using the bathroom's door handle and the heal of his hand. He downed the first bottle in two goes and opened another, the water from the sink dripped down his arm and onto the bathroom floor.

He took the new, full bottle over to the window and sat himself down on the old, wide window-sill. Breathing in the city air and taking in the atmosphere he allowed the alcohol to take effect. Tomorrow would be a new day, a new target. Eventually he would be caught. He only hoped that he could make a difference before the end.

Before too long his mind drifted back to his old friends. Sleep might elude him again tonight. In an attempt to quash the thoughts of the past he downed the beer and went to open another. He delved his hand into the icy water and was transported back, back to a time when he had last felt a biting bitter chill.

Chapter 17

"Friday the thirteenth!" said George, sat in the snow on the other side of the ridge to the Argentinean research base. "Are we sure it's a good idea to do this today?"

"What does it matter what day it is?" asked Bull.

"Just feels like we're pushing our luck," said George. "Don't you think?" George sat alongside Bull and Rory out of view of the base. Cam was still on the ridge lying prone, observing the base, slowly getting covered by the falling snow. The base was quiet. There had been no movement for well over an hour. Cam was growing impatient and cold. He wanted to get moving.

"Speedy," he said, shivering under the thin layer of snow. "Shall we get this show on the road?"

"Yeah, I think so," came Speedy's response through his earpiece. Cam started to crawl backwards down the slope towards where his team sat huddled together. "We'll engage when you go loud."

"Roger that," said Cam, acknowledging Speedy's message. When sure he was out of sight from the base he stood and slid down the rest of the way to meet his team. "OK, are we good?" he said, brushing the snow off his Argentine uniform.

"I'm not sure I can move," said Bull, shivering uncontrollably.

"You'll be OK when we get moving," said George, clambering to his feet, his joints hurting from the extreme temperatures and the lack of movement.

"Guys," said Rory. "I've been thinking."

"Christ!" said Bull, as Rory hauled him to his feet. "What now?"

"On the same lines as before. I think we should be more careful with our comms security."

"Come on guys, mount up," said Cam, clicking on his skis, slinging his rifle on his back and looping the ski pole grips round his wrists.

"We should come up with call signs instead of using our real names," said Rory. He attached his skis and started up the hill to the summit.

"George," said Cam leading the way. "You're with me, we'll take the main building. Rory, Bull you got the barn. Don't destroy the snowmobiles. If you do we're stuck here." The team formed up in their pairs on the summit ready to ski down the slope onto the target.

"So I thought we'd call you the Big Bopper and we'll be Disco King."

"We're not using those call signs." Cam sighed.

"We don't have enough time to come up with anything else," said Rory pushing off down the slope. "We'll give it a trial run." He shouted back to the others yet to set off.

"Shit!" said Cam. "Come on!" He too began skiing down towards the base, chasing Rory. Within seconds all the team streamed down the hill weaving as they descended. Cam and George veered off towards the main building. The perpetual darkness of the Antarctic winter masked their approach.

"Movement!" Speedy announced that he had spotted someone on the exterior of the base. "Barn. White aspect." Rory now alerted to the presence of the enemy skidded sideways to a halt. Through the drifting snow he could see the enemy soldier moving along the front aspect of the barn. Bull, not being the most accomplished skier, slid past. He tried to stop using the snowplough manoeuvre but still he continued on towards the barn.

Rory stabbed his ski poles into the snow forming a bipod. He rested his rifle's barrel on the makeshift platform and took aim on the soldier.

"Going loud," he said quietly, broadcasting to the two teams he was about to open fire. Three cracks rang out. The sound bounced off the snow-covered hills, and the soldier dropped. "Enemy down." Rory skied onwards to the barn. Bull was ahead nearing the barn. He tried to stop but the forward momentum from the slope slammed him into the barn's wall.

"God damn it!" Bull cursed, kicking off his skis, happy to be ditching them. He looked back as Rory joined him against the wall.

"Dick!" said Rory, loosing his skis. The two men put their backs to each other and covered the length of the barn with their M4s. From their position they could see Cam and George ski up to the entrance of the main building and prepare themselves for entry.

Another crack echoed off the hills. The shot, not fired by the four assaulters but by Speedy's team, eliminated a second target.

"Enemy down," said Lugsy. "Main building, second floor window." Cam and George instinctively looked up to the window involved but they saw nothing.

"Barn doors opening!" said Speedy, his over watch position proving useful. Rory advanced on the large sliding doors, rifle up on aim. Bull advanced with him backwards covering their rear. A double tap from Rory signified more enemy movement.

"Enemy down," he said as he moved. An enemy soldier now lay half in half out of the barn. More sniper shots flew over Cam and George's heads, smashing windows and taking out more of the enemy. Each time Lugsy would announce the kill.

"We're going in," said Cam. He looked at George and after a slight nod he turned his back to the wall and backwards kicked the door in, keeping covered by the side of the wall. He spun round and entered the main building up in the aim. George followed, moving smoothly round the door frame.

Rory arrived at the barn's door. It was open but not fully, only enough for one person to fit through. The body of the soldier filled the gap. Rory peered round into the barn and immediately pulled back.

"Shit!" he said.

"What?" said Bull, facing the opposite direction and wanting information.

"We got a problem."

"What?" he demanded.

"I think they're all in there!" Rory turned to Bull with a mixed expression of concern and surprised excitement on his face. "All bloody hundred of em!" Bull stared back, eyebrows furrowed in intense thought.

"What we gonna to do?" he said. His New York accent pushed through.

"OK, two frags and in!" he said, geeing himself up. "You ready?" Bull nodded. "OK, OK." He pulled two fragmentation grenades from a pouch on his belt and pulled the pins and threw them round the door frame, one to each side of the barn. A series of shouts and the sound of frantic movement preceded the explosions. What followed was a short silence, peppered only by the sound of debris falling to the ground, then the shouts of the injured. "Go! Go! Go!"

Rory swept in firing well-aimed shots with his M4. Bull was on his back, his aim lowered to avoid blue on blue. Rory dived for cover behind some industrial machinery, Bull behind some scrap metal piled in the corner of the barn. Before the enemy could re-group and recover from the initial assault, Rory and Bull continued the fight from behind their cover.

Cam and George moved down the corridor clearing the main building. Doors on each side of the corridor passed by being systematically cleared by the two Assets. Civilian researchers huddled in random rooms, some protecting the others with their own bodies.

"Up the stairs," said Cam as they came to the end of the corridor and the staircase loomed. They bounded up, taking two or three stairs at a time. On reaching the top Cam paused, leaning on a wall before the corner that would lead along the top floor corridor.

"Cordon coming down now," said Speedy over the radio. Cam didn't reply. He knew that Kosta and Luca were skiing down to take up positions to cover their withdrawal. In the confusion of the assault Cam had lost count of his rounds. He removed the magazine from his M4 and looked into the mag. It still had enough rounds to be used but he decided to fit a fresh mag. The half full one was thrown down the front of his smock, to be used later.

"Cordon in place." Kosta's Greek accent let them know that they had some cover ready to support them extracting from the buildings. Cam, once re-loaded, peeked round the corner. Being right handed he had to lean right out to see the length of the corridor. He switched hands, holding the rifle into his left shoulder, and looked down the red dot reflex sight on the top of his rifle. It didn't matter what hand he shot with, all the Assets could fire from both shoulders.

Cam took in the corridor and swung round the corner with George on his shoulder. Both men had their weapons up on aim. The corridor was long and empty, only four doors, two pairs, one pair five metres ahead and another set at the end of the corridor twenty-five metres away. They had to clear the building before they could safely withdraw. Cam described the corridor to George as they moved.

Bull had thrown all his grenades and was re-loading his M4. He was getting low on ammo. Rory was firing at the surviving enemy who had hidden themselves behind cover and were periodically popping out to return fire. Rory fired on one then switched targets, keeping their heads down and taking some out where he could.

When he ran dry he ducked into cover and re-loaded while Bull took over. Rory pulled the pin on another grenade and flung it blindly over his head at the enemy. It exploded, sending shrapnel in all directions and shredding the soldiers unlucky enough to be in its path. More screaming and shouting.

Bull and Rory looked at each other as the incoming fire grew worse and bounced off the metalwork of their cover. Rory grinned a nervous smile whilst Bull shook his head in disbelief. The process repeated. Bull covered, Rory fired at the enemy. Then they swapped.

"Luca," shouted Rory. "We could use some help in here." Rory and Bull were running low on ammo and needed support, that support could only come from Luca and Kosta.

"Roger," replied Luca." On our way." They broke cover and ran to the open barn door. Both had a quick look at the situation within the barn, looked at each other and without words agreed on what action needed taken. They opened fire on the enemy over the top of their colleagues, who remained hidden behind their cover.

Cam and George cleared the first two rooms half way down the corridor. Two long rooms, empty apart from crying scientists and one shooter that lay dead by the window. A victim of Speedy and Lugsy. Cam moved smoothly along the corridor supported by George. Lugsy had been firing at other targets in the building and hadn't called out 'enemy down.' His threat assessment was high.

With four Assets involved in the barn firefight, the battle was slowly being won. Each time Bull and Rory fired from their position they took in more of the barn. The incoming fire slowly dwindled into the odd shot here and there. Rory took a good look above the machinery he was hidden behind. What he saw did not look good.

Cam was near the end of the corridor, and he had a bad feeling there was at least one more enemy waiting in one of the other rooms on either side of the building. He slowed instinctively, were there anymore? Then his question was answered, the soldier emerged firing wildly in all directions. The rounds went wide, hitting the walls the whole length of the corridor.

Cam engaged the enemy. He fired six rounds in quick succession then his rifle jammed. He followed the immediate action drill and cantered the weapon over to the left and looked at the ejection port.

An ejected round sat lodged in the breach. With no time to clear the stoppage, he pulled his rifle into his chest cradling it in his arm. He pulled his pistol with his right hand from his thigh holster and raised it, firing as he walked. He held the pistol out with both hands, arms outstretched, rifle lying across his forearms.

He advanced towards the last known position of the panicked enemy, pistol on aim, walking carefully with knees slightly bent to provide a stable platform. When the enemy emerged and darted down the corridor towards them, Cam emptied the rest of the thirteen-round clip into him. The rounds hit him in the chest knocking him to the ground.

Under cover from Kosta and Luca, Rory and Bull advanced deeper into the barn, keeping low. Bodies littered the barn. They stopped periodically to listen for movement, they knew there were more left alive somewhere in the barn. The odd burst of fire flew over their heads, fired by either Kosta or Luca. Rory and Bull stayed low, weaving between machinery and boxes of supplies, looking for survivors.

George and Cam cleared the last two rooms at the end of the corridor. They stepped over the body of the last enemy in the main building as they went. They stayed in the last room and re-grouped at the door. George peered out down the corridor, leaned his rifle on the door frame and waited.

"Rory, Bull. It's Cam." He cleared his M4's stoppage in the safety of the room. "Main building clear and complete. What's your sitrep?" Nothing came back. "Rory, it's Cam. Can you hear me?" He walked over to the window and tried to see the barn but it was just out of view. "Rory, can you hear me?" Cam sighed and his shoulders dropped. "Disco King, this is Big Bopper. Can you hear me?"

"Roger Big Bopper, this is Disco King," said Rory content his radio procedure was being followed.

"Where are you, Disco King?" said Cam, faking a jolly voice.

"We're still in the barn," said Rory. "We may have a slight problem".

"What's the problem?" asked Cam.

"Well," said Rory. "We may have wrecked our ride outta here."

"What?" said Cam. "Shit!" George, who heard the conversation relaxed his aim slightly and looked back into the room. Cam stood in the room, his hand raised, pressing the earpiece further into his ear.

"What are we going to do now?" Cam barely looked at George; he simply looked down at the floor and shook his head.

"How long are you guys going to be?" Cam said eventually. He knew the silence that followed his question was being used by Rory and Bull to make a quick assessment of their situation in the out of view barn.

"We'll be a porno or two," said Rory. Cam shook his head again and sighed.

"Come on mate," he said patting George on the shoulder. "Lets get back outside." They picked their way back to the exit, confident they had taken out all the enemy in the building. Some scientists attempted to flee the building only to be scared back into the rooms as Cam and George passed.

"OK," said Cam on reaching the doorway. "We need to think of a way out of here." George agreed and looked out into the frozen night. The snowstorm had intensified and even their tracks into the building had been covered over. Shots rang out from the barn indicating Rory and Bull were still clearing out the enemy.

As he looked around, squinting through the snow, he saw the helicopter sat on the pan.

"What about that?" he said, staring at the Bell 205 thoughtfully. Cam joined him in the doorway and took in the view of the helicopter and considered their options.

"Speedy," Cam said. "Can any of your guys fly a helicopter?"

"Hey!" said Rory, loudly over the radio. "Screw them guys, I can fly it." Cam and George looked dubious at this new claim from Rory.

"You can fly?" asked Cam with a hint of disbelief.

"Err yeah!" he said, annoyed that he wasn't being believed. "Just get out there and secure the chopper, I'll be out in half a porno." More shots were fired in the barn. To Cam they sounded like the shots of someone finishing off the last stragglers of resistance. Within minutes Rory and Bull appeared at the doorway to the barn just as Cam and George arrived at the chopper.

"Cover us guys!" shouted Rory, running past Kosta and Luca. "Cam, release the rotor blades." He pointed as he ran, to the front blades connected by wire to the front landing skids. "George, clear the windscreen." Cam set about the rotor blade anchors that were designed to support the flimsy blades in areas of bad weather. George climbed up onto the steps outside the crew's door and began to wipe the snow from the windscreen.

Rory opened the side door under the main engines and climbed aboard. Bull stopped outside and knelt down, keeping a good view of both buildings.

"You better know what your doing in there!" shouted Bull, still surveying the buildings.

"Chill out, sweetheart," he shouted back climbing into the pilot's seat. "You saw me fly that unmanned aircraft back in Yemen didn't you?"

"What? Is that your flight experience," argued Bull. "I saw you crash that bloody thing! Twice!"

"I've flown in enough choppers to know how to do it!" he screamed. Cam had un-leashed the rotor blades and was climbing into the chopper. He could see George outside, frantically wiping the snow away only to have it replaced by fresh falling flakes.

"Tell me you know what you're doing, mate," said Cam, leaning on the back of the pilot's seat.

"Umm, yeah," he said, scanning the control switches. "It's just been a while that's all." Rory tentatively reached forward and began flicking some switches. Cam watched, yet to be convinced. Some lights flashed on the dashboard and the sound of what could only be described as a small motor began to whir. Rory looked up at some handles on the roof. "I'm sure I've got to do something with those," he said as he grabbed them and slid them up and down.

"He better get this thing started," said Bull. "I sure as hell don't want to be marching out of here." Bull desperately wanted to get back to the closest friendly research base and re-warm.

"Ah ha, yes!" shouted Rory when he heard the whine of the engines. He leaned forward in his seat and looked up at the rotors, they started to turn, albeit slowly. "See told you!" he shouted, pleased with himself. Cam patted him hard on the shoulder and climbed into the co-pilot's seat and strapped himself in.

"Guys!" he commanded, "everyone in." Cam saw Kosta and Luca abandon their covering positions and turn and run for the helicopter. Bull was already inside and strapping himself into one of the passenger seats. "Speedy! Get yourselves down here. We're getting the hell out of Dodge." Speedy and Lugsy skied down the hill, abandoning their observation point, leaving cloud trails of powdery snow behind them.

The blades turned faster, George continued to wipe the windscreen. Rory, now that the engines were running, had power to the wipers and activated them, knocking George off the front, down into the snow below the chopper. Rory smiled.

"OK," he said. "Everybody in." Speedy and Lugsy arrived at the chopper and helped George up out of the snow. George was bundled into the helicopter mumbling expletives.

"OK, we're all in," shouted Lugsy, sliding the side door shut and dampening the sound of the engines. "Get us the fuck out of here!"

"OK, hold tight." Rory pulled up on the collective stick giving the engines more power. The helicopter started to buffet on the pan. He pulled up on the stick more until the chopper left the ground only to lose lift and drop back down onto the landing pad.

"Woaah, come on!" shouted Lugsy, steadying himself in the back of the chopper. Rory tried again, this time giving it more power. The helicopter lifted off with more speed, jumping into the air. As it lifted it began to spin, slowly at first then with more speed.

"Ohh, uhh," Rory said, looking wildly from side to side. "Cam, help me with the pedals. Press down on the left one there. We need to counteract the motion of the blades." Rory mimed a rotating motion with his hand. Cam did as he was told and the helicopter began to steady itself. "There, sweet!" he said. "Right, that's going to be your job, OK? If we start to spin, counter it with the pedals."

"Yeah OK," said Cam, concentrating on his new job. The helicopter shakily hovered over the Argentine research base. Snow continued to wrap the helicopter in a blanket of thick, white flakes.

"I need a bearing!" shouted Rory into the back. Speedy opened his map pocket and pulled out an ordnance survey map of the area. "Just a rough one." Speedy un-folded the map and spun it around a few times.

"Shit!" he said. "Thing looks like a blank piece of white paper."

"Just give me a rough direction," he repeated. "We only need to get closer than we are. Then we'll ditch this thing."

"North, mate," shouted Speedy. "Head north to Palmer station. It's a US base. It has a heliport."

"Great," said Cam. "Do you think you can put it down on the helicopter pad?" Rory looked at Cam with a less than confident look.

"Don't know," he said. "Never actually landed before."

"What?" shouted Bull, over the noise of the engines. "Did he say he's never landed before?" Bull threw his hands in the air. "Son of a bitch. Told you we shouldn't trust that God damn idiot."

"How many hours have you got in choppers?" asked Speedy.

"Well, I've been flown around enough times," said Rory. "You're bound to pick up a few things."

"So you've never actually flown?" Cam asked.

"In a way yes," said Rory. "But then again in a more accurate kind of a way, no."

"Christ!" said Cam. "How did you get it started?"

"I've been watching. Look, just have a little faith, I'm doing alright. Now, you might want to hold on." Rory pushed the left rudder pedal and faced the helicopter in a rough northerly direction. Next he carefully pushed the cyclic stick forward putting the heli into a dive giving it forward momentum. He pulled up the collective stick to counter the dive. The helicopter kept its height and began its bumpy journey to the American research base.

"You can fly this in these conditions," said Cam quietly into the mic. "Can't you?"

"Don't be silly," replied Rory without shifting his concentration from the front windscreen. "You don't fly in weather like this. That's why it was lashed down."

Cam sighed, accepting he was wrapped up in one of Rory's games.

The flight however, was going well. The team was surprised at Rory's piloting. Rory was flying faster and faster, the more he pushed the cyclic forward the faster it went. To counter the exchange of height for power he continually pulled up on the collective. Snow flew past the helicopter like a star field in a cheap science fiction movie. It was almost hypnotic.

A shrill beeping brought Cam and Rory out of their confident daze.

"What's that?" asked Cam.

"Umm, not sure," said Rory, looking around, trying to locate the source of the noise. "Can't be a good noise though."

"No," said Cam looking at Rory. "An alarm rarely is."

"I'm sure it'll be OK," said Rory. "We're nearly there." As soon as he finished speaking the helicopter started shaking. The aircraft vibrated with increasing violence as it flew north. The first alarm was joined by another, then another. Lights flicked on the dashboard some on permanently, some flashing. Rory didn't know which was worse.

"Um, yeah," said Rory.

"Look, there. Lights." Cam pointed into the distance. "Must be Palmer."

Rory fought against the controls, trying to keep the aircraft on course towards the research base. He pulled up hard on the collective stick using all the power the engines had. As soon as he had yanked it fully up another alarm joined the others. And this one was louder than the rest.

"What's going on?" asked Cam, his voice vibrating along with the airframe.

"Don't know," said Rory, shakily.

"Just put the thing down! We're close enough." The helicopter dropped violently causing everyone to gasp and reach out for a handhold. More alarms as the helicopter plummeted to the Antarctic dessert.

"Autorotate! Autorotate!" shouted Rory.

"What?" Cam shouted in response to the un-known command.

"We're going down! We need to spin with the rotors." Rory was barely audible over the noise of the struggling engines and sound of multiple alarms. "Right rudder! Right rudder." Cam pressed down hard on the right foot pedal. The helicopter spun faster and faster in a right spin. With the helicopter spinning the same way as the engines were rotating the rotors, the helicopter's descent slowed.

"As you can see we have started our descent," said Rory calmly with his best airline pilot's voice. "Please put your seats in the upright position and stow away your…" Cut short by a sudden drop of altitude that tightened Rory's grip on the controls.

"Come on, come on," shouted Cam. "Hold on, were going in." Cam and the passengers in the back braced themselves as best they could.

"Rory!" shouted Bull. "If we survive this I'm going to fucking kill you. Then I'm going to resuscitate you and kill you again!"

"Shit! Hold on," shouted Rory so everyone could hear him. "Shiiiiit!" With a crumpling sound of metal hitting a soft bank of snow the helicopter slammed into the ground. The passengers closed their eyes tight and gritted their teeth, mentally preparing for the worst.

The snow cushioned the crash. The spinning of the helicopter flopped it onto its side and the spinning rotors cut into the ice and snow. The shouts and insults aimed at Rory became more audible as the rotors came to a standstill. The chopper rested on its side held in place by the bank of snow the crash created.

Rory, held in by the straps of the pilot seat, looked over at Cam strapped into his seat.

"Came in a little hard there," he said as if nothing had happened. "My bad, but they say any landing that you can walk away from is a good landing." Rory smiled. Cam closed his eyes and sighed.

"Well," said Bull dangling from his side-mounted seat, arms and legs hanging down into the fuselage of the aircraft. "It's our fault really. Should never trust that idiot."

"You live and learn," said George, also hanging from his seat.

"Christ," said Speedy holding the side of his face. "I think he's knocked my fillings loose."

Chapter 18

Friday 29th March 2013
1000hrs CET
Piazza del Popolo, Rome, Italy

The name literally meant 'square of the people', and it was full. A large crowd of people swarmed the piazza like an army of ants. The scene was that of a typical tourist attraction. The elongated oval piazza, with churches to the north, was packed.

Tourists of all nationalities milled around taking photographs whilst standing in various poses. The throng of people swirled around the central, Egyptian style obelisk like a sandstorm.

Cam stood on the high-rise viewing platform to the east. The Villa Borghese park sprawled out behind him. Beautiful green parrots flew from tree to tree singing songs in the mid morning sun. For a moment Cam allowed his mind to drift, taking in the panorama before him. Beyond the piazza, in the foreground, the Castel Sant'Angelo was clearly visible. Further west, the Vatican was almost hidden in the haze.

From his elevated position he watched the sellers of useless trinkets and children's toys. The piazza was the second of Rome's tourist attractions he had visited that morning, he had already been through the Piazza Navona. Much the same was going on there, peddlers of crap that children would annoy their parents for.

There were so many of these migrants everywhere that they must have been making a small fortune for his target. He hoped they would reveal his prize. If not, he might have to get the information out of one, by force if necessary. But to do this he wanted to find one he wouldn't mind punishing.

He left the platform and walked down the stairs to the piazza. He wove through the tourists towards the centre of the square. The migrants seemed to be treating the tourists with respect. He watched them speak nicely to the families and leave them well alone when they wanted their space.

He felt for them, all they wanted was a better life and were being exploited by their captor. They might never make it to their intended destinations; instead they were trapped in Rome, almost like modern day slaves.

Cam stopped at one of the water fountains that dotted the city and filled his water bottle. He spotted a group of migrants stood around selling squeaking toys. A family stopped when their child became interested and asked his parents for a toy. The sale was made and the seller patted the young boy on the head as he ran off with his new toy. The parents paid the seller and he gave them their change, which the parents offered the seller. He waved his hands, not accepting the tip.

Cam watched, amazed. The migrant didn't want the extra money. Then he realised that it would only be taken from him anyway. They seemed like good people put into a difficult situation.

The bottle, still under the free flowing water fountain, filled and started overflowing. Surprised by the stream of water running down his arm and dripping off his elbow, he retracted the plastic bottle.

He took a sip from the completely full bottle and screwed on the lid, then turned from the group of migrants and left the people's square. He headed south past the Spanish Steps and through the fashion centre of Rome.

He arrived at his next stop, the Trevi Fountain. Crowded as ever with people throwing coins over their shoulder into the water. Every inch by the edge of the water was taken up with people, shoulder to shoulder, most enjoying the local ice creams.

Cam found a position where he could observe the scene, near to one of the Gelaterias. It didn't take long to find what he was looking for. He was one of a group of migrants, but this one worked on his own, slightly older than the rest and of north African origin. He stood out, to Cam at least he did. The tourists didn't see the danger; he was like a shark circling his prey.

He blended in well, wearing bland clothing so as not to stand out. Pick-pockets have a particular skill set, similar to surveillance operators, and it took one to know one. The pick-pocket moved unnoticed through the tourists, he stopped and surveyed his prey then moved in.

A young couple stood near the babbling water taking photos of the statues of aquatic men taming horses. They were crushed up among the other tourists and the pick-pocket knew they wouldn't feel him invading their personal space. The pick-pocket slunk in. He wove through the crowd, eyes locked on the young couple.

He had his jacket draped over his left arm, to disguise his arm movements and also to have a place to hide his prize. It took less than a second to deprive the young man of his wallet. Between the jostling of the crowd, he never felt a thing. The pick-pocket was smooth with his movements and was away, disappearing into the sea of tourists.

Cam had found his man; he followed. He watched the criminal leave the area and move south, passing through the other tourist attractions. Cam observed him stealing twice more on his journey through the city. He also saw him collecting money from the groups of sellers, treating them badly with contempt as he did so. Cam concluded he was higher up in the pecking order. This was good; he might lead him to his target.

The day passed by with Cam stalking his prey, who travelled the city in all directions collecting money and taking extra from innocent tourists. The African pick-pocket didn't suspect he was being followed and never checked his back, not that he would have seen his tail. Cam stayed well out of the way.

He watched the sun start to set over the ruins of the Forum from the bus he was riding. The African stood at the front by the driver. He was hanging from the pole by the front door. He seemed chilled out after his day. Cam had entered the bus via the middle door and was holding the rail in the bend of the articulated bus. The pick-pocket stopped the driver as it passed along the side of the Circo Massimo. Cam jumped off the bus after him.

The Circo Massimo was a long, narrow racetrack from back in the Roman chariot days. They both walked along parallel to the track, heading to the southern end. Cam noticed they were the only two in the area and grew worried he would be spotted by the pick-pocket. Cam sped up and closed in on the thief.

They neared the end of the racetrack and would soon be on the main north south road. The end of the ancient racetrack was a collection of ruined buildings. They were being renovated and had tarpaulins and metal fences surrounding them. Cam took his chance. He wanted to get it done before they came into view of the main highway.

Cam increased his pace and placed himself on the right shoulder of the African. From this position, if he felt spooked and was to spin round, he would be put off balance and would find it harder to launch an attack. That was if he was right handed but Cam had to play the odds.

The thief turned, as if sensing someone was closing him down but before his field of vision found his stalker, Cam struck. He went in with his left hand, hitting the heal of his palm onto the pick-pocket's forehead, stunning him and forcing his head back, exposing his chin.

From the stance he was in, slightly lower than his target and with a good steady footing, he followed up with his right hand. Coming up from below and using his legs for extra power he delivered a powerful strike to the underside of the thief's chin. The fleshy area of his palm smashed the pick-pocket's bottom teeth into his upper, causing devastating damage.

He was out. He fell to the ground like a rag-doll; he made no attempt to shield his fall. Cam intertwined his fingers into the African's hair and dragged him quickly across the dusty gravel. Cam pulled him into the shadows and threw a discarded sheet of wooden panelling over the unconscious body.

He looked around to see if he had been seen. It looked clear so he began the search for a way into the derelict buildings. Not too far from the blacked out thief, Cam found an unlocked sheet metal door. He forced it open and peered inside. He decided that it would do. He went back to the thief and scuffed him over to the empty building.

The metal door boomed shut and sealed the two of them inside the building site. The thief moaned, face down on the floor, Cam gave him a swift kick to the side of the head. He lay again in silence. Cam scanned the dark dusty room he found himself in. Certain they were alone, he checked the thief's pockets. He removed everything he had stolen from the tourists and dropped them to the floor near the door to the street.

An upturned metal-framed chair sat in the corner of the room. Cam picked it up and set it on its feet. A grey, chalky dust covered everything in the room and powdered up into the air when he moved around. Builders' supplies scattered the floor. Cam sifted through the items, setting aside some tough zip-ties and strong black tape.

He hauled the unconscious thief up onto the chair and began zip-tying him to the metal frame, his wrists and elbows to the armrests and his knees and ankles to the legs of the cantilever style chair. He fastened more zip-ties to wherever he could, locking him to the chair. He then took the black tape and began to wrap it round his torso; he would find it near impossible to escape these bonds.

When Cam was satisfied his prisoner was going nowhere he stood back and looked at his work. On the floor near to the chair was a pile of rags. He picked one up and shook it clean, adding to the dust cloud. Finding a tear, he ripped the cloth into a more manageable size.

With his finger and thumb he raised the thief's chin, the pickpocket moaned as his head lolled back. Cam crumpled the dirty, dusty rag and stuffed it into his prisoner's mouth. He forced the rag as far as it would go until it was all in, and then wrapped more black tape round the African's head.

The pick-pocket's eyelids flickered and his eyes rolled as he slowly came too. Cam took a step backwards and watched the thief rouse from unconsciousness. The look on the thief's face showed his head was clearing. He looked frantically around his prison desperate to figure out his situation.

Cam wanted to make sure he could still breathe. He watched as the thief started to struggle. His nostrils flared trying to get enough air in to activate his muscles as he strained against his lashes. Cam was happy he would at least survive the night. The thief tried to scream, to call out for help, to anyone that might be passing by. It was no use; his voice would not travel through the filthy rag.

"Calm down asshole," Cam said flatly. "Save your strength, you're going to need it." The thief realised the futility of struggling and stared at Cam whilst he tried to steady his breathing. Snots and slaver streamed from the pick-pocket's nose. He tried to blow the mess clear so he could breathe better. "Urgh, nice," Cam continued, a hint of loathing in his voice.

Cam walked to the metal door, squatted down and picked up the thief's possessions. "Thanks for this," he said showing the thief the wallets and phones he had stolen earlier. "You sit still and I'll be back." Cam opened the door. The metal hinges screeched under the weight of the heavy metal. Before he slammed it shut he looked back at the thief. "Have a good night now." And he slammed the door shut behind him.

Out on the street, Cam looked along both directions, making sure he was alone. He set off back towards his accommodation. The sun had well and truly set and the stars were out, lighting up the ruins of Rome. He headed north, back to his flat. All the way his mind was mulling over how to get the information out of the thief. He rounded a corner onto a narrow Roman street to see an ambulance parked up alongside the pavement. The lights were still flashing, sparkling up the tall, old buildings.

Cam approached the rear of the ambulance and, out of curiosity, tried the door handle. It opened. Cam peered inside; the vehicle was empty. Instinctively he climbed inside and began to search the cupboards. One suitcase-sized bag caught his eye. He unzipped it and rummaged around the contents.

"Perfect," he said to himself, closing the bag. Before he left the vehicle, he spotted some clear plastic drawers on the ambulance wall. He could see the contents and thought he may need what was in them. He grabbed handfuls of spare equipment and jumped from the back door and moved off down the street at a quickened pace. As he speed-walked away he thought it was strange how opportunities presented themselves.

2325hrs CET
Oppio caffé , Via Nicola Salvi, Rome

Cam sat sipping his double Jack Daniels, his fourth since he had arrived at the corner café. He had dropped the paramedic's bag off at his apartment and decided to have the night off. The thief was safely tied up in the derelict building where he shouldn't be found. If he were to be found, it wouldn't really be a problem.

Also, if he died overnight he would lose nothing. He'd always find another way of getting to his main target. He would leave him where he was until the next night. After twenty-four hours being tied up and gagged he should be ready to talk. If not, the medical supplies would tip the balance.

He inhaled deeply and sighed. He straightened his back against the backrest of his chair. He took another sip and beckoned over the waitress. Raising the near empty glass he indicated he'd like another.

"Would you like me to bring the bottle, Sir?" asked the waitress. Cam thought for a second, shrugged and nodded. The waitress smiled and wove her way through the empty tables back into the bar area. She reappeared a few seconds later with the bottle and placed it on the table.

Cam filled his glass way beyond the point the bar tender would have and took a large sip. After another sigh, Cam looked out over the stunning view. The café was situated up on a terrace above the Colosseo metro station. The outside tables looked down on the Colosseum and the Roman Forum. Cam drank his drink, topping up as he did and felt great. For the first time in a long time he felt relaxed.

Even at this time of night the Colosseum was still surrounded by tourists. The piazza of the Colosseum ringed the ancient monument and it was covered with human activity. The west side of the Colosseum was the busiest. Cam could still see the Roman centurions milling around having their photos taken and asking for way too much money for them.

Looking at the group of tourists and street performers Cam raised his glass but stopped before he reached his lips. He slammed down the glass and leaned forward on the table. He zoomed in his vision like a hawk, ignoring everything else.

Mixed in amongst the tourists, sat on a low wall was a stocky man. He blended in well, considering his bushy beard should have made him stand out. He sat inconspicuously looking around, scanning the whole area section at a time. Cam took a quick look left and right. How had he been traced so fast? How were they onto him?

He had to get back to his accommodation, and fast. He left the payment for the whiskey, including a large tip, under the ashtray and left the café. On the way back, he passed by the shore of the Tiber and disconnected the battery from the phone taken from the thug in Poland. He flung the dead phone and battery into the water. That had to be how he had been found. He wanted no traceable item they could use to track him with.

Chapter 19

"How's the search going?" asked Bull, talking into his phone, outside a sandwich shop to the side of the Pantheon. "Has he found anything to go on?" Bull shoved a pastry into his mouth and dropped his weight down onto a low wall that surrounded the Pantheon.

"Not really," said George from his hotel room. "Italy doesn't have too much of a problem with extremists." Bull nodded along with George. "They have a few internal problems like the Red Brigade, but nothing on the international stage. Not in Rome anyway."

"Damn," sighed Bull. "What's next?"

"Look mate, you've been out all night. Get yourself back here and get your head down. I'll take over. I'll have Colin out as well. We'll find him."

"OK," agreed Bull finishing off his breakfast pastry. "On my way back."

"Good, I'll be gone when you get here. There may be a few leads to check out. I'll get Colin to brief you when you change over."

"Cool," said Bull heaving his tired body off the wall. "Good luck."

"Thanks, and goodnight. Or day," laughed George. He disconnected the call, Bull's name disappearing from the screen. George stood in the hotel room booked for them by Al. He was ready to head out and continue the search for his ex-colleague. He picked up his backpack and sighed. He hesitated as he went to throw it onto his shoulder. He knelt down next to his larger travel bag and pulled out a pistol. He looked at it deep in thought before adding it to the other items in his backpack.

Stepping out onto the street outside the hotel, George blinked in the sunlight. He looked around, up and down the street. He didn't expect to see who he was looking for, but was sure he would show up when he least expected it. He looked at his watch; it was time to go. He made his way to his first lead Al had given him.

2200hrs CET
Roman Forum, Rome, Italy

The day had passed slowly, Cam had been knocked from feeling safe and secure to knowing he was being hunted. Hunted by people who knew him, knew how he worked, and knew his thought process. After destroying his stolen phone, the only thing that could possibly be traced to him, he had been out during the day to buy himself a small Netbook.

Onto the Netbook, he had transferred the files, although he was now considering the fact that if he continued with these targets he would be found far easier. If he had this information then Al had it too. They would be monitoring the individuals in the documents. Al Hammed was one of his own choosing so he should be left to conduct his business unnoticed.

Cam had been in the Forum for most of the afternoon, taking in the spring sun and watching the world go by. Always on the look out for anyone acting suspicious, he was confident he would spot someone hunting for him. The tourists passed him by pointing at and talking about the surrounding ruins, completely unaware of him sat quietly on a bench under a tree.

As the sun began to set on another day in the Italian capital, Cam's mind turned to the African strung up in the Circo Massimo. Had he survived the night? He may have suffocated. Cam hardly cared. If he found the African dead, he would simply locate his target another way. If he was still alive he was about to have a very bad night. Cam looked at and ran his hand over the paramedic's bag.

He slung the bag over his shoulder, left the Forum and crossed the road to the Circo Massimo. The streetlights were on now and gave the old ruined racetrack an orange glow. Cam slowed his walk towards the metal door that hid his prisoner, as a bendy bus drove down the street. The bus disappeared towards the river allowing Cam to continue to the door unnoticed. It was closed tightly, as he had left it.

He had one last look along the street then prised the door open, the screeching of metal on metal was followed closely by muffled cries from within the darkened room. Still alive then, Cam thought.

Cam slammed the door closed and some dust and mortar fell from the ceiling. Cam could make out, in the gloom, a dark lump on the floor. Not moving. The stifled screams stopped when the door slammed and the room fell into silence. Cam heard the gravel floor crunch under his feet as he walked to the middle of the room, his other senses heightened in the darkness.

Cam snapped a chemical light stick. The room was illuminated as he shook the stick, mixing the two chemicals together. He threw the stick to the floor and snapped another, then another. With chemical lights scattered over the floor the whole room was lit with a green light.

"Well look at you," Cam said placing the paramedic's bag onto the dusty floor. "Hurt yourself have you?" Cam squatted down next to the motionless African. During the day he had been trying his bonds and in doing so had toppled the chair. It looked, to Cam, like he had fallen forwards and landed square on his head. Blood had leaked from a gash on his forehead and since dried, leaving dark red streaks down his face. He now lay on his side; dirt and dust had mixed with his blood and sweat and was caked onto his skin.

"Up you go," huffed Cam lifting the chair and the dead weight back up onto its feet. The African looked at him through the top of his eyes, his head lolling forwards after so long in an uncomfortable position. Cam picked at the tape wrapped round his face finding the end and began to pull it free. The African grunted as Cam, who wasn't being gentle, ripped the tape from his face.

Before it was pulled completely off his face, he stopped. Cam pulled the Chechen's pistol from the back of his trouser waist, and let the African see it. His eyes widened at the sight of the gun.

"No shouting now, understand?" He waited for a response. The African nodded after a few seconds of thought. "Good." Cam ripped the last bit of tape free and pulled out the rag from the pick-pocket's mouth. He gasped and dragged in a full lung full of air for the first time in twenty-four hours. Immediately on inhalation, he coughed as the dust cloud aggravated the back of his throat.

"Dry throat?" asked Cam, faking concern. The thief tried to swallow but was unable to lubricate his throat after the dusty rag had soaked up all moisture. The African slung him a look of hatred. "Hmmm." Cam raised his eyebrows. "Shall we get started?"

Cam replaced the pistol into the waistband of his trousers, raised his foot and slammed it into the pick-pocket's chest. With the wind knocked out of his lungs he was sent sliding backward across the floor. He crashed into the wall, hitting the back of his head. Cam followed up with a punch to the side of his face. The thief's head flopped forward. Cam grabbed the thief's hair and lifted his head exposing his face, fresh lines of blood dripped down between the lines of dried blood.

"Hmmm," said Cam dropping the thief's head. "Better put on some gloves, don't know what diseases you bastards have." He snapped on a pair of blue latex gloves that he found in the paramedic's bag. "There." Re-lifting his prisoner's head he delivered a series of punches to the thief's face, taking away his consciousness.

Cam had time to work now, even though the African was zip-tied tightly to the metal frame of the chair, he could still squirm and make the next step very difficult. He dragged the paramedic bag over to the unconscious thief and zipped it open. Knelt down next to the thief's left arm, Cam slapped the back of the pick-pockets hand, searching for a vein.

Due to being tightly zip-tied to the chair, there was no need to apply a tourniquet. Cam selected a cannula, the biggest size there was; he didn't care about hurting his patient. Also, he forwent the alcohol cleaning swab. Infection wasn't a concern.

He inserted the needle and pushed it a couple of centimetres under the skin until he saw some blood flashback into the cannula, confirming correct placement. Cam took a pair of medical scissors and cut the zip-tie around the thief's elbow, releasing the makeshift tourniquet.

He held the needle still and advanced the plastic catheter fully into the vein. He applied pressure further up the arm on the vein and retracted the safety needle. After plying the bung to the end of the catheter to stop the blood running free, he tossed the sharp needle to the corner of the room.

Cam secured the thief's elbow back to the chair with another loosely placed zip-tie and taped the catheter to his arm, holding it in place. Cam hunted through the medical bag and selected some vials of drugs, drawing up needles and large plastic syringes. He stood up and lined up the equipment on a boarded-up window-sill.

After attaching drawing-up needles to the syringes, he picked up and shook the vials of clear liquid. Suxamethonium Chloride, a paralytic, and Naloxone Hydrochloride, an anti-opioid. Removing the sheath from the drawing up needle he inverted the vials and filled two syringes, one of each drug. Again, he threw the used needles to the corner of the room.

Cam turned his attention to the unconscious thief, who sat slumped in his seat unaware of what Cam had just done and what he was about to do. He waited patiently for him to come round, planning every detail of his questioning. He contemplated the drugs he was about to administer. Although it was all theoretical, he was sure it should work.

The thief woke. His eyes fluttered. His pupils focused in and out, finally settling on his jailer. He tried to say something but the words were incoherent. His dry, damaged throat was incapable of forming sounds.

"OK, lets try the simple method," said Cam, casually. "I'm looking for Hakem El Hammed." He stared at the thief who was looking back, straining his eyes upwards. Cam was used to the look of defiance with these people. "OK." He sighed. "Who is it you give the money to when you take it from the immigrants?"

The thief said nothing he simply stared back at Cam, his eyes narrowing. "Yeah, OK," he said. Cam's demeanour changed visibly, immediately from calm to angry. "Where is he? Where!" he screamed wildly. The thief remained obstinate.

Cam pulled his pistol and held it in view. Still nothing from the thief. Cam, in one quick motion jammed the barrel into his face. The thief panicked and tried to speak, his dry throat not allowing him to.

"What? What is it?" Cam said unfairly. He knew the thief was unable to speak. "Where is he? Where is he?" Cam's raised voice sounded more menacing. He put the gun away and punched him as hard as he could in the stomach, winding him. "Where is Hakem? Where is he?"

The thief was trying to speak but Cam didn't listen. Part of him wanted to know if the drugs would do what he thought they would. Cam turned from the spluttering man. He picked up his syringes and held them up and flicked the air bubbles to the needle end. He pushed the plunger until the liquid squirted out of the needle.

"So, this," said Cam, calm again, not looking at the thief, "is a paralytic. It will paralyse you and stop you breathing." Cam looked back at the thief. "A respiratory depressant." He confirmed. "You won't be able to breathe or move. But you will be completely aware." He knelt down next to the thief and, after removing the bung, inserted the plastic syringe into the end of the catheter. "Let's see, shall we?"

Cam pressed the plunger and administered the dose he thought should do the trick. He stood back and watched the thief's reaction. He started to convulse slightly, and then he gasped and fell limp, his eyes still open but completely lifeless. Cam reached in and felt for a pulse; it was there. He was alive.

Cam waited, the second syringe in his hand. He gave it a good thirty seconds then plunged the second drug into the thief. Again he waited for a reaction. He shuddered and Cam saw some respiratory effort. He gasped in a deep breath and blinked his eyes. Surprised his drug therapy had worked, Cam began asking where his target was. The thief however, was in no state to reveal anything and could only gasp for breath.

"OK, well lets try a full minute." Cam gave the thief more Suxamethonium and watched him enter a paralysed state again. The thief was brought out of his coma and re-questioned. Still unable to talk, Cam offered him some water. The thief said nothing only struggled to breathe. Cam put a small bottle of water to his lips and allowed him to drink. "Shall we try two minutes?"

Before the thief could make any form of protest he administered another dose of the paralytic. Cam looked at his watch and stood over the thief. His open, blank eyes stared back.

Cam knew he was able to see but do nothing else. The glazed eyes hid the panic of suffocation.

"Where is Hakem?" said Cam, after giving him a dose of Naloxone. "Where is he?" Cam's tone was more calm and friendly. "Just tell me where you hand over the money." The thief still under the influence of the drugs struggled to part with the information. "Come on, where can I find him?" Cam was almost whispering now, as if he himself was parting with a secret.

The thief blinked slowly and spoke softly, barely audible.

"What? Say that again," said Cam leaning in.

"Colosseum," whispered the thief under his breath. "East side. The old gladiators entrance. Every night at midnight."

"Good, well done," said Cam, standing up. He looked down on the thief, assessing if he was telling the truth. He was too exhausted to lie. He was breathing slow and deep and blinking his eyes hard. "Good. Now I have to go. And, unfortunately so do you."

The thief panicked and thrashed with the last of his strength against his bonds, the natural human survival instinct kicking in. Cam plunged the rest of the depressant into the thief's vein. He convulsed and drifted away. Cam didn't know if he was aware still, it was a large dose he had given him but he assumed he was.

"You've got a few minutes of consciousness left," Cam said, looking into the African's eyes. "Then you'll start to suffer brain damage. You may dream, you may not. Nobody knows. You'll find out soon." Cam squinted his eyes and tried to read the thief's feelings. Blind panic must be coursing behind the glazed look. "It'll all be over in six or seven minutes."

Cam turned and went to leave the building. Before opening the door to leave and let the African sit to wait for his body to be discovered, he turned and faced the paralysed, dying body.

"I don't know if it does. But I hope it hurts like hell. Because that's where you're going."

Al was exhausted, pulling twenty-four hour shifts and sleeping at his desk was starting to grate. He had been in contact with Italian authorities in an attempt to discover why Cam had gone to Rome. The Italian secret service the S.I.S.M.I hadn't been able to shed any light on the subject.

Italy had a few internal problems but nothing that should have interested Cam. Al threw the documents he had been perusing onto the large pile of files that covered his desk. He leaned back in his leather office chair and slid down, slumping in the seat.

He pinched the bridge of his nose with thumb and index finger and massaged the corners of his eyes. Maybe a few minutes shut-eye, he thought. Then he might spot something he'd missed. He rested his head on the headrest and placed his hands on his stomach, intertwining his fingers. He closed his eyes and inhaled, holding the air in his lungs. He was drifting, about to sleep, when his phone buzzed on his desk.

"Damn it," he said jerking forward. "Hey George." Al held the phone up to his ear after reading the name of the caller. "Anything today?"

"No, nothing," replied George. "Any new leads?" he asked, after he heard Al sigh.

"No." Al shook his head. "Very, very little. Could it be he's simply hiding out somewhere?"

"Could be, but why Rome? He could have gone somewhere more quiet."

"Sometimes it's easier to hide in plain sight."

"Hmmm, not Cam's style. He's a no people person." Al got up from his chair and walked over to the window, leaving the chair swivelling behind him.

"I'm at a loss, George," Al said, looking out of the window towards the lights of Harwell science centre. "I have no idea what to do."

"I think we're doing all we can at the minute," said George, trying to comfort Al. "The Carabinieri gave me a few more avenues for tomorrow. Right now I've got Bull and Colin out working on a few things."

"Good," said Al. "How's the new guy doing?"

"Fine Al, diligent. He's going to be a good team player."

"Good, good." Al paused. "I've got to leave this up to you George. There's no more I can do from here."

"Look Al, we're all over it. If he's still here we'll find him."

Chapter 20

Three shadowy outlines stood at the bottom of the stairs to Via Celio Vibenna. The concrete staircase split halfway to the street, to the left and right. Thousands of years ago, gladiators would have walked this route from their training camps to the arena. Now, the camps are long gone, replaced by apartment blocks.

The three men had no idea they were being watched from another shadowy recess across the piazza. They were becoming agitated, arms being thrown in the air as they spoke to each other, pacing back and forward.

Their collector hadn't turned up last night and they looked like they were angry. They probably thought he had disappeared with their money.

From his concealed position close to the Colosseum, Cam could see his target. A positive ID; it was him. He hadn't made it in time for last night's meeting. By the time he had finished off the African it had been too late. Tonight would be Hakem El Hammed's night. He had collected the last of his ill-gotten gains to send off to his commanders.

Cam had been preparing himself to finish the African's journey all day. He had been on his way to the nightly meeting when Cam had intercepted him. Now he was dead and so was El Hammed to be soon.

Cam drew his pistol from the inside pocket of his jacket and studied the MP-443 Grach. The pistol he had taken from the Chechen in Poland was similar to the ones he had used before. It was also the same pistol that had killed his good friend. Cam had decided that it was fitting to use it to complete his tasks.

He double-checked the state of the pistol by slightly pulling back the slide. A 9mm round could be seen in the chamber. Cam knew the state but always went by the old saying – check, check and check again.

He placed the pistol back in his jacket pocket and left the cover of the shadows.

He kept his hands in his pockets, his right hand gripping the pistol, and his head down, covered by his hooded top. Across the piazza, the three men had noticed him approaching. With his head down and face almost covered by his hood, he could only use his peripherals to view the targets. All three were stood near to each other watching him.

At fifteen metres, with his trigger finger out of the trigger guard, Cam clicked the safety down to fire with his thumb. When Cam drew to within ten metres of the men he looked up right at the middle of the three. He knew El Hammed's face from the intel photos and identified him right away.

He drew the made ready pistol and sent one round, in quick succession into the foreheads of the two men stood either side of him. They both fell backwards, dead. El Hammed had no time to react, he tried to speak but Cam, with his pistol raised in the face of El Hammed, grabbed his throat. Cam's fingers gripped into both sides of El Hammed's trachea, he tried to scream out but only gurgling, scratching sounds came.

Cam swept his legs out from under him and he slammed to the floor, knocking the wind clear from him. El Hammed lay flat on his back, his hands pulling at Cam's wrist.

"Still!" said Cam forcefully but quietly and jammed the barrel of the Russian pistol into the middle of his forehead. El Hammed winced and moved his head away from the pistol but Cam kept it in contact with his skull. "I said still!" he said quietly, moving closer to his target's ear.

Cam kept a grip on Hammed's neck but lengthened his arm putting distance between the two men's faces. The pistol was digging into the bridge of Hammed's nose so hard, a trickle of blood dripped round the side of his cheek to the back of his neck.

"Good," said Cam quietly. He knew the sounds of gunshots would bring passers-by sooner rather than latter. "Now," he continued looking into his victim's terrified eyes. "I am going to kill you." Hammed stared back, eyes wide.

"Your last words are going to be chosen by me, do you understand?" Hammed barely moved, he only shook with fear. "I said do you understand?" He now raised his voice as much as he dared in that public place. "You've collected the last of your blood money." The pistol was pressed harder, between his eyes. "Did you really think you'd get away with it? Fake charities, taking money from the people you want to kill."

In the distance, the tones of sirens could be heard over the ambient sounds of the city. Cam knew he didn't have long.

"You deserve to die, you all do!" Cam continued, whilst monitoring the approaching emergency services. "You people need to learn your place. Say you need to know your place." Cam waited for Hammed to repeat the sentence. "Come on! Say it!" he demanded fiercely. Hammed tried but the grip on his neck wouldn't allow him to speak. Cam released slightly. "Say it! Say you need to know your place."

"I, I need to know my place," said a terrified Hammed, stammering.

"Say, Islam needs to learn its place in the world!" Hammed hesitated, his faith was holding on. "Say it!" Cam slammed the barrel of the Russian pistol hard into the bridge of his nose three times, opening up the wound further. "Say it! Say Islam needs to learn its place in the world!" Cam was now shouting uncontrollably.

"Islam needs to learn its place in the world." Hammed repeated the sentence out of pure fear, all he wanted was the pain to stop. Happy at the man's last words, Cam released Hammed who gasped and started to shuffle backwards away from the man with the gun. Cam allowed him to get a few metres away, to allow him a little hope of escape, then fired two rounds, one into each shin bone.

Hammed screamed in pain, his escape stopped in its tracks. Cam released another round, into Hammed's shoulder. Hammed who had been crawling away on his elbows, collapsed to the floor. Blood began to pool on the cobbled ground of the piazza.

"You will learn!" said Cam, raising his pistol. The final shot silenced the screaming.

Cam now heard the sirens were close. Hammed's cries had masked their approach. Cam holstered the pistol under his jacket and turned away from the crime scene. He broke into a run and melted into the shadows of the Colosseum, the opposite direction from the sirens.

Monday 1st April 2013
0100hrs CEST
Hotel Hiberia, Via XXIV Maggio, Rome, Italy

"What? What is it?" George croaked, woken from a well-needed sleep.

"You're never gonna believe this bro," Bull said into his phone. Lights of a crime scene lit the whole piazza around the stone staircase behind him. "There's been a hit. I think it could be our boy."

"What's the situation?" said George, rubbing his eyes and sitting up in bed. He had only had a couple of hours sleep after scouting around the city all day.

"Three guys, all of Asian origin. Two executed in a professional way with a single shot to the forehead." Bull paused as he turned to face the bodies. Police and crime scene investigators swarmed the area looking for clues, casting long shadows over the ancient ruins. "The other one," he sighed choosing his words. "The other, was shot multiple times. From what I saw, whoever did it seemed to choose his shots to prolong the pain."

"Damn," said George taking in this information. "This ain't some April fool's joke is it?"

"I wish it was, bro."

"Any identification?"

"I'll get it," said Bull. "George, get some sleep. I've got this covered. I've got Colin on his way to the airport in case he tries to skip country. I'll get details of this hit and send it directly to Al." Bull changed the tone of his voice to a jokey, more friendly manner. "No offence, but you're not needed right now. Get your head down, you'll take over in the morning."

"You sure you got this?" said George, already half dressed.

"I got it!" reiterated Bull. "Sleep! Now! That's an order." Bull hung up his phone before George had a chance to argue. He cleared the screen of George's name and swiped down the list of contacts. "Col," said Bull when the call finally connected. "Sit rep."

"Nearly there, Bull." The sound of fast driving and other traffic could be heard in the background of the call. "ETA, five or six minutes."

"Good, when you get there, liaise with the cops. Get them to help you, we must get him if he tries to fly out."

"Understood."

"Good, keep me informed." Bull ended the call and slid the phone into his pocket. He took a moment to collect his thoughts. He watched the buzz of people all over the crime scene. He looked around for someone of authority. A Carabinieri officer stood back away from the crowd of investigators. He too looked like he was collecting his thoughts.

Bull bided his time, for a few seconds, giving the officer some breathing space. He approached the Carabinieri and introduced himself. The officer had been made aware of their presence in the area and the two began to swap notes. Bull was given time to examine the scene. He took some photos of the three men on his phone and was present when the police investigators searched the bodies.

It was three in the morning when Bull left the scene. He checked his watch before calling Al. He knew he would be in his office. Al hadn't left it since this had all begun. Bull had the feeling that Al blamed himself for this mess.

"Hello Bull, what do you have for me?" Al, as polite as always, sounded exhausted.

"I'm emailing you some photos. I don't have any names for you though," Bull said. "I was hoping something might come through on the facial recognition."

"Right, OK, just got the email. I'll have Donald run it through the system." Bull could hear the keystrokes and mouse clicks as he spoke. "What's your feelings on this?"

"It's him."

"Yeah," Al nodded as he slowly agreed with his man in the field. "Too much of a coincidence."

"Damn right. It seems wherever he turns up, someone dies."

"Yeah, our problem now is, where is he going next?" Al sounded as if he was genuinely thinking about what he was saying.

"Who says he's going anywhere. He has no reason to believe we're here after him. He may be in no hurry to leave."

"Well, I'm going to leave you guys there for a few days in case you're right. But from what we've seen he's become very paranoid."

"Become?" Bull laughed. "He's always been a little uptight." Al didn't reply. Bull heard what sounded like a knock on a door followed by Al inviting someone into his office. Then, some muffled conversation that Bull couldn't make out.

"Bull, it's Donald."

"Hey Don."

"Bull," said Donald. "All three are known to us. But one in particular is very interesting." Bull could here papers being shuffled. "Hakem Al Hammed, ran from the UK after escaping charges of fundraising for A.Q. Your guys were looking to extradite him so he legged it."

"So now we know where he went," added Al.

"Yeah, and sounds like the sort of thing that would piss Cam off," said Bull.

"What didn't piss him off?" said Donald. "The other two aren't worth bothering about, must have just been in the way."

"Right," said Bull. "What do you want us to do?"

"Keep your phones on, I'll alert you if we hear anything from the Italian authorities. Bring back Colin from the airport. The Italians will take over, take some time for yourselves." Al sighed. "Will you brief the others?"

"No problem boss."

"Cheers, Bull. Get some rest."

Chapter 21

"I don't think he's here anymore," said George.

"I never met the guy," said Colin. The three Assets sat round their breakfast table. The same table they had met and exchanged information at for the past few days. "But from everything I've heard he seems the type to do one as soon as he can."

"Yeah," said George agreeing with himself. "He ain't here." He looked over at Bull who was sat in silent thought. "What do you think?"

"I know you know him best but," Bull paused, mulling over his thoughts. "I have a feeling he's still here."

"Do you think he knows we're here though?" asked Colin.

"He's a sneaky son of a bitch," said Bull. "Maybe he does and he's chilling out until we go and it starts to settle down here." Bull took a bite of toast. "Maybe he has more business here."

"I'm sure Al would have found something if he had," said George.

"He didn't know about this guy," said Bull, crumbs falling from the corners of his mouth, some getting caught in his beard.

"Oh, speak of the devil," said George, noticing his phone vibrating on the table.

Bull raised his eyebrows at Colin in anticipation of what could possibly be about to happen next.

"George, it's Al."

"Yeah I know, Al what's up?" Bull and Colin listened to the conversation only getting George's half. Bull continued with his breakfast. Colin drank a coffee. "Well," said George, hanging up the call. "The story continues."

"Go on," said Bull, wiping away the crumbs stuck in his beard. Colin sat back and waited to hear the next chapter in their hunt.

"Still no sign of Cam, but some builders found something this morning. Another body."

"Serious?" said Colin. "Who?"

"They don't know. Some illegal immigrant, African origin. He was found restrained in the renovation area in the Circo Massimo."

"If they don't know who he is, how do they know it's connected?" said Bull. "Could be some gang feud, nothing to do with us at all."

"You're right, could be anything," said George. "He was drugged, cannulated, respiratory depressant." George looked at Bull. "Sound familiar?" Bull bit his lip and nodded. "He died of a huge overdose of Suxamethonium Chloride. Also, he had traces of Naloxone Hydrochloride. So whoever did it was pulling him in and out of consciousness."

"That's a nasty way to go," said Colin.

"It's a known technique," said Bull cutting Colin short. "What does Al want us to do?"

"He's pulling us back to the UK. We've lost the trail. He thinks it's best if we're all centralised. We can be mobilised anywhere in the world from HQ."

"That's a good call I guess," said Bull

"Al has booked us flights for this evening. He's emailing us the details." As George finished his sentence his phone buzzed on the table. He pointed at it as it stopped. "That'll be it."

"Better get packed up then," said Colin.

Al was pacing his office. It seemed to him like he hadn't left the building in days. His mind had been filled with theories. Why hadn't Cam tried to travel on the passport he used before, or on one of the others Al knew he had? Why had he avoided the airports? Had he even left Rome?

Was Cam aware he was being hunted? That might explain why he had disappeared without a trace. He stopped pacing near his desk. Paperwork covered the entire surface. Most of the documents were the ones that Al thought Cam had in his possession. If he knew they were after him, Cam would surely stay clear of these targets. Making them useless.

Al continued his pacing; he rounded his desk and headed back to the window. The shutters were closed, as they had been for days. He peeked through the vertical slats out into the night. He carried on his route around the office. He could see a worn trail across the carpet where he habitually paced.

Al caught sight of the wall clock in the corner of his eye. His team should be arriving at Fiumicino airport on the outskirts of Rome. Was he missing something? He felt like he was moving backwards in bringing his team back, but it was the only logical course of action.

Al was brought out of his confused thought pattern by a knock on his door. Before he could acknowledge the request, it opened. Donald stepped into the office, paperwork in his hands and an urgent look on his face.

Al raised his hands and wrinkled his forehead, silently asking a question.

"Sorry Al," said Donald. "But I think you need to see this." Donald moved quickly over to Al's desk and swiped the piles of documents to one side, some falling to the floor. "Sorry," said

Donald again at Al's obvious confusion. "I've been working on something all day."

"What have you got?"

"I've been monitoring all free Wi-Fi hotspots in Rome," Donald said hurriedly. "Now, people are logging on and off all the time from cafés, restaurants, pubs etc. Every time someone does I've been taking a snapshot of them through their Web cameras."

"OK, but Cams been disabling his camera."

"Yeah, I know." Donald sounded excited. "One has logged on at a café and the picture I got back is blank, just black."

"Shit!" said Al. Donald, too flustered to notice one of the rare occasions Al swore, showed him a sheet of paper. The sheet had example snapshots of civilian faces; one was blank. "When was he logged on?"

"That's the thing, he's still on."

"Now?"

"Yes, now!"

"Show me." Donald unfolded a map of Rome and pointed to a street near to the centre of the city. "Ops room now, come on." Al ran out of his office followed by Donald, leaving the door open. Down the corridor to the ops room Al ran awkwardly in his suit. He entered the dark room lit only by computer monitors. "Can we see the city's CCTV cameras? Concentrate on the area he's in."

Donald began work, frantically typing and operating the computer's mouse.

"He's just west of the Tiber," Donald said, scanning the bright screen as he zoomed in.

"There!" shouted Al, pointing to a graphic of a camera near to the café that hosted the computer in question. "I want to see what that sees."

"No problem." After more mouse clicks another screen flicked on, displaying a grainy image of a street.

"Can we control it?" asked Al.

"Yes, wait a second." Donald opened up the control menu on the screen. "There." He moved the mouse pointer over the on-screen arrows and directed the camera's view into the café. "There." Donald moved in closer to the screen. "I don't see him."

"No," said Al, looking at the screen. The café only had a few patrons and were clearly not who they were looking for. He stood up straight and crossed his arms. "Cam sees cameras wherever he goes," Al said thoughtfully. "He would never put himself in view."

"Shall I call the guys back from the airport?"

"God damn it!" exclaimed Al, unfolding his arms and covering his face. "Yes, yes. Can't believe I forgot."

"I'm on it." Donald lifted one of the office's phones to his ear and dialled. He looked at Al, who was having a hard time forgiving himself. "It's all right, Al."

"No it's not." Al shook his head. "Minutes count."

"You're tired, don't beat yourself up. They'll get there. Bull, listen." Donald turned away from Al and began the brief. Al shifted his attention back to the monitor screen. A courting couple and a family sat at different tables outside the café. Holidaymakers. Al found it hard to remember how it felt to be in their position. He folded his arms again, one hand rubbing his chin.

"Done," said Donald hanging up the receiver. "They're on route. I told them not to spare the horses." Al nodded, his index finger scratching his top lip as he watched and waited.

"Don," said Al setting up a question. "What about local police? Should I get them out there?"

"I think you'll know what'll happen if you do," said Donald. "It could be carnage. Do you want to risk an international incident?"

"No, no. You're right. We'll keep this to ourselves." Someone walked past the café, along the street across the CCTV image. Both men's eyes followed the pedestrian, examining and taking in every detail. A bleeping sound came from another of the computers, catching their attention.

"Shit!"

"What is it?" asked Al.

"The signal from the Wi-Fi," Donald said, disabling the alarm. "Whoever was using that computer," Donald turned back to Al, "has logged off." No further words needed to be said. They turned back to the monitor screen. The family and couple were still there. They had no idea they were being watched from another country.

The door to the café opened and a man exited, throwing a rucksack over his shoulder as he navigated a path through the outside tables. Al and Donald stared in silence, Donald seated, and Al stood.

"Jesus Christ!" said Al. "Where are the guys?" Donald slid the chair backwards, rolling across the floor to a spare computer. He booted it up and the powerful computer came to life instantly. Donald started the program that tracked Asset phones.

"On the outskirts," he said as Al leaned on the computer desk and manipulated the camera to follow the man along the street. "They're moving fast."

"How long?"

"Maybe ten or so minutes."

"Not good enough," said Al standing back upright. The CCTV was now pointed down the street, the man's back to the lens. "We're going to lose him."

"No we're not," said Donald, rolling back to his original computer. He studied the map of Rome's cameras and began typing a series of numbers on the other computer's keyboard. "There." Another image leaped onto the screen.

Donald angled the camera down and left, centring on the man who was now approaching.

"That's a positive ID," said Al. "That's Cam, no doubt." Donald nodded in agreement and looked for the next camera along the street. They followed Cam, jumping from one camera to the next. All the time Donald kept an eye on their team's progress.

"We're going to run out of cameras," said Donald.

"What?"

"Here, look." Donald jabbed at the map on screen. "Only two more CCTV then it gets a little lighter in coverage." Donald switched to the next camera. "Then we could lose him." Al said nothing. He swallowed hard and rubbed at his temples.

"That phone box," said Al without emotion. "Can we call that phone box?" A public phone lay ahead of Cam, near a deserted bus stop. "We need to stall him."

"Wait," said Donald. "Wait." He worked furiously at finding the number for the payphone. "OK, OK." Donald held the receiver in his hand but not up to his ear.

"He's going past," said Al.

"It's dialling." They watched as Cam walked past the phone. They couldn't tell if it was ringing over there or not. "It's ringing now." Both men held their breath when Cam stopped and looked at the phone. An audible sigh followed when he carried on along the street, away from the phone.

"Down the street," said Al raising his voice. "Is there another one?" Donald activated the next, and last, camera.

"Yes, wait." Donald dialled again and they both waited, their heartbeats raised. Cam drew adjacent to the second payphone. His head flicked to the phone that was obviously ringing. He stopped and turned to face the phone. Al watched, transfixed on the screen, open-mouthed.

Cam, now stood still, looked along the street to the right then left. His look lingered back to where he had just been walking, and then he looked up. Al saw him look straight into the camera lens like he was staring directly at him. A feint dial tone could be heard coming from the receiver that Donald held.

Cam walked over to the phone and without hesitation picked it up and held it to his ear. Donald pressed a button on the phone's base station and a dull static sound flowed through the speakers on the wall. Cam turned his head slowly back to the camera. Al and Donald could hear him breathing, but still he said nothing.

The wait was unbearable. Al was dying to speak but didn't know what to say. They both stared at each other across the telephone lines.

"I know it's you," said Cam. The words echoed around the walls of the ops room. The silence that followed flowed like electricity buzzing in their heads. Cam lost interest in the CCTV and looked away. Al got Donald's attention with a wave then motioned to the wall speakers. Donald nodded.

Al opened his mouth ready to say something then paused, unsure of what to say. He closed his eyes and spent a few more seconds in thought.

"Cam, I want you to come in. This isn't going to end well." Al waited nervously for a response.

"I know how this is going to end," said Cam eventually, his voice sounding metallic through the speakers. "Don't think I don't."

"Cam please."

More silence. Donald turned from checking the position of their intercept team. He caught Al's gaze and signalled one minute. Al nodded. He needed to keep Cam where he was.

"Cam, don't do this."

"You knew what I was about when you recruited me!" Cam said angrily, but keeping his voice low so as not to attract the attention of passers by. "I have to finish what I started." His voice returned to a normal level.

Al fidgeted, his mouth opened but nothing came out. He tried in vain to compose his words. He knew the next sentence could take this situation off in any direction. Cam turned back to the camera and looked again at Al, stopping him before he began to speak again. Something took Cam's attention, his head flicked away, down the street. He dropped the phone and ran, leaving the camera's field of view.

"Shit!" Al swore for the second time in one day. "Has he seen the guys?"

"Yeah," said Donald checking the map display. The dot representing the team had rounded the corner onto the same street. "They're on him." Al inhaled and rubbed his face.

"So, this is it then."

2200hrs CEST
Rome, West bank of the Tiber, Italy

"There he goes!" shouted George from the drivers seat. Cam was off and running away from their car. "He's near the junction up ahead." Bull, who was in the back seat with his gun in his hand, was under no illusion what needed to be done. Colin too, sat next to George in the front, prepared his weapon.

"He's going right," said Colin.

"He's not stupid," said George, accelerating towards the junction. "He's going to take us down the one-way system." Cam had taken a right followed by an immediate left, taking the one-way street close to the bank of the Tiber. He pushed through the pedestrians out for an evening walk, knocking some over as he ran full out north.

George spun the wheel one way then the other, multiple gear changes made difficult by being a left-hand drive that he wasn't used to. The car snaked through the traffic; horns blared and people shouted.

Cam was getting away but the car started to gain when George realised that he had to push his way through. He began to scrape past vehicles knocking off mirrors and grinding against bodywork. Up ahead, the Ponte Palatino bridge came into view. Cam had run six or seven hundred metres at full sprint and showed no sign of letting up.

Cam stopped short of the turn to the bridge and looked back where he had come from, his chest heaved from the physical excursion. The street was a mess, loud with shouts, horns and screeching tyres. The car containing Bull, George and Colin was gaining.

"He's taking the bridge," shouted Colin over the noise of the street.

"Yep, got it," replied George, concentrating on navigating the vehicle through the carnage that was the evening traffic of Rome.

"Let me out here," said Bull, leaning through to the front.

"What, why?" asked George.

"He's going north," said Bull. "I can cut him off if I go across Tiber Island." Bull pointed further up the street with the barrel of his gun.

"OK." George skidded their vehicle to a halt on the junction to the bridge. "Get going." Bull jumped out slamming shut the door and ran for the footbridge to the island. George didn't wait. He stamped on the accelerator and the car's engine screamed as it dragged the vehicle onto the southern of the two bridges.

Now back into two-way traffic, they gained on the running figure less than a hundred metres ahead of them. They closed in on their target, who now drew alongside the Rotto bridge, an ancient bridge of only one arch in the middle of the Tiber. He stopped and turned to face the approaching car.

Cam pulled out his pistol and aimed at the windscreen that was growing larger the closer it got. For a brief second George made eye contact with Cam for the first time since he had disappeared. Cam hesitated. He didn't fire. The time frame lasted less than a second but felt an hour. George waited for him to fire.

Cam shifted his aim and opened up with his pistol. George could see the flash from the muzzle and glint from the empty cartridges as they spun to the ground. Cam had shot out the driver's side tyre.

George felt the car pull to the left. He fought the turn but the tyre had been shredded. The car slammed into the decorative stone railing that lined the bridge.

Colin pounced out of the passenger door leaving it wide open. He left George in the car desperately trying to force open his door. Colin saw, past the crowd of cowering pedestrians, that Cam was off and running again. Colin pursued, weaving and jumping over the panicked tourists and locals.

Seconds later George forced open his door, fighting and grinding the damaged hinges. He climbed out of the door hard up against the stone rails and up over the buckled bonnet. Some brave civilians came over to see if he was OK. George ignored the helpful people and looked dejectedly at the distance Cam and Colin had put between him and them.

"Yeah, yeah. I'm OK, I'm OK," George said to the crowd that was congregating round him. They spoke a variety of languages as they patted him down, checking his condition. "I'm OK, I'm OK," he said again, trying to convince the people he was unhurt, and all the time watching Cam and Colin disappear into the distance.

Cam cleared the bridge and turned left, heading north, paralleling the shore of the Tiber. Colin kept up the pace, hot on his heels. Further north, Bull was sprinting through the piazza of Tiber Island. He ran past tourists sat around the monument who turned to see what was happening. The old island hospital towered on his left as he entered the shadows cast by the café, before the second bridge connecting the island to the east side of Rome.

Cam ran alongside the river. He could not let up. His pursuer was almost on him. Colin's chest burned as he accelerated after his target. He considered a shot but there were too many innocents around.

Bull got to the far side of the Ponte Fabricio bridge as Cam drew adjacent to the sandstone stairs up to the main road. Cam slid to a halt as the two men made eye contact. Bull leaned on the railing wall and stared down at Cam who stole a quick look behind him at his approaching tail.

Cam raised his pistol and fired one solitary shot. The slug hit a decorative figurine on the wall less than a metre from Bull. Cam lowered his pistol and observed Bull wince next to the shattered statue. Bull composed himself and looked back realising the shot was a warning. He swore he saw Cam grin before he darted up the stairs and vaulting over the rail into the trees that separated the riverside path from the main road.

Colin continued to accelerate after Cam. He entered the tree line to see Cam sprint across the main road causing the traffic to sound their horns. Colin followed. Cam jumped over some ruined walls barely slowing at all. Colin, forced to pause by the braking traffic, put in the chase. Bull joined the race.

Al and Donald, back in the UK, wanted to help. With the team on the ground caught unaware and their earpieces not in, they were unable to assist.

"Come on!" said Al twitching and biting his bottom lip. No satellites were prepped to assist, no unmanned drones were circling, nothing. They could only watch through the increasingly dwindling CCTV.

Colin searched the gardens of buildings through which Cam had run. Bull stood, spinning, in a car park desperately looking for their target. Only when Bull heard a commotion to his north did he see Cam emerge onto the main road, still at a dead sprint. Immediately he turned and followed. Bull closed the gap. Cam veered left following the street. Bull lost sight of him for a second but heard more of a commotion up ahead.

On rounding the bend he saw Cam lifting a Vespa scooter up onto its wheels, a few civilians tried to fight him but backed off when Cam presented his pistol in their faces. Bull's lungs burned, he had to catch him.

Cam twisted the throttle and the Vespa zoomed off down the narrow street knocking pedestrians down like skittles. Bull had no chance of keeping up but pushed on none the less.

Cam jerked the handlebars right and clattered down a small set of steps entering a narrow street. Bull ran faster than he had ever run before. Scores of people huddled against the old buildings protecting themselves.

Bull knew it was now or never. He reached the top of the stairs Cam had ridden down like Evel Knievel and brought his weapon up to bear. Cam was in his sights but so were innocent tourists. Bull pulled up the tension on the trigger but there were too many people in the way. He relaxed the pressure and lowered the weapon.

"God damn it!" he shouted. He looked slightly left and right and, for the first time, noticed the civilians hiding, looking on in horror. "God damn it!" he said again at a lower decibel, as he turned away from his target.

He holstered his pistol, a look of anger spread over his face. He hated being beaten. He turned and left the area where he was seen as the danger, took out his phone and dialled Al.

Chapter 22

"Anything?" asked Al. He had only woken minutes ago, still in his office. His neck ached from sleeping slouched in his chair. He had rushed down the corridor to where Donald was monitoring the situation.

"No." Donald shook his head in the darkened operations room. "Nothing yet." Donald had been analysing all activities in Europe – every nationality's police computers for any unusual criminal activity. He had tapped into facial recognition databases hoping one might catch Cam at a bus or train station.

Donald had started his search in Italy then, after calculating how quickly Cam could get out of the country, widened his search. He had now taken the surrounding countries into account. The hunt was growing by the hour.

"I've widened the search to Switzerland, Austria, France and southern Germany." Donald looked at Al and saw his expression. Al looked defeated, Cam had escaped them in Rome and could now be anywhere. They might have blown their best chance of stopping him.

"He's not going to show himself," he said dejectedly. "Now he knows we're after him."

"I've been monitoring ports, airports, train stations," said Donald. "He hasn't tried to get out that way."

"Are you sure?" asked Al.

"As sure as I can be," Donald said, sitting back in his chair. "I've got facial recognition on line here." Donald pointed to a computer monitor. "Well, the countries that have them that is. There's a slight delay in getting the info but at least we'd know if he's on some sort of public transport."

"OK," said Al. "What about using an alias we don't know about?"

"Possible," said Donald. "But I'm pretty sure we know all his identities." Al shot him a look suggesting he was being naïve. "OK, OK," he replied. "Look it's all we got at the moment. I'm hacked into all car hire companies in Europe, watching for car thefts. Everything. Now, excluding the possibility that he just dug in around Rome and didn't go anywhere, it's just a matter of time. He can't stay off the radar forever. He isn't that kind of guy."

Al nodded silently and patted him on the shoulder.

"Good work, Donald," he said. "The guys should be in today, I'll get you some help when they arrive."

"They're here, Al."

"What?"

"Yeah, they're here already." Al raised his hands, palms upwards, and showed a look of shock and disbelief.

"Why didn't you wake me?"

"You need rest. You haven't slept properly for days," said Donald. "Besides, they are working on changing the ops room in the exercise hangar into an operational one."

"They're there now?" asked Al.

"Have been for a couple of hours." Al spun and almost ran out of the control room. He jumped down the stairs and fast walked along the corridors to the building entrance. He burst out of the double doors into the sunlight, blinking as it stabbed at the back of his eyes.

Al moved across the facility, away from the headquarters building, towards the main exercise hangar. The large hangar eclipsed the sun allowing Al to fully open his eyes again. He made his way along the edge of the hangar in the shadows until he reached the main entrance.

Inside he rushed past the signs directing people to the different areas of the hangar. Al followed, without needing directions, the sign for the ops room/observation platform. He climbed, the metal stairs clanking under his leather, dress shoes, up to the highest level.

He entered the observation room where he had entertained the visitors watching Cam's last exercise. He stopped in the doorway and saw his team in the room. Their heads were bent to their tasks, but they looked up when they saw him on the threshold.

"Hey Al," said George. Al felt a wave of security upon seeing his team. He had known George for many years and trusted him more than anyone. "You OK?"

"No," said Al after a sigh. "Not really."

"Yeah," said George. "This is pretty messed up." George stood, leaving the computer monitor he was wiring up. Bull walked past Al on his way across the room. He patted Al on the arm and the two men exchanged greetings. Colin extended his hand and shook Al's.

"Right," said Al, closing his eyes and shaking his head clear. "Sit down guys, we have a bit of time."

"Well, that will make a nice change," joked George, taking a seat.

Al's lips tried to forge a smile, but failed in their attempt. He sat down in front of the remnants of his best team.

"OK, this is where we're at." He started bluntly. "We have no idea where he is." The three team members burst into laughter. Al hadn't meant to make a joke. He forced a smile.

"Sorry Al," said George, motioning to the others to hold their laughter.

"We um," continued Al composing himself. "We're monitoring everything we can, watching for any sign. Anything out of the ordinary and we'll have him."

"What do you need us to do?" asked Bull.

"I'm going to have Donald watch the continent, if you could watch the UK." Al looked at his team. "Donald knows what to do, have a chat with him and he'll give you a good head start. The slightest suspicion, anything, even if you don't know why it feels dodgy, act on it."

"Are we completely in the dark here Al?" asked Colin. "I mean, nothing at all to go on?"

"Nothing," said Al. "Nothing at all."

"So we have to wait for him to either slip up or decide to continue with whatever the hell he's doing," said George.

"That's it," said Al. "You have this control room, once you've got it up and running that is. We're almost certain he's still on the continent so you have a little time before we have to factor in him being here."

"Is there any reason you think he's coming back home?" asked Colin.

"Your guess is as good as mine."

"This is no time for guessing, Al," said Bull. "We need intel, something solid to go on."

"Yeah well," said Al rising from the chair. "We can only wait and hope for a lead."

"Right," said George with a renewed sense of vigour. "Between us and Don, we got this. You get yourself away from here, we'll be in touch when we have something."

"Huh, wish I could," said Al. "I have another eleven teams to run." Al turned to leave. "I've got more than Cam to worry about."

"Anything interesting?" asked Bull.

"Your old op over in Afghan actually," said Al, turning back to Bull who was now very interested. "Speedy's team have got a new assignment. It's so important I'm going out there myself."

2025hrs CEST
Kolding, Denmark

The petrol station was deserted, clouds were low and the air was damp. The town's lights blurred through the mist. An old car, German plates, pulled into the forecourt and parked out of the sight of the two attendants in the shop.

Cam turned off the engine by intentionally stalling it and switched off the headlights, the shop's lights cast a faded glow over the petrol pumps. Cam remained in his driver's seat. He was tired. He had been on the road for two days now, ever since he had escaped Rome. The drive, this far, could have been done in eighteen hours but he'd had to cover his tracks.

He had taken this car, the fourth he had stolen, from a train station car park. Hopefully, the person it belonged to wouldn't notice it was gone until he was done with it. He scanned the station for cameras. There were none, apart from ones recording number plates so people couldn't drive off without paying. His eyes flicked down to his fuel gauge, it wasn't far off full.

This stop wasn't about fuel. He needed to shut his eyes for a minute or two and get some food. He didn't know what time this small, family-run, station would close so food would be first. He opened the door and climbed out, the cool fresh air hit him. He arched backwards and looked up at the clouds.

He slammed the door with the palm of his hand. He felt the rainwater on the roof of the car. It felt cold but refreshing, he rubbed his fingers dry with his thumb. Without the key to the car, he couldn't lock the door so he left it insecure. He took three steps from the car and stopped, the air filled his lungs and nose. The fresh rain on the forecourt delivered a familiar smell that had stopped him in his tracks.

He breathed in again, eyes closed. The rain was settling on rotting vegetation in the nearby fields. Mist coated his face; the air was crisp. He stood still taking it in. He had another lung full, his mind wandered. A bird sang in the distance, he felt like he could have been anywhere in the world right now.

The bird chirped again, the sound carrying along on the light breeze. He felt his knees go; he dropped slightly but opened his eyes and stepped forward, stopping himself from falling. He had nearly fallen asleep standing where he was. A car sped past on the main road. The noise pulled him from his daydream.

He was hungry, needed food. The station had a good selection of home-made sandwiches, which would have been there all day but still looked fresh. They didn't have the pre-packed factory sandwiches that lined the shelves back home. He chose more than he needed – extra rations for later. Paid with the roll of money from his pocket and returned to his car.

Mist had covered the windscreen and was starting to run, leaving water trails down the glass. He started the engine by reaching under the steering column and twisting the ignition barrel that hung by its wires. He cranked the heating up, directing it to the windscreen. The wipers wiped away the rain but still he couldn't see through it, not until the blowers started to eat away at the moisture. The sandwich was good but he hadn't eaten in a while so anything would have felt like gourmet, he wasn't really sure what was in it, it simply did its job. Having satisfied one human urge he needed to address the other, sleep. Nervous, he wiggled back into the car seat and folded his arms to keep in his body heat. If he could get fifteen minutes, he would be able to continue his journey. He only hoped his mind would allow him this time.

2110hrs BST
Asset HQ, South Oxfordshire, England

"Could he be back in the UK?" Colin said to George who was sat going through documents from Donald's team.

"I doubt it," he said without looking up. "But anything's possible. He could be, but that quick after Rome, I think we would have noticed." George closed the document and swivelled his chair in Colin's direction. "No, he'll sit tight and if he's on his way back we'll have to find him. He'll choose when he shows himself."

"You know him well?"

"Yeah," nodded George. "Very well."

"So what do you think he's planning then?" asked Colin. George thought for a second. About to answer, he was stopped short by the door to the operations room opening. Bull strode in carrying more documents.

"More leads to sift through." Bull dropped the cardboard folders on the bank of computer keyboards. "Been talking to Al. Speedy lucked out in Afghan."

"What do you mean?" asked George.

"Tell you about it later," said Bull. "You found anything yet?"

"There's nothing, well no, that's not true," said Colin. "There are literally thousands of car thefts, minor robberies, assaults. You name it but none of it fits our boy." George shook his head.

"Guys look, we gotta just wait. One will stand out, it'll look out of place and that one will be him."

"So what? We just hope we notice it?" said Colin.

"No mate, we have to skim over everything, but we can't concentrate on every single item, we don't have time."

"He's right," said Bull walking over to the viewing platform. The hangar was in darkness but the same scene was still there from the demonstration a few weeks ago. The South American village surrounded by a palm tree jungle could just be made out. "Cam's out there somewhere, what we have to do is find him."

Chapter 23

Monday 8th April 2013
1200hrs AFT
Camp Bastion, Helmand, Afghanistan

A C-17 Globemaster rolled along the runway under the instruction of the ground control tower. Four turbofan engines idled but still churned up the dust from the edge of the asphalt runway. Speedy and Lugsy had watched the giant aircraft swoop in from the north, reverse its engines and slow to a taxi.

The two men had been waiting for the aircraft for over an hour and had taken a seat on the bonnet of their Landrover, soaking up the midday sun. Al was on the aircraft accompanying the guests who were the subject of their mission.

"You ever heard of this girl?" asked Speedy, his gaze never leaving the turning aircraft. Speedy had been with the Asset program since it grew from its original formation two years ago. He had joined with Lugsy, a fellow Scotsman, with clumsy looking, protruding ears. Speedy also had a look of clumsiness about him. Rather short and accident prone, he came across as a bit of a joker but was a fine, reliable operator.

"Nah, it's all fuckin shit!" said Lugsy in his thick Glaswegian accent. Although one of the most dependable soldiers in the program he had the same attitude to most things.

"What is?" asked Speedy, not surprised by his reaction.

"That music," said the ex-paratrooper. "It's all fuckin shit." Speedy nodded and shrugged his shoulders. Speedy was from the far north of Scotland and had come to the Assets from the police force. His firearms background had brought him to the attention of Al. The pair made a good effective team, and with the addition of Luca and Kostas, they had become Al's number two team. However, if they were asked, they were the best.

The Globemaster slowed to a halt and started a slow turn on the pan. The aircraft pointed its large rear door towards the terminal buildings and, after stopping the turn, lowered the ramp. A figure appeared at the top of the ramp and, when sure the ramp was fully down, ran down to the pan and across the runway.

"Fuckin hell, look at this," said Lugsy.

"Ha!" Speedy laughed. "Is that Al?" He was running, crouched, a ballistic helmet and body armour covering his suit. He got to his team, out of breath. Speedy climbed down off the vehicle to meet his boss, Lugsy stayed where he was.

"Hello guys," said Al pleased to be with his Assets. "Phew!" He breathed an audible sigh of relief through his smile. "How are you doing?"

"Fine, Al," said Speedy. "Absolutely fine." Speedy had a confused look on his face as he tried to figure out what was going on. "What you doing, Al?"

"I'm uhh," the smile ebbed from his face. "I'm checking it's safe before I bring them off." Al thumbed over his shoulder towards the aircraft.

"It's safe Al," Speedy looked around at the ground crew going about their daily duties. "Of course it's safe."

"Right, right," Al agreed. "They're just uh, they're just uncoupling the vehicles." Al turned to the aircraft. "Shall I just bring them off?"

"Aye." Lugsy shrugged, sliding off the Landrover's bonnet. "Follow us, we've got a whole accommodation block for them."

"Right, OK," said Al. "It's just…" Al looked at Lugsy.

"What?" asked Lugsy.

"The tour manager," he continued. "Can be a bit um…"

"A prick," interrupted Lugsy. "Is that what you're trying to say?" Speedy stood between them, looking at each in turn, knowing fully what Al was trying to say.

"Just, go easy," said Al.

"Aye, right," he said sarcastically. "Get them to follow us." Al ran back over to the waiting C-17 having been cut short by Lugsy. Speedy joined his colleague in the Landrover and they drove out onto the pan, behind the aircraft. There they waited for the vehicles carrying the visitors to descend the ramp.

Three armoured vehicles, brand new looking, made a convoy behind the Landrover. They drove slowly at the camp's speed limit towards their accommodation.

As they navigated their way across site, passers-by stopped and tried to get a view of the passengers. It was no secret who was here. It had been widely publicised.

"Fuckin pop stars!" said Lugsy. "So fuckin up themselves." He sneered whilst twisting his passenger side mirror so he could see the tailing vehicles.

"I know," sighed Speedy gripping the steering wheel through his gloved hands. "But you heard Al, go easy on them, remember," he said, turning to Lugsy. "They're the bait."

Speedy brought their vehicle to a standstill creating a small sandstorm outside the large marquee-style tent. They exited their vehicle and waited for the visitors to alight from theirs.

"What the hell is this?" said a man dressed in clothes far too young for his age. "We're not staying here are we?" He waved his hands at the desert camouflaged semi-permanent tent. Speedy and Lugsy looked at each other in despair.

Al stepped out of the vehicle and tried to calm him down over the roof of the vehicle.

"It's more comfortable than it looks," said Al rounding the car. "We're in a war zone, remember." The irate man turned to look at Al with a face full of contempt. "Give it a chance, it's private and safe." The man pursed his lips and shook his head.

"Who the hell are they?" said the man, waving the back of his hand in Speedy and Lugsy's direction.

"This is one half of your protection team whilst you're here," said Al, ushering him over to where the two men were standing. "These guys are private military contractors, the best in the business."

The man looked at the two scruffy-looking men.

"These two!" scoffed the man. "These two are the security for the industry's biggest rising star this decade?" He gave Speedy an up and down look and moved on to Lugsy. "This is the best you got?" Lugsy visibly tensed up. "Whoa! At ease soldier." Said the man sarcastically at Lugsy's reaction. Lugsy focused past the man and saw Al's look of silent pleading.

"Fuck you!" said Lugsy, regaining eye contact with the man. Al threw his hands up in the air.

"OK, OK," said Al, positioning himself between the two men. "Mr Smith, this is Speedy and Lugsy. Guys this is Mr Smith." Smith glanced at Lugsy and snorted a laugh.

"I will fuckin kill you," said Lugsy, staring down Smith.

"Alright," interrupted Speedy. "Where's um, where's what's her name?" Smith raised his hand, index finger outstretched and walked back over to the last vehicle in the convoy.

"Look," said Al once Smith was out of earshot. "He may be an idiot but we need him for now."

"He's a fuckin prick!" said Lugsy.

"Two days, two days. That's all." The three men watched Smith open the door to the last armoured vehicle. He leaned in and spoke to the occupants.

The other rear door opened and a large man climbed out followed by a small, teenage girl. They walked as a group back over to their protection team and the girl stood in front of the two close protection operators.

"I'm Ilya, hi." She raised her hand and gently shook Speedy's. She moved over to Lugsy and waited for him to take her hand. "Have you heard of me?" she said when he didn't respond.

"Nah." Lugsy looked at the large man that accompanied the girl, obviously her personal bodyguard. He stood cross-armed behind his client.

"How can you have not heard of Ilya," said Smith, almost angry. "Where the hell have you been?"

"What type of music do you play Miss Ilya ," asked Speedy, trying to bring back some form of pleasantry.

"Kind of new wave sort of a thing, I'm trying to bring back the eighties scene I suppose," she said.

"Oh, sort of like a new Cindi Lauper," smiled Speedy. "You kind of look like her too."

"Who?" said Ilya, a confused look coming over her.

"From the uhh, you know the hair and things." Speedy looked for help but none came. "You've got the makeup and stuff," he continued stuttering. "With the uhh." He motioned towards her earrings and necklaces.

"Shall we go inside," said Al saving Speedy from more embarrassment.

"Let's get some rest for tomorrow." Al led the way leaving the two operators behind. "I'll introduce you to the other members of the protection team."

"Come on granddad," said Lugsy following on. "You're really showing your age."

"What?" said Speedy, catching up with Lugsy. "I'm thirty four! Who doesn't know who Cindi Lauper is?"

"You're a dick!"

2220hrs AFT
Camp Bastion, Helmand, Afghanistan

The tent they would call home for the next few days had been set up with the accommodation for the visitors in the back. The front, near the door, was for the team. They had their camp cots set up between the boxes of equipment.

The team sat around, feet up on the boxes, speaking quietly so as not to disturb the visitors sleeping off their flight.

"The concert's tomorrow night," said Al. "Over on Leatherneck. Then the next day, Wednesday, we're going on a drive out to a couple of the firebases. It's supposed to be a surprise visit, but we've not been as tight with the information. And the route we're taking has been leaked."

"Do they know about this?" asked Kostas, motioning to the back of the tent. Kostas was the third member of Speedy's team, coming from the Greek island of Kos and a former member of the 1st Raider/Paratrooper Brigade of the Greek special forces; he was strong and dependable. Short and stocky, he could carry huge weights all day and still be ready for a drink every night.

"Christ no, we'd never get them to agree to this if they did," said Al. "Anyway, we have strong intel that one of A.Q's best bomb makers is setting up a trap for our visitors back there. And, he's here in the area to monitor it himself."

"How sure are we about this?" asked Speedy.

"We're pretty much hundred percent sure," said Al. "We know he likes to film his hits for his propaganda videos."

"Are you talking about Awrang Shinwari?" said Lugsy. Al nodded, confirming Lugsy's suspicion. "That bastard! I've seen them videos. He's killed hundreds of our guys."

"That's why we're willing to take such a risk in taking him down," said Al, dropping a document in a cardboard folder onto one of the equipment creates. It read Shinwari.

"How much of a risk is this?" asked Luca, picking up the document. Luca was from the Italian Navy's Operational Divers Group.

Unconventional for the military, he was into protecting the environment and wore thin bands with beads on his left wrist and a peace symbol hung round his neck.

"I won't lie," said Al. "We only know he's in the area and he plans on hitting our visitors." Luca passed the file to Kostas. The two had become good friends since they had joined the Assets. Along with Speedy and Lugsy, they formed the rest of Al's number two team. "We don't know how he'll do it, we do know it'll happen when we're out visiting the firebases."

"How do we know that?" asked Speedy, taking the file from Kostas and flicking through the contents.

"Profiling," said Al. "He's a coward."

"Aren't they all?" said Lugsy grumpily hinting his contempt for them.

"Actually we're surprised he's here at all," said Al. "He normally only hits easy targets, films them from afar and well, you've seen the results. We think he's been ordered here, purely because we handed them the information on this lot." Al pointed, through the walls at where the visitors were resting.

"So, what's the plan?" said Speedy.

"You guys are the P.M.Cs, you two in the lead car with Smith and you two in the rear with the girl." Lugsy groaned at the thought of protecting Smith. "The bodyguard," Al continued ignoring Lugsy's objection, "will drive the car with the girl in it and I've got you a driver for the lead car."

"Who?" said Lugsy, gruffly.

"A US Air Force Pararescue. Call him PJ. He'll be useful if anyone gets hurt. So, you will be taking them on the 'surprise visit' to the firebases surrounding Bastion," Al said, making air quotes. They know the route, so it will happen somewhere along the way."

"What do you think, a roadside bomb?" asked Speedy.

"Most probably," said Al. "He'll want the footage for his propaganda, so he'll be nearby somewhere."

"Not sure I like driving into a fuckin IED!" said Lugsy.

"Those vehicles are heavily protected, they weigh tons," said Al. "You should be OK."

"Should be! Fuckin hell, Al. This ain't right."

"Don't worry," Al tried to stop Lugsy going off on one of his rants. "They've been tested, they're as good as a tank. If you can spot it before, obviously that would be better. Just hunt him down, he'll be in the area."

"Right," said Speedy. "What have you got for us?"

"Luca." Al said handing over to the Italian member of the team.

"OK," said Luca. "I got us FN P90s. It's a personal defence weapon, nice, small and light. Fifty-round mags – you can carry hundreds of rounds and not even know about it."

"These as well." Kostas opened one of the crates and moved aside the foam protectors, revealing M32A1 multi shot grenade launchers.

"Whoa," said Speedy. "You're serious about getting this guy aren't you?"

"Six shots, ready loaded in each and a satchel of spare rounds." Kostas closed the crate lid. "One per vehicle. Hand grenades too, the usual stuff."

"And," added Al. "We'll have a drone up, so if we spot him first we'll have a pop at him before he has a go at us. As long as we don't scare him off, that's the most important thing." Al looked at his men. "He will run if he gets a sniff something's up."

"So we have to get blown up so they can get their fuckin man?" said Lugsy.

"That's why we're used," said Al. "Because no one else is capable or has the guts for it."

"Alive or dead, Al?" asked Kostas, breaking his silence. Al made a face and shrugged his shoulders.

"There are merits with both," he said squinting his face. "If we catch him we can 'interrogate' him." Al made more air quotes. "Get what we can from him, let him go, watch where he goes, who he speaks to."

"We could get a lot from a capture," said Speedy.

"Yeah," Al nodded. "And his superiors will want to know why we let him go, what he told us. Allsorts."

"Divide and conquer," said Lugsy.

"Exactly, we could spread suspicion within their ranks. Sometimes that's our best weapon."

"He'll end up dead no matter what," said Speedy. Everyone agreed.

"Good fuckin riddance."

"So," said Kostas. "What you're saying is what happens, happens, dead or alive?" Kostas looked at Al, needing some kind of confirmation.

"Yeah, dead or alive. I really don't care at the moment," Al sighed. "I could do with as little extra work as possible."

"Where are you going to be Al?" asked Speedy.

"I have to get back to HQ, there's lots going on back there at the moment." Al looked forlorn.

"Yeah, we heard," said Speedy with a hint of condolence in his voice.

"Aye, let them fuckers know we're with em."

Chapter 24

Tuesday 9th April 2013
0200hrs CEST
Vagen Harbour, Port of Bergen, Norway

Cam stood on the edge of the bay, up above the quay, looking down on the berths. The night air was cold and damp, his hands were in his pockets, fingers clenched keeping his thumbs warm. The cold ground conducted the body heat away from his feet; they felt like blocks of ice. He stamped his boots on the ground, trying to warm them, water splashed out of the cracks in the pavement.

The fishing vessel, not long moored, bobbed on the water as the waves washed past its hull. Its flag fluttered gently. With little wind Cam could hardly make out the offset red cross with a blue lining on a white background. The vessel was in darkness, only a small internal light showing through a porthole gave it any life.

Cam breathed out a misty breath, and took in the fresh sea air. He could see movement on the inside, shadows cast by the light in the small, round window. He bounced on his toes and looked right, back towards the town of Bergen, to the historic part of the town. Above the multi-coloured, wooden sea houses, a faint green glow was only just visible. The northern lights were making their last appearance of the season.

He was tired, on the run for nine days, nearly two thousand miles across the continent. Made longer by having to change vehicles multiple times and avoid a ferry crossing. Forcing him to take the long route, the road bridge between Denmark and Sweden.

Out to sea, the mist lined the horizon, blurring the line between water and sky. He looked out of the corner of his eye to the bushes next to the railings. His bag was barely visible, hidden nearby in the undergrowth, in case any passing police officers took it upon themselves to question him being there.

The bag contained his pistol. He had ditched his other weapons and kept the MP-443 that he had taken from the Chechen. He felt the need for a signature weapon, what better than the one that had killed his good friend. This weapon represented revenge. Also, the bag was full of money, a vast quantity of money. But not all his funds, the rest was back in the UK, hidden in various places.

Movement on the deck of the fishing vessel caught his eye, he honed in on the figure working on the stern. The figure ducked under framework and coiled ropes, conducting general work on the boat. Cam had been watching for hours now. He had seen them take a delivery of ice, ready to pack the fish they would be catching. Too small to have it's own ice machine, it relied on deliveries before setting sail.

It was time. They were getting ready to leave. He leaned down and grabbed his bag from the bush, slung it and walked along the path towards the steps to the quayside. Down to the side of the water, he kept an eye on the figure on the boat. As he drew closer he could make out more detail of the man. He wore what Cam thought to be stereotypical fisherman's clothing: wax waders held up by heavy-duty braces, thick woollen jumper and a warm hat.

He drew up next to the boat, the man stopped work. He put down the rope work he was winding away. The two men didn't speak the same language – they both knew that. Cam took his hand from his pocket and held up a roll of notes, whilst holding eye contact.

The man paused, as if thinking about what he was seeing. Cam replaced the notes into his pocket, he held the gaze of the fisherman. Cam looked out west and motioned out to sea with his nose. The fisherman stared back, looked left and right with minimal head movement and nodded one slow nod.

0730hrs BST
Asset HQ, South Oxfordshire, England

"Anything?" Bull burst through the door to the control room in the exercise hangar, a tray of takeaway coffees in hand.

"Don't know mate," sniffed George. "Didn't know how much crime there was till I started reading all this." He lifted piles of paperwork and dropped it, scattering it over the desk.

"What's all that?" Bull said placing the tray on the desk next to George and handing him one of the paper cups.

"Well, I've decided to print out anything that might be of interest to us," said George snapping open the plastic tab on the cup's lid. "So as things come over the system we can dismiss it or if we want to check it out we print it, then we can keep the system as clean as possible."

"Cool," said Bull taking a seat and swivelling side to side. "And all that got your attention."

"I don't know mate," said George shaking his head. "There's just so much." George sighed. "I mean, anyone of these could be him."

George pushed the papers around the desk. "None of it jumps out, it's all so…" He pondered, hunting for the correct word. "Normal."

"If it don't seem right, then it ain't right," said Bull. "We don't even know if he's come back." Bull walked over, again, to the large viewing window and looked down on the training area where they had practised for so many hours. "Shit," he said, gripping the cold metal railings. "Back here would be the last place I'd come if I was on the run."

"He's coming back," said George. "He's got an agenda."

"What do you mean, agenda?" said Bull, spinning round leaning on the glass, the railing pressing in the small of his back.

"You know," said George. "The Poland thing, then the other hits. A target that had been active in the UK."

"You think it's revenge motivated?"

"Definitely the Chechen was," said George, taking the first sip from his coffee. "Shit that's hot! Damn. Anyway, trust me he's on his way back. We just have to find him before he does anything else."

"He might not have anymore targets here," said Bull blowing into his cup. "He must know we're monitoring everything he had access to."

"Perhaps," sighed George. "I just have this feeling, there's something in the back of my mind, I just wish I could put my finger on it."

"Until then bud," said Bull, "we have to wait, cut down on the paperwork." He pointed to the mess of papers on the desk. "If it don't jump out at us then dismiss it."

"Yeah, you're right." George slid all the papers off the side of the desk, some landed in the bin others fluttered across the floor.

"Anyway get outta here," said Bull. "Get some rest, have you seen Col? Should've been here by now."

"Yeah, he's over with Donald, catching up with the rest of Europe stuff." George stood from his seat and arched his back. The night shift had seemed to last forever and his back felt like it was twisted in knots. "Glad I'm not working on that team, you should see the intel they're trawling through."

"I bet," said Bull taking George's seat in front of the main computer. "How many are they monitoring now?"

"Every county mate," said George. "From last night we opened it further. It's been long enough. He could be anywhere by now."

"Yeah," said Bull. "Go. Get some sleep, have a beer. See you tonight." George nodded and raised the coffee cup.

"Cheers for the brew." George walked to the door and left the control room. Bull watched the door shut then turned to the screen, more intel was arriving. He read the latest reports starting from the coastal countries.

"Where the hell are you?" he said, his right hand stroking his beard.

1900hrs AFT
Camp Leatherneck, Helmand, Afghanistan

The stage had been set atop a line of blast barriers. Large green sandbag walls made stronger with metal, wire wrap. Sound engineers and the small road crew, brought in on a separate flight, busied themselves prepping for the show. Backstage, Smith ran round trying to control everything and everyone.

"Look at that fuckin prick," said Lugsy.

"Leave it," said Speedy. "Let him run around, if he's bothering that lot he isn't bothering us."

"Aye, alright."

"It's just one more day. After tomorrow we don't have to worry about them." Speedy bumped into him with his shoulder. "Stop watching him, or he'll come over here." Lugsy only grunted a reply.

"He's a good manager." The voice came from nowhere. The two men armed only with their pistols, turned to where Ilya was sitting having her makeup and hair done.

"Eh?" said Speedy.

"I can tell you don't like him," she said. "But he's a good manager, he got me this far, got me all this."

"Still a prick," Lugsy muttered under his breath.

"Shhh," Speedy whispered back. "You must be doing well, you know, to have been asked to come out here." Lugsy scoffed, stopped by Speedy jabbing at his ribs with his elbow.

"I can't believe you haven't heard of me," said Ilya. "Don't you listen to the radio?"

"Don't really have the time," said speedy.

"Well if you did," said Ilya, "you'd have heard my songs, I'm all over the air at the moment."

"That's good, I'm pleased for you." Lugsy shook his head and turned away, not sharing Speedy's sentiments. "Just be careful, might not last forever."

"What do you mean by that?" said Ilya, keeping calm. "Do you think I'm a one hit wonder?" She giggled at her own comment.

"No, no." said Speedy. "That's not what I meant. I mean just make good choices now, while you're young, it'll avoid you having to do things later on in life you don't want to."

"Like you? Are you talking from experience?"

"Yeah, I am," said Speedy. "I'm not going to pretend, I'd rather be at home being paid shed loads for doing very little than be out here. With him."

Speedy flicked his head in Lugsy's direction.

"Fuck you." Lugsy laughed.

"So what did you want to be, you know when you were my age?" said Ilya smiling.

"Can you remember that far back?" said Lugsy.

"I'm thirty four," said Speedy defending himself. "Jesus Christ!" He rubbed his chin and cheeks, feeling the two-day-old stubble.

"Hey dick, don't get a fuckin complex," said Lugsy. "So you had a hard paper round." Speedy shook his head, looking defeated and a little embarrassed in front of the young singer.

"So," said Ilya. Speedy looked at her, confusion covering his face. "What did you want to do?" she continued. "You said you didn't want to be here."

"Well," Speedy said clearing his throat. "When I was your age I was in university, studying art and design."

"Fuck off!" said Lugsy. "You went to university?"

"Yes!" said Speedy, bluntly. "Christ! Do you want to hear this or not?" Lugsy shrugged pretending not to be interested. "I was good too, but I'd never met such a bunch of weirdoes in my life. I wanted to be a graphic artist and they were doing this modern art shit."

"So?" asked Ilya.

"Well, I was drawing graphic novels and getting into computer animation and they were piling up bricks or covering themselves in paint and rolling around on the floor. It turned out in that class I was the weird one."

"So you just left?" Ilya said.

"Yeah, I suppose I did," said Speedy. "I gave up and found myself in the police. I still go to watch all those computer animated movies, not for the movie but for the animation. I like watching the things most people miss, like the way the characters' hair moves, each strand individually like."

"Well, you gave up on your dream," said Ilya. "I've had to work hard to get this far. I've had so many rejections you wouldn't believe it and there's no way I'm going to give up and let it go." Speedy nodded. He knew the girl was making sense, he had learned that lesson too late in his life.

"You know I went to see some of that modern art shit," blurted Lugsy. "In that Baltic Mill thing in Newcastle."

"You went to an art gallery?" said a surprised Speedy.

"I'm more cultured than you are, highlander," he replied, without looking at him. "But it was shit. Floor after floor of rubbish, some rooms were empty, fuck all in em. I stood looking at one for fuckin ages, like you said piles of bricks, paint pots fuckin stepladder. Anyway," he said opening his pocket and offering the contents of a packet of cigarettes to Speedy. "Turned out they were just renovating the room."

"You're an idiot," said Speedy.

"What? Simple mistake to make, I mean there weren't any difference between that room and some of the others. Just because a builder put those things there instead of some arty farty artist, does that make it meaningless?" Lugsy offered Ilya one of his cigarettes. "Don't suppose you smoke, do you love?"

"No thanks," she said unsure of how to take the gruff Glaswegian holding a packet of cigarettes in her face.

"Aye, I didn't think so," he said, replacing the packet in his pocket. "And don't start either," he added quickly.

"I won't," she laughed. The hair and makeup stylist finished her work and Ilya spun herself round in their direction and stood up.

"OK, my darling are we all ready?" Smith came over to where Ilya was, pushing his way between Speedy and Lugsy. Lugsy went to push him back but was stopped by Speedy. Smith, completely oblivious to anyone else but Ilya, took her by the hand and led her towards the stage. "Good, good," he said as he pushed back through their two protection officers, dragging Ilya behind him.

"I'm gonna shoot him myself tomorrow," said Lugsy through gritted teeth. The sound of the crowd on the other side of the stage curtains nearly drowned out his comment.

"Jesus, don't say that," said Speedy. "I think we're gonna have enough people shooting at us."

Chapter 25

Wednesday 10th April 2013
0900hrs AFT
Firebase Fiddler's Green, Helmand, Afghanistan

The air was tense, at least for the team of four protection officers. The entertainment team were oblivious to the danger. The personnel of Fiddler's green loved the teenage star and followed her and Smith as they were shown around the firebase. Smith lapped up the attention, more than Ilya. Speedy watched over the pop star and her entourage, he was waiting, wondering when the strike would come.

"Probably fuckin nothing!" said Lugsy, scanning the surrounding country. The road back to Bastion was normally a safe route. Battered old cars sped along it, leaving sand trails and car fumes. "Bet nothing happens."

"Is that optimism?" said Speedy without shifting his gaze from the crowd of military personnel swarming round Ilya. "Never heard that from you." Realising their client was safe here on the base, Speedy looked over towards the other members of his team. Kosta and Luca were by the vehicles with Ilya's bodyguard and PJ. Kosta was talking to the bodyguard, who had been constantly asking questions about how to get into their line of work.

"That guy's really starting to fuckin annoy me!" sneered Lugsy, stealing a glance over to where Speedy was looking.

"Doesn't everyone?" Speedy jumped down from the barricading onto the gravely sand. "Come on, we have to get moving."

"Aye, suppose so." Lugsy turned and looked out over the desert road. Traffic had slowed right down; the road was virtually empty.

"Hmm," he mumbled to himself before jumping down and following Speedy who hadn't heard his moan.

"You guys ready to mount up?" shouted Speedy on approach to the idling vehicles. His question was met with a series of nods, the bodyguard seemed excited to be working with the private military contractors. He was however, the only one apart from Smith and the girl who didn't know what was possibly about to happen.

"That road back is lookin fuckin quiet, guys!" said Lugsy, following along behind Speedy.

"What does that mean?" asked the bodyguard. Speedy stopped on arriving at the black, armoured vehicles. He slung a look at Lugsy who realised he should have kept his mouth shut.

"Nothing mate," said Speedy shrugging off the question. "How long they gonna be?" He gestured to the girl and her minder.

"They'll be done when they're done," sighed the bodyguard obviously used to waiting on them. Speedy nodded and turned, leaning back on the vehicle. Lugsy spun round too, cradling his weapon in the crooks of his arms.

PJ opened the driver's door of the lead vehicle and slid into the driver's seat. Lugsy, through the corner of his eye, saw PJ crack the door and strode over to the open vehicle. He leaned down and pushed past PJ, slammed his palm onto the steering wheel sounding the horn in two long, loud beeps.

Smith's face changed on hearing the sounds. He looked over at the team stood around, leaning lazily on the vehicles. Lugsy straightened up and locked eyes with Smith. The stare lingered. Lugsy tapped his wrist in an over exaggerated manner.

Smith re-engaged the crowd, leaving Lugsy's stare. Ilya was busy signing pictures, hundreds had been signed that day and she was still passing them out like cards from a deck.

"OK guys!" shouted Smith over the noise of the mob pushing for signed photos. "Sorry but it looks like we got to get going." Smith gestured over his shoulder with his thumb, blaming his protection team. "Come on sweetheart, let's go." He gently held the corner of Ilya's arm, pulling her away from the crowd.

One of the firebase's ranking officers tried to get in between the pop star and the crowd, stopping their progress but taking abuse from the soldiers. Ilya waved back as she was ushered to the vehicles.

"How dare you tell me when…"

"Shut the fuck up!" said Lugsy, cutting Smith short. "Get the fuck in the car." Kostas was waiting. He got the girl's attention with a wry smile and led her back to the rear vehicle. "I said get in the fuckin car." Lugsy drew his pistol and tapped on the rear door of the car.

"I'm putting in a complaint when I get back," said Smith opening the door and climbing in. "I just want you to know that. You'll never work at this level again."

"I fuckin hope so." Lugsy slammed the door with his foot forcing Smith to wince as it smashed shut. He holstered his pistol and a hint of a smile spread across his face. "What?"

"That," said Speedy. "Might have been a bit too far."

"Who gives a fuck!" said Lugsy, moving around to the front passenger seat, the same seat he had on the way to the firebase. "Probably gonna be dead by the end of the day."

"Shit," said Speedy. "What happened to the optimism?" Lugsy ignored the remark and entered the car next to PJ. Speedy shook his head as he walked around the car to his seat, next to Smith. The doors closed one at a time, dampening the sound of the running engines. "Girl's in," he said straining over his shoulder. "Let's go."

PJ stole a look in the rear view mirror, Speedy noticed and his eyes flicked back to the dusty windscreen. The car rolled forward and lurched right towards the main gate of the firebase. Some US marines held open the gates, waving at the vehicles as they passed, allowing the two armoured civilian vehicles to leave the protection of the high sand banked walls.

The second vehicle left the compound and the gates swung shut behind them. Lugsy took control of the passenger wing mirror, angling it so he could see what was going on to their rear. Luca and Kostas' vehicle could barley be seen through the sand trail their vehicle kicked up. Through the cloud he could see Luca sat in the front, the pop star's bodyguard drove.

Lugsy peered over his shoulder and met Speedy's gaze, Speedy raised his eyebrows communicating his anticipation of what was probably about to happen. Lugsy tapped his ear, making sure his colleague in the rear of the vehicle saw. Speedy did the same and Lugsy heard the soft bleeps as Speedy joined the communications net.

Lugsy sat back in his seat and scanned the road ahead, watching for signs, for any clues. After a minute of driving, more soft bleeps sounded in their ears signalling that Kostas and Luca had joined the net.

"Morning guys," Al's voice resounded in the ears of the operators in both cars. Unheard by the other occupants in the vehicles. "Just so you know, the drone is up. Nothing so far but, if there is any strange movement or chatter I'll let you know. OK?" Nobody answered; they kept eyes forward. They let nothing show they were listening to live intel.

The vehicles crawled along the dusty road back to Bastion. The traffic had now virtually ceased to exist, making Lugsy nervous. Speedy shared his concerns; the lack of traffic was common before an attack. Locals always knew what was about to happen and would stay clear of the danger area. Whatever traffic did pass them, the occupants stared in, exacerbating their worries. The looks made them feel uncomfortable. They knew something they didn't.

"Traffic's thinned right out," said Lugsy, his eyes taking in every detail of their surroundings. "It ain't right, something's fuckin up."

"Aye," said Speedy slowly and deeply whilst nodding his head and looking around. PJ remained quiet. He had seen all this before on his ops in the area.

"What?" said Smith. "What's going on?"

"Shut the fuck up!" said Lugsy. Smith was silenced but still was on the hunt for answers. He squirmed in his seat and stared at Speedy, who he considered to be his only friend in the car. Speedy ignored him at first but as his bouncing began to annoy him he held up his hand stunning him into submission.

"Movement!" said Al sharply. "Two storey building, left hand side." All four who could hear him snapped into action, their vision now on the offending structure. "Round the back, figures running. One on the roof."

"Fuck that's it!" said Lugsy.

"What? What's it?" shouted Smith. His question remained unanswered; his protection team were in a different world now.

"I see him!" said Speedy angrily, ignoring Smith. "The bastard's on the roof. Look north corner. He's watching us through binos."

"He films us," said Kostas via the comm, his accent breaking through. Remarking about his modus operandi.

"Fuck!" shouted Lugsy. "Stop the car. Disturbed ground." PJ stamped on the brakes, throwing the occupants forward into the seats and dashboard. The rear vehicle narrowly missed rear-ending the lead vehicle. He had spotted some disturbed ground, leading from the edge of the road back towards the two-storey building.

"Shit!" exclaimed Speedy. "It's him…" That was all he got out, he had seen the man on the roof lower his binoculars. The explosion, from an IED, disguised as a rock, lifted the front of the lead vehicle. The occupants inside the vehicle lifted with the chassis, and then felt a moment of weightlessness before the jaw-jolting smash back down onto the stone road.

"Out!" screamed Lugsy amongst the chaos. "Get out of the fuckin car!" He kicked the damaged car door open with his foot, pushing hard against the twisted metal. The sound of creaking metal on metal was overpowered by the sound of automatic gunfire coming from the rear vehicle. Were they under fire? He thought, or were his colleagues covering his lame vehicle?

Lugsy rolled out of the seat, keeping low below the level of the roof, and grabbed at the handle of the rear door. PJ struggled, with his full assault kit, to drag himself through the cab from the driver's side. He slid out, onto the battlefield, through the same door as Lugsy.

"This way!" shouted Lugsy at the terrified Smith, sat frozen in his seat. "Come on you fuckin prick! Get the fuck out." Smith's head slowly turned to look at Lugsy, his eyes wide. "This way!" he shouted, grabbing Smith's clothing on his shoulders. His round eyes winced as Lugsy pinched his skin along with the fabric. "Fuckin come on!" Smith was pulled to the ground in a heap. Speedy followed, protecting the useless Smith.

The four men from the destroyed vehicle huddled by their smashed-up car, hidden from the structure where they assumed the device was detonated from. Lugsy and Speedy scanned left and right, trying to assess the situation. They could see behind them Kostas and Luca firing on the structure.

They stood by their open vehicle doors, PDWs in the shoulder, laying down fire onto the building. Speedy raised himself, still leaning his back on the vehicle, sliding up for a sneak at the building. He could see movement as figures with rifles ran from cover to cover.

"What we looking at Speedy?" shouted Lugsy.

"Uhh," said Speedy, his head bobbing, looking for more information about the building that was now their target. "We got multiple contacts. Long weapons. Maybe eight or more." He relayed calmly and efficiently. "No sign of our man."

"What do you want us to do Al?" said Lugsy.

"He's in there guys," said Al. "We have thermals on the building. Ten armed enemy, and one more hiding in the top floor rooms. If I know Shinwari, and I do know that coward, that's him cowering in the corner."

"So we're going in?" asked Lugsy, shouting over the noises of combat.

"Yes," said Al after the shortest of pauses. "Go get him! But first get our guests out alive." Speedy and Lugsy, the only two from the lead vehicle who could hear Al, looked at each other and nodded.

"Come on asshole," said Lugsy forcing Smith to his feet but keeping him bent double. Lugsy forced Smith's head down with one hand and, with his PDW in the other, ran him towards the rear vehicle. "Run you fuck!" Smith was pushed blindly to the others, under covering fire from PJ and Speedy.

Bundled into the rear vehicle, guided by Kostas with a push from the side, he landed on top of Ilya. She cowered in the corner of the back seats of the vehicle, her knees drawn up to her chest. She pushed him off her with her feet.

"Don't you fuckin move!" shouted Lugsy through the open door. Some rounds from the direction of the two-storey building hit the side of the vehicle, causing the people in the vehicle to cower even more. The team around the rear vehicle returned fire in the general direction. Lugsy slammed the door shut sealing the two visitors inside.

"They're re-grouping," said Al, watching through the cameras of the drone circling high above. "There are six outside the building, leaving four inside."

"Right!" shouted Lugsy above the noise of the incoming rounds. Everyone back to the lead vehicle. Speedy, PJ. Keep their heads down." The guys intensified their firing, and the incoming faded. "OK. Go, go, go!" Lugsy led the way, Kostas and Luca followed. Seconds later they slid to a stop in a cloud of dust behind the front vehicle.

"PJ, Get them the fuck out of here." Lugsy pointed to the rear vehicle, idling fifteen or twenty metres away. "Back to the Marines at the Green."

"OK, yeah, got it," he said. "Ready?"

"Yeah, go!" shouted Speedy, still up on aim, firing containing fire onto the building. PJ ran for the vehicle. Other members of the team stood and leaned on the wreckage and opened up on the building.

Lugsy stayed low, watching PJ. He saw him reach the vehicle and open the driver's door.

It wasn't audible but Lugsy knew he was ordering the girl's bodyguard over, away from the controls. He climbed in, staying as low as he could. Lugsy saw his hand on top of the steering wheel and the top of his head peeking over the dashboard. The car reversed off. After it made some ground, away from the destroyed lead vehicle, it spun on its handbrake and sped off back towards the firebase.

Speedy ceased firing and ducked down next to Lugsy. He looked along the road they had come noting the vehicle making a good escape.

"What we got then?" asked Lugsy.

"What Al said, about six to eight of them. I've only seen four out front," Speedy said, re-loading his P90. "The rest must be inside with Shinwari."

"How do you wanna handle it?" Speedy thought for a second, glanced up at Kostas and Luca letting off carefully aimed bursts at targets as they presented themselves. He bit his lip and ruffled his brow.

"You got your grenade launcher?" he asked.

"Aye," he said. "In that fuckin mess somewhere." Lugsy beckoned to the twisted wreckage of the vehicle.

"Find it mate," said Speedy. "Al, any intel. What we heading into?"

"Speedy," said Al. "We can see a trail from the road to the building. Hard to make out with the naked eye but it's there. Eleven x-rays in total, one has to be Shinwari. The others seem to be armed mostly with AKs. We see no other movement, civvies seemed to know it was coming."

"Right we're going in," said Speedy. "Lugsy?"

"Aye, got it!" Lugsy dragged the launcher from the smashed cab of their vehicle.

"Guys!" screamed Speedy, forgetting Kostas and Luca could hear him through their comms devices. "Call out that building for Lugsy."

"Two-storey, flat roof. No targets on roof," Luca said calmly between the well-aimed shots. "Floor one from left to right, four windows, door, two windows. Second floor five larger windows. Door, wooden. Windows, no glass, some with ripped sheets. X-rays outside on the corners of the building and some in windows, moving on firing."

"Stand by!" said Lugsy. He stood and pulled the launcher into his shoulder. He pulled the trigger and sent a grenade through the air towards the rickety wooden door. Before the first grenade hit the second was on its way towards one of the ground floor windows.

The building shook with the six explosions from the grenades, the door was blown in and, along with the selected windows, dust and smoke plumed out. Incoming fire stopped, Lugsy lowered the launcher.

"That was fuckin awesome." The barrel leaked smoke from the grenades propellant. He dropped the spent launcher and swung round his slung P90. Speedy stood up, alongside his team.

"OK guys," he said. "Extended line, call out your targets."

Chapter 26

Waves battered the hull of the small fishing vessel, cold spray spilled over the sides and onto the deck. Some of the water seeped under the door that led down into the bowels of the ship, Cam sat in the storeroom that the crew had set aside when he had paid his way onto the ship.

Cam splashed the thin film of water that was under his feet with the sole of his shoe. He rocked back and forth and side to side as the boat rode the crests of the waves, diving into the troughs and climbing the peaks. Over and over.

Cam swigged the last of the Akvavit. He had bought the Scandinavian liquor from the Faroese fishermen. He had downed two bottles of this yellowish, caraway-flavoured spirit in the twenty-four hours he had been aboard. He threw the empty bottle of 40% liquor into the bin; the bottles clanked together but didn't break.

He leaned forward placing his head in his hands, he couldn't take much more of this sea sickening motion. Cam could hear the crew moving around, frantically keeping the ship operational. He knew they were wary of him. They talked in groups, glancing at him as they spoke. He decided to stay out of their way until they got him to his destination.

A white-crested wave pushed the boat to port, sending the bin scuttling across the storeroom. The bottles spun, aquaplaning on the layer of salt water, past Cam's feet. He would need more booze if this was going to continue for the whole voyage. He groaned and rubbed his closed eyelids with the tips of his thumb and forefinger. He needed sleep but it still eluded him. Faces of people long gone plagued his subconscious, mostly friends but some were less friendly.

The face of the Chechen was the latest to take a spot on the roll call of the dead. His was the face that had started this chain of events. Cam reached into his shoulder holster concealed by his jacket. He studied the pistol, every detail. How many lives had it taken? There were five he knew about.

"God damn it!" he said to himself. He needed more drink. It was the only way to keep the memories at bay. He held the pistol close to his face; he could smell the cordite, the brass cartridges. He leaned the top slide on his forehead feeling the cold metal on his skin.

"Damn it!" he repeated. He tapped the edge of the pistol on his head, again and again. "Urghh." Cam rocked back and forward the gun hitting his forehead, getting harder and harder. "Everything ends, nothing lasts forever. Everything ends."

One of the Faroese fishermen passed by the door to the storeroom. Knowing the strange Englishman was in there he stole a glance. He saw him hunched over, rhythmically rocking, gun in hand. His face was covered, the gun was in the way and he was muttering in a foreign language to himself. He didn't hang around in the doorway long. He was off to tell the captain what he had seen.

Cam, with another sigh, looked at the gun again. He pressed the magazine-release catch and the magazine fell out the bottom of the pistol. He caught the ejected mag and counted the rounds.

The small holes in the back of the mag showed it was full, fifteen 9mm bullets.

He re-inserted the mag seating it back into position with a click. He slid it back into his shoulder holster. One of the empty bottles floated back past his feet, bouncing of the toecaps of his boot. He swiped it up and undid the screw top, there were a few more drops left.

1030hrs AFT
Close to Firebase Fiddler's Green, Helmand, Afghanistan

Speedy and his team advanced cautiously over the sandy ground towards the two-storey structure, still smoking from its windows from Lugsy's grenade assault. Weapons up on aim, each man scanned the building for enemy movement.

"That's the white aspect, with the door." Speedy wanted to make his team's target indicating easier by designating colours to the correct sides of the building. "Keep your spacing guys."

The team moved apart, they knew one good burst from the enemy would take out most of them if they bunched up.

"Contact, white one three," said Luca, letting off a burst from his P90. His indicating let the rest of his team know that he had spotted a target on the lower floor, third window from the left on the front aspect.

"Contact, white two four." Kostas indicated he had seen, and was firing on, a target in the second floor, fourth window along.

"They're moving inside," said Al. "There are none left outside. From the heat sources I have three not moving; one seems to be crawling. You got at least four with your grenades."

"Luca, Kostas. You take the front door," said Speedy. "We're going round the back. Let me know when you're making an entry."

"Moving now," said Luca. The team split when they were close to the building. Kostas and Luca took up positions either side of the front door. Speedy and Lugsy peeled off round the left-hand side of the structure. All the time, weapons up in the aim. Ready for anything.

"Corner!" said Speedy, slowing as he approached the rear of the building. He took the corner wide, moving sideways in an arc. His view opened up as he moved round. "Contact!" Speedy pulled his trigger in a smooth motion and rounds hit his target. The enemy soldier, who was half in and half out of a doorway, fell out onto the ground. "X-ray down."

Speedy quickened his pace towards the doorway, the threshold now blocked by the dead enemy combatant.

"Speedy, this is Luca. We're going in." Speedy and Lugsy didn't need to reply, there was no need, this team was battle hardened. They knew their trade. Speedy heard their transmission but concentrated on the door and the body.

As he approached the lifeless form half out of the door, he lowered his barrel and fired a volley into the man's back. The soldier didn't move, apart from the transfer of kinetic energy from the bullets, telling Speedy he was already dead. He stopped short of the door, keeping his muzzle from clearing the frame and showing his presence to anyone inside.

"Frag it," said Speedy. Lugsy grabbed a grenade from his team mate's tactical vest and pulled the pin, holding in the safety lever. He reached over and squeezed Speedy's shoulder, telling him he was about to post the grenade. He held it at waist level next to Speedy so he could see it was ready. The lever let out a metallic sound as it flew free, spinning to the ground.

The grenade was tossed in through the door. They heard it bounce off the wall on the other side of the room. They heard no shouts from within; there was nobody in the room on the other side of the door. The explosion rocked the building, its foundations seemed to crumble and the structure moved.

"What the fuck!" shouted Lugsy. Speedy, who was nearest the door frame took a step back, bumping into Lugsy.

"Christ!" he said, the wind knocked out of him by the massive shock wave. "What the hell was that?" He looked around at the building, assessing its state. "Al?"

"I think we've got a problem," said Al. "They're not moving." Speedy pressed his earpiece into his ear and narrowed his eyes against the rising dust cloud forming around the trembling structure. "Damn it! I think they're down."

"Kostas! Luca!" Speedy desperately wanted to get a response. "What's happening, Al?" demanded Speedy, coughing the dry dust from his throat.

"Huge heat signature," said Al. "Resembling a blast. Kostas and Luca are down. They're not moving!" Al's voice was tight with anxiety. "IED in the first room, white aspect. I think the guys triggered it."

"I'm going back round!" Lugsy was on his way before he finished the sentence. Speedy turned to see him rounding the corner leaving his view. He went to verbally stop him but only got out half a syllable.

"Shit." He turned his attention back to his door. He entered the dark building, swathed in smoke and dust, stepping over the body of the soldier.

He cleared the room, sweeping his muzzle round it, and then moved to the next doorway, which would lead him deeper into the building.

Lugsy found the front door, swung back against its hinges. The blast had forced the door flat against the wall. He peered in, his eyes adjusting to the gloom. He focused through his sights, visually clearing the room. Only on making the room safe did he notice the bodies.

"No! Fuckin no!" He tactically moved into the room and made his way towards the first of the bodies, covering the doorway across the other side of the room.

"Sit rep!" demanded Speedy, moving through the tight corridors.

"They're down!" said Lugsy. "Man down, man down!" Speedy listened, waiting for more details. He continued on his part of the mission, to capture or kill the bomber.

Lugsy checked the room for any danger to himself. He knew something had triggered the blast. It must have been a trip or a pressure mat; they were Shinwari's favourites. He could see Luca, laid flat, face down, near the wall. He was in one piece but unconscious, covered in blood and smoking from shrapnel wounds.

Kostas was on his back. He had taken the full blast. Possibly protecting Luca from the device. His body had been ripped apart. He had lost both legs, one above the knee and one below, his lower shin splintered. Keeping one eye on the un-cleared doorway, Lugsy knelt down and felt for a pulse on Kostas' neck. As he desperately needed tourniquets, he was already a priority one casualty and needed stabilising first. He had one. Weak, but palpable.

Lugsy had to stop the blood loss. He ripped open the Velcro on his first-aid pouch and pulled out a tourniquet and lifted what remained of Kostas' leg. Blood pumped from the stump, coating both Lugsy and Kostas.

Lugsy tried to fit the tourniquet to Kostas' upper thigh. Blood covered his hands as he struggled to get the tourniquet into position. His hands slipped as he tried to buckle the strap. He began to twist the plastic stick; the tourniquet tightened slowly squeezing the iliac femoral artery against the thigh bone.

"We're gonna need a fuckin heli!" said Lugsy. "Al, get us a fuckin evac, now!"

"On its way," said Al, the helplessness evident in his voice.

"I have two P1 casualties Al, we have to get them out now!" Lugsy couldn't twist the tourniquet any further. Kostas' thigh muscle was as thin as his wrist. Lugsy could only hope it was enough to stop the bleeding, he couldn't tell. Sticky red fluid pooled on the floor, around Lugsy's feet.

"Kostas!" shouted Lugsy. "Kostas. Can you hear me? Wake up, buddy, come on." There was no reaction. Lugsy opened Kostas' first-aid pouch and found his own tourniquet. He began the same process on the other leg, still trying to rouse his colleague. He could feel the splintered bones crinding as he moved the shattered limb.

Once the second was in place he checked for a pulse and breathing. Despite his injuries he was breathing and he could feel a pulse. He shifted his attention to Luca, there was no more he could do for Kostas. Not without putting life-saving fluids into him, he didn't have the means for that. Not till the heli medics arrived.

He slipped on the blood under his feet as he moved over to Luca, almost losing his balance. He regained and bounded over to his unresponsive friend.

"X-ray down!" Lugsy could hear Speedy taking out one of the enemy. He mentally counted how many should be left. "X-ray down!" Another one out the picture, he counted maybe three more and Shinwari himself.

"Luca, Luca." Lugsy shook his friend. "Give me something, mate." Luca's body was limp, completely lifeless. There was no pulse, no respiratory effort and no signs of life. His skin was charred and showed signs of shrapnel wounds, clothes ripped and torn from the sharp, shards of metal that would have been slung at them from the explosion.

"Luca's dead," he said hardly believing what he himself was saying. "P4 Al, he's gone."

He left his friend; there was nothing he could do. Lugsy had lost comrades before but immediately he knew this was different. He had worked with this team solidly for two years now. They were brothers. He felt blood soaking into his trousers from where he was kneeling and he shuffled backwards, away from the body.

Something caught his eye; in his peripherals someone had presented themselves in the door frame to the room. Lugsy spun on his heels into a kneeling fire position. He pulled his pistol from his drop holster and slammed a round into the figure in the door. The figure fell back into the unexplored corridor.

The pistol grip slid in Lugsy's hands, his friend's blood squeezed through his fingers. He dropped the pistol, which dangled on its coiled lanyard. Lugsy gasped. He tried to breathe in but his body was in shock. His throat spasmed in an attempt to bring in air but his chest refused to rise. In a panic he fumbled at the clip attaching it to his belt, finally releasing it. He crawled, crab-like, backwards into the corner of the room. A corner clear of blood and bodies.

"Fuck, fuck, fuck!" he said to himself. He wiped his hands over and over again on the thighs of his trousers. "Get off! Get off!" Some of the blood that was fresh was transferred to his trousers but the rest was dry, staining the webs of his fingers. "Get off! Get off."

"Speedy," said Al. "Heat signatures are coming from the far corner of the building. I think the last three are huddling together in one room. The rest of the house is clear."

"Cheers Al," said Speedy shifting his aim to the last door in the corridor. "You hear that, Lugsy?" Speedy waited for a response while he walked cautiously down the corridor. He had heard Lugsy trying in vain to help the others. "Lugsy?"

"He's OK, Speedy, he's seeing to the guys." Al knew it was bad and Lugsy was out of the fight. Speedy was his only operational Asset still on task.

"I'm at the door," whispered Speedy. He kept his body flat against the wall, away from the flimsy wooden door. "Going in." He reached over for the handle and cracked the door open, slightly. He darted back a few feet putting both hands back on his rifle. He knew an AK could easily fire through the wall. He wanted to be away from the area immediately adjacent to open the door.

He waited a second or two. When no slugs came through the wall he un-hooked a flash grenade from his kit, pulled the pin and rolled it into the room. The canister exploded, blinding the people in the room, silencing their shouts of, what Speedy could only assume was, grenade.

Speedy was done waiting; he followed the grenade in. Three figures were on the floor, stunned by the flash bang. Speedy's muzzle swept the room, the floating red dot sight flicked from one figure to the next. He identified his main target and fired a burst into the other two figures. Without losing momentum, Speedy moved across the floor space and planted a kick into the torso of the un-injured man.

The groans continued from the man bent double on the floor. Speedy cleared the rest of the room with a sweep of his rifle, firing more rounds into the two downed figures. He took a closer look at his prisoner, coughing on the floor, confirming he was un-armed. A secondary examination of the room revealed the recording equipment set up by the window, just as Al had suspected in his briefing.

"Got recording equipment, Al," Speedy said, moving in for a closer look at the small camcorder device set up on a tripod.

"Can you confirm we have him?" asked Al.

"Yeah," said Speedy gazing down on his prisoner, still sprawled out on the floor. "That's him."

"Good," Al sighed with relief. "Condition the son of a bitch."

"With pleasure." Speedy took a step towards Shinwari and swung in his boot, directly into his midriff. "Didn't quite work out for you did it?" Speedy followed with a second kick into the winded bomber. "Gonna try and record us being blown up were ya?" A third kick. "You've made your last movie."

"Get him up!" Speedy stopped, shocked to hear the voice from the room's doorway. Lugsy stood, anger spread across his face like a mask of hate.

"What?" said Speedy.

"Up, get that fucker on his fuckin feet!" Lugsy stormed over to Shinwari, grabbed his clothing and hauled him to his feet. "Up!"

Lugsy was screaming now. Shinwari wobbled on his shaky legs. Lugsy threw him against the wall. Shinwari steadied himself on the brickwork.

Lugsy took the tripod from the window and set it in front of the bomber. He aimed the camera at Shuinwari and started it recording. Speedy watched the red LED light on the camera flash, thinking that he was the intended star of that movie.

Lugsy reached over and grabbed Speedy's pistol from his holster and walked into frame alongside Shinwari. He pressed the barrel hard against his head.

"Kosta's dead too," said Lugsy without looking away from Shinwari. "Smile for the fuckin camera." He took up the pressure on the trigger. "This is your big finish."

Chapter 27

Wednesday 10th April 2013
0730hrs BST
Asset HQ, South Oxfordshire, England

"Why don't you get yourself home bud," said Bull finishing his takeaway coffee. He had brought some in every morning, today George was still hanging around. "You look exhausted." George looked at him through red bloodshot eyes and shook his head.

"I want to meet these guys." He picked up his empty coffee cup and agitated the last of the thick, dark liquid at the bottom. He swirled the remaining coffee hoping to dilute it, make it drinkable. "We might get something out of them we can use."

"Well, we need something," said Colin. Bull and George agreed without speaking, they knew he was right, they were clutching at straws. Nothing they had seen had shown the slightest trace of Cam, he had simply vanished from the face of the planet. They all threw their empty Styrofoam cups into the bin in succession. George turned to the computer screen he had been staring at all night, in the hope something might have appeared in the last few minutes.

"George," said Bull tapping his friend on the shoulder. "Get up, let us take over. You can barely see."

"Yeah." George tapped the desk and slowly got to his feet with a groan. "Yeah." The roller chair slid back the seat rotating as it rolled on its casters. George staggered over to an empty desk and leaned on it.

He crossed his arms and rested his chin on his collarbone. His eyes blinked a few times then stayed shut.

Bull took George's seat and scanned his handwritten notes. George had briefed him on the night's findings, not that there were any. He spun in the swivel chair and opened his mouth to say something but stopped when he saw George sleeping where he stood.

Colin snorted a laugh when Bull motioned with a smirk at George. Bull returned his attention to the computer that was in sync with the police national computer database. He needed to send some emails with a few ideas he'd had overnight.

He stopped typing when he heard footsteps approaching the door to their ops room. Colin too heard them; he ruffled his eyebrows and watched the door through the corner of his eye. A figure appeared in the frosted glass panel in the door. Both men recognised the silhouette as Al's.

The door opened and Al stood in the doorway, he didn't enter. His suit was crumpled as if he had been sat down all night. His eyes, like Georges, were red and dry looking. He was gaunt and looked like he had aged overnight.

"Al?" said Bull. His one word question woke George and snapped Al out of his trance like state. "What the hell happened to you?"

"We had an op last night," said Al, his voice low and monotonous. "It uhh, didn't go well."

"What happened?" asked Colin.

"Where?" asked Bull. Al snapped from Colin to Bull following the assault of questions.

"Speedy," said George. "Afghan?" Al shifted his gaze to George's eye line.

"Uhh, yeah." Al composed himself by pulling his suit jacket taut and entered the room, leaving the door open. "The details will have to wait, the G.R.O.M are here. Donald's meeting them now, they'll be up in a few minutes."

"You've met them before haven't you?" asked George. Al nodded. "What did you make of them?"

"Do you trust them?" added Bull.

"Yes," said Al confidently. "I went out there to recruit them when they were working with Rory."

"Recruit them," said Colin. "Why them?"

"They are the best G.R.O.M team in the Polish military," said Al. "The Poles want in on our program so are willing to send us the best."

"Do we have space for more teams?" asked George who had been with Al and the Assets from the beginning. He had helped set up the program and knew the numbers.

"We do now," said Al gloomily.

"What do you mean?" asked Bull.

"Never mind." Al dismissed the question with a wave of his hand. "Besides we need their language skills for some potential ops against the Russians." Bull rolled his eyes.

"Urgh," he groaned. "Russians."

"Why are these guys gonna help us with the Russians?" said Colin, asking the question that Bull hadn't.

"What do you know about the crash that killed the Polish president back in 2010?" said Al.

"Weren't they on their way to some anniversary from the war?" said George, starting to wake up.

"Yes," said Al positively. "The Katyn massacre, the 70th anniversary."

"Another conspiracy theory," said Colin, dismissively. "Lady Di, JFK, Malcolm X. There's always crazy conspiracy theories around the deaths of the famous and politicians."

"Look, we all know what the Russians are like," Al responded. "Relations have always been tense, the Poles want revenge and they can blend in as Russians better than anyone we have."

"You sure bout that?" said Bull, butting in.

"Oh yeah," nodded Al. "They may not like it but most speak Russian and I'm pretty sure that'll come in handy for us."

"Why do they want revenge over what was an accident?" asked Colin.

"Their President, Lech Kaczynski, was popular with the Poles. The anniversary was for the massacre of 22,000 military personnel killed by the Russians in Katyn forest during the war. His aircraft crashed after being denied landing permission four times. They went down near Smolensk, so close to Katyn forest. It just left a bad taste for the Poles, as if the Russians didn't want them to be present at the ceremony."

"Didn't I see a video of what sounded like gun shots at the crash site?" asked George.

"Yeah," said Al. "Look, who knows if it's true or not. The Poles see some symbolism in the crash. The Russians deny all involvement, just like they did with the original event."

"Al." Al whipped around to see Donald stood in the doorway with those he recognised as members of the G.R.O.M team hovering on his shoulder. "The G.R.O.M are here."

"Ahh, come on in guys," said Al changing, both subject and mannerisms. "I have some people here for you to meet." Bull moved over, between Colin and George. The G.R.O.M team shuffled in. Al stood between the two teams and Donald left the doorway for the corridor.

The G.R.O.M stood together, shoulder to shoulder. The remainder of Al's best Asset team studied the four men in front of them. This was the team Rory was working with when he died. They were itching to get out of them what happened that day.

"These," Al motioned towards the three tired and scruffy looking men who occupied the dark operations room, "are my best men. You may one day be working together." The two teams nodded to each other in a silent introduction. Bull studied each member of the G.R.O.M team in front of him.

One, the youngest, looked like he had recently been beaten up. He had the yellow tint around his eyes that represented healing black eyes, many cuts to his face and a split lip. Another had his arm in a sling but still looked like you shouldn't mess with him. The other two, one young and one in his fifties looked un-injured.

The oldest one was looking back at him, his gaze lingered and Bull locked eyes with him. He was of a similar height to Bull and just as weathered looking. The oldest G.R.O.M straightened up and momentarily ruffled his eyebrows before equalising his features and looking away. George noticed the exchange and cleared his throat.

"Which one of you was there?" he asked. Colin stayed quiet; as he hadn't been part of the group back then he felt he had no part in this interchange.

"Me," said the youngest. George and the rest were taken aback by his blunt, brave reply to the probing question.

"They all were, George!" said Al almost reaching anger. "But Mats was the one in the car with Rory." George and the others looked uncomfortable at the mention of their friend's name, apart from Colin who silently watched the conversation from the sidelines.

"So, why are you still here and Rory's not?" asked Bull directly.

"He was unconscious," said the eldest, once again locking eyes with Bull. "They must have thought he was already dead, he was badly injured."

"Hmmm!" mumbled Bull, refusing to break the G.R.O.M commander's stare.

"Bull," said Al. "These guys are now a team here with us. We will learn to work together! Do we understand?" Bull had never seen Al like this. He was showing anger and aggression for the first time.

"Yeah," said Bull. "Yeah, of course." He analysed Al's face. He looked tired, stressed and upset. "Everything alright, Al?" Al straightened up and looked back at Bull. "Anything to tell us?" Bull said.

"No," said Al. "Nothing, I'm going to show the guys around our facility. Get them on the ground as soon as we can." The Asset team nodded, unsure of what else to say. "Follow me gentlemen, this way."

Al ushered the G.R.O.M from the room. As he left he fixed his two longest operators with a short but intense stare. Then he joined his new team and followed them down the corridor away from the untidy, makeshift ops room.

"What do you think?" said Colin, finally piping up. "Anything to do with it?"

"Don't know," said Bull. "I think they're genuine. Young lad stood up for himself."

"And what was that with the main guy there?" asked George. "Looked a little intense for a while there."

"Not sure bud," said Bull. "There's something, not sure what." Bull collapsed back into the swivel chair that he took from George, exhausted from the mix in his head. "Feel like, like I've seen…" Bull spun the chair and resumed typing his emails. "Never mind, I'm sure it's nothing."

2345hrs BST
Scrabster Harbour, Caithness, Northern Scotland

The small Faroese fishing vessel didn't stay moored long; it dropped off its passenger and set sail. He knew, as he watched it sail away, that the crew were wary of their illegally paying passenger. They had cut the voyage short, by at least three days. The captain, who agreed to take him back to the UK, seemed just to want him off his boat.

He had spent the time on board drunk, watching and listening to the crew talk about him. He didn't speak the language but the whispering and stolen looks spoke a thousand words. After being self confined to the storeroom he was pleased to be back on shore.

So used to being jostled around on the waves, he felt as if the solid ground around him was moving.

He shook off the land sickness and walked along the harbour path. Tall streetlights, each with three separate bulbs, shone spots of light at regular intervals following the route of the path. Misty drizzle soaked into his jacket and settled on his cheeks. A biting, midnight breeze dropped the ambient temperature and started to numb his forehead.

He stopped in the shadows between a set of streetlights next to a small café and surveyed the scene before him. Heads of seals bobbed on the surface of the harbour water around an orange lifeboat. A crew member could just be seen through the mist. Cars parked in the ferry terminal car park looked like easy targets, until he looked up at the stalks of parks lighting. Cameras!

He carried on, leaving the harbour behind him, ascending a set of stairs, overgrown with vegetation up to the small harbour settlement. He shifted the weight of his rucksack and looked over his shoulder at the fading glow of the harbour, streetlights creating an orange haze through the drizzle.

The top of the stairs led to the intersection of St Clair and Clett Avenue. To the left, his view obstructed by a line of bottle banks, ran a street of bungalows. The right, a collection of ex-council houses. He was looking for the right car. He needed an old car, one that would be easy to start and wouldn't be missed until the morning.

Some houses had cars parked directly outside the front door; he would leave them alone. One car, an old style Fiesta, sat to the side of an abandoned looking garage. Interested, he approached, watching for security lights. The car had a layer of dirt, smeared from the streaking moisture on the rusting paintwork. The area of windscreen swiped by the wiper blades blended seamlessly to the edges of the glass. Bits of twigs and grass rested on the blades. Nobody had used the car for a while.

He stood with his back to the car, leaning on the rear passenger door. He chewed his bottom lip and scanned the streets. The rear window broke easily with a jab of his elbow. The centrally locked doors opened with a thunk, proving the battery was charged. Confident he had chosen well he moved around to the driver's door and climbed into the seat.

Finally out of the fine rain, he reached around under the steering column finding a seam in the plastic covering. He forced his fingers into the seam and ripped off the panel exposing the ignition drum. He pulled the drum free from it's housing and removed the outer section. He inserted a stubby, flat-end screwdriver. The old car's key had been inserted and removed thousands if not millions of times and the drum's pins were worn down. The engine started with a twist of the screwdriver.

He slammed the door shut, sat back in the seat and sighed at the full weight of the situation he found himself in. He had a long drive ahead of him with multiple car swaps along the way. Squeaking wiper blades pushed the debris to the edges of the windscreen, taking three wipes to clean the glass. Slipping into reverse with a crunch of the gears, he began the journey.

The car chugged along the coast road. Thurso beach half-mooned on his left and a lighthouse glinted on the far peninsula. No traffic gave him an empty road. He drove into the town and through a set of red lights taking a left at the town square. Red-lettered lights spelt TESCO as he left the small, most northerly UK town. South was the way he needed to go, he couldn't get lost, there was only one road.

He read the sign on the roadside of the A9, Inverness one hundred and ten miles.

Chapter 28

Thursday 11th April 2013
0800hrs BST
Asset HQ, South Oxfordshire, England

Sat in front of the computer, Colin read the notes from the previous night. Paper documents scattered over the keyboard. George had handed over to Colin and Bull giving them a few things to investigate further during the working day. The hunt had stalled; it was getting repetitive. Leads turned out to be nothing and they had no idea where their target was headed.

Bull stood cross-armed peering into the training area, forty metres below. The training area, still decked out like a tropical village, was bathed in darkness. The only light source was the light from their ops room, tucked away in the roof space of the giant hangar.

"What you thinking about?" asked Colin, knocking Bull from his dream-like state.

"Huh," was Bull's only response, still staring into the darkness. He focused on the broken wooden staircase Cam had fallen through on the last training day.

"You look deep in thought mate," said Colin. "I was just asking what you're thinking about."

"Uh, nothing much bud," said Bull, turning his attention away from the training hangar.

"Wondering how long we're gonna be doing this for."

"Till we find him I suppose."

"Come on, Col, we may never find him." Bull left the large glass window and grabbed the back of a swivel chair, spun it round at sat down. "Not if he doesn't want to be found that is."

"He can't be that good," said Colin. "If he's coming back he can't stay off the radar. Not here, it's impossible."

"We've no reason to believe he's coming back, all this…" Bull motioned to the notes Colin held in his hands. "Is probably a waste of time."

"George thinks he's on his way back."

"Yeah well, I hope he's wrong." Bull rolled the chair back, away from one of the empty desks, lifted his feet and placed them cross-legged on the edge. "Let's all pray he just disappears and is never seen again."

"George seems to think he ain't that type of guy."

"Unfortunately George is right," sighed Bull. "He could be very dangerous, as we've seen. But, he's also not stupid. He'll probably leave a good period of time before his next hit."

"So you think he's still planning to carry on?"

"Hell yeah," said Bull. "If he's anything, he's persistent. He won't leave anything unfinished."

"Hmm," said Colin sensing the conversation was over. "Yeah." Colin clenched his jaw and nodded to himself. Bull stretched, arching his back. He relaxed and interlocked his fingers behind his head, took a deep breath and closed his eyes. "Hey, what was that yesterday with the G.R.O.M?" Bull opened his eyes but didn't move. "You and their boss seemed to have a moment."

"Yeah," said Bull cracking his neck to one side. "I've seen that guy before. Can't place where though."

"Well he knew you too, have you worked with G.R.O.M before?"

"No, never." Bull cracked the other side of his neck. "I'm gonna have Al look into his past."

"You'd hope Al's done his homework. He seems sure about them..."

Colin stopped mid sentence as the door opened and Donald entered the room.

"May have something for you," he said breathless, storming across the room to the computer Colin was sat at. "I've been monitoring ship ports, airport... Morning by the way. And this caught my eye."

"What you got?" said Colin, moving out the way so he could access the computer.

"One thing I've been checking is car thefts." Donald stayed focused on the computer screen as he spoke.

"So have we," said Colin. "But there are far too many to investigate. Folkstone and Dover are a nightmare."

"Yeah," said Donald. "But this one." He tapped the screen, Bull wheeled his chair over to the desk and the two guys studied the information. "A small harbour town near Thurso, way up in northern Scotland. Virtually no crime. But, early this morning a car was reported stolen."

"And? What's the big deal?" said Bull.

"The car was found north of Inverness, ditched in the river. Police Scotland reported it to us."

"So, normal car theft," said Colin. "Just some kids."

"Could be," Donald continued. "But it needs looking at because Kessock Bridge has police automatic number plate recognition on it."

"So you're thinking someone arrived in Thurso, stole a car and dumped it before it was pinged on ANPR?" said Colin.

"Yeah, that's about the size of it," said Donald. "Especially when there was another car stolen south of the bridge, taken around three am."

"Alright, got to admit that's strange," said Bull.

"Why ditch it in the river? If it was a joy ride the car thief would normally burn it out." Colin said.

"Burning it would attract police sooner," said Bull, sitting back in his chair. "Whoever it was wanted to slip away. And running water destroys DNA traces just as well as fire."

"Any CCTV on the bridge?" asked Colin.

"No," replied Donald. "Well, there is, but not working at the moment. I requested it but, nothing." Donald tailed off when a phone began to ring. Colin silenced the phone by lifting the receiver.

"For you Don," said Colin. "One of your team." Donald took the phone and listened to the message.

"OK, good. Cheers." Donald handed back the receiver. "The car stolen in Inverness has been found. Dumped, north of the Forth Road Bridge."

"Burned out?" asked Bull.

"No, rolled into the Firth."

"ANPR on that bridge?"

"Oh yes," said Donald. "We have a pattern here. Someone is moving south, stealing cars and trying to avoid police national computer."

"There will be CCTV on the bridge into Edinburgh," said Colin.

"Yeah, on it." Donald began composing an email to Police Scotland. "Should have it soon, they're generally pretty good." Donald quickly finished the brief message and hit the send button. "There, done."

"What do you reckon?" said Colin. "This him?" Bull looked at Donald but said nothing. "You guys know him," he continued. "What do you think?"

"Could be nothing," said Bull. "But we need to see that footage from the Forth Road Bridge."

"Shall we get Al?" asked Colin.

"He's been acting weird these last few days," said Bull. "Any idea what's going on with him?" Bull looked directly at Donald and waited for an answer.

"Uh, yeah," sighed Donald realising he wasn't getting out of this explanation. "Look, keep this quiet. Not supposed to say." Donald shifted uneasily, eyes darting around. "Speedy and his team have been hit pretty hard."

"Shit!" exclaimed Bull. "Who's down?"

"Kostas and Luca, KIA. The others are OK but they're out of action for the time being. G.R.O.M are replacing them."

"God damn it!" Bull looked down. "We'll leave Al alone, he's got enough on his plate. We'll tell him when we have something concrete to go on."

"Here, got it." Colin said reaching for the computer mouse. "Looks like they've sent the whole tape." Colin opened the file with a double click. "I'll run it through the software. The footage downloaded and was run through their computer program, picking out movement on the pedestrian side of the bridge.

The screen of the computer displayed a grainy image of a bridge walkway. The image jostled, the cameras shook in the wind. The software had skipped the long portions where there was no movement. A man walked towards the camera, hiding his neck from the wind.

"No, next." Bull dismissed the man. Even Colin, who didn't know Cam, knew it wasn't him. "Keep going." Donald skipped to the next detected movement, going backwards in time. "No." Back further.

They kept going, sometimes skipping the obvious ones, sometimes watching them fully. The camera also switched from front to rear, watching them walk away. Still not the man they were looking for. A couple appeared on the screen and Donald clicked past them.

"Wait!" Bull said loudly. "Go back." Donald brought up the previous clip. The couple walked along the bridge, getting closer. The smaller figure, female, held onto the taller figure's arm. Their shoulders hunched, protecting them from the early morning wind. "There! Look."

Bull pointed to the screen. A second figure, tailing them, followed at a distance. This lone figure was male, had his hands in his jacket pockets, hood over his head and walked also hunched over.

"Is that him?" said Donald. He knew Cam, had worked with him on the operation that had injured him so badly he would never get back out into the field again. He looked at Bull who also knew Cam well.

"Could be," he said. "Can't say for sure. Just that distance he's keeping, looks like he's doing that on purpose."

"What, do you think he knows we would use the software and we'd skip when we saw the couple, missing him in the background?" Bull raised his eyebrows, reflecting the question right back at Donald.

"Maybe we're looking too much into this guys," said Colin, playing devil's advocate.

"Perhaps," said Donald pressing the back button, starting the clip from the beginning again. The couple repeated their walk together along the bridge. The lone figure followed, his feet only just showing as the couple's heads left the screen. "But that just looks like it's done on purpose." He looked around for approval. Even Colin had to agree when he saw it again.

"Can't make out if it is him though," said Bull. "I'm gonna call George in, he's the only one who knows him just as well as Al."

"Hope he won't mind being woken up," said Donald as Bull picked up the phone and jabbed at the number pad with his finger. "He's probably only just got his head down." Bull didn't answer; he turned, pulling the coiled phone cord as far as it would reach.

Bull mumbled into the handset, waited for a reply and turned back round. The cable returned itself to its original shape when the phone was hung up. Bull looked at the screen as it played over on a repetitive loop. The others looked at him, waiting.

"He'll be in," he said without averting his gaze. "In a few minutes." Bull crossed his arms and raised one hand to his face and rubbed his beard. They waited in silence for George to arrive.

George, looking tired and with wrinkled clothing, flew in through the door to the ops room. He sidled up to the others and studied the screen. He didn't even get through the full clip. He turned and looked at Bull, who looked back through the corners of his eyes and gave a slight nod.

"We're gonna need to set up a gatekeeper exchange," said George matter-of-factly. "We must have all forces and agencies working together on this one, we have to make sure we share all information. No egos!"

"Don," said Bull. "Can you get in touch with Al?" Donald nodded accepting his order. "Also, ANPR. Check out those number plates; see if he's following anyone, or being followed. Look for any links."

"No problem," said Donald.

"What about car thefts in Edinburgh," asked George. "Were there any after that CCTV image?"

"Yeah, quite a few."

"Well let's follow them," George continued. "I want to know where they're heading."

"All of them?" asked Donald.

"Yeah, every single one of them."

"OK, I'm on it," Donald said, striding to the door with a sense of purpose.

"So," said Colin interjecting. "I take it that's our man." Donald paused in the doorway and glanced back into the room where George and Bull had concerned looks on their faces.

"Yeah," said George, his voice filled with confidence. "That's him."

2120hrs BST
North East England

He sat in the drab hotel room. On the flaky painted, bare wooden desk, lay a number of components. Only a few components were missing, these he would be acquiring soon. Two devices were

264

under construction; one was for his main purpose, the other to help him escape should he be located.

He had done all he could do without the final components. He sat back and looked out the window above the desk. The wooden backrest of the cheap furniture dug into his back. The dirty curtains fluttered in the breeze that blew in through the open window.

He could smell the sea on the wind. He stood, sliding the chair causing it to scrape on the floor. Reaching forward he moved the nicotine stained net curtain to one side. Although run down, this area of the Northeast was still popular with people looking for a night out. Small groups of people made their way, too and fro up and down the street.

Games arcades and takeaways lined the street along the seafront where the cheap B&B he was staying in was located. The crashing waves were eclipsed by the clatter of a train as it screeched to a stop at the local platform. A silver moon, cut by a thin line of cloud, hung high in the sky. He sighed and closed his eyes.

The hotel room had no glasses, that he could find, so he picked up the bottle of Jack and took a swig. Perhaps tomorrow night, he thought. If he could stay off the drink for one day he would be able to get hold of the last components he needed.

Sleep, need to get to sleep, he thought. He had drunk enough; he should manage to sleep until morning now. Then the process would start again. He would have to stay sober and rested tomorrow, to be clear of mind to break in to the facility.

Chapter 29

The people of the Northeast had opposed the open-cast mining operation for years. Now however, they were on the side of the miners. It had brought jobs to the area and boosted the economy. The owners of the mine had also built a park for the local population to enjoy.

Shaped like a women lying down, the park boasted miles of walks through the Northumbrian countryside. As well as injecting some life into the surrounding towns, the owners had promised to return the land back to its original state when done. Most of the locals were happy to be back in the mining business after so many years.

At this time of the morning the mine was silent – the only people on site were the security staff. Some, employed full time by the mine, others such as dog handlers were contracted in. Whoever they were, this time of the day most were asleep at their posts or bleary-eyed and inattentive. They certainly hadn't noticed the intruder creep past them as they slept at their desks.

He was a professional. He had gained access to facilities far more secure than this one. A hop of a fence, dodging a sparse network of CCTV cameras and avoiding the un-armed guards was all it had taken to get this far. Only now was he looking at his first obstacle. He rubbed his chin with a latex gloved hand feeling stubble through the thin, skin-tight rubber.

The single manned post at the entrance to the site had posed no problem. The patrolling dog handler seemed to stay external, no threat. Now he was stood in a room, his back flat against the closed door through which he had entered. A camera, above his head, was trained on a door along the right-hand side wall, the door to the next room where he needed to be.

The door had a swipe card access. Being of an incredibly sturdy construction meant he had to find the card to be able to gain entry. Right now he couldn't move; if he did the camera above would pick him up. Although the guard watching it was asleep, he didn't want his image recorded.

Looking up, he opened his shoulder satchel slung around his neck. From the bag he pulled a small digital camera. Hanging from a USB port was a short cable. Holding the cable in his teeth he reached up and grabbed the top of the door frame and hauled his weight up. He jammed his feet on either side of the frame and held himself steady a metre or so off the ground.

With his hands now free, he manipulated the small camera next to the lens of the CCTV camera. His legs started to shake under his weight, the unusual placing of his feet made the position impossible to hold for any length of time.

Fighting the disco dance in his calf muscles he pressed record on his digital camera. Three seconds later he stopped the recording.

On the loose end of the short USB cable was a small, square plastic box. He flicked it open revealing a series of metal spikes. He pushed the spikes into the wire leading away from the CCTV. With the cable block squeezed shut, pushing the spikes through the plastic casing deep into the copper cabling, he pressed play on the digital camera. The camera, pre-set earlier, began repeating the three-second scene over and over back to the display in the site's control room.

He dropped to the floor and shook his feet, the blood supply had been cut off with his ankles at a strange angle and he waited for the pins and needles to start. Blood rushed back into the soles of his feet, the familiar tingling feeling jabbed at his skin as he stepped to the locked door.

There was no other choice but to search the building for the access key card. There were two guards in this single storey building. One was asleep in a small rest room, flat out on an old sofa. The other was supposed to be manning the building's main security lodge. He was fast asleep too, elbow leaning on the desk that the hacked CCTV's camera feed came back to.

He left the room through the door under the tampered camera and entered a corridor that led to an open area within the building. The open area was viewed by the security officer through a large glass window. Two doors were the only other features in this area, the front entrance and the door into the security lodge.

From where he was stood he was just out of view of the guard, not that the sleeping man would have noticed him. He didn't notice him first time he slipped past him, now he would have to get closer to find the key card. The open area in front of the security lodge was lit up by artificial lights. The lodge was in darkness. The sleeping guard had turned them out.

The intruder sidled up, following the wall line, to the lodge door. He crouched next to it. The door had a mechanical keypad, but it wasn't going to cause him a problem. The guards had left the door unlocked. He had pushed a bolt up into place, missing its bolt hole. This held the door slightly open and allowed the guards free entry and exit.

The intruder pushed the door; it opened silently without a squeak. He slid into the lodge staying in the crouched position. An automatic door closer began to close over the door. He helped it shut, allowing it to stop quietly against its misused locking bolts.

Inside the lodge was a partition screen and he moved in behind it, using it as cover. He stood slowly and poked his head up over the partition and took in the rest of the lodge. The guard was still asleep, oblivious to the infiltrator.

On the desk he could see keys but no cards. He looked closer at the guard. He had a bunch on his belt, attached to a sprung-loaded hook. Around his neck was a lanyard that would normally hold an ID card. It seemed like the best option or at least a place to start.

He moved in on the sleeping guard, carefully and slowly. Taking deliberate, controlled steps he closed in. He stared at his prize, the ID card lanyard. He concentrated on the guard's breathing. He watched for any sign of him becoming aware of his presence.

Placing his feet carefully, heel first then rolling round the outside of his foot to the ball. Knees bent, like suspension springs, taking his weight. He balanced with his arms, which he held slightly away from his side, fingers spread. He froze as the guard took a deep breath, his back inflating then deflating with a sigh. He waited, like a living statue, still staring.

When he felt it safe, he continued. He was right behind the guard and could hear his shallow breathing. He leaned over his shoulder and followed the line of the lanyard down his chest. On the end was a card, in a plastic cardholder. There was a photo of the guard on one side with his information; on the other side was a magnetic strip. That had to be it, he thought.

Carefully, he hooked a finger under the company logoed lanyard and softly lifted the hanging ID card. Lifting the card released the minute weight of it away from the back of the guard's neck. He waited again for any reaction. When none came, he swiftly but cautiously lassoed the lanyard off the guard's neck, taking care for it not to brush against the man's face.

He retreated out of the lodge, never losing sight of the guard. With the door closed softly, he re-entered the corridor back to the secure door under the camera. He looked up at the camera, confident he had complete control of it. He slid the ID card out of the opaque plastic holder.

He lined up the card with the slot and held it in place above the reader. He held his breath and swiped the card's magnetic strip through the reader.

A soft bleep and a clunk followed. He tried the door, it swung open. It felt heavier than it looked. The room behind the door was pitch black, no lights and no windows. He knew he had found what he was looking for.

A two foot by two foot metal safe sat in the middle of the dark room. The contents of the safe needed to be kept away from heat and stored in a dark, dry environment. Otherwise the dangerous contents would cook, the safe acting like an oven. He closed the heavy door behind him locking himself into complete darkness.

A barely audible snap of the glass vial was followed by a slow build up of glowing yellow light as the chemicals mixed inside the plastic light stick. He dropped it to the floor, near the safe door. He snapped another, then another. He threw them down, scattering them around the small windowless room.

He knelt down next the now illuminated safe. He studied the locking mechanism on the front of the safe. A sturdy iron construction, bolted to the thick concrete floor. He didn't want to deface the safe, he wanted his actions to remain unnoticed for as long as possible. He wanted to get as far away before it was discovered, so he couldn't drill, this was going to take patience.

He made himself comfortable, sat on the floor leaning his left shoulder on the safe. He placed his shoulder bag on the floor and opened the zip. He took out an A5 notebook and pen. He placed them on the floor and put his hand back into the bag. He found his stethoscope, which he coiled and placed next to the pad, hoping he wouldn't need it.

He turned to the first page of his notebook. Some scribbled notes were scrawled over the page. Some research earlier had provided most safe's pre-set combinations. These were the combinations that new safes were set to for transit. Some people didn't alter them.

He tried them all. It was a long shot but worth a try, but they had changed the combination from the factory set one. He looked around for any scribbled numbers, on the sides and back of the safe, the walls and back of the door to the room. He hoped lazy guards had made a quick note of the combination somewhere, but there was nothing. He resigned himself to the fact he was going to be there for a few hours.

With the stethoscope's earpieces in place, he tapped the diaphragm end, twisting it so the metal bell faced away from the safe door. The diaphragm would vibrate higher pitched frequencies to the earpieces, the bell, lower frequencies. He placed the diaphragm against the door near to the combination wheel.

He slowly turned the wheel, normally smooth and silent he heard the click of the internal mechanisms through the stethoscope. The click of the spindle and flywheel created acoustic pressure waves that travelled up the tubing to his ears. He listened for minute differences in the clicks. One would make a slightly different sound as the drive pin fell into the notches in the flywheel.

He noted numbers down that could be possible combinations. Each mistake reset the lock, this was a group one or two safe meaning it had many internal wheels making it possible to have six or eight numbers. He turned the wheel right and left, noting numbers each time. After an hour his back started to ache, he was hunched over spinning the dial.

He flexed his arm, his hand felt cold, lack of blood in its elevated position and contact with a metal dial sapped away his body heat. He blinked his eyes hard, a headache was forming. He sighed and continued. Each notch had to line up inside the lock, when it did the bolt could be operated and the door opened.

Pages and pages of notes and graphs covered the notebook. A combination was slowly filtering out of the pages, numbers repeated. He wrote those numbers along the top of the page. He only had one more number to find. He checked his watch, he had been there nearly two hours. He turned the dial carefully, not wanting to miss the last click. If he did he would have to re-start the process again, he needed to get out of there soon.

His tired, cramped arm spun the dial, notch by notch. He was nearly there. He held his breath and closed his eyes, hoping to heighten his hearing. His eyes opened wide on hearing a slightly louder clunk than all the others. He still didn't breathe as he dropped the end of the stethoscope from the dial.

He grabbed the silver handle and pulled it down from the horizontal to the vertical. It moved without any problem and the door popped open.

The rubber strip, that stopped the metal door and frame hitting each other, moved it from its closed position.

The door, now fully opened, revealed his prize. He leaned back and looked inside, he could now breathe again. Piled inside, wrapped in a brown greaseproof paper, the mouldable plasticine-type bricks sat waiting to be placed in his satchel. He nearly had all he needed.

0600hrs BST
Asset HQ, South Oxfordshire, England

At first he didn't believe what he was reading. He read it again, concentrating on every individual word. It was the end of his night shift and George had just been sent an email from Northumbria constabulary.

"Jesus Christ!" he said, reading the message for a third time. He involuntarily reached for the phone but stopped. By this time Bull and Colin would be on their way in anyway. "Shit!" He held the receiver halfway between the base unit and his ear, the phone's dial tone bleeped continuously through the earpiece.

George replaced the receiver, cancelling the tone. He had no choice but to wait for his team to get to him. He rested his elbow on the desk, chin on his hand and re-read the email again.

"Morning," said Bull walking into the ops room closely followed by Colin. The cardboard tray of takeaway coffees landed on the desk spilling slightly from the impact. The tense atmosphere stopped the two men in their tracks; they knew something was wrong.

"Guys," said George to their two staring faces. "We've got one hell of a problem."

"What?" said Colin. George rolled back on his chair and motioned to the computer screen. Bull and Colin approached the screen and read the email. "We don't know it's him."

"No," said George. "No, we don't. But a couple of the cars stolen this side of the Forth Road Bridge headed that way. ANPR tracked them before they were dumped. Two got into Northumberland."

"It's not much of a trail but it's all we got," said Bull. "I'm going north to check it out."

"OK, good," said George as the phone rang. "Hello," he said into the receiver. "Al, we have something." George pushed the loudspeaker button.

"I know," said Al through the speaker. "Turn on the news." George grabbed the remote and pointed it towards the wall-mounted TV in the corner of the room. He flicked channels until the news appeared. Al remained silent as the three men watched. The newscaster told the story of the email from Northumbria constabulary.

The story segued into the next and held their attention. A photofit of their ex-colleague filled the screen with the newscaster telling an inaccurate tale of the hunt for the fugitive wanted for murder.

"Doesn't look like they've linked the two," said Bull.

"No," said Al. "But I think it's only a matter of time. Some bloody reporter will link it."

"Shit!" said George. "This is going wrong."

"I've got an idea," said Colin. "How about we leak some info to the media." He looked around at his audience. "We know he isn't in Rome anymore, so why don't we give them some CCTV images of him there."

"That's not a bad idea," said Bull.

"It'll shift attention away from the UK, give us a bit of breathing space," Colin said, reinforcing his point.

"What do you think, Al?" asked George, looking at the phone. The TV blared in the background. George muted the newscaster and continued waiting for Al to answer. "Al," he said again. "What do you think?" The silence lasted.

"Do it," said Al finally. "Send it."

Chapter 30

Saturday 13th April 2013
2240hrs BST
Small Heath, Birmingham, England

Days had gone by since his last hit. He was beginning to hurt. His habit had taken all he had. He needed multiple hits daily, by now he was shaking; cramps and uncontrollable sweating came and went. He could barely move from his empty house. He had sold everything to feed his habit and now he was in his boarded up living room, huddled under a worn blanket on a filthy mattress.

His name was Edward Barrington and he was brought up in a wealthy home. His parents had disowned him after he had abused their good will for his own addicted needs. He had strung his brother along for longer, but now he too shunned him, he was well and truly alone. Despair was setting in knowing he would have to continue his burglary streak to fuel his need. More people were going to suffer from the repercussions of his crimes, but he didn't care. He needed the drugs.

He pulled the blanket up over his head trying to stop the shivering, but it wasn't the cold damp air in the dark house that was causing that. He couldn't find the strength to react when he heard the back door being smashed in. The cramps and hunger pangs were too much. He even struggled to look up at the man who had just kicked his way into his slum of a home.

He blinked, hardly able to see the figure in front of him, the torchlight shining into his face. He scrunched up his face baring his Methadone rotted teeth. A figure stood in front of him looking down, his features hidden by shadows. Edward tried to make out the man's face but he lifted the torch higher directly into his eyes.

"Arrgghh," he groaned shielding his pupils. "Stop it," he said feebly. "Who are you? What do you want?" The figure didn't reply. He leaned over and grabbed Edward by the jaw, he groaned again from the heavy-handed pressure on his mandible.

The mystery figure turned Edward's face to both sides then pulled the blanket off the top of his head. His dirty, greasy hair was probably a light brown under the weeks of filth. The figure pushed Edward's head back as he stood up, hitting it off the wall. He turned off the torch allowing him to be seen in the gloom.

The figure un-slung his shoulder bag and opened it up. After fishing around he pulled a wad of cash from the bag. He threw it down onto the floor next to Edward.

"I'm going to be staying here for a couple of days," said the figure in a monotone voice. "There's more where that came from if you keep your mouth shut and don't ask questions. Understand?" Edward picked up the money and counted it, stunned at the amount. "Good." The figure backed off to the only piece of furniture left in the room: a rickety old wooden chair.

He sat and pulled out a pistol from the back of his trousers resting it on his thigh. Edward watched from his huddled position and pulled the blanket back over his head. The two sat silently in the darkness, Edward struggling to think through his physical pain. He was trying to sum up the strength to get out and buy more product.

An hour passed, and neither moved. Edward could wait no longer. The hunger for chemicals was too strong. He strained as he climbed to his feet. The blanket dropped to the floor landing half on, half off the stained mattress. The stranger didn't move. A shard of streetlight streaked through the boards on the window.

The stranger's face could just be made out. The two men had similar features and looked a lot alike. Edward didn't much care, he needed to feed his craving.

On shaky legs Edward hobbled to the front door, unlocked the various bolts and chains and left the building. The stranger watched him leave without moving from the chair. The door slammed shut. He had time to get to work.

He stood, re-placed the pistol in the waistband of his trousers, clicked on his torch and began scoping out the rest of the house. Each room bore a similar resemblance to the living room. Carpets ripped up, boarded windows and basic, paint-stripped wooden furniture.

In the far corner of a bedroom he found a table, cluttered with drug taking paraphernalia. He swept the items off the table's surface with his forearm. Dumped his bag down on the table and began pulling out some of the contents, spreading them on the table. He took a knee, lowering himself near to his belongings. He had all the components now, everything needed for an improvised explosive device. He peeled the greaseproof paper from two of the blocks of Semtex and started to mould it into shape. The malleable orange plastic explosive was easily shaped into long strips. These he put down amongst the other pieces.

He picked up the main component, the switch. The heart rate monitor had already been programmed to the state he needed it to be. He also had opened it up and soldered four, colour-coded, bare wires protruding from the chest sensor.

He opened a hardened plastic container to reveal some small, cylindrical metal objects. He carefully removed one from the container. About the size and shape of a half broken pencil, this would be responsible for the detonation of the device. He inserted it into one of the strips of plastic explosives, pushing it all the way into the malleable plasticine.

He held the moulded explosives against the chest strap and wrapped it in black tape, securing it to the strap. He then took two of the bare wires and connected them to the wires on the detonator, twisting them together. He took a strip of electrician's tape and covered the bare twisted wires, protecting them from the possibility of short-circuiting.

He repeated the process for the other shaped brick of Semtex, taping it to the other side of the chest monitor. He placed the finished device on the desk, straightened up stretching his back and admired his work. He looked at the other bricks of Semtex and spare detonators. He had one more device to make and this one was going to be big.

2345hrs BST
Asset HQ, South Oxfordshire, England

"So," asked George. "What's your opinion?" Bull hadn't long arrived back. He had been flown by helicopter to the Northeast, checked out the crime scene and came back.

"Well," he sighed surveying his entire team. Even Donald had come along with Al to the case conference. "Whoever it was got in and out without being spotted by human or electronic means. They had guards, cameras and dogs and still nothing."

"Not that hard," said Colin. "I'm sure most of us here could do that."

"Yeah," he agreed. "The guards swear they were doing what they were supposed to be doing but the intruder managed to take a key card from around the neck of one of the guards."

"What?" said Al.

"Yeah, exactly," continued Bull. "Now, he got away with twelve, five hundred gram blocks of Semtex."

"Shit!" exclaimed Colin. "What damage could that do?"

"Take down a fair sized building," said Bull. "Easily."

"Bull," said George. Bull snapped his view from Colin to George. "Honestly, what do you think? Is it him?" Bull tightened the muscles in his jaw, his eyes rolled down and to the right. His eyelids blinked as he nodded his head.

"Yeah," he said. "Yeah, it's him." The room was left in silence following Bull's answer.

"OK." Al rose to his feet and walked to the centre of the room attempting to inject some enthusiasm into the group. "We need to work out what he's up to." He looked around the room, at the people he had assembled, these men who had worked with him. They knew him, knew how he operated, how he thinks. If anyone can stop him it would be these men. "If anyone has any thoughts, any feelings, no matter how insignificant, I want to know about them."

"We should come up with a list of all possible targets," said Donald. "We've got surveillance units watching all the terrorist cells and persons of interest that he might have got from our records. If he goes near one of them we'll have him."

"He isn't that stupid," said George. "He knows we're on to him, he'll go nowhere near any of them."

"So it'll be personal to him," continued Donald. "Something he has a grudge against."

"Christ!" huffed Bull. "If we're gonna talk about all the things Cam's got a grudge against, we'll be here all night."

"He's right," agreed George. "It could be bloody anything."

"I think you knew him best, George," said Donald. "You got any inkling to what he's doing?"

"Like I said, it could be literally anything." George shrugged off the question. "Your guess is as good as mine. You mention it, he's got an opinion on it."

"Yeah but twelve blocks of Semtex, that's a lot of bang for 'an opinion'," emphasised Colin.

"It's very particular," said Bull. "He could easily mix up some home-made explosives. Why risk laying a trail by breaking into a mining compound?"

"What do you mean?" said Al. "Explain."

"Well, it's seems very specific. He wants manufactured explosives, so he'll want manufactured detonators." He paused to look around, gauging if the others were following. "Otherwise what's the point?"

"He's right," said Colin. "We need to be on the lookout for dets going missing."

"Mmm," moaned Al. "Not that easy." Al stood cross-armed, one hand rubbing his chin. "He knows where to get detonators. We're having a problem keeping track of them at this point in time."

"Yeah," said Donald with a hint of amusement. "Tracks being the word."

"So what we have to decide is whether it's one big device or twelve or so smaller ones," George posed.

"That's the million dollar question," said Bull.

"But also we've no idea what the targets are," said Colin. "Only that he has the devices."

"We don't even know where he is," said Al. "Only he was last in the Northeast."

"Nearly twelve hours ago," said Colin. "He'll always be one step ahead of us. He could be anywhere now."

"At least we've knocked the media off the scent," said Al. "But I can't guarantee that will last."

"It won't," said Bull. "I think they're on this one. Won't be long till they piece it all together. Then we're screwed big time."

"We're screwed already," said Colin. "He's running the show this time."

"All we can do is wait." Al sounded like a defeated man. "He'll show himself eventually. There's a purpose to all this; it's a waiting game now. We're here round the clock from now on. Sleep in shifts. We monitor everything." Al rubbed his tired face. "And I mean everything. The most insignificant detail could be what we're looking for."

"OK," George said with forced enthusiasm. "Lets get some food in, it's going to be a long haul."

"Another curry?" sighed Bull. The others nodded as if he had asked a stupid question. "You Brits and your damn curries."

"I'll pay, if you pick it up," said George in an attempt to persuade.

"Fine," said Bull, agreeing to a free meal. "At least it can't smell any worse in here."

Chapter 31

George stirred. He hadn't had a full sleep since they had started staying twenty-four hours at the HQ. After two hours of restlessness, he decided to give up on sleep. He unzipped his sleeping bag and kicked his feet out of the bottom of the foot well.

He swung his legs over the side of the camp cot, placing them down next to his boots. He rubbed his face and ran his fingers through his hair, his face felt warm and his eyes heavy. He had been awake all night, checking everything. All reports from all agencies that came in needed to be examined for clues.

A plastic moulded chair placed near the head of the bed carried, along with a few of George's possessions, a glass of water and a handheld radio. From the makeshift table he grabbed his watch and looked at the time. He sighed as he strapped the watch to his wrist.

He picked up the radio and checked the battery level and that the volume was up. This would be the means that the team members who were on down time would be alerted that something was happening. George stood, aiding himself up by placing his hands on his knees and pushing. He stretched his back and groaned, forcing his shoulder blades together.

He looked around the room, light kept out by thick blinds. The other camp cots were empty. Everyone was working through, tension was high and George wasn't the only one who couldn't sleep. He swung his jacket on and pocketed the radio. Leaving the room he left the door open to let in some air to the sleeping area.

George walked into the operations room like a ghost. Bull and Colin glanced over as he slumped into a swivel chair by one of the desks.

"Am I disturbing something?" he asked.

"No man," said Bull. "Just going over some old stories with Col, you know, about you guys and Cam." George turned the chair left and right nodding slightly with his whole body against the sprung-loaded chair. "Remember Yemen?" he said, raising his eyebrows, knowing full well the answer.

"Huh," he huffed. "Christ, how the hell do you forget something like that? That was one of the closest calls I've ever had."

"Rory got hit," Bull droned in his New York drawl, continuing with the story. "Donald was blown up and coughing up his lungs. I fly over in a chopper and I see him and Cam dragging them both out through a desert town chased by a God damn army."

"What the hell were you doing in Yemen?" asked Colin. George looked over at Bull and snorted through his nose.

"Don't ask," he said. "Long story."

"First and last time Don was in the field," said Bull taking the subject away from the reason why they were there. "Damn near coughed his lungs up right there in the desert."

"Guys!" said Donald loudly appearing in the doorway as if summoned by being talked about.

"Whoa, speak of the Devil," said Bull, greeting Donald who ignored the comment rushing by the group. He thumped some papers down on the desk nearest his team. His hands shook and he sounded over-excited.

"I may have something!" he continued, still blanking his colleagues. "I've been, umm." He paused for breath. "I've been, uh, trying to watch everything." He only now turned to his team. His eyes were flicking, red from exhaustion.

"Don mate," said George. "Calm down, collect your thoughts." Donald took in some air and blew it out through clenched lips.

"You know how we were monitoring certain things during the Olympics," Donald said, calmer. "Well for the first time something's flagged up."

"What?" said Bull when Donald paused again. "What's flagged up?"

"Mail cart," said Donald looking at each in turn. "A motorised postal mail cart."

"OK," said Bull.

"No, no," said George. "He may be onto something here. Postal vans, British Telecom vans, they're seen everywhere. Sat on street corners every day, nobody asks questions when they see them. Intel came in that some terror cells were considering using something that's seen everywhere to hide devices."

"Exactly!" Donald pointed with exclamation. "Postal workers push these motorised carts around, leave them chained up to lampposts and nobody bats an eyelid."

"What does this mean to us?" asked Bull. "Could be any punk kid stealing birthday cards for money."

"Yeah but the mail was all dumped in a post box," added Donald. "The nearest one to where the cart was chained up."

"What? Un-tampered with?"

"Yeah, just re-posted." Donald made a face of amazement. "It's in Birmingham. Confused the hell out of the police over there, that's why it kind of stood out."

"Wait!" interrupted George. "Where in Birmingham?"

"An area called Small Heath." George's muscles tightened, he grew an inch taller. His eyes widened and he gulped, he couldn't speak, his jaw was clenched shut. "Now, I looked for CCTV footage in the area but whoever it was either dodged in and out of cover or was simply lucky to avoid it."

"You seem convinced this is something," said Bull. "What does Al think about it?"

"Haven't briefed him yet, thought I'd run it by you guys first," said Donald. "Get your opinion."

"Might be worth a look, what do you think…" Bull turned mid sentence to George.

He cut himself short when he saw his friend, normally un-shakeable, tensed up. His stare cut into the distance, through everybody in the room. "George!" Bull verbally shocked George out of his trance. He blinked and his eyes flicked to Bull's. "What's going on?"

"I know what the target is!"

1145hrs BST
Small Heath, Birmingham, England

The old school house, converted into apartments a few years ago, was five storeys high and overlooked the local Mosque. The side of the apartment block, in the shadows of an alleyway, hid a metal fire escape that scaffolded up the side of the building. All he had to do to reach the flat roof space was jump for the lowest rung of the ladder and haul himself up to the first level.

The roof looked the same as it did five years ago, he wondered if anyone had been up here since he was last there. The thin layer of gravel crunched as he walked over to the railing wall, a cold gust reminded him the air would cool soon with the setting sun. The same breeze block, the one he had placed there last time, lay near the low wall.

He looked down on the Mosque. The door swung open and shut as people came and went. Years ago this place had been identified as a bomb factory and a place where the young were being groomed into fighting for the struggle. The government was too scared of starting an international incident by getting in there and shutting it down. After all, the land is classified as belonging to Islam, no longer British.

Soon it wouldn't be standing there anymore, no longer a portal from which evil materialised. His plan was in place. Its days of creating acts of treason were numbered. He leaned forward and looked down on the building that would soon be nothing more than a crater.

He had studied the plans of the building and identified the weak points. In an attempt to squeeze as much into the space as possible, the architect had butted the Mosque up against the existing buildings either side. A tiny alley next to the Islamic Bank Of Britain led to a cut away in the Mosque, this created a small walkway to the Mosque's kitchen door. A device left in that walkway could potentially destroy the building.

Then, along the street, from the right walked a postman. Following his motorised post cart, he passed the bank and went to the front door of the Mosque. The postman delivered some mail then reversed back towards the bank and took a left, straight down the alley. From his elevated position he watched the postal employee disappear into the shadows. It was all he needed to see; his plan had just been confirmed.

He looked up and down the street, taking in the surroundings. It hadn't changed, but he had. The community was still, for the most part, peaceful. He however, was not. Years of fighting against the forces of Islam had made him hate anyone who was connected to it. Before, he hadn't wanted to cause any harm to any innocent civilian. But now, he didn't care. To him they were all the enemy. The device would probably take down most of the bank too, but to him it was acceptable collateral damage. They were all the enemy.

Enough watching, he knew all he needed to know about the Mosque and it was time to leave. Birds circled above his head, the trees of the small park to the west gave home to flocks of blackbirds. He paused and watched as two tangled in the air, fighting for food. Twisting and turning, diving in turn as one dropped some food. These birds had been in the sky, fighting over scraps, every time he had visited to check over his target.

With the aerial fight over he glanced down at the Mosque before turning and crunching his way across the roof. He climbed down the metal fire escape and jumped the last floor to the ground. On his way back to his dilapidated home base along the streets of Small Heath, he passed by ethnic families going about their daily business. He watched them pass with a cold stare and they eyed him, the loathing apparent.

The back door was still broken, hanging off its hinges. He entered the foul-smelling property and lifted the door back into place. Edward was in his normal position, slumped on the mattress enjoying the product his temporary lodger was paying for. He looked up as his renter entered the boarded-up living room.

"Hey," he croaked. "Where you been?" He realised as soon as he said it that it was a stupid question. The stranger had barely spoken to him during the five days he had been there. "Hey uh, you got any more money." He continued. "It's just I could use a bite to eat."

"Really?" was the stranger's contemptuous response. Edward shifted uncomfortably, knowing he wasn't believed. "Here." He threw more notes onto the floor by the mattress. Showing great restraint, Edward left the notes where they fell.

"So, how long you gonna be here?" said Edward trying to gauge how much more of a free ride he was going to get. The stranger moved across the room in a semicircular motion, past Edward. Ignoring him and his question. Edward watched him leave the living room and heard him climb the stairs, clomping on the wooden steps, the carpet having been ripped up years ago.

Edward drew the blanket up around his shoulders swept up the money and stood. Wobbling on the springs of the mattress he shoved the notes into his jeans pocket. He followed the stranger and stood at the bottom of the staircase, looking up at the door that had been locked since the stranger had arrived.

He had tried earlier that day to see what was in that room but the stranger had put extra bolts and locks on both sides of the door. He knew better than to poke his nose in, the stranger gave off an air of ruthlessness. Also, he wanted the money to keep coming.

The stranger heard the front door slam from the locked upstairs room; he stopped what he was doing but didn't turn. He kept his eyes on his creation. Two devices rested on the table in front of him.

One, the larger, made up of multiple blocks of Semtex and a plastic box of components, all taped together, he lifted carefully and placed into an old rucksack. The other, he examined, hoping he would never be forced to use it.

1400hrs BST
Junction 4, M42 North, West Midlands, England

"I don't want anyone to go near the Mosque!" Al said over the car's internal speakers. "If it is him, and that's the place, we can't risk alerting him to the fact."

"Exactly Al," said Colin. "However, this could be nothing at all, we have to remember that."

"That's why I've got Donald carrying on the search," Al said. "You'll be there no more than two or three days, tops. Just to confirm or negate. Donald can handle it for a few days by himself."

"What's the plan Al?" asked George, butting in.

"OK, I'm monitoring the Mosque and surrounding area with satellite and drones on stand-by if the satellites are taken away from us. I've cancelled the G.R.O.M from going to Afghan. They're on their way to the area, they will be kitted up for an assault and only used if needed. Bull you're on over watch; be ready to take the shot if he presents himself. George, Colin, if we find him, confront him."

"You seem to think this is a kill mission, Al?" Said Bull. Al paused on hearing the question. The occupants of the car heard him sigh, his breath flowing over the microphone.

"No, well," another sigh rustled across the mic. "I hope not, but if there's threat to life we may have no choice."

"So if I can get to him, make him see sense," said George concentrating on the road layout ahead of him. "I mean, how do we take him back after all this?"

"I don't know," said Al. "I just don't know." The car fell silent, everyone deep in thought.

"What have you got on the Mosque?" asked Bull, shattering the silence with his gruff voice.

"This damn place has been a thorn in our side for years. Cam and his old team worked on it ten or so years ago. Even back then it was radicalising the community and we are sure many extremist acts have come out of there."

"So why don't we bust it open?" said Colin. "Shut it down. Shit like that shouldn't happen in our own country."

"Now you're sounding like Cam," said George as Bull nodded. "He's wanted to do that very thing, he's even tried before."

"He's done this before?" asked Colin.

"Not to this degree," said George. "It's a long story. Continue, Al."

"I've got the postal route from the postal service. They deliver a couple of times a day, first to the bank next door then to the front door of the Mosque. They then back up and take an alleyway between the two, accessing the street behind. That's about it."

"Times?" asked Bull.

"Around midday, then afternoon. But we can't expect him to use the same times."

"If it is him!" said Colin, a hint of frustration in his voice.

"Yes, if it is him. You never see two posties together do you? If it is him!" Al emphasised for Colin, "he'll turn up at any time, he'll try to stay unnoticed."

"Where do you want us to deploy?"

"I'm emailing you addresses, maps, and everything else we've got. Donald's working overtime on this. I'm putting you to a stand-by location near to the Mosque, we'll be watching. Everybody OK?" Nobody answered. "Alright," sighed Al. "Best of luck, anything starts and we'll be on comms."

The dashboard bleeped to let the driver know the call had ended. Everyone looked around the car, the expressions on everyone's face was different.

"It's him," said George looking ahead as they drove into Birmingham. "Just… something he said. I know it's him."

Chapter 32

Blue sky hung over the Mosque; white wispy clouds lay to the east. In the west, the clouds were thicker with the sun barely getting through. With about three hours left of daylight, George started to feel the chill of early dusk.

From the top of the opposite building, George observed the Mosque. Below the wispy clouds, Bull could be made out perched on the edge of another building. Out of sight, Colin was waiting. He had spent the last few days hanging around the street's coffee shops, internet cafes and charity shops.

"This ain't happening," said Colin, sipping his umpteenth coffee of the day and wiping the salt grains off the gingham plastic tablecloth. "He's not here." He obscured his mouth with his coffee mug as he spoke, hiding his secret conversation from the other patrons in the café.

"This is the one, I'm sure of it." Bull, ever vigilant surveyed the street. They had been lying in wait for the second full day. Genuine postmen had made deliveries at the correct times, nothing more. Bull had zeroed in on each, scanning their faces through his telescopic sight, looking for their target.

"I'm never going to sleep again at this rate." George was sure he could hear a shake in Colin's caffeine-riddled voice.

"Try switching to decaf, mate." George yawned. He rubbed his hands together, warming his fingertips. There was a chill in the air, which was starting to bite. He blew into his cupped hands. Sitting around and not moving was causing him to shiver. "I think the drone's back," he said looking up.

"Must have lost the satellites again," said Bull trying to spot it.

"At least we've still got cover," said George. "Over in the west," he continued seeing Bull searching for the drone. "In a wide arc, circling us." George puffed his cheeks and blew out a long breath. He shifted his body weight on the breeze block and arched his back. He took one last look at the small black dot, watching them from above, then back to the street.

"Stand by! Stand by!" Donald's voice broke through the three men's earpieces. George bolted to a low position and peered over the wall. "We may have something, stand by!" George looked over to Bull. He too was keeping a low profile, leaning forward looking through his telescopic sight on the sniper rifle.

"You see anything, Bull?" asked George.

"No," he answered eventually. "Nothing." Colin, sat covertly in the coffee shop on the street level, could do nothing but wait. He couldn't give away his cover. Without moving he surveyed the street outside the coffee shop through the dirty, condensation-covered window.

"Don, what have we got?" George asked – knowing Donald would be listening, back at HQ.

"Wait!" came the response. George shuffled on his brick seat. Bull swept the whole street with his sharp shooter.

"Take cover," Donald said. "Down, everyone." On command, George and Bull abandoned their position, taking cover behind the low walls that railed the rooftops. "I don't want anyone visible."

"Come on, Don," said Bull. "Fill us in man."

"We've picked up an individual," said Donald obviously concentrating. "Postman, with a cart." George and Bull, out of sight of one another, tensed up. They listened intently with wide eyes. "There's no delivery expected."

"Aye, we know that," said George. "It's six in the evening. Have we got an identification?"

"Not yet, stand by."

"We need to ID him!" said Bull.

"Stay down!" said Donald, his voice raised. "Stay in cover." Donald composed himself after a rare outburst. "If this is him, we can not give him any reason to think someone's onto him."

"He's right," said George. "He'll be watching the roofs."

"He hasn't looked up yet," said Donald. "Trying to move the drone into an angle to zoom in but he's looking down, face hidden by a postman's hat."

"CCTV?" asked Bull anxiously. George shook his head, confidently, knowing the answer.

"No, not on the route he's taking." Donald could be heard typing in the background of the open mic. "Guys, there is an evening prayer – Isha, a few minutes past six. It's the last prayer of the day. The Mosque will be full in a hour or so."

"Christ," said George. "This is it. What's the plan, Don?"

"Try to get a positive ID, let him plant the device. EOD are on stand-by, they'll deal with it. The drone will track him to his LUP, then it'll be over to you guys."

"Where's Al?" asked Bull.

"He'll be with us immanently," said Donald quickly. "Here we go, he's on your street now."

"Bank CCTV?" said George.

"I'm on it," said Donald. "It's above the main entrance, no good unless he looks up."

"I have him," said Colin, his voice muffled. "Across the street from me. Heading east to west."

"Well?" Bull said, asking the question on everyone's mind.

"Yeah, it's him." The answer was met with a short moment of silence. Every man on the OP now knew this was it; they had found him. "What do you want me to do?"

"Stay put," ordered Donald. "If you can keep eyes on, all the better but don't leave that building. We let him plant the device." For a few seconds there was no new information or commands. The airwaves went silent allowing the operators to weigh the gravity of the situation. "Al's here."

"Guys, it's Al." George shook his head again with the unnecessary introduction. "We have first hand visual confirmation. We must be cautious, we all know who we are dealing with here."

"Wait!" interrupted Donald. "What's he doing?" George sighed forcefully through gritted teeth. He abandoned his position and crawled towards the fire escape. Once he was far enough from the edge of the building, and out of street view, he stood and ran for the metal staircase.

The postman had stopped, unexpectedly, still on the main street just outside the entrance to the alley that separated the Mosque and the bank. The postman stood still. Colin watched from the coffee shop. He turned his head slowly to the left, without moving his body, his head stopped naturally at almost ninety degrees.

"He's looking right at me!" said Colin, forcing himself to remain still. It took all his will power but he stayed rock steady, in a relaxed pose, arm draped over the chair next to his.

"What's he doing?" said Al. "Is he on to us?" The postman forced his head further, over his shoulder, past the coffee shop's smudged window.

"He's looking past me."

"Could be a bluff," said Al. "He won't let on." The postman then shifted his view up, to the opposite building's rooftops. "George, don't move."

"I'm on my way down."

"What!" said Donald. "Stay out of sight. Do not enter the street."

"I'm no use up there," said George clanking down the metal fire escape. "I'm only of use on street level."

"Do not enter the street!" repeated Donald.

"Christ, Don! I know, just concentrate on him. Let me worry about what I'm doing."

"Colin, report." Al was desperate for first hand information. The drone, with its camera zoomed in, still wouldn't give the same level of detail as a human eyeball.

"He's not moving," reported Colin. "He's scanning the rooftops. About where George would have been." The man in the postman's uniform followed the line of the buildings, realigning his head to a more neutral position. "Tell me you can't be seen, Bull."

"No chance, bud," replied Bull. The postman looked right, down into the alleyway. He still didn't move. Colin could clearly see the look of contemplation that filled his face. He looked up, straight up into the dusk sky.

"He's looking for something," said Colin. "Do you think he can see the drone?"

"Should be no more than a dot to him," said Al. "He has no reason to suspect that he's being tracked. Remember we only found him on a hunch."

"Shit Al, he's on to us!" said Colin.

"Relax!" demanded Al. "We follow the plan." After a long, lingering skyward stare, the postman returned his attention to his motorised cart. He operated the controls and steered it down the alley, enveloped by the shadows. "He's in. Colin, George, follow Donald's commands. He'll lead you from now on. Bull, I'll direct you. You'll stay up top and provide cover for the boys."

"The G.RO.M, Al?" asked Bull.

"They're mobile," said Al. "If you need a team they'll back you up. Bull, North, stay high. Go!"

"Col, George." Donald took over the commands. "The alley. Go!" Colin left the café as George entered the street, they converged on the alley, one either side. "Wait!" Donald ordered his men to stop. "Satellites coming back online."

"Can you see him?" asked George, resisting the urge to peer round into the alley.

"Yes, there he is," said Donald. "He's out in the open, heading away from the Mosque."

"The device?"

"He doesn't have the cart," said Donald. "Move in guys, watch yourselves. Could be a trap."

"We know the drill," said George as the two of them, in a fluid motion, slipped round the corner into the alley. From their waistbands, they drew their pistols once they melted into shadows and out of public view.

They advanced down the alley, looking over the top of their pistols. In their earpieces they could hear Bull being directed by Al, over the rooftops, following the target from above. Concentration etched on their faces, Colin and George scanned the alley for any sign of booby traps. Natural lines on the ground and the points where shadows meet the light could hide any number of trip wires.

"Got the alcove," said Colin. "Going round." Colin motioned with his hand for George to watch the alley ahead. Colin took the corner, wide so he had the most view around. "Clear!" Colin moved into the alcove, George advanced to the far corner. He took a position, using the corner as cover, aiming down towards the end of the alley.

"Shit!" said George, the cart caught the corner of his eye, chained to a pipe near to the rear door of the Mosque. "Careful, Col – wait for EOD."

"They're on their way guys," said Donald. Colin pushed his pistol down the back of his jeans. He cracked his fingers, stretching them back against the ligaments. Gently, he placed one hand on the top of the cart, one on the zip.

"Jesus, Col!" said George, not leaving his aim. "SF EOD are on their way, leave it for Christ's sake." Colin relented, backed off and drew his pistol.

"Alright, lets go." George moved off, relieved to be putting ground between him and the possible device.

"Don't leave the alley," said Donald. "We have him on satellite. Bull's got eyes on too if he needs to take the shot. Let's see where he goes."

Donald and Al tracked their target; they watched his every move, directing their operators like chess pieces. George and Colin stayed ground level, Bull jumped from roof to roof. The G.R.O.M, although not seen by the team, could be heard being moved from street to street in their blacked out van.

They watched as he circled round the suburb of Small Heath, coming back towards the Mosque. Finally, four streets from the Mosque, he entered a house.

"OK," said Al. "Lets put a containment on that house. Bull you got eyes on?"

"Yeah," said Bull extending the tripod on his sniper rifle.

"Good. Colin, George. You get round the back. I'm going to put the G.R.O.M down the street. They'll be ready to deploy if you guys can't end this. We wait for dark then you're going in."

1925hrs BST

Edward heard the door, he heard it shut and the chain being put in place. The stranger walked into the living room. Edward struggled to focus on him. He failed to notice the uniform; he was beyond caring. Drugs flowed through his veins. The chemicals controlled him.

The stranger stood in the centre of the living room, looking down on the junkie. His stare lingered, like he was examining him, taking in every detail. Edward pulled the hood of the grey-hooded top off his head.

"What?" he said.

"There will be some people coming," said the stranger, emotionless. "They're going to try and kill me. I suggest you hide yourself."

"What? I'm not going anywhere!" Edward squirmed on the mattress, he settled against the wall and pulled his knees up close to his chest.

"Up!" The stranger grabbed Edward's hood and dragged him to his feet. The neck of the hooded top strangled him and he chocked as he was shoved against the wall. The stranger didn't have any trouble over powering the weak junkie, he spun him around and pushed him face first into the wall, knocking him senseless. Edward slowly slipped to the floor.

The stranger hog tied and gagged the drug addict and roughly dragged him across the living room. He opened the cupboard that ran under the staircase and bundled him in.

"If you have any sense you will shut the hell up." Before closing the small door he took Edward's mattress and, after folding it in half, covered the junkie who was lying on his side at the bottom of the storage cupboard. "If you want to stay alive I suggest you do not move."

He closed the door, locking Edward in the under stairs cupboard, he turned the key and placed it in his pocket. Knowing he was short on time, he left the living room and climbed the stairs over the cupboard that Edward was held in. He unlocked the room he had been using since his arrival and, after stopping for a short period to listen for noises, entered the room.

Once inside he locked it behind him, sealing himself inside. He took off the postman's uniform, replacing it with an old jumper and dirty jeans. He walked over to the table where he built his devices; one was left. He reluctantly picked it up with a sigh. He lifted the grey jumper and strapped it to his chest.

A wristwatch lay on the desk, this too he picked up. He strapped it to his wrist and pressed and held a button, the watch bleeped. He closed his eyes realising this could be the end. He felt under the table, taped underneath was an old Russian pistol. He pulled it free and racked the top slide back.

With another sigh, he sat down on the floor, his back in the corner of the room, knees up by his chest. He rested his forearms on his knees. Pistol in hand he started the wait.

2200hrs BST

Silent hours passed by. The light outside faded. The streetlights turned on and off a couple of times before coming on permanently. Orange artificial light streamed into the dark room through holes in the closed curtains, creating thin beams of light. Too much time had passed and he hadn't heard the bomb go off. That confirmed everything. Someone was on to him.

Quietly he sat in the darkness, ears strained, listening for any sign of intruders. The house creaked. He hoped Edward had taken the warning but couldn't be sure. A floorboard squeaked outside his room, his eyes narrowed. Instinctively he clicked off the safety. A second squeak, closer than the first, prompted him to rise to his feet.

From this angle, the hinge side of the door, he would have more notice than anyone coming through. He could sense someone on the other side and levelled his nine mil at the centre of the wooden door. He focused on the foresight, the door and rear sights blurred. He didn't breathe. Someone was there. He stood rock still. He could hear his own heart beating, pounding in his ears, drowning out vital evidence. Oxygen depravation forced him to take in a breath. He held it in, lungs inflated. Seconds ticked by like hours. He swallowed hard, drowning out more clues.

Quicker than expected the door came in, with such power it slammed back against the inside wall. He saw a darkened figure enter the room so fast he had no time to react. The figure swept the far corner of the room with the barrel of a P226 pistol, coming round, settling the sights on him.

He recognised his old friend over the top of his weapon. The two men stood off against one another, not even daring to blink. He stepped to the side, George followed, circling the opposite direction. Neither spoke, they circled each other, trying to gain an advantage.

"How the hell did you find me?" said Cam finally, orbiting the room.

"Come on Cam," said George. "What you were doing couldn't go un-noticed. You had to know we'd be on to you sooner rather than later." Cam didn't reply he continued to circle around the room. "You know why I'm here, don't you?"

"Yeah," Cam said in a monotone. "But can you do it, George? Can you kill me?"

"I'll do what I have to do," George answered, without emotion, still moving round the room. On his next step to the side he moved into one of the shafts of light emanating through the curtains. It dazzled him, he was forced to blink and step back. His target smirked.

"Could have killed you, George," he said. "Could've had you."

"But you didn't," said George. "It's over Cam, EODs made your bomb safe. It's done! Over."

"Do you know," he said, his face half-hidden in shadows, "what that place is doing?"

"Cam." George tried to answer.

"That place!" he continued, forcefully, "is one of the reasons this country is in the mess it's in."

"We still can't go blowing up innocent civilians."

"Innocent!" he said, his voice rising with anger. "Innocent! Not one of them is innocent."

"What?" said George. "Can't you see what you're doing, what you've become?" George paused, hoping for some form of realisation. "You're the terrorist now! Not them."

"I'm a freedom fighter!" he shouted lurching slightly forward. "Fighting for my country! Fighting for the freedom of the British public. Don't you see, George, there's fucking thousands of them here? They outnumber our police, military, everyone! They could take our cities from us. What would we do then, eh? Bomb em? Our own cities, our own capital. When our own civilians are being used as human shields."

"Cam…"

"No, no! No, no, no!" he shouted, struggling to keep control. "This will happen! Come on, you've seen the reports. You more than anyone should know."

"Can't you hear how crazy you sound, Cam?"

"Crazy! Crazy!" He let out an involuntary snort of derision. "What's crazy is letting it get to this stage." Cam and George kept their aim on each other. "You know the statistics, you just choose to ignore them like the rest. They tell us only seven percent of Muslims have been radicalised. Sounds like such a small amount doesn't it?" Cam paused.

"Cam…"

"But when there are one point seven billion of them in the world that's still a huge number." He paused again. "Well I'll do the maths for you! One hundred and twelve million. That's how many are coming for us. Christ, George, our population is only sixty-two and a half million, and not all of them are on our side."

"George," Al spoke to George, unknown to Cam. "Do you need assistance?"

"No," replied George.

"No?" said Cam. "Who you saying no to?" Cam eyed him quizzically. "He's listening isn't he?" George said nothing. "Of course he is."

"Colin, stay out," said Al ordering Colin to remain at the back door, knowing only George would hear him. "Donald hold G.R.O.M back."

"What's he saying, George?" whispered Cam. "Al! What's he saying? I know he's talking to you. Voices in your head. And you're calling me crazy."

"Cam, it's over. You can't win," said George.

"I can't win?" said Cam, huffing. "I've already won," he smiled. "You see, I've got an insurance policy." George tilted his head slightly at this new development. "A message. If I don't go online and keep delaying it, it'll get sent to the media. Giving a location where I've left files on everything – who we are, what we've done and what's coming! Everything!" His voice cracked with anger.

"What's coming?" said George. "And just what are you saying is going to happen?"

"Come on, George," he said shifting his emotions back to calm. "You know fine well what's being planned. When it happens, and it will happen." He made his point with a look of his eyes and an exaggerated point of his pistol. "When the war starts, their army is already here. They have us! Why are we pretending it ain't happening?" He laughed as if George should join him in his views.

"Cam…" said George, unnerved by his old friend's erratic behaviour.

"Oh I know, George." He sighed, nodding, faking acceptance of his fate. "You think there's no way out for me." He lifted his jumper, revealing the device strapped around his chest. "Heart rate monitor. Shoot me, my heart rate drops below a certain level, and…" He leaned his head to one side and whispered. "Boom!"

George took a step back, still aiming, but Cam advanced two steps forward, a grin on his face. George studied the device. He could see the shrapnel imbedded in the explosives, ready to shred him apart if he took the shot.

"Back!" said George. Cam stopped; there was no need to get any closer. George analysed the look in his eyes, hoping for some answers, and some kind of solution.

He saw Cam's pupils constrict, as if his focus had shifted from his target to his foresight, George knew he was about to fire. "Don't do it, Cam!"

Cam paused, the barrel of the pistol pointed at George's head started to tremor. His facial muscles tightened, he flicked his eyes to the side then settled them back on George as if re-setting his thought process.

George took his chance. He leapt forward, taking advantage of Cam's hesitation, gripping Cam's clothing around the neck line. George trapped Cam's shooting arm under his own and carried on the forward momentum slamming him into the bedroom wall. Cam winded by the impact pulled the trigger, firing into the floorboards.

George brought his knee up hitting the underside of Cam's elbow, he did it again, then again until the pistol dropped from his hand. Cam retaliated by head butting George on the bridge of his nose. Immediately his eyes watered and blood flowed from his nostrils. Cam continued his fight by placing his leg behind George's and pushing him backwards, George started to fall back.

George fell but brought Cam with him, they both fell to the floor. The collision and resulting jolt caused George's gun to go off. Cam let out a pain filled growl, George rolled the two of them onto their sides and let go. Cam no longer had a hold of George, he was gripping his left shoulder. George struggled to see through his streaming eyes, Cam was only a blurry figure writhing on the floor.

George climbed to his feet and levelled his pistol at the blur and fired. He wanted to run, if he hit Cam with a fatal shot the device would go and take down the house but he needed to make sure the job was done. He fired two more shots in the general direction then turned and ran.

"Clear the building!" shouted George running down the stairs, three or four at a time. "Device! Get away!" George clattered to ground level, his shoulder bashing into the landing wall. "Out, out!"

"Everyone's pulling back, George," said Al. "Report, what's the situation?" George just ran, he didn't explain, he bounced down the corridor of the dark, damp house. All the way he attempted to clear his eyes, he wiped at them with the back of his hand. He blinked but they stayed bleary.

He burst out of the back door. Colin wasn't there. Where he had left him in support, he must have moved back. Back to safety, where he needed to be. He pushed through the rear garden, over the crap in the yard and through the fence line. He caught a glimpse of the G.R.O.M, kitted up for an assault, disappearing into the surrounding streets.

"George get the hell out of there!" Al shouted loudly in their earpieces. "We still have containment."

"I have eyes." Bull's distinctive voice boomed through. He could see the house from his elevated position, vectored there by Donald. George, rattled by the situation, ducked behind the first hard cover he could find.

"I hit him!" he said, gasping for air. "I got him." He leant against his cover, crouched behind a low wall. "He's wearing a suicide vest, on a heart rate monitor." He didn't need to explain any further. All the operators had a good knowledge of IEDs, they knew what they were up against.

"Why hasn't it gone?" said Colin.

"It could go any second," replied George. He poked his head round the hard cover wall. He couldn't see the house. "Bull you can see right?" he said, collapsing back around the safe side of the cover.

"Yeah bro," he said. "All over it." Bull peered through the scope of the magnified sniper rifle.

"George, confirm a solid hit on the target," Al asked, looking for confirmation.

"Can't confirm," said George. "He's down though." He sighed. "Cam's down." The radio went silent with the first time his name had been mentioned on the air. Up until now, it could have been someone else. Against all hope, it might have been someone else. But now, it was confirmed it wasn't.

"Movement!" said Bull as calmly as ever. "Black One two, the rear door." He indicated the position of the exit point that was under observation.

"What do you see, Bull?" gasped George, only now starting to get his adrenaline under control.

"Door open, possible target!" Bull explained what he was seeing, describing the scene. "I have a target!"

"Confirm!" demanded Al.

"Possible target," Bull continued, squinting through his sniper scope. "Cannot confirm, I say again, cannot confirm."

"We have a signature leaving the building," said Al, using the satellites orbiting tens of miles above the earth. "I need you to confirm Bull!"

"No, I can not confirm." Bull watched the target stagger out of the back door of the property, collapse on the ground and start to crawl. "Are you seeing this, Al?"

"Yes," he acknowledged. "Bull," he said as blandly as he could. "I need you to ID this. We have seconds here." Al waited for a response. "Bull," he said, after a pause, with a hint of concern. "Confirm!"

"Can't," he said. "Can't. No ID." Bull kept his sights over the target, his trigger finger out of the trigger guard. All he needed was the word. George, behind his wall, panted to regain his composure. He wanted to move to a better position but he knew Bull had it in hand. He was useless.

"Bull!" said Al. "I've just received orders to go for a critical shot."

"I have no ID here, Al." Bull watched the subject crawl along the ground, "I say again, I have no ID."

"Take the shot!" said Al.

"Confirm you want me to take this shot?" asked Bull searching for verification of the order he had just received.

"Confirmed," said Al. "Take the shot!" Bull kept aim on the subject and placed his finger on the trigger, without any undue physical effort, he squeezed. He fired the shot without any disturbance to his position. The target dropped lifeless to the ground. It lay for less than a second until the explosion ripped apart the body. Leaving nothing but a small crater.

Windows of the surrounding houses shattered in the eruption, car alarms sounded as the vehicles were hit by the blast wave and street lights went out. Bull lowered his rifle, looking over the weapon at the scene below him. Dust and debris swirled as it started to settle around the creator in the street. He folded up the tripod and clicked the legs back into position against the body of the rifle.

"Extract!" called Al. "Everyone out of the area. Now!"

Chapter 33

Tuesday 23rd April 2013
1600hrs BST
Far From The Madding Crowd, Friars Entry, Oxford,
England

The small Oxfordshire pub, its bar adorned with real ale signs, was almost empty apart from the six men sat around the small round, wooden table. Another one of their number was at the bar. They sat in silence, this was the first time they had been all together since the OP in Birmingham had ended.

Colin, being the newest member of the team, felt like he should get the first round in. He placed the order, turned and propped himself up against the bar. His colleagues sat in silence none of them knowing what to say.

"You know, he was kinda right," said Speedy. He and Lugsy had joined Al, Donald, Colin and George for the meeting. "The country is in a bad way." He looked around to judge how his comment was received. Most seemed to nod slightly, except Lugsy, who sat in continued silence, looking down at his hands and picking at his fingernails.

"No matter what our opinions are, we can't advocate violence on our streets." Al sounded like a politician.

"Well we just blew someone up in our second city," said George. "Is it OK that it was one of ours not one of theirs?"

"What are you getting at?" asked Al.

"Ughh," sighed George. "I don't know, just seems they've got us over a barrel."

"Yeah," said Bull. "It's messed up. You guys are too polite for your own good. You don't want to upset anyone even when they hate you and want to kill you." Bull showed a rare hint of a smirk.

"How have they done it?" said George. "People come from European countries to work and all we do is complain about them taking our jobs. They aren't wanting to kill us. But God forbid we ever say anything about all them others, that would be racist."

"Yeah, somehow they've got us. Don't know how they did it." Said Speedy. "They just did it right."

"He who shouts loudest, gets heard." Said Bull leaning back in his chair, arching his back. The others nodded whilst a thoughtful silence fell across the group.

"We're uh, we're the good guys right?" asked Speedy breaking the silence and looking around the group.

"What do you mean?" said George.

"Well, we always assume that we're the good guys," said Speedy. "But they must think they're on the right side. I mean nobody thinks they're the bad guys."

"Come on," said George. "You only have to watch the news mate. It's plain to see who the trouble makers in the world are."

"But couldn't all that be propaganda from our lot, you know like in North Korea." Continued Speedy. "Couldn't it all be designed to steer us into thinking one way."

"No." Said Bull. "Look at us and look at them. We all know what they do, they still stone people to death. They don't allow their women to be educated, why should we respect a nation that treats half their population like second class citizens."

"Yeah," said George. "Think about this. During the Gulf conflict when one of our pilots was shot down, they're dragged through the streets. They're kicked, beaten and spat on by the ordinary people."

"What's your point?" asked Speedy.

"If it was the other way round, and an Iraqi pilot was shot down over the UK, would you expect your mother and father to go out into the streets and beat the pilot to within an inch of their lives?"

"No, no. You're right." Said Speedy. "We must be the good guys. So, why don't they see they're in the wrong?"

"Cam thought what he was doing was right." said George.

"Suppose, did you even try to bring him in?" asked Speedy. "He's, sorry was, one of our own."

"His mind had gone mate," said George. "If you could see the look in his eyes you'd understand. I hate to agree with Al, but it had to be done." Al flicked his gaze to George, then quickly away again.

"Here you go," said Colin returning from the bar, feeling he had disturbed something. He began placing the drinks down on the table from the silver tray he was carrying.

"Four ales, Guinness for the cliché Irishman and some American piss for the Yank." He placed the frosted bottle down in front of Bull.

"At least my beer's cold," said Bull, reaching for his bottle. Still a smirk hidden beneath his beard.

"Yeah, yeah. We drink warm beer," said Colin over his shoulder as he walked the tray back over to the bar.

"Where do you guys get that from?" said Speedy. "We never drink warm beer." Bull just shrugged, sipping from his bottle.

"So," said Colin returning to his colleagues, his chair scrapped as he sat down bumping into the table. "Crazy couple of weeks huh?"

"That's putting it lightly." Said George wiping the froth from his top lip with the back of his hands.

"Look, it's over," said Al. "Cover story in place and we're in the clear. His cottage in the lakes is being combed through as we speak. It's over."

"What about what he told me in the house?" said George. "The message."

"We're working on that," said Al. "Leave that to me, I've got my best people on it."

"I thought we were your best people," said Donald trying to lighten the mood with an uncomfortable laugh.

"It's in hand," Al emphasised.

"OK," said Bull changing the subject with a visible show of relief from Al. "So, all we have to do now is sort ourselves out."

"Well, we need to re-group," said Al. "We've lost people, so we need to shuffle around. I thought Speedy could join you guys, to make up the four."

He motioned towards Bull and George's side of the table. "Lugsy, I've got another team for you to slip into." Lugsy finally looked up, Al could see the look on his face. He hadn't bounced back since he lost his two team mates.

"I need to talk to you guys about that," he said. "I think I want out. I can't do it any more. Not after… Well, you know."

"Oh, umm." Al stuttered. Lugsy was one of his strongest operators. He was as steady as a rock and although he constantly moaned, he was dependable. "Well, I can't keep you if you've made up your mind."

Lugsy nodded, he had thought about it ever since the incident. "I suppose you've earned the right to go."

"What?" said Speedy. They had been firm friends since joining the Asset program at the same time three years ago. "You're leaving? Where you going to go? What the hell you going to do?"

"I don't know." Lugsy shrugged. "Maybe I'll get my bar started up, got the money, just need to find the place."

"Sounds good mate," said George encouragingly. "If I can help out in any way let me know."

"Yeah, me too," said Donald.

"Count me in too," said Al. He had to let his operator go. He knew he was done.

"I want to be invited to the opening," said Speedy sadly, realising his friend and closest colleague was actually leaving. "Where you gonna head to?"

"Back home I think, maybe the highlands," said Lugsy. "Always liked Aviemore."

"All the better mate," said Speedy. "A good pint and a burger, that's what you need after a downhill session."

"Aye, maybe work for a few months in the winter then take the rest of the year off. Live the life."

"I think you could get a great contract from the program, for rest and rehabilitation," said George. "What do you think, Al?" Al agreed, half-heartedly, with a shrug and a nod.

"Wait a minute!" interrupted Bull. "Are you saying I'm going to be working with an Englishman, Irishman and a Scotsman?" A few low grumbles of laughter appeared round the table. "We're gonna be a living joke."

"So what's fuckin new!" said Lugsy, laughing.

"Anyway, that's what we were thinking," said Al with a smile that hadn't been seen for a while on his face. "Also the G.R.O.M are going to be a permanent team with us." Bull looked uncomfortable at the prospect. "Problem, Bull?" Al's smile faded.

"No," he said. "It's just, I know the commander from somewhere. Have you properly looked into these guys?"

"They've been vetted," said Al. "Just like all you have. They're Polish SF, they are going to be a great benefit to us."

"Well, that remains to be seen," said Bull. "Mark my words, they need watching."

"Vetting means fuck all!" said Lugsy. "As soon as the fuckin interview's over, it's invalid.

"They're good!" said Al. "We're going to need them and their skill set, trust me." Al wanted to say more but the vibrating in his pocket stopped him short. "Al!" he said confidently into the phone. He listened for a second then brought the phone down to his leg, muting the speaker. "Excuse me gentlemen, need a minute on this one."

Al got up to leave. He tried to finish his pint but couldn't. He spilled some of it down his expensive-looking tie.

"Still got that drinking problem, Al," said George, making light of the situation. Al smiled, choking, and left the pub. As he opened the double door, he came face to face with the G.R.O.M. Al stopped in his tracks. He looked between the two teams, unsure of what was about to follow. He had invited them, hoping the two teams would get to know each other, but wasn't sure if they would turn up.

Silence and tension filled the small bar, Al's team looked at each other. The G.R.O.M did the same. One still had his arm in a sling, the youngest-looking one's cuts and bruises seemed to be healing well. Everyone in the bar looked uncomfortable at the situation.

"Can I get you guys a beer?" said George, standing up.

"Uh, yeah. Sit down guys," said Colin, following George's lead. He and Donald began moving chairs around to accommodate the new patrons to the bar.

"Four beers?" asked George holding up four fingers. The G.R.O.M nodded and started to filter in amongst the Asset team.

"Thank you," said Karol moving the chair with his un-injured arm. "I would offer to give you a hand but I only have one." Al, feeling relieved, left the bar to continue his conversation.

"I go," said Radek patting Karol on his shoulder. "You never see him near the bar." Karol rolled his eyes at the comment. Bull greeted the Polish team leader with a small nod; who returned the gesture. A look lingered between them before Bull broke the stare by taking a sip of his drink.

"We are sorry to hear of your loss," said Mats to Speedy and Lugsy. "It was quite a task by all we have heard." Speedy and Lugsy acknowledged the condolences by raising their glasses.

"And your man, Rory," said the team leader breaking his silence with a rare comment. "He was a good man, I never met anyone like him before."

"No," said George re-appearing with the round of drinks for their new colleagues. "None of us had."

"He was unique," said Donald. All the men raised their glasses and toasted the memory of their deceased friends and colleagues. Radek returned from the bar with a round of shots.

"Vodka!" he exclaimed. "Not Polish, but never mind." He placed one down in front of each man; one shot remained. "This, for Rory. We only knew him for a short time but he felt like one of us." Radek raised his glass, leading the second toast. "Na zdrowie!" The shots were slung back and the glasses slammed back on the table, all but Rory's.

"Well gentlemen," said Bull scraping his chair backwards and rising to his feet. "If you'll excuse me, I need to be getting home. Got the school run to do." Bull patted George on the shoulder as he passed him.

"How are the family?" said George.

"Well I haven't seen them much for nearly four weeks, but they're fine I guess. I'm hoping to spend some time at home for a while." Bull moved round the table towards the main entrance. "Nice to meet you guys." He said as he passed the G.R.O.M team.

The door opened before Bull could grab the long vertical metal handles. Al appeared in the doorway, a flustered look across his face. Bull didn't want to know, he wanted to get home to his wife and daughter.

Although he was taken away from them regularly, they were still always his number one priority. He passed Al, a slight nod between the two men.

"Donald, George!" Al beckoned from the door, half hidden by the frosted glass panels. "Quick!" he added when they slowly left the table. He led them outside and ducked into a side street when he saw Bull walking away from the pub.

"What's going on, Al?" asked George, his eyes re-adjusting to the light of day compared to the dimness of the bar.

"We've found the location of the files." Al spoke fast. "I want you to get moving south, back towards HQ. I'll contact you en route with the details."

"How'd you find it?" asked Donald.

"No time for questions," said Al. "Get going, I'll be in contact." Al lifted his phone before he turned and hurriedly moved off down the street. "Go!"

1800hrs BST
A34, Heading South Towards Newbury, Berkshire, England

The car weaved in and out of the traffic as if it was stationary. Expertly George swung the car left and right smoothly, making steady progress through the rush hour commuters. The engine revved high as he changed gears, allowing the front wheel drive car to pull them forward towards their destination.

"Guys! It's Al!" Al's voice sounded through the car's speakers via the Bluetooth function.

"We know, Al!" said George, concentrating on the road and smoothly steering the wheel left, pulling the car back into the slow lane and undertaking a stream of vehicles. "We've been waiting!"

"What do you have for us?" asked Donald. Being the technical one, he was still interested how they had tracked the files down.

"Right, I'll be brief," continued Al. "I've had our I.T guys working overtime, they've managed to dig into the communal Wi-Fi that he was using in Europe. He logged into an email account whilst at that café in Rome, just before you chased him. Remember?"

"Kinda hard to forget, Al," said George.

"Anyway, they hacked into it or whatever they do and they discovered an mpeg and a location for the media to go to. It was set up to be sent in three days time. I can only presume that he would just re-set the send time to prevent it from being sent. If something was to happen to him it would go to a pre-arranged list of newspaper editors and journalists."

"Did it get sent?" asked Donald.

"No, luckily. We might be in time for this. I'm sending the video to Donald's phone." No sooner had Al finished speaking, the phone bleeped at the arrival of the mpeg file. "Just secure the files, they are in lockup 1435 of Newbury Business Park storage facility, just off London Road. Keep me informed." The speakers fell silent.

Donald thumbed at the screen of his phone until the video started to play.

The small screen struggled to show the detail of the video. George leaned over, catching glimpses of the movie between manoeuvres. He made out a white room and a figure emerging from behind the camera and sitting mid frame.

The engine drowned out most of what was being said, but he recognised the figure as his old friend. Donald raised the volume and he heard him speak.

"If you're watching this you've worked everything out and I'm probably already dead." Donald watched as Cam explained what the reporters would find at the drop site. George stole the odd glance between lane changes.

"Turn that bloody thing off," said George palming the wheel and sending the car down the slip road off the motor-way. "We're nearly there." Red signs for the hospital's A&E department flew past the windows of the car; the business park came into view. "Here." George announced their arrival at the storage facility.

The tyres screeched to a halt outside the glass double door to the reception, creating a burnt rubber smell. The two front doors flew open, bouncing back against the door springs, Donald and George jumped out. The reception hall was empty apart from the receptionist.

George approached the man sat behind the long desk cluttered with computers and printers. As he moved he reached into his pocket and pulled out a small black leather wallet. He opened it and flashed an ID card to the receptionist.

"George Hassler, National Crime Agency." The man behind the desk stood up, unsure of how to greet the two NCA agents. "This is my colleague Donald." Donald remained silent, he only managed a nod after his introduction.

"Um," said the receptionist shakily. "How can I help you?"

"Lockup 1435," he said. "I need the keys." The receptionist, without acknowledging the request, began fumbling through the drawers under the front desk. He held out a key with a small cardboard tag. George could clearly see the numbers 1435 written in black felt tip pen. He looked at the key in the man's hand then looked him in the eyes. "Take us to it."

Nervously he led the two agents to the lock up, turning sharp right-angled turns along a bright corridor. George noticed CCTV cameras in the corners of the corridor.

"These cameras," said George. "Are they recording?"

"Uhh, yes. Yes they are."

"Good," said George, making a mental note to have the footage impounded. The lockups all had tall orange metal doors, each padlocked shut. In his head he counted down the numbers of the lockers, then he saw one with a different, sturdier padlock.

"Here," said the receptionist. "This one." The three men stopped outside the metal doors. George held out his hand and beckoned for the key.

"What's with the padlock?" asked George, taking the key from the man. "This one's different from the rest."

"Uhh, yeah," said the receptionist. "Sometimes people want their own padlocks, and as long as we have a copy of the key it's alright."

"Hello, Al," Donald said into his phone, turning away from the others. "We're here. What do you want us to do?" Donald listened for a moment. "Open it." He said in George's direction, still listening to Al.

"EOD?" asked George. Donald relayed the question to Al. Donald lowered the phone, looked at George and shook his head. George knew Al would want to keep this in house, no outside agencies involved. George turned to the doors, looked down at the lock and the key in his hand. "Anyone been in this lockup? One of your staff members I mean?"

"Uhh, yeah. We enter all our lockups. To check for anything that might be illegal."

"So people have been in and out of this lockup?" The receptionist nodded. "You're sure?" He nodded again. "This is important!" He raised his voice hoping to get something a little more concrete out of the man. "Tell me someone has been in there!"

"Yes, Christ! I'm sure. We go in all the time."

"Have you been in?" asked George.

"No."

"Right, back." He pushed the receptionist away from the doors and slid the key into the lock. The padlock snapped open and he carefully unhooked the shackle from the hasps. He opened the doors.

The storage room was empty apart from a single filling cabinet standing in the centre of the floor like a metal column. There was nothing else in the room. Donald joined George in the doorway and looked inside.

"Getting déjà vu," said Donald. George, without replying, entered the lockup. Donald gave a whispered commentary to Al. George circled the filling cabinet, taking in every detail. "Al wants to know what's in there George."

"Alright Don mate, Jesus!" George gritted his teeth and snorted with disbelief at the risk he was being asked to take. He grabbed the handle to the top drawer and placed the other on the top corner, holding the cabinet steady.

He looked over at Donald, stood in the doorway with the phone pressed against his ear.

George opened the top drawer, only an inch. He put his face close to the open drawer and examined the space between the drawer and cabinet. He systematically moved around the drawer making sure nothing was going to put him and the files in danger.

With the thought that the storage staff members had been in the room and it's whole purpose was to pass on the information held within, he slowly opened the top drawer fully.

"Nothing," he said, closing the top drawer and moving down to the middle one. Again, the drawer was empty. He told Donald who passed the message to Al. "Last one," he said kneeling down. The bottom drawer slid open and George stared into it.

"What is it?" asked Donald. George turned his head towards Donald, his eyebrows furrowed.

"Nothing mate," he said. "There's nothing in it, Don." He slid shut the drawer. The metal casters grinding on the slides echoed around the empty lockup. It clunked shut, the sound bouncing off the bare walls.

"Empty, Al," said Donald into the phone. George appeared on his shoulder, leaving the storage room.

"Ask him what he wants to do now," said George.

"Well, why don't you look at the CCTV footage?" said the receptionist. George looked at him and gave a slight nod. They were going to anyway, for a positive ID. "I mean, he was here the other day, you'll be able to see him on the film."

"What?" said George. Donald stopped talking to Al. "He was here? When?"

"Couple of days back," he said shrugging, nonchalantly.

"When, think!" George shouted at the staff member who flinched at the outburst. "Exactly when, it's important!" He took a few steps closer to the receptionist, moving past Donald.

"Ummm," stuttered the receptionist. "Well, uhhh."

"Think!" he yelled, scowling.

"Sunday, yeah Sunday," he said nodding. "Definitely Sunday. Guy with his arm in a sling." George stared for a second, judging the information just gleaned from the receptionist.

"Were you in that day?"

"Yes Sir," he said.

"And you saw him?"

"Yes Sir."

"I'm gonna want to see that camera footage!" he said, turning his back on the receptionist. He wrenched the phone from Donald's ear.

"George?" said Donald, as he watched his colleague walk away, along the corridor, putting ground between him and the receptionist. "George!" he said again, still no reaction.

George reached the end of the corridor and turned to the right. He took a few steps along, out of sight of Donald and the receptionist. He stopped and leaned back against the wall, hitting it hard with his shoulders. Phone in hand, dangling by his side. He looked up to the roof of the building, his eyes flicked left and right.

His mind raced. He placed the phone to the side of his face. The sound of an open line echoed into his ear.

"Al!" George said into the phone. "We may have a problem."

The End

ND - #0254 - 270225 - C0 - 234/156/21 - PB - 9781908487490 - Matt Lamination